THE RISE OF HENRY MORCAR

PHYLLIS BENTLEY

BLOOMSBURY READER

LONDON · NEW DELHI · NEW YORK · SYDNEY

This electronic edition published in 2012 by Bloomsbury Reader

Bloomsbury Reader is a division of Bloomsbury Publishing Plc,

50 Bedford Square, London WC1B 3DP

ISBN: 978 1 4482 0393 2
eISBN: 978 1 4482 0334 5

Visit www.bloomsbury.com to find out more about our authors and their books
You will find extracts, author interviews, author events and you can sign up for
newsletters to be the first to hear about our latest releases and special offers

Contents

Prologue: To Remember

The Siren warbled for the seventh time that night. Morcar, busy with the agenda of the committee on wool textile reconstruction which he had come to London to attend next day, called in a preoccupied tone:

"Keep away from those windows, girls."

Receiving no reply, he pulled off his new reading glasses quickly and looked up from his desk, first at the large sheets of glass-once a pleasure, now in the summer of 1944 a menace— and then across the room. Through the windows—from habit the amount the view added to the flat's rent came into his mind, then he remembered he was trying not to think that kind of thought nowadays—through the window the Park over the road made a beautifully calm and sunlit picture, and the two young women by the hearth made a beautifully calm and sunlit picture too. In both cases the appearance of calm lied, thought Morcar, for the Park lay under the threat of an approaching bomb, and Jenny and Fan bore perplexities in their fair young heads and griefs within their breasts. Indeed, it was not like them to be so still; in the odd, bright, careless clothes the young affected nowadays, made for movement, their immobility looked strange. But it seemed they were both deep in reverie; Jenny's handsome intelligent face, Fan's usually so shrewd and saucy, were both blank as if their owners had withdrawn from the façade. Well! They had plenty to think of, certainly, with the problems of their future all unsolved. Fan's young man, if he could be called hers, was in the Normandy battle; while as for Jenny! Now that Morcar looked more searchingly, he saw that there was tension and not relaxation in their pose; Jenny upright on the settee, Fan folded in acute angles on a low stool, maintained their balance by a brooding concentration.

The two girls, who were friends in spite of their different natures, had dined with him, as they often did nowadays when he was in town; they found his flat easier to meet in physically than the cottage attic Fan occupied up at Hampstead, easier psychologically than the house of Jenny's parents in the select Kensington square. Morcar loved to have them with him; he had recently discovered that he was by nature a genial, lively, sociable man who liked the company of young people, lonely through no fault of his own. If he had discovered this afresh after so many arid years, it was through these young men and women who were especially dear to him; for if Cecil was his son, David Oldroyd had been better than a son to him, and Fan was David's sister, while Edwin and Jenny were Christina's children; the lives of the five were interwoven with Christina's and his own.

Christina! His mind flew to the blue door, once so richly glossy, faded now in wartime but to him always the symbol of elegance, beauty and romance, which would swing behind Jenny when he took her home to-night. It was not in his code to approach the mother by way of the children; he kept Edwin and Jenny out of the problem, never used them as a means of meeting his love, would not accept the casual invitation to enter which

Jenny was sure to offer to-night; indeed it sometimes seemed to him that half his life was spent in hiding his feelings for Christina from those whom it might hurt. But to be near Christina's daughter was to be near something of Christina, and so Morcar liked to be near Jenny. Outwardly she did not resemble her mother, for everything about Jenny was strong and fair and candid, while Christina, with her dark thick curls, her lovely tragic eyes, her sweet profile, her delicate skin and charming hands, had an air of uncertainty, of indecision; but the mother and daughter shared a loftiness of soul. Jenny was always complete and staunch and whole, whether in grief or joy; Christina ever frustrated— her very dress, though so delicious, was often marred by some slight careless omission, some unexpected roughness, which betrayed her deep inner trouble; but the generous warmth, the delicate integrity, of their spirits was the same. They loved each other, too, in spite of Harington. At the thought of Christina's husband Morcar's heart filled, as always, with rage and pain, for though he hated Harington he found it impossible to despise him. Sir Edward Mayell Wyndham Harington was no weakling and no fool; he knew his job, he was high in his Department, his acquaintance with powerful people and his sophistication were both immense. He was in the inner circle always, he knew how things were done. In his own way, too, he loved Christina, though it was a way which blighted, frosted. "My darling", thought Morcar with tender pity. Oh, if only the war were won! Now that we've landed in Europe, thought Morcar hopefully, surely it can't be very long And then? Would Harington yield? Bracing; himself for the struggle, Morcar wondered.

In the distance a faint throb, like a distant road-drill, began to pierce the air, and steadily though at first almost imperceptibly grew in volume. There was something unpleasant, even sinister, in the persistence of the long-drawn-out unceasing very gradual crescendo, the endless murmured repetition of the same vibrating note.

"Here she comes," said Morcar. He sighed with exasperation, shut his glasses in their case with a snap and rose.

The murmur was now much stronger and more clearly defined and not to be mistaken for anything but the sound of an approaching flying bomb.

"It's coming this way," said Morcar, putting a hand under each girl's elbow to help them up. "Best get into the hall."

"You always think they're coming this way," pouted Fan, nevertheless rising obediently, for the murmur had now become a penetrating grind.

The absence of glass in the entrance hall window, whence it had disappeared in an earlier raid, made it a useful refuge when fly-bombs were overhead. Fan lounged at the side of the boarded-up gap, Jenny sat down on a stiff hall chair. Morcar looked around and unhooked the mirror from the wall.

"What are you doing with that, Uncle Harry?" said Fan as he clasped it in his arms.

"Admiring the Morcar profile, love," said Morcar genially. "What else?"

He laid the mirror carefully face downwards on the floor.

The noise in the air grew and grew, until it seemed as if a heavy railway train rolled overhead. They all looked up, expecting a diminution as the bomb passed by, but the sound increased to a clamorous roar.

"Down! Down!" cried Morcar suddenly. "Under the table! Quick!" The girls slipped obediently to their knees, Fan in a single graceful jerk, Jenny heavily, for she was with child and near her time. "I'll have her out of this tomorrow, Admiralty or no Admiralty," thought Morcar, helping her: "I'll get her up to Yorkshire where she'll be safe. She owes it to the child. If there is any tomorrow," he added grimly. He felt something at his knees, and found the girls trying to pull him down; but there was no room for him beneath the table, and he shook his head. The raucous thunder of the fly-bomb now crammed the air. "Nay, this is ours, this is it," he thought. "If the engine cuts out now, we're for it." The noise abruptly ceased. "Ours! Well," thought Morcar, jocularly speaking Yorkshire to himself to keep his spirits up: "If we're bahn to die, we may as well die thinking o' summat fine, choose how. England!" thought Morcar.

He wondered what went on within the two fair heads below. The girls were looking up at him; Fan wore a sardonic defiant grin, Jenny a fine quiet smile. Suddenly there began to race through his own mind pictures of his life; things he had not thought of, people he had not seen, for years, came up before him, fresh and vivid as when they were real, but with the added significance lent to them by later events.

"Scenes from the life of Henry Morcar," he thought sardonically. "Well! I hope this is not the last of the series."

In silence they waited for the bomb to fall.

I

Education

1

Home and Mill

Henry Morcar was born in the very middle of the English middle class, the son and grandson of solid but not wealthy West Riding cloth manufacturers. He might have been the great-grandson of such a manufacturer too, for all he knew, but he set little store on great-grandfathers and never troubled to enquire. A good-natured, even-tempered, affectionate boy, healthy always, fair-complexioned, burly for his age, Harry spent a thoughtless and carefree childhood which included no poignant moments of anguished intensity. Accordingly his recollections of this period were scattered and overlaid. Certain places, people and incidents however were still vivid in his mind.

One of these was his grandfather's house, Hurstfield, which stood in Hurst, a suburb of the town of Annotsfield in Yorkshire, on the well-thought-of Hurstholt Road, where a group of similar houses looked across at the new Hursthead Park with the sober satisfaction of substantial ratepayers. Old John Henry Morcar's house was built of good local stone, with bay windows in the rooms each side the door, to which two large flat steps whitestoned at the edges gave access. Its air of prosperity verging on affluence was emphasised by a family of steep gables, two above the attics and a smaller one over the front porch, two well-painted iron gates and a short curving gravel drive between, circumnavigating the front garden. The letters JHM in the rubber mat on the top step were always in complete repair, the pointing of the walls was fresh, the lace curtains were always spotless in their handsome symmetry, the front door was magnificently grained, the laurels by the gate were well pruned and the flower-beds and plot of grass were held in check by small plum-coloured tiles in the interests of neatness. Hurstfield lacked the pink marble pillars and glass conservatory of the more impressive house on the right, but was superior to the semi-detached houses on the left where the Shaws lived, which had a straight asphalt path to the front door and only one gable. The marble-pillar house had three maids, the Morcars two and the Shaws one of a more general kind. In the same way Alderman Morcar did not keep his own carriage, but never scrupled to take a hansom when occasion really required, offering a lift sometimes to Mr. Shaw from the station. Yes, the Morcars were middle middle-class, the backbone of England as Morcar's grandfather often proudly told him.

Down the hill to the right the road became suddenly precipitous and turned into Hurst Bank, and at the bottom of Hurst Bank lay a nest of mills and workmen's houses, and one of those railway viaducts of which the hilly West Riding has such an abundance. Amidst this industrial cluster at Hurst Bank Bottom lay his grandfather's mill, built in 1871, a substantial stone building with a couple of extra weaving sheds at the back and a shortish hexagonal chimney which had been added to at the top, so that it looked as if it wore a collar. The brass plate at the side of the door announcing that this was the abode of J. H. MORCAR & SON always gleamed with what Harry's grandfather mystifyingly called elbow grease. Within, the office was fitted along the walls and in the centre with massive sloping desks of gleaming mahogany, divided along the top by a gleaming brass rail. High cushioned stools without backs were ranged along the desks, where inkpots, ledgers, round black rulers and letters to which were pinned snippets of cloth lay in geometrically neat array, quite dustless. A door on the far side of the office led into the mill; when this was opened the restless clacking of the looms rushed in and drew Harry towards the weaving sheds.

His father and grandfather were very willing that he should wander about the mill as he liked, provided he were wearing a navy blue sailor suit and not a white one. There had been tears from his mother when he returned once with a white drill suit all smudged; it was a new suit, she had finished machining it, pressed it and attached its black silk tie and whistle cord only that very morning, so that he should look well when walking out with his father, and now it was all smeared with textile grease. She wept with vexation at the sight and since tears were rare with her, both husband and father-in-law were appropriately impressed. But in a blue sailor suit of cloth from the mill Harry was free to wander as he chose, and accordingly he could not remember a time when he was unfamiliar with looms. He stood at the end of a loom-gate watching and wondering, his mouth perhaps a little agape, his sailor hat on the back of his round fair head, and occasionally his father—solid and cheerful in those days—passed by and smoothing his fine straw-coloured moustache threw out some information about picks or reeds, or his grandfather paused beside him and taking his hand explained the whole loom mechanism in technical language. His grandfather, a plump fresh-complexioned man with a round white beard, had a marvellous gold watch-chain— it cost a pound a link, said Harry's mother—with two remarkable gold coins swinging from the centre; the coins and the loom divided Harry's attention, so that he did not always hear all his grandfather said; but the incident occurred so often that imperceptibly he acquired a deposit of knowledge. The weavers too would smile at him and calling him "lovey" allow him to approach quite close and watch while they put fresh bobbins into their shuttles; he was a sensible boy, they felt, who would not get hurt or into trouble. In those days the weavers wore clogs at their work and shawls in the street, and sang hymns (or sometimes more secular songs) as they stood in the loom-gate. Harry early acquired the knack of talking and hearing through the noise of the looms and scorned those ignoramuses who tried to shout above it.

2

Sunday

On Sundays the Morcars attended the important Eastgate chapel in Annotsfield, where Alderman Morcar was one of the trustees, Harry's father took a Young Men's Bible Class and Harry's mother was prominent in the Dorcas meeting, cutting out materials for the garments they sewed. She was young for this post, which she held because of her skill, and the whole family were proud of her on this account.

On Sunday afternoon in the crowded school Harry sang *Onward Christian Soldiers* and *Dare to be a Daniel* with great gusto, feeling clean and good in his best velvet suit, his white silk scarf and his Sunday coat of pilot cloth (made by his mother from cloth from the mill of course) with its brass buttons and astrakhan collar. The volume of shrill sound was enormous, almost drowning the harmonium's powerful roar; the lilting rhythm of the tunes made Harry feel excited and jolly.

After the hymn and some prayers to which Harry did not listen very much the children filed out to the sound of a ceremonial march into the small classrooms which fringed the large assembly hall. Here, where glossy brightly coloured pictures of Bible scenes looked down on them from the walls, they were told a Bible story by their class teacher: Daniel in the lions' den, David and Goliath, Jacob and Esau, Elijah and Elisha, the call of Samuel, the miracles of Jesus. Harry liked the Old Testament better than the new, for the stories were more exciting and concerned people more like Harry Morcar, but the parts in the New about the fishermen disciples had interest, because of the background of the bright blue lake and boats with sails and nets filled with silvery fish, such as Harry saw on his summer holidays at Scarborough. And the parts about sheep and shepherds were very good. There were sheep on the hills round Annotsfield. Harry made David his hero, admired Daniel, preferred Esau to his brother but supposed there must be something hidden in the story which he would understand when he grew up, to account for God's preference for Jacob. For Samuel he felt little enthusiasm, but was suitably shocked by the spectacle of a High Priest whose sons robbed the people—it must have been terrible for a man in Eli's position to have sons so completely lacking in respectability. Elijah was grand, so fiercely independent and somehow *Yorkshire;* it served Gehazi jolly well right to be turned into a leper and the ravens were splendid; Elisha in spite of the widow's cruse seemed rather soft and disappointing. Towards the end of the class one grew a little tired and one's attention wandered, for one was not a saintly boy who knew everything and won Sunday School prizes. On the other hand, one was not a bad boy who threw pellets and pulled the girls' frocks from their gathers and was rude to the teacher when she read one's name from the register. That would have been unkind, and Harry had no capacity for being unkind. Harry knew the Ten Commandments and (with a little prompting) the

Beatitudes, and could recite the parables of the grain of mustard seed and the sower who went forth sowing, with reasonable accuracy, and furnish their explanations. A parable was an earthly story with a heavenly meaning. A miracle was—Harry was not quite sure what the teachers said a miracle was, but he knew a miracle when he saw one, perfectly. He believed in the miracles completely, of course, but found them a trifle irrelevant. What was clear was that one should be brave like David, honest like Eli, kind to children like Jesus; one should defend the right like Daniel and not tell lies (look at Ananias!) or heap up wealth (look at the rich man who died the same night). One should honour one's father and mother, believe in God, love one's neighbour and keep Sunday different from other days. God was one's Father in heaven, and nobody could come between. Talents must not be buried but used; cleanliness was next to godliness; in the sweat of his brow man must eat his bread.

When the lesson was over the children marched back into the big room and sang *There's a Home for Little Children Above the Bright Blue Sky*. They were rather tired by now and sang in a sentimental yearning tone. Harry was not particularly anxious to seek a home above the bright blue sky, for he was perfectly satisfied with his home in Annotsfield, but it was nice to know such a home was there; it gave one a safe, well-provided-for sensation which was very cosy. One came out into the bright windy afternoon with a comfortable feeling that one had done one's duty and that provided one continued to do it all would be well, probably in this world, certainly in the next.

Looking back on it now, the world of his childhood seemed to Morcar completely safe; a strong smooth firm fabric without a single rent in it, a world without a crack, without the tiniest fissure.

3

McKinley

There had been a slight crack once, it seemed, but it was now smoothed over, a damage in the fabric which had been mended. This damage, the child Harry knew, had something to do with his birthday.

"You were born on a black day for the textile trade, love," his grandfather sometimes said in a solemn monitory voice, shaking his head. "Aye, you were that!"

Harry's self-esteem was vexed by this attack on a matter so closely connected with him as his birthday, and one day he riposted sharply: "Well, it wasn't my fault!" At this his grandfather laughed heartily, his father said: "The child's right there!" and his mother, exclaiming: "For shame, Fred!" drew him to her knee and smoothed his hair. Finding his sally so well received, Harry thought the moment opportune for further enquiry. "Why was it a black day, Grandpa?" he demanded. By this time the two elder Morcars were again discussing the business affairs which his grandfather's apostrophe had interrupted, and made no reply. "Why was it? Why was it a black day, Grandpa?" repeated the child. He put his hand on his grandfather's knee and shook it vigorously. "Why was it a black day?" he shouted.

"Hush, love, don't worry your grandfather. It was because of the McKinley tariff," explained his father hastily, seeing the question framing again on Harry's firm wide mouth.

"What's a McKinley tariff?" demanded Harry, staring.

His mother pulled him away: "It's something the Americans did which made the trade in cloth much less."

"You may well say that, Clara," interjected his grandfather, unable to keep out of a discussion on a matter which upset him so much. "Export trade dropped from sixty-three to nineteen million running yards in four years, that's how much less the McKinley tariff made it. What's nineteen from sixty-three, Harry?"

"Forty-four," said Harry promptly. "What's a running yard?"

"A yard in length," explained his father.

Harry pondered.

"He's sharp for his age," said his father proudly.

"He'll need to be," said his grandfather, grimly jocular.

"He will if that tariff gets reaffirmed," said his father in a sober tone.

"Nay—we've done with that, I reckon," said Alderman Morcar.

Harry's father seemed less certain, shaking his head doubtfully.

4

Jubilee

Victoria, great and glorious, firm and free. Ever victorious may she be. In white letters on a red ground. With a portrait of the Queen above, flanked by Union Jacks.

The waggon, which had been held up by the crowd in the square long enough for Harry to read this patriotic inscription where it hung over the façade of the railway station, suddenly jolted forward. The packed children were thrown against each other, the well-brushed curls, the starched drill suits and muslin dresses tossed like flowers in a breeze, screams of delighted laughter filled the air. The fifteen thousand Annotsfield Sunday School scholars were on their way in procession to celebrate the Queen's Diamond Jubilee in the new park. ("Why Diamond?" wondered Harry, but not with sufficient interest to put the question into words.) On his breast a Jubilee badge, a round tin medallion bearing the Queen's picture, hung from a bow of red white and blue ribbon. Church bells were ringing, older children on foot around the waggons were singing. Now they were lined up on grass in front of a platform decked with flags; the Mayor, in a cocked hat and red robes and a big gold chain, was making a speech; at the back in the middle of the row sat Grandpa, resplendent in his best silk hat. The Mayor was delighted, he said, that in Annotsfield on this wonderful day the sun was shining upon them, and he hoped it would be the same for the great celebrations now being held in London. This was the first time it had occurred to Harry that weather might be different in English places at the same time; he was awestruck by the thought and missed much of the Mayor's speech, rejoining it at the peroration. "May the sun continue to shine upon Her Majesty, and Her throne continue to set an example to the world, for many years to come. God Save the Queen!" The band played; then everyone cried Hip Hip Hooray.

Now the crowd of children was breaking up and dispersing; his mother came towards him looking very pretty; the white hat perched on her piled-up light brown hair was trimmed with red white and blue ribbons and she wore three flowers of the same colours pinned in the bosom of her best heliotrope dress.

"Come over here, Harry; don't you want to go in for the races?" cried his father.

"He's too young, Fred," pleaded his mother, as Harry hung back.

She took his hand and led him to the side of the roped-off space where Sunday School officials were marshalling the seven-year-olds for sports and games. Harry gazed, fascinated; they were tying couples of boys together with handkerchiefs round a leg of each. One heat of the three-legged race was run; some children tumbled on the grass, the antics of others as they strove to synchronise the movements of their arms and legs made the watching grown-ups laugh and clap. Suddenly Harry snatched his hand from his mother's and ran across the grass.

"That's right, Harry," said his father, pleased.

He knelt and tied Harry firmly to another boy. Harry looked up from the knots and found it was Charlie Shaw from the house next to his grandfather's. Charlie was thin and taller than Harry; he had wavy dark hair, an oval face broad at the temples, sparkling hazel eyes and a clear delicate skin which coloured easily. The two boys exchanged a look and felt friendly. Harry had no idea how to run a three-legged race but intended to do it as well as the other competitors and possibly rather better.

"I think this is the way," said Charlie in a light quick tone, passing his arm round Harry's waist.

Harry gripped him in the same way, firmly. Charlie's thin body was quivering with joyous anticipation. The starter fired the pistol.

"Come on!" cried Charlie eagerly.

The boys ran expertly down the course, Charlie setting a quick pace. There was a moment when Charlie stumbled and almost fell, but Harry's grip held him upright. They reached the end of the course almost before the rest had started. They won the heat and presently the whole race, and sat on the grass together, surrounded by their delighted families, triumphantly drinking ginger-beer from a brown stone bottle. In the distance some older children performed drill with long white wands.

Now it was twilight and Harry stood in front of the Town Hall, which was festooned with coloured fairy lights spelling: *God Save Our Queen: 1837–1897*. He was footsore, for Charlie had scorned the slow delays of the children's waggon, but completely happy— or rather, he would be completely happy as soon as the monster bonfire was lighted. A councillor whom his father identified as the chairman of the gas committee came out with a long

rod lighted at one end and handed it to his wife, who helped by
her husband timidly inserted it into the mass of logs and twigs
and thus ignited the fire. At first the results were disappointing,
only occasional gleams of fire within being seen; then suddenly a
red tongue leaped up, the crowd cheered; soon the bonfire was a
blazing mass throwing out sparks and smoke and long red flames,
so hot that the crowd to leeward had to run from it. In its flicker-
ing light the banners on the warehouses at the other side of the
square were clearly visible: *Long Live Our Noble Queen*, read Morcar:
Victoria, the Greatest Queen on Earth.

5

Tariff

It was not long after this, on a very hot summer's day, when Harry, coming to the mill one afternoon with a message from home for his father, found his grandfather alone in the office, looking very glum. His fresh face was strangely sunk, his round blue eyes perplexed and disconcerted. He gazed at Harry in silence for a moment and then sighed and shook his head.

"What's the matter, Grandpa?" asked Harry practically. Without understanding why, he often felt a need to moderate his grandfather's reactions to life. They seemed to him altogether excessive and exaggerated—like a too highly inflated balloon they urged him to apply a pin.

Before the Alderman could reply, the foreman came in and said: "They're ready now." John Henry Morcar rose stiffly, and taking Harry's hand in his, led him silently through the door towards the mill.

Harry hung back. "I've got my white suit on, Grandpa," he said.

"Never mind," said his grandfather in a loud hoarse tone.

He led Harry across the first weaving shed. The door to the next shed stood open, wedged with a block of wood, and Harry felt a shock of surprise as he saw the looms within stood still and sheeted. His grandfather paused in the doorway and looked around, then stepped back, kicked away the wedge, closed the door and gave a signal to a couple of men in aprons, strangers to the mill, standing by. These joiners lifted slats of wood into position across the door and hammered them fast.

Harry's heart quailed. To nail up looms and abandon them like that was like leaving people to starve and die alone. To watch this murder, in his white suit too, gave him an extraordinary feeling of guilt and shame.

"This is the Americans' doing, this is," said Alderman Morcar in the same strange loud tone. "You'll never forget this day's work, Harry; you'll remember the Dingley tariff as long as you live. Won't you, eh? Won't you?"

He bent down so that the child's face was on a level with his burning red-rimmed eyes.

"I thought it was the McKinley tariff, Grandpa," said Harry stoutly.

"They took that off and now they've put it on again," wailed Alderman Morcar. "Grass will grow in the streets of Annotsfield, love, you mark my words."

Harry felt sure that this was nonsense. Nevertheless the thought of the dead cold looms lay heavy on his mind, he never forgot them all his life.

6

Shaw Family Album

The next scene in Morcar's mind was his grandfather's deathbed, which was irretrievably comic and tragic, so that he always laughed when he thought of it and then shook his head at his own heartlessness. Alderman Morcar in a very clean white linen nightshirt, his white beard beautifully brushed, lay propped up on pillows embroidered with his monogram, a peevish expression on his harassed but still fresh-looking face. His son and grandson had been summoned by his housekeeper suddenly in the middle of the night to take their last farewell; they had hurried into their clothes and run down Hurstholt Road and panted up the stairs, and now it seemed they were not welcome. When they entered the room old John Henry Morcar lay with his eyes closed, his face pale and very thin, his respiration heavy; he appeared on the point of death. His son went to him and took his hand, and Harry followed trailing after. Unluckily he left the bedroom door open. A draught blew in and ruffled the pillow-frills, and his grandfather opened his eyes and snapped out irritably: "How many times have I to tell you to shut the door, Harry?" He raised himself on one elbow to watch his grandson cross the room, and urged: "Don't bang it now," as the boy struggled with the large black slippery knob. When the door was safely shut he lay back on his pillows and sighed. "If you two hadn't come I should have gone by now," he exclaimed in a tone of unalloyed vexation. In spite of the solemnity of the moment Harry could not keep back a slight snort of laughter at this, for to be eager to die seemed to his young mind really ludicrous. His grandfather turned his head and stared at him sourly. Suddenly a strange look crossed the Alderman's face; his eyes widened; he whispered; "But it doesn't matter," and let his head fall back upon the pillow. His breath fluttered and he was gone.

Next, Harry stood in Annotsfield cemetery in a storm of rain. A man in decent black whom he guessed to be the undertaker murmured: "Let it go," and four labourers, panting a little, for old Mr. Morcar was a heavy man, lowered the coffin jerkily into the grave. One of the four, a young man with big clay-smeared boots, stood beside the minister at the graveside, and at the words *ashes to ashes, dust to dust* threw in, rhythmically, seriously, but with an inescapeable effect of brutality, two handfuls of earth, which fell with damp plops on the coffin lid.

Then there was the cemetery in sunshine, and a huge grey marble slab like the head of a bed, on which was engraved below the name of John Henry Morcar, the proud words *Alderman of this Borough.* The stone also contained references to the Alderman's long dead wife, and to an infant perished ten years ago named Clara. Who was she, wondered Harry.

It was about this time that Morcar saw a picture which later recurred too often: his mother in a long white cooking apron with her sleeves rolled up, removing china from a vast cupboard.

It was her back that he saw: the high-piled light brown hair, the sloping shoulders crossed by the broad linen strings of the apron, the smooth white elbows, the neat tape bow at her firm waist. He had no idea of the meaning of her actions, but something in her attitude alarmed him, he felt disaster in the air. He went up to her for reassurance. Clara Morcar smiled at him, straightened his flat bow, exclaimed at the state of his eton collar, and receiving an affirmative reply to her question whether he was hungry, suggested he should visit the kitchen, where she had been baking currant buns. Harry went off and came back munching but not entirely cured of his disquiet. A large wicker skep from the mill stood by the cupboard and Mrs. Morcar was carefully packing into one corner a pile of red and gold dessert plates, hand-painted, which were the family's pride.

"Why are you packing the plates, Mother?" enquired Harry.

Mrs. Morcar smiled. "Never mind, love," she said.

She looked at the clock and made to untie her apron and gave no further explanation, for an invincible reserve was interposed between her and the rest of creation. Why? At this moment Harry suddenly found in his mind the knowledge that the infant Clara mentioned on the gravestone was his own younger sister, and that his mother was still sad because she had lost her. He put his arms round her waist and tentatively inclined his head towards her breast. Mrs. Morcar, smiling maternally, somewhat perfunctorily patted his head and Harry was confirmed in his belief that she did not much care for caresses. "Silly boy," she said. Her tone was kind and not meant to wound, but Morcar changed his embrace into a playful attempt to untie her apron strings, and their relationship was settled. Henceforward, though their affection was staunch and loyal it was practical and calm, neither outwardly demonstrative nor deeply passionate.

20

Did this scene take place in Hurstfield, or in the smaller house the Fred Morcars then lived in, of which Harry retained little recollection? Probably in Hurstfield, because Harry soon knew that they were not to live there, and that this disappointed long-cherished expectations. No explanations were made, but it seemed they were to move to one of the semi-detached Sycamore houses, next to the Shaws.

From that time Harry's recollections were clearer, for the Shaws were for years the main thread and still the deciding factor in his life.

The Shaws were a large and bustling family; Mr. and Mrs. Shaw had four children already and more seemed to be continually arriving. "Let 'em all come!" cried Mr. Shaw, cheerfully dandling the latest infant on his knee: "There's nothing so lovely as a baby." "Isn't she beautiful?" he would cry, gazing admiringly at his offspring, who, from the violent shaking he had administered, was wont to give him a somewhat sour look in return and show a tendency to vomit. When this occurred John William Shaw called loudly for his wife and his eldest daughter. "Annie! Winnie!" he shouted disgustedly. "Come here and take this child! Come and take this child, can't you?"

Mrs. Shaw, a large fair comely perplexed-looking woman, arrived on the instant of these summons, panting, but Winnie deferred her arrival to suit herself. If Mrs. Shaw was out of hearing at the kitchen range this cool delay of his daughter left Mr. Shaw uncomfortably landed; his cries grew louder and his irritable distress mounted to a pitch when he was apt to dump the baby into the arms of anyone who stood handy—his eldest son Charlie, for instance, or even Charlie's school-friend Morcar. But Harry did not like Mr. Shaw well enough to submit to such an imposition. Mr. Shaw's exiguous body, usually quivering with some vehement vexation, his scrubby dark pointed beard and thin dark hair, his bright irascible brown eyes and sallow complexion, made a disagreeable impression on Harry, he did not at first know why.

Luckily Charlie, though his slight stature and dark hair were his father's, had inherited much of his mother's disposition as well as her fresh skin and clear colour. He was a lively restless boy, full of invention, an admirable mimic, always crying: "Come on!" and leading the way at the double to some new and usually risky activity. But he was also warm-hearted, generous and loyal, and fully cognisant of the value of Morcar's staunch solid qualities. The boys were friends; at the height of their many swift quarrels it never occurred to them to break the partnership of Shaw and Morcar.

They attended Annotsfield College together, rushing off each morning in their Norfolk suits (of blue cloth from their father's mills), wearing their school caps with the Annotsfield crest, with satchels slung over their shoulders, to catch one of the steam trams down the long hill from Hurst to Annotsfield. Morcar was, always ready first; it seemed to him now that he had spent hours of his life standing on one foot in the Shaws' asphalt walk by the side of the house, from time to time shouting "Are you coming, Shaw?" and listening to the sounds of disturbance within. Occasionally Winnie would throw up a window and, thrusting out her pointed pert little nose and round bright-coloured cheeks, advise him of the progress of her brother's preparations and the altercation he was having with his father. She too, at least until she tied her smooth hazel hair back with a big brown bow, went down to Annotsfield to school, but it was a point of honour with her never to start till she had seen Charlie off the premises. Suddenly Charlie would rush out of the back door—Mr. Shaw from time to time had the notion that the children should use the back door so as to save the front hall carpet—and shouting: "Come *on*, Morcar! We shall be late," run exceedingly fast up the road, Morcar following steadily after. They arrived on the school steps just as the bell ceased to ring.

At school they shared a double desk together; assistant masters of timid disposition sometimes tried to separate them, feeling the pair to be a focus of disorder, but separation proved injudicious, driving them merely into disorder of an angrier kind. In lessons Charlie was quick and untidy, Morcar neat and slow. Charlie always finished his sums or French sentences or chemical experiments before the rest of the class, and had plenty of time to fly paper darts, play miniature knur and spell (that old Yorkshire game) with ruler and indiarubber, or beat Morcar at noughts and crosses. He never tempted Morcar to play till Morcar's class task was also finished, but this loyalty made him all the more impatient with his friend's lagging understanding. He explained what the teachers had failed to make clear to Morcar in a sibilant whisper which grew in volume with his impatience.

"No talking there, Shaw," commanded the master.

"Please sir, Morcar's so *slow*," cried the exasperated Shaw.

Indeed Morcar recalled absolutely nothing of what he had learned at school except some arithmetic and a little geometry, together with the fact that a Saxon earl of his name in northern England had rebelled against the Norman William the Conqueror—though when and why remained obscure to him. Oh, and the Spanish Armada, of course. Imagine any foreign nation thinking they could invade England! But Morcar remembered vividly Charlie's eager face, his witty schoolboy retorts, his thin pointing finger (rather dirty), the élan with which he shot up his hand when he knew the answer to a question, his disgust when Morcar got a written answer wrong. Morcar also remembered a rather handsome box of crayons given him by Charlie for a birthday present, which he used to colour maps at school. As regards maps and painting-lessons Morcar to his own surprise was rather effective, whereas Charlie's choice of colours was somehow ordinary and crude. But this was the exception to the general rule of Charlie's superior success in school, for Charlie usually took second or third place in class, while Morcar hovered comfortably halfway down.

It was not school in Annotsfield, however, but out-of-school hours which Morcar remembered all his life. Football, in which his solid vigorous body was more effective in the scrum though less speedy in the field than Charlie's slight frame; cricket, in which Charlie was a really graceful and effective bat and Harry a slow bowler with a sly twist which took many a wicket. At the back of the two Sycamore houses, behind their joint garden, lay a small rough field, reasonably level, which belonged to the Sycamore property and could be entered from either house; the two boys contrived a cricket pitch there and spent hours on it, whole days in the summer holidays, improving their play. Their different talents were admirably complementary, and if they could secure a young Shaw or two to field for them, their happiness was complete. Charlie was a very kind elder brother and took pains to instruct his family in cricket, which Harry entirely approved. If Eric or Hubert or one of the girls played well, Charlie applauded them heartily, crying: "Well done!" even when it was himself they had caught out. Harry thought this very good and right in Charlie.

Winnie would never consent to play cricket; she strolled out sometimes to watch them when her domestic and amatory preoccupations allowed, made a few scathing remarks on their crimson faces, tousled hair and dirty hands and shirts and strolled away again, shedding her brown hair-ribbon as she went. The two boys were not upset by her comments, however; they took them in good part because Winnie, especially after she was removed from school in her middle teens to help her mother in the house, was an invaluable ally and staunch friend. She warned them when Mr. Shaw was in a rage; she secretly repaired damages to their clothes, represented in a favourable light accidents caused by cricket balls to windows or to Mr. Morcar's cherished plants and coaxed money for gingerbeer from her mother's household purse. She egged on Mr. Shaw into buying a bicycle for Charlie, which secured one for Harry too; when her father gave them a dilapidated old shed he had bought at a sale to keep their bicycles in, it was Winnie who furnished it with decrepit but recognisable chairs and found two cushions and urged Harry to beg an old table from his mother, so that it became quite a private room for them, known as the Den. Winnie took care of their precious bats and cricket balls and footballs, preventing the younger Shaws from using and ruining them in their absence; she greased their skates; in successive stages she fed their goldfish, their mice, their beetles, their canaries. Winnie was a year older than Harry and Charlie. With her bright hazel eyes and unexpectedly dark eyebrows, her small even white teeth, her fresh colour, her dimple, she was considered a pretty girl; her manners were easy and her retorts provocative, and she always had a boy or two on hand. These swelled quite agreeably the concourse of young people always to be found in the Shaw half of the Sycamores.

At times indeed Mr. Shaw burst into a rage and complained that all these many guests were eating him out of hearth and home. Then all the Shaws, the suitors, the friends and Harry

25

dispersed rapidly, so that the stairs and doorways seemed full of flying ankles. Mrs. Shaw was left to soothe her husband, and after they had sat together quietly for a time the temperature seemed to lower; Mrs. Shaw's faded and small but rather sweet voice could be heard mildly singing an old-fashioned ballad— *I Stood on the Bridge at Midnight* or *Juanita*—and the children crept into the room again, taking care to wash and brush rather thoroughly before doing so. Mr. Shaw would be found smoking a cigar and listening to his wife with a great air of benevolence, but this was still unstable, and woe betide any young person, Shaw or other, who then disturbed his mood by untoward speech or action. Morcar was rather apt to incur frowns on these occasions, for he was as clumsy as a young puppy and chairs seemed to fall if he approached within a yard of them.

For some reason, he never told tales at home about Mr. Shaw's rages. The parents of the two families were in a sense quite intimate. Mr. Shaw and Mr. Morcar paced up and down the common back garden on summer evenings discussing textile problems, argued pleasantly about the same topics while Mr. Morcar planted out his seedlings, and went to football matches together in winter. Mrs. Morcar helped Mrs. Shaw to cut out and sew the innumerable garments required by the large Shaw family, and Mrs. Shaw who was an admirable cook assisted her younger neighbour with recipes for baking and preserving. They often visited each other's houses for high tea, on Saturdays and holidays. But Morcar felt that there was not the confidence and approval between the families at the parental level which existed on his own. Mrs. Morcar sometimes murmured darkly that Mrs. Shaw had a good deal to put up with; Mr. Shaw sometimes addressed to Harry sarcastic textile remarks about his father's business which Harry understood perfectly though he pretended not to. Frederick Morcar had recently become a Town Councillor, and Mr. Shaw had a habit of referring to Councillor Morcar with a mock-respectful inflexion which Harry found disagreeable. It was better to ignore parental comment, which in any case was sure to be incomprehensible, and pretend a respectful affection for one's friend's parents, even if for some reason one did not altogether feel it.

There were times, of course, when owing to family tension it was better to leave the Sycamores behind altogether for an hour or two. In their young days on such occasions Harry and Charlie played at Red Indians, or Boers, or robber chiefs, on the wooded steeps of Hurst Bank. Presently part of the land was devoted to building operations, the lower fringe of trees was cut down and in its place appeared stacks of clean white planks, interlocked to form hollow triangles. These tall stacks could be climbed, Charlie discovered, and the hollow space within formed a completely private retreat, hidden from the eyes of all the world. Winnie, who was let into the secret of these timber nests and sometimes consented to play the chief's wife or captive maiden which such fine lairs seemed to demand, climbed in skilfully without damage to her long ribbed black wool stockings but thought the planks insalubrious and threatened to betray the boys' whereabouts to their mothers if they haunted the Bank too closely.

So then they took out their iron hoops and drove these before them with looped iron rods on long excursions, trotting all the time. The distances they accomplished thus were quite prodigious. Turning from Annotsfield they pressed up the hill through Hurst, came out on the moorland road, bowled along rapidly, with the wind fresh in their faces, between the rough grass and the heather, till they reached the remote Moorcock Inn on the wilds of Marthwaite Moor, then turning to the left they coaxed the hoops over the white sand and dark rock of the narrow winding path towards the bluff of Scape Scar. To keep the hoops erect and turning along the hazards of this path, almost buried beneath overhanging ling and heather, demanded a skill which they were proud to give and an attention which left them little time to observe the landscape, though occasionally they paused and gazed at the various rocky Pennine summits rising about them, sombre beneath the swift grey clouds, with a vague sense of pleasure. From Scape Scar the descent to the Ire Valley was agreeably risky, for the path became so precipitous that the hoops continually threatened to escape and leap down the hillside, to destruction against a jutting rock, burial amidst deep russet bracken, or drowning in the dirty waters of the Ire. They crossed the river by the bridge at Marthwaite and bowled down the busy paved Ire Valley, lined with mills, to Irebridge. Sometimes they went on to Annotsfield, glancing at Mr. Shaw's mill on the way; more often they crossed the Ire again at Irebridge and found themselves at the bottom of Hurst Bank. This hill was a considerable trial at the end of a long day's run—the boys' faces grew crimson, their foreheads wet and their breath uneven, for the hoops needed innumerable applications of force to drive them up the Bank and it was considered dishonourable to allow them to cease rolling and carry them. But the disadvantage of the severe gradient was outweighed in their minds by the fact that this route enabled them to make a complete circle from the Sycamores without retracing a single yard. When they had topped the worst of the rise they argued agreeably as to which of them felt the hotter: Charlie who was wiry though slight or Harry who looked stronger because more solid.

As they grew older they grew to scorn the hoops, and their excursions shortened because they were not very fond of mere walking, which they found dull, but after the bicycles came they travelled far afield—to Hudley, to Bradford, or over the Pennines into Lancashire. For the longer of these trips they were allowed to be absent all day. The initiative usually came from Charlie. On a bright holiday morning there would come a knock on the back door while the Morcars were at breakfast; a pause followed while the Morcars' maid—like the Shaws they now had only one—climbed the steps from her kitchen in the cellar; then there were sounds of brisk colloquy; then Charlie bounced into the room, his cheeks very pink, his hazel eyes very bright, and twisting his schoolcap in his hands announced breathlessly that his mother wanted to know if Harry could go out for the day with him—Winnie was buttering a teacake for him now. The Morcars smilingly agreed; there came a long five minutes' wait while Mrs. Morcar's slender fingers sliced a teacake too, and a further delay later in the Shaws' kitchen when Winnie, exclaiming: "Wait!" vanished into the cellar and reappeared with some especial delicacy, such as a treacle tart, some ginger snap or a handful of rock buns. Smiling, yet looking apprehensively over her shoulder in case her mother should appear, to the accompaniment of scolding from the Shaws' loud-voiced maid, Winnie swiftly tucked these into neat white paper packages.

"That tart's for dinner, Miss Winnie," grumbled the maid: "I don't know what Mrs. Shaw will say if you give it those boys."

"Well, Master Charles has to have some dinner too, doesn't he?" riposted Winnie sharply.

The maid muttered and grumbled and looked askance at Morcar, but was not inhospitable enough to say what was in her mind. "There won't be enough to go round," she usually ventured.

"Then somebody can go without," said Winnie tartly, holding out the packets.

Morcar, ashamed, had once attempted to decline the delicacy and put aside her hand, but at this Winnie's cheeks flamed, her eyes snapped, she scolded him in a voice which rose, and crying: "I suppose you think it isn't good enough for you!" she threw the package down on the kitchen dresser so that it burst and the piece of apple tart within dissolved. Morcar gaped at her, astounded and alarmed, while she stood before him breathing anger.

Suddenly the tension of her slender body relaxed, her very hair seemed to sink to rest about her head. "Well, never mind," she said in a soothing, calming tone. She snatched a fork from a nearby drawer, and swiftly restored the sticky mess to the semblance of something eatable. In a moment she had tied the parcel round with string and was offering it to Morcar. Colouring and hanging his head, he took it; his fingers touched her warm pulsating palm.

"Come *on*, Morcar!" shouted Charlie.

Winnie followed the boys to the door and watched them as they crammed their parcels into the small black leather pouches attached to the saddles of their machines. Morcar's fingers were clumsy and the pouch would not close.

"Never mind, Harry," said Winnie again, watching him from the door.

"It's all right," muttered Morcar, sniffing. His voice, which had recently broken, sounded very gruff—he was profoundly hankful that it did not go off into one of its tiresome squeaks. He mounted and rode off along the asphalt path. There were some tin buckets full of water standing about, containing the Shaws' pots of aspidistras receiving their weekly immersion; on an impulse—for though he understood Winnie's resentment and was sorry to have caused it, he felt a sturdy determination not to be put down more than he deserved—Morcar steered the bicycle skilfully in and out between the buckets so as to weave a well-curved figure eight. At the corner of the house he looked back at Winnie and gave a cheerful grin. She smiled a trifle uncertainly. He touched his cap in cheeky salutation. Winnie frowned, but the dimple in her cheek betrayed her.

Next time the boys set off on a cycling expedition Winnie put their parcels on the dresser, then withdrew to the hearthrug and stood there without a word, her amber lashes resting on her cheeks. After a moment's pause Morcar took up his parcel and muttered: "Thanks." Winnie said promptly: "You're welcome."

In Morcar's estimation the matter was now settled and he thought no more of it; it troubled him not at all as he munched Mrs. Shaw's admirable cakes, until one day his mother found some alien crumbs adhering to a small parcel of sewing materials which he had fetched for her from town and which had of course travelled to the Sycamores in the saddle-pouch. A few questions revealed that her son had been eking out his provisions by accepting additions from the Shaws. A hot flush stained Mrs. Morcar's cheek and she rebuked Harry with real anger. Councillor Morcar chancing to enter the room at the moment, she explained the situation in a rapid flow of speech very unlike her usual reticence. Her husband looked grave.

"You shouldn't have done so, Harry," he said in his kind if grating tones: "always stand on your own feet, you know."

"And from the Shaws, of all people!" cried Mrs. Morcar.

"What's wrong with the Shaws?" said Harry with resentment.

"Nothing, love. Charlie's a grand lad," they said hastily.

It was the very next day that the incident occurred which clarified these parental discontents and made the boys deep friends for life. It was a Saturday in September; the Morcars were at the

Shaws' for tea; the meal was over and Winnie and the maid were clearing the heaped table. Councillor Morcar and Mr. Shaw had attended an exciting football match that afternoon, a cuptie in which Annotsfield had gloriously triumphed, and accordingly they were both in an expansive mood. After discussing the match in great detail, they wandered off into business matters and began to tell textile anecdotes in which each mildly boasted of his own skill. In this sort of competition Mr. Shaw was soon far ahead of all rivals and the conversation became a monologue tending always to the glory of John William Shaw. Harry found it tedious, and after a while heard only snatches, replaying the football match to himself during the duller parts. He was suddenly recalled to Mr. Shaw's meaning by a feeling that something uncomfortable was being said. Mrs. Morcar's lips were compressed, Mrs. Shaw looked pink and worried; Mr. Morcar was very busy filling his pipe.

"I could see they were just what I wanted," chuckled Mr. Shaw triumphantly: "So I out with my scissors and cut a strip off the lot."

"And didn't he object?" enquired Mr. Morcar in a very dry tone.

"Nay, he was in the inner office," explained Mr. Shaw, laughing. "What the eye doesn't see, the heart doesn't grieve at. I'm having 'em all made up now, in cheaper yarn of course—they were just what I was looking for."

Could this story possibly mean what it appeared to do, wondered Harry, aghast. Mr. Shaw appeared to be saying that in the outer office of the warehouse of some great manufacturing firm—Armitages', perhaps, or Oldroyds'; yes, he had said Oldroyds'—he had perceived some fine patterns which were just the kind of thing a customer of his own had wished to buy. He had cut a strip from the pattern and was having them copied in cheaper stuff—thus stealing the designs. How or why anybody had been such a fool as to give John William Shaw access to a place where a rival's next season's patterns were lying about, Harry could not understand, and he had missed the part of the story which described this interesting detail. He leaned forward and cried out:

"But how did you get into the Oldroyds' warehouse, Mr. Shaw?"

"Harry, fetch me some more tobacco," said his father quickly. "There's a packet in the bookcase drawer. I'm waiting," he added on a sharper note, as Harry did not immediately move. "Run along."

Everyone seemed to be gazing so sternly at Harry that he was confused; he blushed, uncurled his ankles from the sofa legs and ran quickly from the room.

It was some minutes before he returned, for in the place indicated he found a packet of tobacco of another kind than that habitually smoked by his father and ransacked the drawer before resigning himself to credit that this was the one meant. When he eventually completed the errand, none of the Shaw children was in the room, the two sets of parents were sitting alone and talking town politics. His father's pipe lay on the table at his elbow. Harry put the tobacco beside it and tiptoed out to look for Charlie. The house seemed quiet, so he went out to the back field, where some of the younger Shaws, who were playing at rounders, told him that their brother was in the Den. Cheered, he went towards it rapidly and pressed down the latch, shouting his friend's name. To his surprise, the door did not yield; he pushed it resolutely, it gave and he found himself face to face with Winnie in a tearing rage.

"You can't come in," she said abruptly. Her bright cheeks were mottled with anger, her round chin trembled. She made to shut him out.

"I don't mind Harry," came in a muffled version of Charlie's light pleasant voice.

Winnie threw back the door angrily and stepped aside. Charlie was standing with his back to the door with his hands in his pockets and his head bent down. His whole attitude expressed a deep wretchedness.

"What's wrong?" enquired Harry in alarm. He squeezed round his friend to look into his face and found his worst fears confirmed, for Charlie showed unmistakable signs of having shed tears. "What's up, Charlie?" he said in his gruffest tones.

"I shall never forgive him," said Winnie. Her tone was low and vicious. She flounced from the shed, slamming the door.

Harry cleared his throat. "But what *is* wrong?" he said.

"The same as it usually is," said Charlie bitterly. "You heard him about those patterns. It's so … He does things … He isn't *honest,*" he broke out with a sob. He gulped and sniffed and got his voice under control, then said with infinite sadness: "My trouble is always Father."

A warm love and sorrow filled Morcar's heart. He wanted to console, to assure his friend of his understanding, his sympathy, his eternal loyalty; but none of those things could get themselves said. And indeed if they were said, they would deepen Charlie's trouble by revealing how deeply troubling Morcar thought it. There in the hot musty bicycle-house, surrounded by watering-cans and tins of paint, old cricket gloves and wickets, some sunflower seeds which the children were growing on flannel, a pair of gardening shears and a rake in one corner which fell over as he moved, starting off a sleepy bluebottle to buzz once more up the pane, there in the garden shed he was faced, felt Morcar, by one of the great moments of his life. What could he say? All he could do was to put himself on Charlie's level by confiding the deepest trouble that he himself owned.

"Mine's money," he blurted.

Charlie turned, astonished, and Morcar was astonished too. Until he spoke he had no idea that he was worried about the Morcars' financial position, but now he knew he had been anxious about it for years. McKinley. Dingley. The closed weaving-shed, never yet reopened. The Sycamores instead of Hurstfield. A pink printed form with *Annotsfield Borough Council* on top and sums of money written in below, to which was gummed a red slip saying FINAL NOTICE. Mr. Shaw's jeering jokes, and his mother's vexation about his accepting the Shaws' sandwiches.

"I'm sorry. But you're lucky if that's all," Charlie said bitterly. "I didn't know. But I own I thought it was a bit funny at the time, your father selling Hurst Bank Wood in such a hurry."

There was a silence. Morcar felt the blood rushing to his face at this blunt confirmation of his unconscious fear. He had known neither that his father owned the land nor that he had sold it, but a hurried sale was only too clear an indication of the state of Morcar affairs. Charlie was looking at him with pity in his eyes.

"He's sold our part of the Sycamores, too," said Charlie softly. "To Father. Your father owned them both, you know."

Morcar could not speak.

"Well, never mind," said Charlie warmly, catching his arm. "Let's take out our bikes."

From that moment the boys were true, deep, lifelong friends, who concealed nothing from each other.

7

Death of a Councillor

And yet the sale of Hurst Bank Wood and half the Sycamores was not the worst thing Morcar learned that day, for if the gradual relinquishment of the property Alderman Morcar had carefully collected indicated a failing prosperity, the change in Councillor Morcar's tobacco indicated a failing health. His pipe, his unfailing friend for so many years, no longer tasted sweet to him. Having no idea at first that the change lay in himself, he sought to remedy it by sampling a fresh brand. For a few days this seemed to satisfy, then an expression of distaste crept over his face as he smoked, he leaned forward abruptly and knocked out the still burning dottle from the pipe.

"I think I'll go back to my Owl Cut, Clara," he said.

"I never thought you'd fancy anything else," said Mrs. Morcar in a wise wifely tone.

But a few days later the Owl Cut was again out of favour. A few days after that its position was once more retrieved, and Harry, obscurely relieved, prepared to dismiss the matter from his mind. Somehow it had worried him; no doubt it was only part of the general undecipherable mystery of grown-up behaviour, but the obvious distress it caused his father worried him. Why, his father had looked positively haggard as he knocked out his pipe! It was a pleasure to see him now leaning back in his chair and smoking comfortably. Even as he watched, however, the boy saw a faint look of perplexity creep over his father's face. His heart sank, a core of uneasiness formed in his mind. Sure enough, next day his father came home with tobacco in a different wrapping. The boy watched apprehensively as he unfolded the tinfoil—his father was always neat and careful in his movements—and shredded the tobacco into his pouch.

"Yes, this is milder," he announced with satisfaction.

But a few days later he was again smoking Owl Cut.

This matter of the tobacco, apparently so trifling and even silly, really so significant, dragged on for the next three months till it became a protracted nightmare. A whole collection of half-consumed packets gathered in the bookcase drawer; every time Mr. Morcar opened the drawer he began an irritable lament which lasted dreary minutes. Over and over again he explained to his wife, to his son, to Mr. Shaw, to his fellow Councillors, to his cashier and foreman, to anyone who would listen, that he had smoked Owl Cut for seventeen years and now he could not abide it.

"I must be growing old, Clara," he joked. "That's what it is."

"Nonsense," said Mrs. Morcar firmly.

Mr. Morcar wrote a letter to the manufacturers complaining that they had let down the quality of their product; they replied in affable terms, denying the charge and sending a selection of all their brands for "such a valued customer" to sample. Mr. Morcar was greatly pleased; an almost childish look of happiness illumined his face as he examined the packets and explained to his son the meaning of the various symbols they bore. He took them next door and displayed them to Mr. Shaw, who was not a pipe-smoker. He wrote a polite note to the manufacturers, promising to let them know his preference when he had smoked a pipeful of each brand; but it was a week before he sampled them. Mrs. Morcar and Harry watched him anxiously. He took a pull or two, held the pipe away from him and looked at it. The moment that followed seemed an eternity. At last he replaced the pipe in his mouth.

"Not bad," he said.

Harry gave a long sigh; Mrs. Morcar with a shake rearranged the embroidery on her knee. Presently Mr. Shaw came in, smoking one of his customary cigars.

"Well, how's the tobacco, Fred?" he enquired.

"I don't care for it much," replied Mr. Morcar distastefully.

Mr. Shaw gave him a sharp glance. "Tell you what, Fred," he suggested: "I think your digestion's out of order. You should see your doctor and get a bottle to put it right. What do you think, Mrs. Morcar, eh?"

Mrs. Morcar seemed to have some difficulty in speaking. "I've been telling him so," she said at last in an airy tone.

A doctor! Was his father really ill enough to need a doctor? Harry looked at Mr. Shaw, whose sallow eyelids were lowered, then tried to see his father as his neighbour saw him. He perceived with a pang that his father's mild brown eyes were unnaturally large and burning, the skin tight-drawn across his forehead, his cheeks sunken and pale. He had lost weight too; his waistcoat across which he wore Alderman Morcar's famous watch-chain hung loose so that the chain drooped and sagged. His hands looked wrinkled, fleshless. Harry got up suddenly and leaving his homework unfinished went into the house next door. He found the Shaws and a couple of Winnie's admirers all playing a round card game of a noisy kind in which they had coaxed Mrs. Shaw to take part, so he had no opportunity to speak to Charlie privately. But he had no need; from Charlie's welcoming glance and smile, from Winnie's mild greeting, very unlike her usual pert reception, from the way Mrs. Shaw made room for him beside her, he knew that they had all guessed his trouble.

Next day when he came home from school he met his mother in the hall carrying an empty glass and a spoon on a small tray. She looked flushed and troubled.

"The doctor's sent your father to bed for a few days," she said. "For a rest. It's his heart. He's been rather worried about business lately."

His father never smoked again. All through that winter his pipe hung, empty and cold, in the oak rack beside the hearth. This picture mingled in Morcar's mind with the wet streaky haunches of a dark brown horse beneath the gaslight from a street-lamp, bands of leather harness and reins dangling through the air—the hansom in which his father went hopefully out to Town Council meetings or returned from them exhausted. How many times that winter Harry at his mother's bidding ran along through the cold driving West Riding rain to the cab proprietor at the end of Hurst Road, to fetch a hansom for his father! How many times, at night, he heard the horses' hoofs clop-clopping down the road and halting at the Sycamores' gate. Harry paused in his homework, his mother raised her head and waited for footsteps to come up the path; none came; then they knew that his father was too tired to dismount without help. Harry ran out and unbuttoned the apron and pulled the shiny black leather away, while his father, unconscious of his own delay, fumbled with thin

39

nerveless fingers in his pocket for coins and made slow jokes with the cabman. Then the hansom became a standing order, morning and midday and night, to take his father to and from the mill. Then it came at morning and noon only; in the afternoon his father rested at home.

In the New Year came the picture of his mother in a large white cooking apron with her sleeves rolled up, carefully placing little squares of newspaper between the dessert plates in the china cupboard. It seemed they must leave the Sycamores and go to a smaller house, since his father was giving up the mill. Mrs. Shaw came in to condole, panting a little, her large bulk spread over the drawing-room settee.

"I'm afraid this is a bad blow for you, Mrs. Morcar love," she said.

"It will be better so," replied Mrs. Morcar proudly: "Fred will have more time to give to his Council work."

Winnie came in and helped to pack.

"Winnie's been a real good help," announced Mrs. Morcar at tea-time. "She has indeed."

Her tone implied that this was something of a surprise to her, and indeed for some reason, Harry could not then fathom what, there was always an antagonism between his mother and Winnie.

They moved to a house in Hurst Road, a house which Morcar could not, would not, remember. He excused himself for this because they lived there less than six months, but the real reason for his rejection of its image was that he never had a happy moment there. It was wretched to be so far away from Charlie, for it meant that he seemed always to reach the Sycamores at the wrong moment. When one lived next door, one took soundings, so to speak, one tried the temperature of the water with one's toe before entering and withdrew if the water seemed chill and the

40

moment inopportune. But living a quarter of a mile away made setting out for the Shaws' quite an important step, not easy to retract; one could not hang about in somebody else's back garden and wait for Mr. Shaw's temper to cool or Mrs. Shaw's baking to finish; moreover, Harry had a feeling he was not as welcome to Mr. and Mrs. Shaw as he had been in days of old. Charlie, of course, was always the same, and Winnie's acid was mingled with sweetness quite as before, indeed if anything it was a trifle sweeter. But a shade of vexation passed over Mr. Shaw's sallow face nowadays whenever he saw Morcar, and Mrs. Shaw asked: "How's your father?" rather as though she regarded Mr. Morcar's illness as his own fault, due entirely to his own perversity, as if he could cure himself and cease being a trouble to everyone, if he would only make the effort.

This was not true, for Mr. Morcar made every effort that could be made. Staunch and cheerful always, a smile fixed on his haggard face, he drank whatever medicine was prescribed, rested when he was bidden to rest, accepted a rug over his knees when one was offered, made no complaints about the loss of his business, spoke of the few yards of garden which separated the house from Hurst Road with genuine enthusiasm, welcomed old friends when they came to see him but was content with his family when they stayed away, attended the Town Council indomitably and was persistent at Eastgate Sunday School until the doctor forbade. Then indeed Mr. Morcar shrank and grew sad, and his clothes hung so loose on him it could hardly be believed they were his own. After a week or two of brooding he expressed the view that he ought to resign his ward and his Sunday School class, but Mrs. Morcar would not let him. With a persistence which Harry did not understand and which vexed him for his father's sake, she opposed all suggestions of resignation.

41

Accordingly when a new section of Hursthead Park, with a bowling green and a neat pavilion in the Swiss chalet style, which had long been a pet scheme of his, was opened in the summer, Mr. Morcar was still a member of the Parks and Gardens committee. With infinite precaution he was conveyed to the scene, resting by the way on the green-painted iron park seats, and sat in front of the pavilion with his wife beside him, while the opening ceremony was performed by the Mayor of Annotsfield.

It was a bright July day, warm by West Riding standards, with scarcely any breeze. Mrs. Morcar was very smart in a bright blue dress of net over silk, a black transparent hat with an ostrich feather fastened in with a black velvet bow and a pink flower, and a long white feather boa. The courage of this attire Harry did not at the time appreciate, but he thought his mother looked very elegant. The new turf was a wonderfully fresh light green, the geraniums were very scarlet and gave forth a strange musky scent, the plants bordering the geometrical beds had deeply indented leaves, alternately purplish and silvery white in colour. Quite a fair-sized crowd had gathered to witness the ceremony, Harry and Charlie modestly concealing themselves in the rear.

"Before asking the Mayor to finish the good work he has begun, by bowling the first wood," said the Chairman of the Parks and Gardens Committee, rising at the conclusion of the Mayor's speech: "I am going to call on our friend here, Councillor Frederick Morcar, who has been interested in this scheme from the start, just to say a few words to us, on account of him being so interested in the scheme."

There was some applause, and Mr. Morcar, rising, smiled with pleasure. His gaunt face, livid cheek and burning eyes impressed the crowd, and the applause deepened. Mr. Morcar held on to his wife's chair and in a thin grating voice began a speech of which very few words could be heard—"Mr. Chairman" and "Parks and Gardens Committee" were all his son could distinguish. After a few sentences he hesitated, cleared his throat, seemed to consider, then waved his hand to the Chairman as if to return the conduct of the meeting to him, and sat down. Mrs. Morcar leaned towards her other neighbour and whispered urgently; the request was passed along through the Mayor, and the Chairman poured out a glass of water and rose with an anxious look to hand it to his colleague in person.

After a brief but hearty round of applause rendered to a sick man doing his duty the crowd turned abruptly towards the green where the next part of the ceremony was to take place; there was a general bustle, and when Harry next caught sight of his father he was being helped into the chalet by Mrs. Morcar and the Mayor. His mother's arm was round his father's waist, his father's head was bowed and he stumbled. Harry turned and pushed towards the chalet roughly, Charlie at his heels. They came out of the crowd to find a policeman guarding the entrance. Harry halted, disconcerted, but Charlie slipped away and beckoning him with a nod, led him round to knock on a side door. There was a pause, then the door opened suddenly to reveal the Mayor's mace-bearer, a man with waxed moustaches and some insignia on the shoulders of his frock-coat. The points of his moustache seemed positively to bristle with outrage at the sight of the two schoolboys and he told them in a sharp emphatic whisper that they could not come in. At this Harry found his question stuck in his throat, so Charlie asked it for him.

"Please, how is Councillor Morcar?"

"Eh, love, he's dead!" exclaimed the mace-bearer distressfully.

So then presently Morcar heard the sound of his father's coffin being bumped down the narrow stairs of the house in Hurst

Road, amid heavy breathings and whispered instructions from the undertaker's men; again there was a sizeable funeral and many wreaths, again Morcar stood by an open grave and shuddered while a handful of earth rattled on a coffin lid. There was a funeral lunch at the house for some little-known relatives and a few friends, including of course the Shaws, while the Shaws' maid and Winnie bustled about helpfully in the small kitchen. Mr. Shaw made what amounted to a speech extolling Mr. Morcar, praising him as a true friend, a kind husband and father, a generous giver of his time and energy in the service of the public. It was all true and Harry felt a lump in his throat and tears in his eyes until he glanced across at Charlie, whose long dark lashes, downcast, could not conceal his air of impatient derision. Harry really wondered at his friend's expression and would have been hurt by it had he not known Charlie's habit of being one jump ahead of everybody else in his perceptions—no doubt his derision was directed at something quite other than Mr. Shaw's mild oration, thought Morcar.

The party broke up at last; Winnie and the maid in spite of Mrs. Morcar's protests finished the washing-up, then quickly went away. Mrs. Morcar and her son were left alone in the silent house, feeling strangely exposed now that the blinds no longer covered the windows. Mrs. Morcar sat silent for a long time, very upright in her chair as always, with her well-shaped hands folded in her lap. Her son sat opposite by the table, acutely embarrassed by his mother's long immobility and silence, but too tender-hearted to violate her sorrow by any speech or movement which she might think unfeeling. At last Mrs. Morcar said:

"Well, he died a Councillor."

She rose and left the room.

8

Entrance to Industry

Some three weeks later—it was in the summer holidays—Morcar came home from a morning on his bicycle to find his mother in her cooking apron with her sleeves rolled up, packing the red and gold dessert service into a large wicker skep marked J.H.M. He looked at these initials enquiringly, to conceal from himself the sinking of his heart. His mother followed the direction of his glance.

"I got your father to keep the skep back when he gave up the mill," she said. She added in a lower tone: "In case we wanted it."

A foreboding of death and disaster so long ago, so practical and so accurately fulfilled, wounded Harry; it seemed mean and disloyal, a treachery against his father.

"When are we moving?" he asked abruptly.

"Next Friday," replied his mother.

In later life nothing struck Morcar with such a sense of tragi-comedy as his mother's immutable preference for indirect communication. Mrs. Morcar never spoke to him directly of their financial situation and their plans, but it emerged in the course of the next few days that his father had left almost nothing on which his wife and son could live and that they were moving into a tiny house, really a workman's cottage, in a row along Hurst Road. The College Board of Governors had been very kind, remarked Mrs. Morcar on another occasion; they had accepted the notice for Harry as though it had been given at the beginning of the term, so that there would be no further fees to pay—this was her method of informing her son that he was to leave school at once. Harry did not care twopence about leaving school, but to leave Charlie was a different matter. The Shaws were away on their summer holiday just then, at Bridlington, and Morcar was missing Charlie sorely. Now he found he was to do without Charlie always—except, of course, in the evenings and at the weekends. It was a bleak outlook. He sat silent, stunned.

"Mr. Shaw is giving you the chance for your father's sake, you know, Harry," observed Mrs. Morcar next day, as mother and son sat at tea together. "So you must work hard and do the best you can."

So he was to go to work at Mr. Shaw's! Immediately Harry's world, which had looked so black, took on a happy, rosy, hopeful hue. He asked nothing better than to go to work at once—he was a big burly lad in his middle teens, he felt strong and shrewd and full of common sense, sure to do well; textile processes, in some way or other, were quite familiar to him and not in the least intimidating. It would be splendid to get out into the world, to earn money, to support his mother; he felt suddenly no longer a boy but a man, with a wide range of adventures opening before him, highly coloured, exciting. If now it had been discovered that his next year's fees at school had been paid by his father, so that he could remain there another year, he would have been disappointed. And to work at Mr. Shaw's! What a piece of luck! In his father's lifetime he had not thought much of Mr. Shaw's place, for Mr. Shaw leased half a brick mill at the bottom of the town between Eastgate and Irebridge, and its interior arrangements had seemed to Morcar incommodious and muddled. But now Prospect Mills seemed Paradise, since Charlie would be working there presently. A gush of joy and hope filled Morcar's heart; he smiled all over his candid pleasant face, and asked:

"When am I to start, Mother?"

"The Monday after Wakes Week," replied Mrs. Morcar. She looked doubtfully at his bright face and seemed to ponder, resting her hand maternally on the top of the cosied teapot. After a while she sighed and said: "Well!" and roused herself. When she had cleared away the meal she returned to the room with one of Mr. Morcar's blue and white check aprons—the kind known locally as a "brat"—in her hand. "Try this on," she said.

Although Harry was not yet full-grown and lacked several inches of his father's height, his shoulders were already broader.

"It doesn't matter—I can leave the top tape undone," he offered.

Mrs. Morcar did not even reply to this suggestion; she took out her sewing basket, unpicked every seam and with her customary skill completely refashioned the overall.

On the following Friday the Morcars moved. Harry was active in the preparations, which he enjoyed, and rode on the box of the furniture van conveying a selection of their previous furniture to their new home. The van drew up at Number 102 Hurst Road, Mrs. Morcar who had gone on ahead opened the door, Harry clambered down and ran in. He stopped, aghast. The

47

room was tiny, with a steep narrow staircase leading directly from the rear. He turned on his mother with an impetuous question, but she was gazing at him with such a look of anguish that he was astonished and alarmed—he had never seen such a naked expression of feeling in her face before—and mumbling instead something about helping to unload, ran out of the house again. As he helped the removal man to let down the back of the van and secure it by chains so that it formed a low platform, there was a tumult of feeling in his heart, which presently settled into the conviction, firm though inarticulate, unclarified, that this was a disaster and he must bear it like a man. Accordingly he became very cheerful and even facetious in his manner of handling the furniture, carrying chairs light-heartedly on his head and shouting "Whoa!" to the removal man as they struggled together to edge the Morcars' sideboard through the tiny door. There was a neat little scullery in the rear with which he professed himself enormously satisfied, but it was beyond his powers of deception to show pleasure over the outside lavatory beyond, reached by a descent of five stone steps into the bowels of the earth.

While they were in the very thick of the removal there came a knock at the front door and Harry found himself ushering in an elderly lady of the Eastgate congregation whom he knew by sight, carrying a parcel about which she seemed to have mysterious business with his mother. The parcel when opened contained, as he saw, a length of crash and a few scraps of brightly coloured material which proved to be intended as patterns. Mrs. Morcar was vexed at being caught in her apron with her sleeves rolled up and repeatedly expressed this vexation by observing that they would be straight tomorrow, but she broke off the work of removal to draw out from a sideboard cupboard a box full of

48

coloured skeins of silk in great variety, and proceeded to match them to the patterns with a good deal of care and animation. Harry hovering in the doorway could not but be interested in this matching process, and approved his mother's choice amongst the bright twisted skeins, which however was overruled by the visitor. As the latter left she remarked:

"About next Wednesday, then?"

"Next Wednesday," replied Mrs. Morcar firmly.

"I'll call about the same time?"

"Harry can bring them round if you like," offered Mrs. Morcar.

"Oh, no, I'll call," said the visitor hastily, stepping into the street. She looked back over her shoulder and added in the high artificial voice of embarrassed kindness: "And you'll perhaps think over that other matter and let me have your decision at the same time?"

"You have my decision now," said Mrs. Morcar fiercely. "What I do for Eastgate I do for love."

"Well," hesitated the other woman. "I honour you for it of course, Mrs. Morcar." She seemed to wish to urge the matter further but to find it impossible in view of Mrs. Morcar's stern bearing, and gathering her skirt into her hand went off down the street.

That very night, though plainly wearied by the removal which in any case was not yet quite complete, Mrs. Morcar cut the crash into lengths for antimacassars, tacked their edges ready for hemstitching, and applied orange-coloured transfers to the ends, pressing the flimsy paper with a hot iron to imprint the pattern on the material.

Harry pondered. He admitted readily that, in the Yorkshire phrase, he was "slow in the uptake," but the process when once accomplished was fairly sure. When he woke in the morning he knew that his mother meant to earn money by her talent for sewing and embroidery, that the Eastgate Dorcas meeting had offered to pay her for her services to them in cutting-out and general direction, that Mrs. Morcar had refused. Then he felt such a restless suspense, such a burning eager desire for the Monday after Wakes Week to arrive when he could go to work, that he could hardly contain himself. He threw the furniture about the house with a strength and energy which astonished his mother; with a slight frown of concentration down the centre of his fair placid forehead he carried in coal, cleaned the rusty range until it shone, rode off on his bicycle to fetch provisions, on his return swilled down the five lavatory steps. He observed that the other houses in the row kept their steps, the floor and the slab on the top of the tiny odorous chamber yellow-stoned, and remembering vaguely the utensils he had seen employed for this purpose, looked about in the scullery and found a bucket containing a brush, a cloth and a knob of the yellow stuff. A rough fibre mat, he seemed to remember, was also necessary. He found one, filled the bucket with water and going out to the back premises, knelt on the second step and began experiments with the yellow-stone. Suddenly his mother rushed from the house and snatched the bucket from him. Her face was white with fury.

"Come in," she whispered in a tone of raging disgust. "Harry! Come in at once."

"I'll just finish this," said Morcar stolidly.

"No!" whispered his mother as before. "Come in at once!"

"Who's going to do it, then? You?" said Morcar.

"It's not a man's work," said Mrs. Morcar, trembling with anger.

Harry considered. "I think I'd better do it," he said presently.

His tone was mild but final; he seemed to know that he was quite as obstinate as his mother. They were both holding the handle of the bucket; Morcar gave it a jerk towards him and the water slopped over on his mother's dress. With an angry exclamation she released her hold and moved with a swift step into the house.

Half an hour later, just as he finished the roof slab, she summoned him to a meal; her face was calm and she made no reference to the incident. Harry made no such reference either; he replaced the bucket and the mat in their proper places, washed his hands at the sink and sat down to the table without a word. He then discovered that—for almost the first time in his life—he was not hungry. But it was necessary to eat, he felt, or the battle would be lost, so he chewed his way through the Saturday's steak staunchly.

The next week was a protracted ordeal. It was Annotsfield Wakes: the holiday week when the mills slumbered and all the Annotsfield inhabitants who could afford disported themselves at the seaside. The town lay empty beneath the bright hot sunshine; the looms were silent, most of the shops were closed. Morcar mooned about listlessly, alone, for the Shaws were still absent. His mother urged him to get out into the fresh air while he still had the chance, but as he had never experienced the limitations to freedom imposed by the hours of regular labour, he took this recommendation impatiently. However, there was nothing else to do; so he rode out on his bicycle every day. His favourite round was one often ridden by Charlie and himself; up the moorland road to the Moorcock, then by the rough path over the brow to Scape Scar, down the steep slope into the Ire Valley and down the valley road to Irebridge. But in Irebridge, instead of crossing the Ire and regaining Hurst by Hurstholt Road, he kept on the road towards Annotsfield so that he might turn off into the small side street where stood Mr. Shaw's business premises.

Prospect Mills was not perhaps a very inspiring sight; low and smoke-blackened, with dirty windows, it belied its name by gazing into a row of equally smoke-blackened small dark houses. To the side, wooden gates, once red now pink with time, gave on the yard Mr. Shaw shared with another tenant—who must be a wool-comber, decided Harry, judging from two or three huge taut sacks tumbled nonchalantly against each other in the far corner. Even in August the yard looked dank and muddy, and the squat brick chimney seemed to exude dirt. The double-leaf door to the office, also pinkish and peeling, was closed to-day, revealing to the full its need of a new coat of paint. But Harry, cycling slowly past, or glancing at the mill sideways from the shelter of a cross street—he would not for the world, of course, have been discovered openly viewing it—found it in the highest degree romantic. It was the centre of his hopes and dreams. That faded door was his entrance to the great world, the world where he would work for his own living, the world where he would be a man. He longed for next Monday with almost unbearable intensity. The days seemed years, and as if in corroboration his very face in the glass looked older by the end of the week.

About Wednesday an idea struck him. The antimacassars were already finished and called for, so he felt at liberty to ask his mother to do some sewing for him. He took his school cap down from its peg and offered it to her. "Can you unpick the badge?" he demanded gruffly. For answer his mother covered her face with her hands and sat thus, motionless. Morcar wriggled irritably; all this emotion! Mrs. Morcar suddenly took down her hands, unpicked the crest and pressed the cap with a hot iron from within, so that the marks of the stitches became invisible.

52

At last it was Saturday, and the people of Annotsfield began to return to their homes to resume their labour. In the evening Hurst Road was full of workers in bright clothes carrying bags and baskets and paper parcels, streaming homeward from the station. Morcar slept wretchedly, tossing from side to side in a feverish though vague ambition. Sunday came. Chapel in the morning passed the time on well, and there were some good fighting hymns which Morcar sang with gusto. The afternoon was terrible. He went down to the Sycamores to see if by some happy chance the Shaws' plans had been changed and they had returned earlier—a picture postcard from Charlie had announced their coming on Monday morning. But the house was empty. Harry went round to the back; he would like to have watered the garden with a hosepipe, but dared not because it was Sunday. He tried the door of the Den, but it was locked. The father of the family who now lived next door, in the Morcars' old house, was in the garden as he returned and spoke to him kindly; Harry coloured and hurried away. Then there was tea, then there was Chapel, rather sad and sentimental so that his mother quietly wept; and then at last as they walked homeward Harry saw thin feathers of smoke beginning to rise from the mill chimneys. The men were re-lighting the boiler fires ready for work on the morrow. Then there was supper; then there was a slight ceremony in laying ready the brat, setting his alarm clock and discussing with his mother what time he would be home for dinner. Harry wished to stay at the mill all day without a break, but his mother was firm for his return at midday—on his bicycle, she said, the distance between Prospect Mills and Hurst Road was small. Mr. Shaw, she said, was sure to expect it. She was equally certain that Mr. Shaw would not require Harry to go to Prospect before breakfast tomorrow morning. Harry, who had envisaged himself climbing the steps on the stroke of six, was keenly disappointed and argued the matter stoutly.

"But Mr. Shaw won't be there himself, child, and he'll be vexed if somebody puts you on to work that he doesn't intend."

Harry yielded on both points only as far as the first day was concerned. "I shall see what Mr. Shaw wants," he repeated several times in an earnest important tone. "I must do what he wants, Mother."

His mother sighed at last, told him he had better get off to bed and kissed him goodnight. To his astonishment he fell asleep immediately.

He woke at just the right moment next morning and sprang out of bed at once. His mother seemed still asleep for no sounds came from the next room and he wondered with some diffidence whether he would need—for the first time in his life—to wake her, but luckily just as the problem became acute he heard her stirring. She was prompt with his meal and nothing occurred to delay him, and soon he was riding down Hurst Road towards Annotsfield. The morning was rather cool and dull, but the birds were singing in the park trees. Morcar was keenly happy. At last! At last! He rode with beautiful precision, but without any school-boy flourishes, down the hill and across the knot of traffic in the centre of Annotsfield and along Cloth Hall Street and East-gate, weaving in and out of trams with sober skill.

At last he reached Prospect Mills. Half the red door stood open. Morcar picked up his bicycle and carried it in, up the four stone steps, depositing it in the dark back passage where his machine and Charlie's had so often leaned before; he took the brat out of the bicycle pouch, snatched off his cap and gave a clumsy pat to his thick fair thatch, then pushed open the office door and entered industrial life.

An elderly man with greying hair, thinnish, wearing crooked pince-nez and a morose expression, sat on a high stool at the sloping desk which ran down the centre of the room. Morcar did not remember to have seen him there before. He looked up at the boy sideways over his glasses and said: "Yes?"

Blushing and twisting his cap in his hands, Harry gave his name. "I've come to work," he explained.

"Oh yes, I remember now—Mr. Shaw told me," said the cashier in an unexpectedly kind voice. "Well—Mr. Shaw isn't here yet; he's coming back from Bridlington this morning. Well now, let me see. I don't just know what Mr. Shaw means to put you at." Harry gazed at him anxiously, and he responded to the appeal. "You can help next door till he comes." Relieved, Harry hung up his cap on a hook by the door and began to unroll the brat.

"That's a fine apron you've got there," said the cashier, amused.

"It was father's," muttered Harry, looking down.

The cashier stood up and turning him round in a rough but friendly manner tied the tapes for him, then pushed him through the inner door of the office into a long light room which was apparently the Shaws' warehouse and place of despatch. Various piles of finished pieces stood about on low wooden platforms and shelves; they were not very numerous—"but of course they'd send everything out they could before Wakes," reflected Harry quickly. A knot of men stood gossiping at the far end of the room; at the cashier's shout they broke up and in a leisurely way resumed their avocations. One was measuring cloth on the long wooden table, golden with use; another was packing; a third seemed to be in charge, and came towards them enquiringly. The cashier explained Morcar.

"Can you write and figure and such?"

Harry said he could, and accordingly he was put to help a dark short solid man, addressed as Booth by the rest, at the weighing machine. They lifted a piece on to the platform of the scales; the man adjusted the weights and called the result to Harry, who wrote it neatly on the ticket attached to the piece, while Booth entered it in a book; then they lifted the piece off the scales to a table, where Booth stitched its number and some particulars into the end of the fabric in an odd-looking sewing-machine. Harry was happy to find his first textile task so well within his capacity and Booth approved his clear figures and careful accuracy, so they got on together well enough. At first Harry could not understand a word his companion said, his speech was so broadly Yorkshire, but after a time his ear adjusted itself, and he began the long slow process of learning his trade. He was allowed to lift the huge iron weights, to feel the cloth, to discuss its design, texture and destination; presently he was allowed to try the sewing-machine. His first attempt with this was not very successful and he was standing with his hands behind his back watching his companion manipulate the machine slowly so that he might see where he had erred when a distant bustle arose which grew louder and nearer, and presently Mr. Shaw rushed in. The effect was that of a whirlwind; the men's slow sure actions were galvanised to a feverish tempo; tickets fluttered in the air, pieces of brown paper fell to the ground, tempers rose; two of the men were sent off on errands and left with hurried steps; Mr. Shaw seemed to examine every piece in the place and be dissatisfied with its appearance or its progress. Eventually his tour of the room brought him back to Morcar.

"You'll have to do more than stand about with your hands behind your back if you're to stay at Prospect, Morcar," he cried hastily. "We've no room for do-nothings. We've no Councillors here."

The men all looked round with interest, and one sniggered slightly. Harry's face burned.

"I were just learning him the sewing, Mester Shaw," said Booth in a vexed defensive tone.

"Work, honest work!" exclaimed Mr. Shaw, vanishing into the office.

As he had not set Harry any other task, the boy remained with Booth, in whose goodwill he found no diminution. But Morcar now felt guilty and unhappy. To be called a do-nothing! And what had Mr. Shaw meant about no Councillors? He had just reached the point of asking himself whether Mr. Shaw could possibly have meant something insulting about his father when his employer stuck his head into the room and called to Booth that the Inspector was at the door, he'd best go help him.

"And you, Morcar," he added on a savage note, frowning: "Make yourself useful—if you can."

Booth accordingly crossed the office and clattered down the steps, Morcar at his heels. At the door stood a flat horse-drawn cart, from which two men were throwing back a waterproof cover, revealing a couple of heavy wooden boxes and some fifty-six-pound iron bar weights of the kind Morcar had seen for the first time that morning.

"Give us a hand with this lot," invited one of the men.

Booth and Morcar took a box between them and staggered up the stairs. Morcar would have descended to help with the iron weights, but was prevented by his companion.

"He's not got all his strength yet, you see," explained Booth to the Inspector. "One o' them weights would pull his inside out."

"Quite right," agreed the Inspector, unhooking the largest box.

A complicated arrangement of wood and gleaming brass was revealed, nestling in faded velvet. The fascinated Morcar watched this become a wooden tripod secured by links of brass; then the stirrup and beam were placed in position, and the two flat round brass weight-pans allowed to dangle from their thick brass chains. The assistant threw back the lids of other coffers, revealing a smaller beam and a set of spherical brass weights, so gleaming and polished that they seemed made of gold.

"Bring out your weights," said the Inspector cheerfully, taking a printed record book from his pocket and licking a thumb to turn its long narrow leaves. "Let's see now; what had you last time? Here we are." He secured the page by an elastic band and laid a well-pointed pencil beside it on the table.

Aided by his assistant, he checked the mill weighing-machine, which proved to be accurate, and then began to test the Shaws' bar weights against the standards, on the official beam. Seeing Morcar's interest in these novel proceedings, all the adults began to explain them to him at once. The Inspector showed him a blank page of the record book, ruled in columns for all kinds of weigh-machines, weights and measures, with *C* for *correct* and *I* for *incorrect*, divided by a thin red line.

"What happens if they're incorrect?" asked Harry.

The Inspector turned up one of the weights so that the boy could see in its base a deep oblong hole, at the bottom of which were stamped some hieroglyphics.

"That's an E.R., you see, for the Crown," he explained: "And that number means Annotsfield. There's '05, that's for last year when they were tested, and that letter means the month."

"But there's no month beginning with G," objected Morcar.

"They go by the alphabet," explained the Inspector. "A for January, you know; G for July."

"Aye, it would be about July last year when they were done," conceded Booth.

"It'll be H this time, then," proffered Morcar.

"That's so, my boy. I see you've got your head screwed on the right way," said the Inspector affably. "If they're incorrect we obliterate the stamp, see? And take them with us to adjust. Unless, of course," he added gravely: "Some fraud is suspected. Then we seize the weight, and court proceedings would follow. Now then, what about the smaller ones?"

"There's some in t'cupboard, Harry," said Booth, busy with the bars. "On't top shelf."

Harry, stooping, dragged out one by one a rather mixed collection, as it seemed to him, of four, two and half-pound weights; they looked so dirty compared with the Inspector's gleaming brass that he felt ashamed of them. As he withdrew his head after one of these forages he found that Mr. Shaw had come into the room and was watching the proceedings benevolently. Morcar was glad to be discovered so obviously making himself useful, and only wished there were more and heavier weights to pull out of the cupboard.

"Is that the lot?" enquired the Inspector at last, pencil poised.

"That's the lot," said Booth.

"No! There's another here," cried Harry joyously, diving into the bottom of the cupboard. "A big one." He drew out with some difficulty a fifty-six-pound weight and displayed it with triumph to the company.

To his surprise his discovery was not well received. Mr. Shaw coloured and barked: "Where's that come from?" while the Inspector opened his eyes and observed on a questioning note: "It wasn't on the list last year."

"Where's it come from, Booth?" repeated Mr. Shaw angrily.

"Nay, I don't know," said Booth, scratching his head.

The Inspector turned over the weight and peered into its hole. "Unstamped," he said.

"Have you seen it before, Booth?" asked Mr. Shaw, his colour deepening.

"I might have—and again I mightn't. I couldn't be sure," muttered Booth cautiously.

The Inspector, tightening his lips, placed the weight on one of the Crown scale pans; his assistant took the cue and laid a standard weight on the other. The eyes of all were fixed on the anonymous weight, which to Harry's horror slowly rose while the standard descended.

"Light," said the Inspector drily, making a note in his book—no doubt, thought the dismayed Harry, he was putting it below the red line. "Any more in that cupboard, young man?"

"No," said Harry, shaking his head emphatically. To be completely convincing he threw back the door. The Inspector crouched and peered in. The expression on Mr. Shaw's face as he watched this was really strange.

"No," said the Inspector, rising. "No more here. I'd best take this one back with me for adjustment, Mr. Shaw."

"Aye, do," said Mr. Shaw affably, turning on his heel and leaving the room.

The mill weights were stamped and the standard weights and beams were repacked rapidly, in silence, and in silence the equipment was carried through the office and down the stairs to the cart. The Inspector, Harry noticed, carried the faulty weight himself; when he had placed it on the cart, he took a label from his pocket and wrote on it *Shaw, Prospect Mills, light* and tied it to the weight's handle. The cart drove off, the Inspector walking at its side, and Booth and Morcar reentered the mill. Just as Harry approached the doorway between the office and the warehouse, Mr. Shaw came up full tilt; he was talking over his shoulder to one of the men, and not seeing Harry cannoned into him violently.

"Sorry!" said Harry cheerfully.

"Get out of my way!" shouted Mr. Shaw, suddenly crimson. "Get out of my way, can't you! Here I take you on to give you a chance, and you do nothing but make a confounded nuisance of yourself all day. Here, Booth! Take him away and find him something to do, can't you? For heaven's sake keep him out of my sight for a while." He pushed Harry out of the office and banged the door.

Harry, dumbfounded, stood quite still for a moment, then turned to Booth.

"Never mind—don't take on—Mester Shaw's a bit hot-tempered," said Booth consolingly. "Ah, there's t'buzzer," he added with relief, as the shrill wail filled the air. "Are you going home for your dinner?" Harry nodded. "Be off with you then— Mester Shaw'll have forgotten all about it by th' afternoon. Best go out t'other way," he concluded, jerking his head towards the back premises.

Harry took the hint, and after dejectedly removing the brat, found a side door which led him into the yard. He came out into the street past the red wooden gates, turned into the mill again and had begun lifting out his bicycle when he remembered his cap, which hung in the office. "I could leave it till this after-noon," he thought. But he did not wish to leave it till the afternoon. Very quietly he approached the office door. To his great joy it stood ajar a few inches. Sliding his hand through the opening with extreme care, he stood on tiptoe, and by extending his arm to its utmost reach managed to finger his cap. But it was

61

too distant; he could not lift it from the peg. After several vain attempts he changed his tactics and gave it a sharp flick upwards; it rose above the peg and fell clear below. With infinite good luck, it seemed to him, he caught it as it fell, and withdrew slowly from the room. The next moment he was safely out of the mill and stooping to adjust his trouser clips by the kerb.

He felt strongly impelled to go home by way of Irebridge and Hurst Bank.

"It's not much further," he muttered to himself, mounting.

This was not quite true and he had no idea why he wanted to go by Irebridge, but the impulse was too strong to be denied. He turned to the right along the Ire Valley Road. Presently he saw ahead of him the huge stone block of Syke Mills, with its tall clock tower, its five storeys, its soaring circular chimney, its two hundred yards of main road frontage. Syke Mills were the premises of Oldroyds', one of the great long-established textile firms of the West Riding. Morcar drew near to the wide archway which led to the interior yard. The iron gates stood open. His front wheel wobbled; he dismounted and propped his bicycle carefully against the kerb. His heart beat thick and fast. He knew now why he had come this way home; he wanted to get a job in Oldroyds', whose name he remembered particularly from Mr. Shaw's odd story about cutting a strip from their patterns. He would try Oldroyds' on his way home, Armitages' on the way back after dinner. If he couldn't get into either place, he would try something smaller next day. He crossed the line of the archway slowly, made out the letters *William Oldroyd and Sons* in curving script on the brass plate let into the wall, almost obliterated by eighty or ninety years of polishing—then suddenly hung back, intimidated. Dare he really pass that impressive glossy brown door, climb those fine brass-bound cork-carpeted stairs?

What should he say? What did one say when applying for a job, especially for a job which did not exist save in one's own imagination? But on the other hand ... He started forward.

"Make up your mind!" shouted a loud sardonic voice almost in his ear.

"Ackroyd!" rebuked another voice severely.

Harry, whirling round, saw that he had been almost run down by a dark-green open motor-car, of which the chauffeur, a young man in olive-green to match the car, was bellowing at him indignantly. Harry sprang to one side, the chauffeur braked with violence; the car stopped a few yards within the archway and the boy found himself face to face with a handsome, dark, sallow man in late middle age who looked rather ill and was frowning sternly. Harry had never been so near one of the new motor-cars before and he was sure the passenger in this one was Mr. William Brigg Oldroyd, the present head of the firm; crimson with confusion, he gaped and fixed his ingenuous grey eyes on the millowner appealingly.

"Do you work for us?" inquired Mr. Oldroyd, stretching out a hand to open the car door.

His accent, his shirt-cuff, his gold cuff-links and the handsome signet ring on his little finger were so superior to anything Harry had known before that his confusion mounted; he struggled unsuccessfully first to open the door then to remove himself from its path, stammering: "No. That is, not yet." Wringing out the necessary courage to add: "I should like to," required the greatest effort he had yet made in life.

"Ah," said Mr. Oldroyd. By this time he had descended from the car and was standing on the threshold of the office building; a man whom Harry at once judged to be the works manager came out with papers in his hand to meet him. "What's your name?"

"Henry Morcar."

"He'll be Councillor Morcar's son, I daresay," offered the manager. Harry nodded. "I thought John William Shaw was taking you on for your father's sake—I'm sure I've heard him say so often enough," concluded the manager, not without a touch of sarcasm at the expense of Mr. Shaw's benevolence.

"I won't go where I'm not wanted!" burst out Morcar suddenly.

"Quite right, my boy," approved Mr. Oldroyd. "What department would you like to be in, eh? What would you like to be when you grow up?"

"A designer," blurted Morcar to his own astonishment.

"You'll have to study hard for that. You must attend classes at the Technical College in the evenings. And even then you may not be a designer—designing requires a special talent," said Mr. Oldroyd.

Morcar drank in the information about the Technical College with rapture. As for talent, somehow he did not worry. He smiled happily.

"Well—have we room for a lad up there?" asked Mr. Oldroyd, turning to the manager.

"I daresay we could find room," replied the manager accommodatingly.

"When do you want to start, my boy?"

"Two o'clock?" suggested Harry, after a rapid calculation.

Mr. Oldroyd laughed. "Put him on," he said to the manager, nodding. He began to mount the stairs.

Saying hastily: "Ask for me here at two," the manager followed him.

The jubilant Morcar pushed his bicycle up Hurst Bank so rapidly that when he reached the Sycamores he was crimson and breathless. He propped the machine against the Shaws' front porch, took off his cap, wiped the sweat from his forehead with a handkerchief which showed marks of the morning's toil, sniffed to reassure himself, and walked into the house. The dining-room door stood open and the room was empty; probably the Shaws were eating their meal in the cellar kitchen, as was their habit on non-ceremonial occasions during the frequent crises when their current maid left them. Morcar listened at the cellar-head; voices floated up from below. He descended cautiously, then threw open the kitchen door. Yes; the whole Shaw family was seated at table, eating one of Mrs. Shaw's admirable raspberry and red-currant pies—Morcar's mouth positively watered to see it.

"I don't want to take advantage of your kindness Mr. Shaw so I've got myself a job at Oldroyds'," he announced breathlessly in a loud shrill tone, then waited for the thunderbolt to fall.

The Shaws' heads all flew round towards him, then flew round towards Mr. Shaw, as if actuated by clockwork. Charlie's face was white, Mrs. Shaw's elongated with horror, Winnie's round and smiling impishly. Morcar turned his eyes, with theirs, towards the head of Prospect Mills. He surprised a strange expression on his late employer's face; a look which he would almost have believed favouring and friendly had not that been quite unbelievable.

"It's very kind of you but I don't want to go where I'm not—needed," said Morcar.

"Upon my word!" began Mr. Shaw. ("Here it comes," thought Morcar.) "Upon my word," continued Mr. Shaw in a surprisingly mild tone: "You know your own mind very clearly, Harry, for a lad of fifteen."

"He's almost sixteen, Father," put in Charlie loyally.

"It's not everybody has two jobs on their first day in business. But I won't stand in your light," continued Mr. Shaw in the same benign strain. "If you want to go to Oldroyds', go, and good luck go with you." He gave Morcar a friendly dismissing nod and applied himself to his redcurrant tart.

Astonished and disconcerted, but yet infinitely relieved, Morcar got himself out of the kitchen and stumbled up the steps. He heard a chair pushed back in the room he had left and hoped it was Charlie's; sure enough by the time he had reached the front porch Charlie had caught him up.

"It won't make any difference, Charlie, will it?" said Morcar, staring at the handlebars of his bike. "To us, I mean?"

"Don't be so daft, Morcar!" exploded Charlie in a furious tone. "How could it make any difference to us? Surely you know by this time what I think of Father? You've found him out too, that's all. You did right to leave. He was always jealous of your father, and he'd take it out on you."

"Jealous of father!" pondered Morcar, astonished. "But why is he so kind about my leaving, then?"

"Nay, I don't know. He's got some idea at the back of his mind, I don't doubt," said Charlie disgustedly. "You're well out of it."

Since Morcar thought this too, he could find nothing to say of a consoling nature. In silence he mounted his machine.

"Come to tea on Saturday," called Charlie as he rode off.

"Will he—will it be all right?" cried Morcar, brightening.

"Yes—Mother said so. Meet me at half-past two at the end of the road."

All this had taken a good deal of time, and when Harry rushed into Number 102 shouting: "Quick, Mother! I have to be there at two," Mrs. Morcar had been waiting dinner for her son long enough to raise her anxiety to a considerable pitch.

"Wherever have you been, Harry? The dinner's ruined," she cried severely, seizing an oven-cloth and whisking out the stew. It was so clearly not ruined that her tone became milder as she added: "I don't suppose Mr. Shaw will mind you being a few minutes late."

"I'm not at Shaws' any more," said Harry promptly.

Mrs. Morcar blanched. "What have you been doing, love?" she wailed.

"I've left and gone to Oldroyds'. Mr. Shaw didn't really want me," explained her son.

"Oh, Harry! Don't begin to be wild and difficult just because your poor father's left us," implored Mrs. Morcar. "You must go back to Mr. Shaw and apologise, this afternoon."

"I won't go where I'm not wanted," said Morcar, setting his jaw stubbornly. "Mr. Shaw agrees I shall leave, and I've got a job at Oldroyds'."

"What sort of a job?" wailed his mother. "What sort of a chance have you in a big place like that? You'll have no opportunity for advancement, you'll be an errand boy all your life."

"There's no opportunity for me in Shaws'."

"There's more there than anywhere else, love, I'm afraid you'll find."

"I won't go anywhere to be called a nuisance."

"A nuisance?" shrilled Mrs. Morcar. Her face twitched; crying: "Oh, Fred, Fred!" she burst into passionate tears. She sobbed for a long time, while her son ate his dinner stolidly.

"There's no need to cry, Mother," he said at last, exasperated by her continued weeping. "I've got a job at Oldroyds' and I'm to be there by two. Mr. Oldroyd gave me the job himself, and told me to go to the Technical and learn to be a designer."

"A designer!" exclaimed Mrs. Morcar, startled. In spite of herself she was rather taken by this idea, which marched so closely with her own talents. She looked up and began slowly to wipe her eyes. "But how shall we manage, Harry?" she said in a tremulous tone. "We can't afford for you to study any more, you've got to go to work at once."

"I'm *going* to work!" shouted Harry. "I'm going now—it's ten to two." Immediately ashamed of shouting at his mother, he hung his head and muttered: "We shall manage all right."

By pedalling furiously all the way down Hurst Bank at the risk of his neck, he reached Irebridge at two o'clock. He was passed from hand to hand till his suspense was almost intolerable, but by two-thirty-five he was inside a small light upper room in the main block of Syke Mills, giving an indignant affirmative to the Oldroyds' head designer, Mr. Lucas, who asked him—imagine!—whether he had ever been in a mill or seen a loom before.

9

Design

The period which followed was reckoned by Morcar as one of the happiest in his life; it was a period of grinding work, but of growing knowledge and expanding fortune.

He rose at five and reached Syke Mills by six, stayed in Irebridge all day and ate his teacake in the large room outside the three chief designers' doors. He left the mill at half-past five in the evening, rushed home for high tea, and was at the Annotsfield Technical College by seven-fifteen, three nights in the week. Two, sometimes three, other nights each week he sat at the table in Number 102, doing homework; Saturday night and Sunday afternoon were reserved for Charlie. Sunday morning he took his mother to Chapel, but his evening attendances dropped during this period, for the burden of his homework was so heavy that it often required Sunday evening hours to clear it off. He had put himself down for the full six-year course in textiles and was learning spinning and weaving, both theoretically and by tending the machines housed in the basement of the College. He also learned textile chemistry and physics, calculation and drawing. By the end of the third year, if he passed his examinations satisfactorily, he would reach the tuition in design. His wage packet contained seven shillings and sixpence a week for his first six months at Syke Mills; after that to his pride and joy it rose to ten shillings. Luckily the fees at the Technical College, designed to attract just such boys as he, were very small, amounting to only a few shillings yearly. But the price of the textbooks presented a real problem.

His mother and he lived on the tiny remnants of his father's savings, the few shillings he brought home and what his mother earned by teaching sewing classes and selling raw materials or finished embroideries. His mother, of course, also kept the house spotlessly clean and cooked and laundered and sewed for her son and herself. She even repaired Harry's suits and coats, tailoring and pressing them expertly, so that he always looked spruce and well groomed.

Morcar loved his job. He loved Mr. Lucas's room, in which every item had reference to his chosen profession. The long wide desk by the windows which gave a north light, the neat weighing-scales in their glass-case, the twist-tester atop, the chart of Oldroyd "standard makes" hanging from the wall, the stack of copies of *The Wool Record* in the corner, the black-covered board heaped with coloured skeins, the innumerable sharp pencils and small oval labels, the roll of blue point-paper, the long strips of cloth cut from the centre of new ranges which hung on a string in Mr. Lucas's locked cupboard—all these seemed to him immensely thrilling and romantic; each morning when he saw them afresh his heart leaped and he smiled with pleasure. The very cushion on Mr. Lucas's chair was covered in Oldroyd cloth. One of Morcar's first tasks was to re-cover this cushion.

"Where shall I find some cloth?" asked Morcar.

"There's plenty about," replied Mr. Lucas sardonically.

Considering the five hundred thousand yards which Oldroyds' turned out every year, this was not an exaggeration, but it did not solve Morcar's problem. "Try the pattern-room," advised one of the assistants. Morcar set off without securing clear directions for the route—a mistake he never repeated—and found himself lost, on the ground floor and in the wool-combing department. The lad he asked the way teased him with contradictory directions, thinking a newcomer fair game. Without any conscious desire on his part that it should do so, Morcar's right hand flew out to a large three-pronged iron fork which leaned against the nearby wall.

"Give me a straight answer," he begged affably, raising and aiming the fork. "Mr. Lucas is waiting."

The men around laughed at the discomfiture of the lad, who sniffed angrily, then laughed himself and gave simple and correct directions. They always nodded to each other afterwards when Morcar passed by on one of his many errands.

For at first Morcar's task was simply to "run and fetch" for Mr. Lucas. Mr. Lucas, spare, grey-haired, baldish, in his late fifties, was an austere and dignified man, as befitted the head designer of a firm like Oldroyds, for the designs of a fancy worsted manufacturing firm are its life-blood. The welfare of the Oldroyds and their thousand employees with all their families depended, of course, Morcar admitted, on the skill and industry employed in every department, but he liked to think it depended chiefly on the ability of Mr. Lucas and his staff to produce fifty thousand new, interesting and tasteful designs each season—a hundred thousand in a year—for customers to choose from. Ten pattern looms existed to try out Mr. Lucas's designs. The difference

71

between a range which took the merchants' fancy and a range which did not was many thousands of pounds' worth of orders.

From Mr. Lucas Morcar learned enormously. It was no part of the designer's duty to teach Morcar, as he sometimes drily remarked, but merely to be able to run and fetch intelligently the boy had to know something of what he was about. He learned what a range-ticket, a make-paper and a loom-card looked like and what their hieroglyphics meant; where the blue-point paper—like the graph-paper he had drawn on at school—was kept, and why some sheets had larger squares than others. He learned to weigh a square inch of cloth and test the twist of ten inches of yarn; he ran down to the colour room and got the men there to scour a few hanks of yarn for Mr. Lucas, since colours were always matched in fresh-washed yarn—Mr. Lucas was horrified to find that Harry had not known that, for to him it was a self-evident axiom accepted by all, like one of the ten commandments. He took a bit of a new range down to be scoured and dried, so that Mr. Lucas could judge of its appearance after this process; he ran between the pattern looms and the designers when anything went wrong. He tidied up the many-coloured hanks of yarn heaped on Mr. Lucas's black-covered board after the designer had been working with them, arranging them in order of shade beneath the two threads which held them in place. Each colour had a number, so Harry need only look at their tickets to get the order right, but he liked to test himself by arranging them only by his notion of their shade first, then check their order by their numbers. He soon knew by heart the numbers of all the shades the Oldroyds usually dyed—their dyehouse was not in Syke Mills, but at a place called Old Mill down by the river Ire.

From the first Harry did well at Syke Mills. His neat figures and clear writing pleased Mr. Lucas's fastidious taste. Days of thought and experiment on Mr. Lucas's part resulted often in a half-sheet of paper covered with meticulous but mysterious pencilled notes in the designer's tiny beautiful calligraphy; presently Harry was interpreting these symbols into the statistical directions from which the quantities of yarn for warp and weft could be prepared.

When he had been at Oldroyds' six months, Harry went one Saturday afternoon into an optician's in Annotsfield clutching five shillings, the savings from his weekly sixpence pocket-money, in his hand, and came out the proud possessor of a "piece glass" like Mr. Lucas's. On Monday morning he drew the inch-square magnifying-glass from his waistcoat pocket, unfolded its cuboid frame and placed it on one of Mr. Lucas's newest patterns. The threads of the cloth leaped up to his eye, large, distinct, hairy; at such close quarters the intricacy and beauty of the design were positively breath-taking and Harry exclaimed with pleasure. Mr. Lucas looked up.

"Got a glass of your own, eh?" he said.

"Why is there a rainbow round the edges?" asked Harry.

Mr. Lucas delivered him a brief lecture on prisms and optics.

It was shortly after this that Harry found his wages increased, and—much more important—Mr. Lucas lent him a book on textile design, which Harry studied as a treat on Saturdays and in bed on Sunday morning. At first on a torn scrap of point-paper, later on a sheet he bought for himself, Harry dissected patterns, practised the twills and stripes and diamonds given as examples in the book, and taught himself to compile those mysterious diagrams known as *drafts* and *pegging-plans*, which directed how the threads of the fabric should be set in the loom and in what order they should rise and fall. Chemistry and spinning and weaving were work to Harry, but designs—colours, drawing, patterns—were pleasure; he turned to colour and weave effects after doing his Technical homework with eager zest, as some people might turn from grammar to poetry. He observed with joy that the more he learned about complementary colours and colour ranges, the more his mother's instinctive preferences and his own were shown to be soundly based on correct principles. By the time he reached the Technical College course on elementary textile design, he knew it all already, and by special permission attended the lectures on colour for advanced students, in its place.

Then all of a sudden, as it seemed between one day and the next, Harry Morcar grew up. One day he was a boy, Harry, who wore a school cap and was always growing out of his clothes, a boy who considering his age was really quite useful and promising, but still a boy. The next he was a young man, Morcar, nineteen years old, a big square-shouldered lively sensible fellow with a good taste in neckties, who shaved every morning and night and was one of the Technical's best pupils and Mr. Lucas's trusted assistant. In his fourth year at the Technical, he won a gold medal in the City and Guilds examination by a figured fabric of his own design and weave. The Principal of the College allowed him to telescope his fifth and sixth years' training, and put him on to mill management and the special textile research class, exclusively. At Syke Mills, he could now map out a range almost as well as Mr. Lucas himself, and translated the head designer's pencil notes into all the instructions needed without any supervision. When the talk turned to the prevention of curled selvedges—as it often did, for that ticklish problem was Mr. Lucas's hobby—Morcar was not only allowed to listen without being rebuked for idleness but even occasionally to put in a word of his own, for his ideas on the subject were not at all silly, not at all negligible. One or two of his colour suggestions, too, were actually adapted by Mr. Lucas and incorporated into designs which proved very popular, though on the whole Mr. Lucas was apt to find Morcar's colours too bright. They were tasteful though, he agreed; yes, really quite tasteful. Morcar was now earning thirty shillings a week, which Mr. Lucas told him was a really remarkable wage for such a young fellow. The truth was that Mr. Lucas was growing older and developing that curse of the bleak West Riding, rheumatism, and when he stayed away to nurse it Morcar, though of course still under the instructions of the other designers, carried out Mr. Lucas's routine work entirely competently.

It was just a fortnight after Morcar's twentieth birthday when one of those pregnant incidents, one of those knots of converging circumstance, occurred which change the course of lives. On a sharp October day which had kept Mr. Lucas at home by the first frost of the season, the works manager came up from the private office in a hurry, asking for the head designer.

"There's a row on about our blue striped suitings," he explained hurriedly. "Butterworth took a lot, do you remember? Mr. Butterworth's here himself—he's brought two pair of trousers—they're all faded and patchy."

All the members of the designers' office gathered together in horror; to have cloth returned was unheard-of, disgraceful, in Syke Mills whatever it might be elsewhere, and Mr. Butterworth was a merchant whose father and grandfather had dealt with Oldroyds' all their lives—a most valued and valuable customer. Mr. Oldroyd was naturally vexed, and the heads of all the departments concerned had been sent for to explain if they could why the cloth had faded in wear. Morcar hastily took out the strip of the original pattern—dark blue with a narrow white stripe—from the string in the cupboard and collected the various papers which recorded the cloth's career, from its design to its passage through the looms and presses a few months ago, then followed downstairs on the heels of the works manager and the second-in-command of the designers.

"It's a pity Lucas isn't here," muttered the latter. "I know nowt about that cloth—it's a pity."

The procession of three entered the handsome private office in considerable trepidation. Mr. Oldroyd had a temper of his own which at that time illness was exacerbating; he knew all there was to know about cloth, was fiercely proud of the good name of Oldroyds', and had a tongue which could be extremely cutting. They saw at once that their fears were justified and that he was ready to be thoroughly angry. He sat erect behind a huge table of gleaming mahogany, frowning, one thin hand stretched out on the table beside the unfortunate garments returned by the customer to the tailor and by the tailor to the merchant; between illness and rage his sallow face looked livid and his dark eyes were burning. Mr. Butterworth, pink, plump and silvery, sat flipping his thumbnails and gazing at the bronze horses on the mantelpiece with an air of an impartial desire to see justice done which was perfectly proper but very irritating. In the rear, by the window, jingling the keys in his pocket, leaned Mr. Oldroyd's only son, Mr. Francis; a big tall handsome young man, a few years older than Morcar, with the clear skin which goes with reddish fair hair, and dark blue eyes. There had recently been an unpleasant scandal about Francis Oldroyd; he had married in a hurry, "because he had to," said Annotsfield, a girl from a working family; last month their child had been born, dead and far too soon—which as Annotsfield said gave the game away properly. Annotsfield and Syke Mills took sides over Francis's marriage; some liked him and turned an indulgent eye on a young man's escapade; others thought the affair shocking. Amongst the latter group was Mrs. Morcar. Harry at twenty was still half in, half out of his mother's tutelage, and regarded her views partly with respect and partly with impatience. He saw little of his employer's son and had not set eyes on him since the scandal of the birth had broken on the public ear; he looked at him now with half hostile, half fascinated curiosity. Francis Oldroyd was wearing a beautifully tailored suit of admirable cloth, and a tie which Morcar guessed to be that of the public school he had attended. But then, Oldroyds' had made the cloth; Morcar himself had made out the range ticket—indeed he had even had something to do with selecting the colours of the decorations—while as for a public school tie, anybody would wear one whose father could afford to buy one by paying public school fees, Morcar supposed. So he was unimpressed, and maintained a suspended judgment.

The works manager was explaining that Mr. Lucas was unfortunately away with rheumatism.

"Is there nobody in the mill who knows about this cloth, then?" demanded Mr. Oldroyd.

His tone indicated that a storm of considerable dimensions would break if Mr. Butterworth had to leave unsatisfied, so Morcar felt that he was not "speaking out of his turn" in saying quickly:

"I made out the make-paper, sir. Could I see the cloth for a minute?"

Mr. Oldroyd picked up the wretched trousers and passed them to him impatiently.

The moment Morcar took the garments in his hand a delightful suspicion assailed him; he drew out his piece glass, examined the cloth and exclaimed triumphantly:

"This isn't ours, Mr. Oldroyd!"

"Yes, yes, it is ours; Mr. Butterworth says so," said Mr. Oldroyd impatiently.

"No, sir—excuse me—our stripe has three ends, this has four," said Morcar, smiling happily. "Here is our pattern, Mr. Butterworth—you can see the difference for yourself. If you'll just count the threads, sir."

He offered the garments, the Oldroyd strip, his glass and the paper to Mr. Butterworth, who, frowning, examined the evidence. There was a moment of suspense.

"You're quite right, young man," said Mr. Butterworth at length curtly. "I apologise, Brigg. My people have made a mistake somewhere."

He passed the two cloths on to Mr. Oldroyd, who, taking his own handsome double-lens glass from his pocket, examined them. He said nothing, but gave a nod to Morcar before pushing the cloths away. Francis bent over his shoulder, then stood up and stepped back. He too made no comment, but it was clear to Morcar that he could see no difference in the stripes.

"Probably doesn't even know what an end is," thought Morcar scornfully, and he despised his employer's son with all his heart. He took up the Oldroyd pattern and the make-paper and looked towards Mr. Oldroyd, who nodded again in dismissal. His employer's manners evidently did not permit any outward expression of triumph over a defeated customer, but there was no doubt about his secret pleasure, for his handsome mouth moved as if to repress a smile, and a grim glee lighted his dark eyes. As Morcar left the room he heard Mr. Butterworth say:

"You've a sharp lad there, Brigg."

"John Henry Morcar's grandson," replied Mr. Oldroyd. "Came to us as a boy. Lucas has trained him."

On the following Friday Morcar found in his wages packet an increase note and a rise of ten shillings, and Mr. Lucas, restored to work by a rise in the temperature, after an absence downstairs told him with some ceremony that Mr. Oldroyd had expressed willingness to "put him through" all the departments in the mill so that he might acquire the experience necessary for a really first-class designer.

To be willing to pay a young man to whom he was not bound by any ties of blood or friendship two pounds a week for an unspecified time while Morcar did no useful work in the mill at all but simply learned his trade, was indeed to take him by the hand and lead him forward. Morcar felt that with his training at the Technical the period necessary would probably not be very long, and to be truthful with himself he also felt a strong disinclination to go again through all that toil of learning textile processes, which with the cheerful arrogance of youth he thought he knew thoroughly already. But what an offer! From the great Mr. Oldroyd! His way to be Oldroyds' head designer—a textile plum—seemed to Morcar to lie clear before him if he chose to tread it.

He could hardly wait for the buzzer to sound at the end of the afternoon before he rushed up Hurst Bank to the Sycamores to tell Charlie the splendid news. "This'll make the Shaws sit up!" he exclaimed gleefully to himself every hundred yards. The impetus of his joy had carried him forward so rapidly that as he approached the Sycamores he saw Mr. Shaw and Charlie beneath a gas-lamp in the distance, descending from the Hurst Road tram by which they travelled back and forth between Hurst and Prospect Mills every day. He hurried to meet them, and almost before he had reached their side cried out Mr. Oldroyd's fine offer.

The news had not the effect he hoped, for both father and son looked glum. There was nothing unusual in this, for during the three years Charlie had worked at Prospect Mills it was customary for Mr. Shaw and Charlie to return from the mill looking glum—close association in daily work increased the friction which had always existed between them. But it struck Morcar that they looked even more glum now than was their habit. True, Charlie said warmly at once: "Mr. Oldroyd must think very highly of you, Harry," but his voice held an undercurrent of disappointment, while Mr. Shaw remarked: "You'll be at Oldroyds' all your life, then," in a dry non-committal tone.

"It was that striped suiting of Butterworths' that did it," exclaimed Morcar with satisfaction.

"What was that?" asked Mr. Shaw.

Morcar described the incident, which was already familiar to Charlie. The three had now reached the Sycamores' gate, and Mr. Shaw stood there with his hand on one of the green-painted spikes, which he patted thoughtfully. At the conclusion of the anecdote he said:

"Come in for a minute, Harry."

He led the way up the asphalt path into the house, and to Harry's surprise turned into the cold, dark drawing-room and switched on the recently installed electric light. The two young men followed him, still wearing their coats, and Charlie shut the door. It was immediately opened by Winnie, who stuck in her head to enquire whether her father wanted tea now, or should she put it off.

"Go away, love, we're talking business," said her father affably.

Winnie grimaced at Morcar and withdrew.

"We were thinking, Harry, that you might have come to us," said Mr. Shaw. His voice was as smooth as sateen and he showed not a trace of embarrassment. Morcar on the other hand did not know where to look. "The truth is," continued Mr. Shaw with a man-to-man air which Morcar in spite of his dislike for Mr. Shaw found deliciously flattering: "Charlie and I are both outside men. We both like selling. We need an inside man, somebody in the mill to keep things straight. What do Oldroyds' pay you?"

"Two pounds," muttered Morcar.

Mr. Shaw winced but said firmly: "I'll pay you the same. At first. More, of course, later."

"What do you say, Charlie?" asked Morcar after a pause.

"I've been wanting Father to ask you for a long time, but he wouldn't before today," said Charlie bitterly. "And now it's too late, I suppose. I don't want to persuade you, Harry. Of course Oldroyds' is a fine firm and it's a splendid chance."

"So long as Brigg Oldroyd lives, it is," argued Mr. Shaw. "But he's very ill, they tell me. Cancer. How can you be sure what'll happen when he's gone? You might be left in the department you happened to be in, and never get back to designing. His son will have his own favourites, you may be sure."

Morcar felt stifled. He stood up. "I must think about it. I'll let you know," he said gruffly.

"Aye, tell us by Sunday evening," agreed Mr. Shaw.

Morcar plunged out of the house into the darkness. The autumn air struck cold on his flushed cheek. He was deeply troubled by the decision which lay before him. On the one hand, his future was assured if he stayed at Syke Mills—provided, of course, he could give satisfaction in the job; but he had no doubt of that, and the same condition would operate at the Shaws' or any other firm. Working through the departments would be a bore, but he could stand it, and he supposed there might still be a few things he could learn. He would have great scope for the exercise of his special talent in a firm which produced a hundred thousand patterns every year. On the other hand, at the Shaws' he would be more or less his own master, which with the Oldroyds he never would. At the Shaws' he would have infinitely fewer designs to work on, but at least he might be able to try the livelier colour and weave effects he had in mind. He felt an antipathy between himself and Francis Oldroyd; Charlie was his lifelong friend. Syke Mills were huge, handsome, well equipped; Prospect was small, old and muddled. Just so; it would be far more interesting to reorganise Prospect than to maintain a standard already set at Syke. At Syke, although it was so large, Morcar had a feeling of restriction, of confinement, because it was so highly departmentalised; in Prospect he would be able to range through the whole place, oversee every process, at will. But then, how greatly he disliked the thought of association with Mr. Shaw! But he was not now an ignorant boy, helpless, an object of charity; he was a knowledgeable, useful, marketable young man. Give him a year or two in Prospect Mills, thought Morcar, keep Mr. Shaw and Charlie busy with their outside duties, and he'd make Prospect hum.

He reached Number 102 and in duty bound laid the alternatives before his mother as they sat at tea. Mrs. Morcar seemed inclined to shed tears of happy pride when he described the Oldroyd offer, but her eyes dried and she sat erect when he spoke of Mr. Shaw's.

"Why should you give up that splendid chance to go to the Shaws', Harry?" she said. "You were eager enough to leave them four years ago."

"And you were eager enough for me to stay, Mother," Harry told her with a grin.

"I didn't know then how you were going to turn out, Harry," said Mrs. Morcar with dignity.

"You should try to have more faith in me," joked her son.

"Most people in Annotsfield will think you unwise if you throw away such a chance in order to go to John William Shaw," said Mrs. Morcar.

"Oh, I don't know," argued Harry. "There'll be more chance of becoming a partner, with the Shaws."

"With all those young boys in the family, I should say a partnership is exceedingly unlikely," objected Mrs. Morcar. "And what will Mr. Oldroyd think of you leaving now? And Mr. Lucas? After all the training he's given you?"

"Yes—I'm sorry about that," agreed Morcar. "I wasn't apprenticed or anything, though."

"You would be settled for life at Oldroyd's," urged Mrs. Morcar.

"I want to be on my own, Mother!" exclaimed Harry impatiently.

As he spoke he knew his decision was taken. His mother continued the discussion all the weekend, but Harry's mind did not change, and on Sunday evening immediately after tea he went to the Sycamores and asked for Mr. Shaw. The maid had evidently received instructions what to do with him when he called, for she led him past the drawing-room where the family, as Harry could hear from their voices, were congregated, and placed him in the dining-room, where he was joined by Mr. Shaw. They sat down with stern expressions at the long table, which was covered, as it had always been in Harry's memory, with a chenille tablecloth in ultramarine blue.

"Well? Have you come to say you'll join us, Harry?" demanded Mr. Shaw in a cool tone.

"Yes—on those terms you mentioned. I suppose in a way I shall be a kind of works manager?" hazarded Harry.

Mr. Shaw winced but agreed, and the matter was settled.

Harry's new employer led him to the other room, where Mrs. Shaw was trying to coax Charlie and Winnie to go to Chapel and not succeeding.

"Harry's coming to Prospect as soon as he can get free," said Mr. Shaw in a benevolent tone, laying his hand on Harry's arm—the young man's shoulder was now too far above him for a benevolent gesture.

"I'm very glad, Harry dear," said Mrs. Shaw kindly, while Charlie exclaimed: "Good!" and thumped a cushion vigorously, and Winnie remarked: "About time too," with her usual blend of tart sweetness.

"Now go to Chapel all together, you three, do," urged Mrs. Shaw. "To please me, Charlie. I know your mother would like you to go, Harry. And bring her in to supper afterwards."

The young men exchanged glances and decided to yield, and Winnie sprang up and said she would accompany them if they would agree to go to Hurst Congregational instead of all the way to Eastgate. This compromise was accepted by Mrs. Shaw, and the three young people went off together. Winnie was wearing a dark green costume, as she called it, and a rich dark green satin blouse with thick, open lace at the cuffs and throat; a black beaver hat with a green ribbon sat at an agreeable angle on her smooth hazel hair, which was dressed high on her head, revealing unexpectedly small and delicate ears. Harry felt proud that they were all three growing up into such important, promising, successful and interesting people. Evening service was always rather sentimental and touching, and as they sang the sweet sad hymns Harry felt deeply happy to be there with his friends, on the eve of their great enterprise together. Winnie sang rather well, in a clear true soprano; the young men muttered comfortably together in the bass. Harry put a shilling (double his usual contribution) into the collection, to commemorate the occasion and show his gratitude to the Almighty for re-uniting him to Prospect Mills, and he could not help noticing that Charlie did the same. Winnie threw in her sixpence with a petulant air— women never took purses to church and could not change their minds about the collection, thought Harry leniently. Outside the Chapel the three parted, the Shaws returning to the Sycamores and Harry going up the road to fetch his mother.

It was clear that Mrs. Morcar did not want to go to the Shaws for supper. She stood by the table listening to his account of the interview, the excursion to Chapel and the supper invitation with a look of deep trouble and anxiety on her face. At the close of his narrative she sighed.

"Well, I suppose you know best what you want, Harry," she said. "But it's not what I should have chosen for you."

She concealed her feelings admirably at the Shaws', however, and the supper went off well.

A sharp bout followed next morning with Mr. Lucas, who on learning of Harry's new job exclaimed angrily:

"I suppose Shaw thinks he'll get hold of all Oldroyds' new season's designs."

"That's not fair, Mr. Lucas," objected Morcar.

"It might be fair to Shaw and unfair to you," said Mr. Lucas bitterly. "You're being a fool, Harry, a young fool. Is there a girl in it, eh?"

"No," said Morcar, astonished.

Mr. Lucas snorted. "The more fool you," he said. "What Mr. Oldroyd will say I tremble to think."

"I'll tell him myself if you like," said Morcar stoutly.

Mr. Lucas's expression changed. "He isn't at the mill today," he said. "He's not so well, it seems."

Morcar remembered Mr. Shaw's odious speculations on Brigg Oldroyd's health. Perhaps they were justified. He hesitated. "Mr. Oldroyd gave me the job here, and it's through his kind offer that I've got this other job now," he said. "I'd like to see him to say goodbye to him and tell him I'm grateful."

Mr. Lucas however thought this quite unnecessary, and Harry left Syke Mills the following week without again seeing his former employer.

10

Springtime

Another calm and happy period followed.

It was true that Morcar received an unpleasant shock when he discovered the coarse, low-quality stuff which Prospect Mills were manufacturing. It seemed to sell well and he supposed it filled a need, but it was not the kind of stuff he had been used to handling at Syke Mills, nor a kind to which he proposed to devote his life. He decided at first to let the matter ride for a time until he had got the mill work reorganised and avoidable defects minimised—heaven knew this was badly needed—and then move on to finer fabrics and better designs gradually. But he learned then that it was impossible to tackle difficulties in neat chronological order; they all presented themselves at once, inextricably entangled. Machinery reached a point of deterioration where it had to be renewed; a decision had to be taken immediately as to what type to buy, and this decision would commit the Shaws for many years to come, to undertaking or declining certain classes of fabric. Workmen who left—and until Morcar's

87

advent workmen often left Shaws'; his old friend Booth was still there, but not another face he recognised—caused similar problems. Then, both Mr. Shaw and Charlie had a maddening habit of accepting commissions which their existing labour and machinery were not adequate to fulfil and expecting Morcar to find a way of fulfilling them. The way he eventually found committed them to further work of the same kind if the steps he had taken were not to prove expensively fruitless. Morcar did not in any case like "weaving on commission", i.e. weaving other men's yarn into other men's pieces for other men to sell—it hurt his pride; but he admitted that it tided Prospect over some meagre seasons. The book-keeping at Prospect had been chaotic; Charlie had struggled vainly to straighten it out but could not do so because the reality it represented, the actual work done in the mill, was chaotic too. Now the two young men together wrestled it clear, introduced reforms and got a fresh system into smooth working order.

There were times, indeed, when Morcar wondered how on earth Mr. Shaw had managed to conduct business at all, never name to do so with any degree of success, for he soon discovered that he himself knew a very great deal more than Mr. Shaw about textiles, while Charlie was much more capable than his father at letters, accounts and soothing customers. But Morcar perceived after a time that Mr. Shaw had one extremely important talent; he knew what the public would like, and was often able to guess what customers would want before they knew themselves that they wanted it. Morcar observed the operation of this talent thoughtfully. He did not possess it himself, he feared; on the other hand, it was barely possible to judge whether he had it, or to develop it, since he never came into contact with customers.

Charlie, it appeared, was a superb salesman. He was honest, tactful and sincerely sympathetic because he understood the customer's point of view; his voice, his manners, his appearance were pleasant and gentlemanly without being so "upper-class" as to irritate solid West Riding merchants. He told good stories, but not till the serious business of the interview was over, and he never capped a customer's joke. He had left school at seventeen and gone into the mill without any technical instruction, so he knew little of textile theory and nothing of economics, but he was always a quick learner and under Morcar's coaching he soon became knowledgeable about textiles.

After a rather uncomfortable and muddled year, at the end of which Charlie and Morcar were privately both relieved to find that the balance in the bank was about the same as in previous years, Prospect settled into a steady routine which offered a fair certainty of reasonable profit. Then Morcar hit on a very charming small dice check design in a range of soft colours which found real favour for ladies' wear; this became the Prospect speciality, and the firm rapidly prospered. It became, in fact, one of those neat, compact, reliable, profitable little family businesses over which harassed men saddled with large sprawling concerns shake their heads enviously. Now that their fortunes had taken this upward turn, the young men urged Mr. Shaw to smarten the mill up a bit and he was by no means unwilling; the premises were repainted inside and out in a tasteful green, the letterheads were altered to please Charlie; a lot of junk was cleared out of the office, a couple of girls with typewriters were installed and the furniture modernised. Mr. Shaw was so jubilant that he positively increased Morcar's salary twice without being asked, and on a third occasion when asked yielded after the minimum of grumbling.

All three men worked hard. Mr. Shaw had a daemonic energy when he chose and selected his periods of indolence wisely. The two young men took it in turn to go to the mill before breakfast, they stayed late, they discussed their plans when they met at the weekend; altogether they took Prospect seriously. During the height of the check boom Harry even occasionally let himself into the mill on Sunday afternoon—though he dared not confess this Sabbath-breaking to his mother—to tidy up a few pressing problems ready for Monday. But the work was light to him after the toils of the previous five years, especially after his Technical College courses finished. (Mr. Shaw jeered at him for continuing these so long, but though desperately weary before the end Harry stuck to them till he passed out a fully qualified student.) It seemed to him then that he had been presented with a gift of boundless leisure, and he turned happily to the enjoyments to which his youth entitled him.

Charlie and Winnie Shaw belonged to a lawn tennis club; Morcar joined it too. In the summer evenings and on Saturday, in flannels of spotless white he careered cheerfully over the green sward in the sunshine. Nobody's white buckskin boots were more consistently, purely white than Morcar's; he cleaned them every night and stood them on his window-sill to dry. Charlie's were white too, but then it was Winnie who applied the caked white to Charlie's boots and sent his flannels to the cleaner's. Winnie herself, in a long white piqué skirt, a white blouse with a stiff collar and a knotted silk tie, white shoes and white stockings, looked extremely neat and trim. They all three played quite a good game and were sensible people, so they soon found them-selves in positions of responsibility in the club. Winnie was a member of the ladies' committee which superintended the teas on Saturdays and match days; the two young men both sat on selection and dance committees. The joy of being elected, by ballot of one's fellow-clubsmen, was quite immense.

Charlie soon became one of the best players in the club, swift, stylish, original; he was elected captain of the team, and he and Morcar formed the first match couple. Morcar's steady persistence often retrieved them from defeat, but it was Charlie always who played the winning strokes. The two Shaws also made an admirable mixed couple. But Winnie and Morcar did not play well together. To Morcar, Winnie seemed always to be in places on the court where she ought not to be; he was surprised and perplexed when they crashed into each other and missed the flying white ball. He said nothing about it but mildly pondered. Winnie, on the other hand, told Morcar he was never in the place where he ought to be—she looked round, she said, expecting a partner, and beheld a vacuum. She grew quite hot about it; this surprised Morcar, for Winnie when playing with her brother was a good loser, joking over their mistakes sardonically. Eventually it was agreed that if Morcar and Winnie played together they quarrelled. A succession of young female partners introduced to him by Winnie therefore flitted past Morcar's eyes; he could remember nothing of them save that they were in white, with puffed-out fair hair, and giggled often. One felt pleasantly protective, however, when playing with them, and giggling on a summer evening was agreeable.

In summer, too, there was the joy of cricket. Sometimes when the weather was fine and Mr. Shaw in an expansive mood, he would allow his traveller and his works manager an afternoon off together to watch Yorkshire playing some other county (inferior of course in their opinion) at Bradford. The train ambled through the winding green valleys and puffed up sombre hills and stopped at the special cricket-ground station, which confirmed its identity by a painted decoration of bat and wickets, with a red ball far too large in proportion. Then the indolent lounging hours on the open wooden benches, the white-flannelled figures on the pitch with famous names, the delicious "chock" of bat on ball, the graceful swift athletic action, the excitement of the mounting score competing with the flying minutes, the long, long discussions of famous innings, of slow bowlers' hat-tricks, of difficult umpires' decisions. Winnie made them sandwiches for lunch and sometimes accompanied them, looking fresh and summery in a thin frock of mauve-figured voile and a large white hat; but Winnie found cricket rather slow and was apt to make audible mordant comments on the batsmen which embarrassed her brother and Morcar.

In the winter came the delights of subscription dances. At first the tennis-club gave "flannel" dances, at which the young people wore tennis attire to spare their pockets, but one or two of superior social standing began to turn up in formal evening dress, and the following year it was generally agreed to drop the idea of summer clothes at winter functions. When Harry first broached the project of a dress suit at home, Mrs. Morcar brought out his father's evening suit and offered to modify it to fit him. But it was far too narrow across the shoulders; besides, the cut was definitely old-fashioned.

"I shall have to have one of my own, Mother," apologised Harry.

"Well, Harry, you deserve one," said Mrs. Morcar with a sudden sprightly staunchness. "And you can afford it."

Harry was responsible for supervising the decorations at this dance, being chairman of the decoration sub-committee; the arrangements of the palms in the pots, the pink and silver design on the programmes, the flowers on the supper-tables to match, were all considered most successful and charming—a good background, too, for the frocks of the gigglers.

Charlie of course was a brilliant dancer, Morcar modestly competent. Winnie was too restless to make Morcar a comfortable dance-partner; full of verve and go, she waltzed him round faster than he intended and pushed and pulled him vehemently through round dances. In spite of this they danced a good deal together; she was Charlie's sister, he was Charlie's friend. Morcar took a mild revenge on her by swinging her completely off her feet whenever the Lancers gave him the opportunity. Winnie was slight in build, light in weight; a lift of Morcar's powerful arms sent her flying helplessly through the air. He could not quite make out whether she liked to be taken off her feet or no; for his part he rather enjoyed doing it and continued the practice. She had a certain evening frock, pale blue satin with an overskirt of flowered ninon, which billowed wildly on these occasions; it became a family joke, expected, licensed, for Morcar to give this frock a gleeful sideways glance as he stood before her writing his name on her programme.

"Now, Harry," Winnie adminished him: "You'd better not take any Lancers."

Of course he took a couple. As the relevant figure of the dance approached, he solemnly unbuttoned his white kid gloves (leaving them on his hands, however) lest the necessary muscular effort should tear the buttonholes. Winnie at once became uneasy.

"Now, Harry," she urged, turning up to him her perky little face and gleaming hazel eyes: "Don't let us have any nonsense about taking me off my feet tonight, if you please."

"I'm not making any promises," replied Morcar mildly, smiling.

The music started; the circles formed; in a moment Winnie

was flying shrieking through the air, supported only by Morcar's arm grasping her. Afterwards, restored to earth, she scolded him while patting her hair, retrieving hairpins, settling her ruffled frock. When they were all children together, reflected Morcar, Winnie seemed far older than Charlie or himself because there was a twelvemonth between them; now he was quite on her level and unafraid of her sharp witticisms.

This was because he was a successful business man now, no doubt. That year he had made rather a hit with an attractive "step" pattern showing zig-zag lines of colour, and Mr. Shaw had murmured something about a possible partnership. True, he had immediately qualified his offer by relegating it to some indefinite period in the future, but the offer had at least been mentioned, and Charlie would not allow it to be forgotten. Morcar felt he was really doing well. Only that night, before he came out to the dance, he had been urging his mother again, as he often did nowadays, to move into a better house, or get some woman to help her with the housework, or give up some of her sewing classes. She could afford to take life easier now that her son was doing so well. Mrs. Morcar as usual refused his suggestions.

"I don't want you to spend your money on me, Harry," she said. "You must save it for when you want to get married."

"Married? Me?" said Harry, laughing. "That won't happen for a while."

Indeed he was not greatly interested in girls at this time. Even without the continual enlightenment offered by Charlie on the subject, he was fully aware of the uses to which girls could be put, but had never yet seen a girl who tempted him to think of her in that connection. It was agreeable when dancing to hold a light warm armful, agreeable to put one's strength at a girl's disposal,

94

to help her carry something heavy, to offer her tennis balls with which to begin service or help her over a stile. But to retire with girls into dark corners as Charlie did, to encircle their waists and kiss them and whisper into their ears, seemed to Morcar a tedious and meaningless occupation. As for any association of a darker and more mercenary kind, Morcar thought that such possibilities existed in great cities but not in Annotsfield; in any case, the idea that he or anyone he knew might be involved with such wickedness never entered his head. The proper procedure between the sexes was as follows: One met at tennis, fell in love, got engaged for three years while one saved and began to buy a house through the Building Society, then married. Some people were known as flirts, of course. Admired by their contemporaries, they were scolded by parents from time to time but no great harm was thought of them, for Annotsfield flirtations in the second decade of the twentieth century were conducted with a decent mildness. Charlie was a flirt and liked girls, Winnie was a flirt and liked boys. Well, let them enjoy themselves. Morcar did not object, so long as he was not called upon to share their pleasures.

These never seemed to last long with either of them. Charlie talked to him of a fresh girl almost every week and he had long since lost count of Winnie's innumerable admirers, but neither of them seemed to be thinking of getting engaged. Morcar hoped that none of them would marry for a while yet. He was prepared to accept with solemn loyalty any girl whom Charlie chose to be his wife, and to tolerate the ass whom Winnie, with her habitual perversity, was almost certain to pick on for a husband, but he hoped the necessity would not arise for a few years yet. Marriage would break up their present way of life, complicate their present relationship, and life in this winter of 1913 seemed to him straightforward, pleasant, satisfying, just as it was.

II

Action

11

Call to Arms

TIME OF TENSION, read Morcar on a summer morning in July. *Europe's Peril. War Clouds Loom. In his rescript the Austrian Emperor recalled that Austria first exerted influence in Bosnia and Herzegovina…. Servia was never reconciled to the forcing of German and Magyar sovereignty over peoples mainly Slav in origin. Nor was Russia ever reconciled to the annexation of the two Slav states … a desire to inflict a blow on the prestige of Russia….*

What on earth was it all about? What in heaven's name was a rescript? Where were Bosnia and Herzegovina? Who were the Slavs?

Morcar got his father's old atlas down from his mother's bedroom, spread it out on the table and went solemnly through the leading article, laying his finger on each place in the map as it was named. At the end he had received a strong impression that a large country (Austria-Hungary) was bullying a small one of different race (Servia) just because some prince or other (Morcar had no use for foreign royalties) had been assassinated in their territory; Russia belonged to the same race as Servia and felt elder-brotherly towards her. So far some sense could be made of it, he thought; but then the paper seemed to say that Germany was supporting Austria because Germany wanted to inflict a blow on the prestige of Russia, and France supporting Russia because she feared a German victory would gain Germany too much prestige.

"Prestige," thought Morcar, pulling a face. "What bunkum!"

Sir Edward Grey proposes a Conference of Ambassadors in London. Very sensible. *But it is not likely to be acceptable, owing to Austria's extreme exasperation. This is the third time in half a dozen years that Austria has mobilised against Servia, and she is determined that this shall be the last.*

"Well, upon my soul!" said Morcar. "Servia might be exasperated as well, I should say."

Next morning his newspaper told him that Austria had declared war on Servia and begun to fight, Russia was excited, Sir Edward Grey was still trying to localise the conflict, Germany had declined to participate in the proposed conference because she thought it offered no hope of success. *Austria cannot appear before an European tribunal like a Balkan State, say the Germans.*

"Why not?" said Morcar, vexed. "Surely there should be one law for all Powers, great or small."

The Powers, urges Germany, being well aware that Servia deserves chastisement, should be content to stand aside.

"Chastisement?" said Morcar, colouring. "I don't care for that word."

On Thursday he learned that Russia had mobilised, but *there is no suggestion of panic or craven fear amongst the British.*

"I should think not, indeed!" said Morcar impatiently.

On Friday, the Servian capital was in flames.

"Well, it's a shame," said Morcar.

Germany had asked Russia to explain her mobilisation; Russia doubted Germany's sincerity in making her request.

"I'm not surprised," said Morcar.

The persistent unanimity of the bland responses made by Austria-Hungary and Germany to Russia's despairing appeals for a hearing compels the unwilling conclusion that all this diplomatic effort has been merely by-play to gain time.

"It's a put-up job. I could have told them that some time ago," was Morcar's comment.

In England, there was to be a party truce, so that the tiresome fuss about Home Rule, for Ireland would subside for a time. *LIBERAL AND LABOUR OPPOSITION TO ENTANGLEMENT: We wish to enter an emphatic protest against an attempt to make it appear that Great Britain is bound to enter the impending struggle. … An island, she can remain unmoved by the storms that may sweep over the Continent.*

"I wonder," said Morcar thoughtfully.

On Monday, Germany declared war on Russia. Over the weekend, German troops had already occupied Luxemburg.

"I wish they'd leave those small countries alone. Aren't there any treaties to protect them?" said Morcar uneasily.

France, it seemed, was mobilising.

"Well, you can hardly blame her, can you?" said Morcar.

On Tuesday, it seemed Sir Edward Grey had sent a note to Germany requesting an assurance that the neutrality of Belgium would be respected.

"Quite right," said Morcar with relief.

We must, in the opinion of the Foreign Secretary, defend against the invader the neutrality of Belgium, which we are pledged by treaty to respect.

"I should think so!" said Morcar.

The bond of honour is one which will appeal more strongly to Englishmen than Sir Edward Grey's vision of German domination over the whole west of Europe.

"Yes. But you have to think of that too," said Morcar: "Since they're the kind of people who regard treaties as mere scraps of paper, you know."

Owing to the summary rejection by the German Government of the request made by His Majesty's Government for the assurance that the neutrality of Belgium will be respected … a state of war exists between Great Britain and Germany as from 11 p.m. on August 4th, 1914.

"Nothing else to be done," said Morcar soberly.

What did one do in a war? Let's see, now, reflected Morcar; there was a war in South Africa when he was ten. That, he understood, had been a wicked war; good Liberals like his father had strongly disapproved. But Morcar could not remember that a war made any difference to ordinary life in Annotsfield. He went soberly down to Prospect Mills and found Mr. Shaw quivering with rage against the Jingoes who, he said, pushed Great Britain into the war.

"Nay, Mr. Shaw, I don't see what else we could do," said Morcar.

"It was nothing to do with us, it wasn't our business, we've been shoved into it by those damned Tories," shouted Mr. Shaw.

"Well, it won't be you who'll have to do the fighting, Father, so you needn't worry," said Charlie.

"You daft young idiot!" exploded Mr. Shaw. "What do you think a European war will do to trade? They're saying in Annotsfield that two-thirds of the operatives won't be needed."

"It's not the time to think of trade," said Charlie shortly.

"The heavy woollen trade will be all right," mused Mr. Shaw. "They make khaki for the Army."

"But surely the Army's fitted up already, isn't it?" said Morcar.

"They'll need more soldiers than they've got, I expect," said Mr. Shaw shrewdly. "Such nonsense! Land-owning Jingoes! That Lord Kitchener has been appointed Secretary for War—I bet he'll ask for a bigger Army."

This prophecy, to Morcar's astonishment, was soon fulfilled, for before the week was out Kitchener had called for a hundred thousand men immediately, and Parliament had voted an increase of half a million. Meanwhile the Territorials were all mobilised; the Irebridge batch marched through the streets to Annotsfield station, passing the top of Prospect Street on the way. One of the new girl typists called Morcar's attention to this by rushing out of the mill, crying: "They're coming! I can hear the drum!" It seemed she had a young man amongst their number. Morcar followed her out and stood at the corner of the street and watched the hundred men go by. At their head marched three or four officers, amongst whom Morcar with mixed feelings perceived Francis Oldroyd. Just as they drew level with Prospect Street the men began to sing *It's a Long Way to Tipperary*—the words had nothing whatever to do with the war, but the tune was a good one to march to, thought Morcar.

"It makes you feel you ought to be in it yourself," he said uneasily to Mr. Shaw as he described the scene.

"Oldroyds can afford it, we can't," snapped Mr. Shaw. "We're going to have a hard time keeping things going here."

All the same, thought Morcar, he would like to have gone with the Havercake lads—especially when the drums rolled and the band played: *Empress of the Wave*. Could he go? Recruits, according to the *Annotsfield Record*, were coming forward nobly. But what would his mother live on while he was away? And if you once got into the Army did you ever get out of it? How did you actually fight? What was one in fact expected to do during a

103

war? He wished to do his duty, but had no idea where it lay. The newspaper carried a special panel one day headed *THE WAR AND COMMERCE*, informing him that non-combatants would best help to beat the Germans by maintaining and cultivating resources at home. *It is the duty of everyone not with the fighting forces to do what he can to promote the country's commerce and to revive business as usual.* But Morcar did not feel quite so sure....

The Germans had taken Liège and were sweeping through Belgium. Now, the British Expeditionary Force had landed in France without a single mishap, so Brussels would not fall. *GERMANS ADVANCE IN FRANCE. SLOW RETIREMENT OF THE ALLIES.*

"Retirement!" exclaimed Morcar, astonished. "The British Army retire?"

GERMANS ENTER BRUSSELS. ENEMY ADVANCING ON GHENT. GERMANS MARCHING SOUTH OF BRUSSELS. POPULACE FLY BEFORE INVADERS. ARE WE DOWNHEARTED? NO! The Kaiser's command is that you exterminate first the treacherous English and walk over General French's contemptible little army.

"Contemptible!" exclaimed Morcar. "Treacherous!"

"Do you know, Charlie," said Morcar soberly, as the two young men left the mill together at noon on Saturday August 22nd, 1914, "I have an idea we aren't doing so well out there? I mean, in France?"

"I've thought so for some time," said Charlie, grim.

They did not speak again, parting only with a nod when Charlie dismounted from the tram at the end of Hurstholt Road.

Morcar jumped off just before the next stop and swung into his home. His mother was busy cooking in the scullery and called to him not to wash and change before the meal, as it would be ready without delay. Harry accordingly rinsed his hands at the sink and sat down, and to pass the time picked up the *Annotsfield Weekly Record*, which lay on the table. A large advertisement attacked his eyes:

THE CALL TO ARMS

LORD KITCHENER ASKS FOR
100,000
for His Majesty's Army.

Annotsfield calls upon its sons to do their
duty and provide its share of the force.

Come and Help to Fill the Ranks of the
Duke of Wellington's Own Regiment.

You can enlist at:
Annotsfield Drill Hall
The Terms of Service are:

Morcar hastily whisked the paper aside as his mother came into the room. He was quiet during the meal, answering in monosyllables her comments on the stories of "hoarding" she read in the papers.

"It isn't right that some should get all and others nothing," she said. "But I'm bound to say I haven't seen any attempts to get more, in the shops."

"Don't buy anything extra yourself, Mother," said Morcar.

"I shouldn't dream of doing so, Harry," replied his mother with dignity.

Morcar washed and dressed and went out.

"Shall you be in to tea?" asked his mother as he was leaving.

"I hardly think I shall," replied Morcar with a considering air. He was perfectly sure in fact that he would not.

Where was the Drill Hall? He had no idea, and felt an insuperable objection to enquiring, yet at the same time could not bear a moment's unnecessary delay. A tram passed; he ran-after it and leaped aboard. There were two or three other young men in the tram who looked thoughtful and embarrassed even as he; perhaps he might follow them, mused Morcar. However, in the centre of the town there was no further difficulty; posters of Kitchener's appeal everywhere plastered the walls, with *Annotsfield Drill Hall* and the name of the street filled in at the foot. Morcar swung round a corner rapidly and found himself at the end of a considerable queue.

"Is this the Drill Hall?" he asked the man in front.

"That's right," replied the man with satisfaction.

"Aye, this way for t'B.E.F.," cried another, and several turned round and grinned sheepishly at Morcar.

Embarrassed by all this attention, Morcar flattened himself against the wall and kept his head down. A hand fell on his arm and a voice said:

"Harry!"

"Have you been here long, Charlie?" mumbled Morcar.

"No—I'm just a few yards up in the queue," said Charlie.

"But I'll come back here with you. We may as well stick together."

The queue moved slowly forward.

"I'll tell you who's going to be fed to the teeth with this," said Charlie with relish. "John William Shaw, Esquire."

"Well, it can't be helped," said Morcar mildly. "Nothing else to be done."

"Nothing," agreed Charlie, nodding.

12

Soldier

They had expected of course to be off to France in the morning to aid the Contemptibles, as the first British Expeditionary Force now began proudly to call themselves; they expected, they were ready and eager, to perform prodigies of valour and endurance in the terrible battle round Mons. Instead, they were packed off to train at Hudley, ten miles away, and learned to number by the left, salute smartly and wind their puttees tight, while the Contemptibles were in spite of stubborn and prolonged resistance driven back, inexorably back, into France. Paris was in danger, and saved by the battle of the Marne, and Shaw and Morcar were still in England, chafing. To get to France became the greatest ambition of their lives.

Morcar took Army life easily. He had a strong physique, a cheerful disposition and a good deal of patience, and these were the three main requisites. Charlie at first found it a good deal harder. It was symbolic that while Morcar's big burly body looked well in soldier's khaki, the neck of Charlie's jacket always appeared too large. Less strong physically, less placid and more acute than Morcar, Charlie fretted against the maddening delays, the everlasting orders and counter-orders, the route marches to nowhere, the muddles over rations and billeting, the endless drill by old-fashioned sergeants, the tent-pegs without notches, which were often the lot of the British Army recruit in 1914. He continually began his remarks with: "Why don't they …" and Morcar had to admit that his suggestions, never of course adopted, seemed more sensible than the official scheme. It was probably owing to Morcar's placid good-humour that Charlie's tendency to fret critically over Army regulations never went so far as to mar his good conduct record, while Charlie's quick grasp of unfamiliar terms, the meaning of which he communicated rapidly to Morcar, enabled them both to be and to appear "keen"—a magic word in the vocabulary of officers at that time. Sergeants and officers early recognised that Shaw and Morcar were inseparable, and more use together than apart. They kept each other out of scrapes in their spare time, too. In the Army Morcar discovered the soothing power of beer and when overpoweringly bored was inclined to drink it to excess. But Charlie detested clouded wits and had no patience with his friend in his sodden, slow, post-beer condition, and his sharp raillery diminished the number of Morcar's pints. On the other hand, on Morcar's side of the balance came an incident when the pair once stood together in front of a house in a sordid street in a seaside town.

"Are you going in?" said Charlie.

"No!" said Morcar emphatically.

Charlie took a step or two towards the door and stood, considering. Morcar turned and walked along the street. In a moment Army boots clattered on the pavement, and Charlie stood beside him.

All these discontents, however, existed only while they were in England. Charlie was splendid once they were in the front line. Lively, resourceful, cheerful, tireless, in two weeks he was a first-class soldier, the pillar and support of all company commanders, liked and respected and listened to by the men. Morcar too was not without his value. Trenches where Morcar dwelt always emerged from his stay improved—sides revetted, duckboards laid, firing-steps in good condition, dug-outs made comfortable by many ingenious devices. Charlie had a thoroughly "offensive" spirit and was always thinking up new ways of annoying and outwitting the Boche; Morcar was best when the enemy after heavy shelling came over on a raid, or made a flanking attack, or blew up an uncomfortably close mine. Charlie joked and jested, always knew numbers and times and mileages and names, wrote long amusing letters home and once had a piece printed in the *Wipers Times*. He was always the first to volunteer for dangerous duty, always the first—that is, until he got a stripe—to discover the inconvenience in a new order and grumble at it. Morcar smiled at his jokes, pondered them during the night and on sentry duty, sometimes added a footnote or an illustration. He understood distances and the directions from which sounds came and had a better eye for a sniper than Charlie, but could not make deductions from observed facts as quickly as he. They both loathed mud, rats and lice, but Charlie felt them more acutely than Morcar, who on his side felt so cramped in the narrow trench that the order to go over the top was almost a pleasure to him.

In a word, they were two typical specimens of the men who from 1915 onwards held the British line—the new armies.

13

Price of a Medal

A certain page in the history of the Regiment:
The main activity of the Battalion at that time was patrolling. In this department Corp. C. J. Shaw (acting/Sergeant) was extremely active. Night after night he penetrated deeply into No Man's Land in his effort to secure prisoners for an identification. Though unsuccessful in this, he secured valuable information as to the strength of the enemy wire, his dispositions, defences and working parties. On October 12th a small party under his control went out, consisting of four other ranks including Pte. H. Morcar. There had been desultory shelling by the enemy during the evening, but mostly directed to the rear. The ground was not easy to cross, being one mass of shell-holes, and littered everywhere with the débris of scattered trenches and wire entanglements. They had reached a point about thirty yards from the enemy's line when a flare went up and revealed their presence. They flung themselves flat but they had been seen, the rattle of machine-gun fire was heard and there were casualties, Pte. Jessopp being wounded. Under the direction of Corp. Shaw they now contrived to roll into a shell-hole nearby, partly filled with water, Pte. Morcar assisting Pte. Jessopp. Unluckily the

Jerries had evidently planned a "strafe" for this night, for shells now began to fall more quickly on the sector and in a moment a full-dress barrage developed. Meanwhile a merciless machine-gun fire was directed towards the shell-hole, Corp. Shaw's previous patrol exploits having probably made the Jerries nervous. After a time the shelling died down and the party repeatedly attempted to withdraw. As soon as the enemy detected the movement, however, heavy rifle and machine-gun fire broke out again. In one of these bursts of fire Corp. Shaw was wounded, and altogether the withdrawal was a very difficult operation. Eventually Pte. Morcar carried Corp. Shaw on his back to safety, receiving two bullets through his clothes and one through his left arm while doing so. He then actually returned across No Man's Land to help Pte. Jessopp, who had lost consciousness owing to the loss of blood from a wound in his face. For his coolness, courage and gallantry throughout this operation, Pte. Morcar was awarded the Distinguished Conduct Medal, and after his recovery from his wound at a base hospital, proceeded to England for a commission. Corp. Shaw …

The shell-hole was luckily a deep one; from the slimy greenish water at the bottom protruded the hand and head of a German soldier killed on a patrol ten days ago. Jessopp touched Morcar's hand and made uncouth moaning noises. Morcar wriggled round on his stomach in the mud so that he could put his ear close to the man's lips, and said: "What is it, lad?" Jessopp made desperate efforts to articulate words but could only moan grotesquely, and suddenly a spurt of blood flowed over Morcar's ear. He shook his head to get rid of it, and the barrage broke out again. Heavy explosions seemed to stamp brutally on the shrinking earth so that it trembled; a vast weight of metal screamed and roared through the air above their heads. From time to time portions of the sides of the crater slid down into the water with dismal splashes.

"Did you cop anything, Harry?" whispered Charlie.

"No. How about you?"

"All right."

"I think Jessopp's broken his jaw."

Charlie crawled over in Jessopp's direction.

The gun-fire died away at last; the hush was wonderful. Crouching in the mud in the darkness—which was not as dark as they could wish, the moon must have risen behind the clouds— the men in the shell-hole listened for sounds from the nearby enemy trench. A harsh and angry voice harangued the Jerries.

"We might go now while the blighter's talking," whispered Charlie.

"Better wait till they stand down—they'll all be there now, listening to the officer," cautioned Morcar.

They waited. The voice went on and on in a jerky rhythmical manner.

"We can't wait here for ever," said Charlie impatiently: "It'll soon be daylight. Besides, we must get Jessopp in. Are you ready, lads? We'll make a dash for it. Can you walk, Jessopp?"

A vague stirring and rustling in the darkness and an uncouth sound from Jessopp signified assent.

"Come on!" whispered Charlie. He leaped up out of the shell-hole.

There was a sharp crack; he spun round and fell on Morcar's feet so that Morcar stumbled over him. He was evidently uncon- scious, for he did not exclaim. A machine-gun rattled venomously.

"Keep down there!" ordered Morcar, pulling Charlie into the crater. "We must wait."

At last, when they had heard no sounds for some time, they tried again. Morcar heaved Charlie on to his back—it was not easy, because the sides of the crater were steep and slippery and he had a horror of falling into that loathsome water. However he managed it at last, got Charlie's arms over his shoulders and tried to link his hands. But Charlie's fingers slipped apart. "Still unconscious," thought Morcar anxiously. Holding his rifle in one hand, he gripped Charlie's left wrist firmly in the other and crawled out of the shell hole. A couple of rifles spat in their direction and the rattle of the machine-gun began again. But it was too late to wait any longer, daylight was threatening. Stooping and crawling and taking all the cover they could find, they crept towards the British trenches. The Jerries at the machine-gun lost them and found them again; Morcar staggered and fell, and finished the distance on his belly. There was a moment when in the dim pre-dawn light the British barbed wire loomed up ahead of him thick and unbroken; with difficulty he heaved himself to the left—Charlie seemed to weigh a ton in spite of his light frame and he wasn't doing a thing to help himself, reflected Morcar irritably. Then he saw the gap he was seeking, just ahead. But now it seemed far, far away; each barb he passed seemed miles apart. He was panting as though he was pushing his bike up Hurst Bank, reflected Morcar, and with a great effort rose to hands and knees. His left arm was stiff from gripping Charlie. Something pulled sharply at his sleeve. He croaked the password. "Harry!" said a voice. Charlie's weight rolled off him—the relief was heavenly. "He's wounded," explained Morcar thickly. "Unconscious." The familiar cry went up: "Stretcher-bearer!" Where was that idiot Jessopp? Charlie, who never lost a man on patrol, would be vexed if Jessopp got left behind. "Come *along*, Jessopp!" urged Morcar angrily, seizing the prostrate man by the band of his trousers and half carrying, half dragging him to the gap in the wire. The enemy artillery was starting up again, though what was the point of such a noisy bombardment unless they were planning a daylight attack, heaven knew; it was a senseless waste of metal.

"Will you and Jessopp go to the First Aid Post now or wait till nightfall? There's a bit of a strafe going on," said Captain Oldroyd to Morcar in the officers' dug-out, where Charlie, wrapped in a blanket whose folds partly covered his face, lay on a stretcher on the floor.

"Somebody'll have to go to take Corporal Shaw, sir, so Jessopp may as well get down too," urged Morcar. "As for me, I'm not badly hurt; it's just as you think, sir."

The Company Officer was silent for a moment.

"I'm afraid there's no hurry for Corporal Shaw," he said at length in a kindly tone.

"Shaw's seriously wounded and ought to have attention at once, sir," urged Morcar, trying to keep the impatience out of his voice.

"I'm afraid it's too late, Morcar," said Captain Oldroyd. "It was too late when he was first hit, I should think."

He stopped and drew back the blanket. Morcar looked down. Charlie's face was leaden, gaping, drained of colour. There was a bullet-hole in the forehead; the lips protruded oddly. It was—yes, it was—the face of a dead man.

Corporal Shaw, who had received a bullet through the head, died before reaching the First Aid Post.

III

Defeat

14

Winnie

"You look very nice in your officer's uniform and your ribbon, Harry," said Mrs. Shaw wistfully.

"Worsted," muttered Mr. Shaw in an explanatory tone.

"Charlie would have looked nice in that kind of uniform," continued Mrs. Shaw.

"Mother!" exclaimed Winnie painfully.

"You're right, he would, Mrs. Shaw," agreed Morcar. "If he'd lived, Charlie would have been an officer sooner than me, you know."

Mrs. Shaw set her rocking-chair moving slowly backwards and forwards in satisfaction. That she looked ten years older than when he had last seen her was not due only to her deep mourning. An expression of harassed perplexity marred the comeliness of her face; her eyebrows were perpetually raised, her fine hazel eyes stared out in perpetual bewilderment. Her left hand, work-roughened, with its rather broad gold wedding-ring, symbol of so many griefs, so many joys, so many toils, wandered vaguely over her ample breast. Harry wished heartily that Mr. Shaw and Winnie would go away and leave Charlie's mother and himself so that they might grieve for Charlie together. He should not at all mind shedding tears with Mrs. Shaw, and this open expression of sorrow would probably ease the hearts of both, for they were both simple creatures. But in the presence of those two restless critical perverse spirits, Charlie's father and sister, simple open grief was not possible; they would in some obscure way feel it to be insincere, an insult.

"Your mother must be very proud of you, Harry," said Mrs. Shaw, still rocking.

"I daresay she is," said Mr. Shaw sardonically, his small features quivering.

"Well, love, I'm sure she is," said his wife, contending against his tone. "Why, I should think Harry's proud of himself. He has a right to be. It's one thing to be made an officer straight out of school because they're so short of them, as they are now, and another being promoted for merit. I only hope he'll be spared to enjoy it."

"I don't enjoy anything much now Charlie's gone, Mrs. Shaw," said Morcar.

"I had a beautiful letter from that Captain Oldroyd," continued Mrs. Shaw in the same childlike placid manner. "Winnie, where's that beautiful letter from Captain Oldroyd about Charlie?"

"It's on the table at your elbow, Mother," said Winnie.

"Oh, yes, so it is," agreed Mrs. Shaw placidly. She handed the envelope, worn and soiled with much fingering, to Morcar. "Open it—read it, Harry," she urged. "It's a beautiful letter."

With a sick heart Harry read the conventional phrases, written a thousand thousand times in officers' dug-outs by the light of candles: *keen and capable … a great favourite … will be much missed …*

you will be relieved to know that his death was instantaneous …

"How will they get on at Syke Mills without Captain Oldroyd?" wondered Mrs. Shaw.

"How do we get on at Prospect without Charlie?" said her husband bitterly.

"What Francis Oldroyd knows about textiles would go on a sixpenny-bit," said Morcar mechanically. He was astonished to find these words, ghosts from another world, on his lips. Textiles seemed so remote from the blood and the mud, the lines of poplar trees, the shelling, the dead bodies, the trench feet, the rats, the boredom and the danger, which were his realities nowadays. It struck him suddenly, with surprise, that the ruined Ypres Cloth Hall had been a *cloth* hall. "But he's a good officer as officers go. He's been promoted twice lately."

"I hear his new works manager is feathering his own nest nicely," observed Mr. Shaw in a tone of satisfied malice.

"When you get back, Harry, you might thank him for that beautiful letter he wrote about Charlie," said Mrs. Shaw.

"He's not with us now—he's been taken off to be a colonel in some other regiment," said Morcar.

"You look very nice in your officer's uniform. Charlie would look nice in that kind of uniform," said Mrs. Shaw placidly.

"Mother!" cried Winnie. She sprang up. "You'd better be going, Harry," she said. "Mother'll go on for hours like this now she's got started."

"Well, goodbye, Mrs. Shaw," said Morcar, rising. On an impulse he bent forward and kissed her awkwardly. She kissed him warmly in return, and her tears suddenly ran over.

"Goodbye, Harry," she said. "Come and see me again soon. You were always a good boy, Harry, and a good friend to my Charlie."

"Come *along*" whispered Winnie in a tone of savage impatience.

Morcar shook hands with Mr. Shaw, who gave him a couple of cold dry fingers, and followed Winnie into the hall. Winnie took down his British warm from the peg and helped him into it, then turning him round towards her began to fasten the buttons.

"I congratulate you on your medal, Harry," she said in a high trembling voice.

"Now, Winnie!" protested Morcar, wretched.

Suddenly Winnie's face was convulsed, and tears poured down her cheeks. She buried her face in Morcar's coat and sobbed bitterly. Morcar put his arms round her and patted her shoulder.

"Now, love, now!" he said, at the same time urging her towards the empty drawing-room. "Think of your mother, you don't want her to hear you." Winnie, shaken by sobs, yielded to his touch, and with his arm round her waist he drew her across the threshold and pushed the door shut with one foot. Winnie put her arms about him, leaned her head against his breast and wept with passion.

"Why didn't you bring him back to us?" she sobbed frantically.

"I did my best, love," said Morcar.

"You were with him—you were with him in that shell-hole. You should have rescued him—you should have brought him back to us."

"I *did* bring him back, Winnie," said Morcar. "It wasn't my fault that he was dead before we started." Although he knew in his soul that this was true and that Charlie had fallen dead on the lip of the crater, he could not help feeling at the same time an entirely inconsistent and unjustified resentment against Captain

Oldroyd, who had not sent Charlie off at once to the First Aid Post—medical aid might have saved him, thought Morcar obstinately, at the same time as he told Winnie what he knew to be the truth.

"You should have prevented him from climbing out of the shell-hole," said Winnie angrily.

"Perhaps I should. But you know Charlie, how quick and impatient he was. He wanted to get Jessopp in—Jessopp was losing so much blood."

"Jessopp!" whispered Winnie in a fury.

"Well, Charlie was Corporal, you see. He was responsible for us. We were under his orders," said Morcar.

"All that is nonsense," said Winnie fiercely. "You should have prevented him! I don't mean it, Harry," she wept again. "Don't take any notice. But Charlie——"

"I know, I know, love," soothed Morcar, stroking her thin sob-shaken shoulders. "I feel just the same." He laid his cheek against her temple, brushed back her hair and kissed her tenderly. Suddenly she was very quiet and still in his arms. "You're all worn out with looking after your mother," he told her. "Come and sit down."

Winnie gave a deep trembling sigh and allowed him to lead her to the sofa. They sat down side by side; Morcar gently pressed her head against his shoulder so that she might rest. A few convulsive sobs shook her at increasing intervals; then she lay there quietly, his arm about her.

At last she gave another sigh, sat up and began drying her eyes with a wisp of a handkerchief. Morcar proffered his own and she took it; its khaki colour made her weep again, but more calmly than before.

Mr. Shaw suddenly opened the door and looked in. His glance

sought and found them as they sat together in the twilight; his little eyes, burning, fixed them sardonically.

"Winnie's a bit upset," said Morcar.

"So I see," said Mr. Shaw. He waited a moment, then as neither of them spoke, withdrew abruptly.

"I'd best be going," said Morcar, rising.

Somewhat to his surprise, Winnie remained seated on the sofa. She gave him a strange fiery glance as he stood in front of her, his newly acquired officer's manners obliging him to wait her pleasure. Then she broke out harshly:

"Are we engaged or aren't we? Because if we are," she added in an angry tone: "I think you ought to say something to Father."

"Engaged?" repeated Morcar in sheer astonishment.

"You kissed me," murmured Winnie, hanging her head.

"We are engaged, of course, if you want to be, Winnie," said Morcar at once staunchly.

"Nay!" cried Winnie, springing up, her eyes, red-rimmed and glazed with weeping, suddenly renewing their sparkle, her round cheeks fiery: "It's for you to say, Harry Morcar! I'll not be beholden to you! Make up your mind!"

An, immense tenderness filled Morcar's heart. Winnie! Charlie's sister!

"We are engaged, love," he said in his kindest tone, and drawing her to him, he kissed her lips gravely. Her slender body trembled within his arm—he found that very touching.

"I always loved you, Harry," murmured Winnie, burying her face in his trench-coat.

Morcar was astonished. Winnie with her endless supply of admirers! Winnie who, from her twelvemonths' vantage, had always scoffed at himself and Charlie, pretending to regard them as hopelessly immature and juvenile! He felt tremendously flattered and exhilarated, suddenly proud for Winnie's sake of his medal, his war service, his manhood. How suitable, how altogether proper, that he should marry Charlie's sister! He kissed her again in a much more lover-like fashion, and cried cheerfully:

"We'll be married on my next leave."

"The next? Why not on this leave?" pouted Winnie.

15

Wedding

Morcar could not imagine why his friends all joked so much about feeling nervous at their weddings. He himself did not feel in the least nervous. Everything was going well and without a hitch. He stood before the minister with Winnie at his side in Hurst Congregational Chapel, on a winter's afternoon, plighting his troth to her in a steady voice which to his relief sounded neither too shrill nor too much of a growl. It was fairly loud, he admitted, but then, Morcar had always believed that the man should speak louder at his wedding than the woman. Winnie's voice was the merest thread; her customary assurance was quite gone from her—but that too was proper. The sun was shining and the polished wood of the galleries and pews gleamed cheerfully golden. His mother, in brown moiré with a bunch of dark red chrysanthemums, sat on his right amid a group of young men in khaki, his friends of the tennis court and the trench. On his left amid masses of Shaw relations sat Mrs. Shaw, in a new black musquash fur coat and a large black hat slightly awry, carrying a bouquet of bright pink carnations. Her mild vacant gaze seemed to rest more often on Morcar than on her daughter, and Morcar understood why it was so—she was thinking of Charlie. Mr. Shaw in a new morning-coat which looked too large for him hovered restlessly in the rear. Winnie had elected to be married in navy-blue, as so many people thought a white dress inappropriate in wartime. Morcar rather regretted this decision, for he thought he would have taken an innocent pleasure in seeing his wife in flowing white silk and lace, tulle and veil and orange-blossom; but of course Winnie must do as she chose; the matter was of small importance. He did not like her navy blue coat and skirt much, and her angular black velvet hat did not suit her, but such details were, again, of small importance. His wedding present to her was a fur coat and cap of grey squirrel, and these suited her well enough. The poor child looked pale and red-eyed, as though she had been crying all night, which was very natural and proper, thought Morcar sympathetically, in view of what lay before her. He himself had never made love to a woman before, but had a modest confidence that he should acquit himself reasonably well—no worse, anyway, than other men. At any rate all should be done with the utmost kindness. He took Winnie's cold little paw in his own—it trembled visibly—and placed the wedding ring on her finger in a firm steady movement. He would like to have given her hand a comforting squeeze to warm it, but supposed that would not be proper. The minister, looking particularly solemn and raising his voice, now pronounced the beautiful and moving words which made them man and wife for ever.

A sigh of relaxed tension came from the congregation, the organist broke into a wedding hymn and after standing through a verse or two Morcar and Winnie were led away into the vestry.

125

There were tears in Winnie's eyes and her mouth trembled as he kissed her; altogether she seemed more upset by the ceremony than anyone who knew her would have expected. This weakness made Morcar feel particularly tender towards her, and particularly determined to give her that strong protection, that love and care which were his duty as a husband. Friends and relatives now burst into the vestry and kissed Winnie and himself, some mildly weeping, others mildly hilarious. Mrs. Shaw laid her bouquet down somewhere and could not find it, and Winnie became more like herself again, throwing off a pert sharp sentence of her usual kind as she retrieved the flowers and straightened her mother's hat. The organ pealed out the Mendelssohn wedding march and Morcar marched down the aisle with Winnie on his arm and in his heart a feeling of calm satisfaction. He had often wondered whether he should ever marry, what shape in general his life would take and whether it would be creditable and manly and like other people's lives; now here he was, a lieutenant in the Army, with a ribbon up, practically a partner in Prospect Mills and a wife on his arm who was Charlie's sister. It was all very satisfactory, and he did not feel nervous.

The reception was like all other Annotsfield wedding receptions, with champagne and patties (rather meatless) and trails of smilax and Morcar's throat growing tired with talking so long through the noise. Just for a moment there was a hush and a deeper feeling as Morcar in his speech replying to the toast blurted suddenly:

"Only one thing could make my wife and myself happier to-day—and I think you can all guess what that would be— if my brother-in-law could be here to greet us."

Just for that one moment Morcar felt as though somebody

was driving over his heart with harrows, as though all this alleg-edly happy scene were unreal except Mrs. Shaw's mild staring eyes, which at that moment had a tragic beauty as they gazed into his own. Then he passed on rapidly to one of the usual bridal jokes, closing the curtains over his for-the-moment too openly exposed heart.

The newly married pair were to spend their brief honeymoon in London in spite of Zeppelins, and a hired car was to take them to catch the afternoon express at Leeds. Winnie vanished and reappeared looking her best in the squirrel coat and cap; her cheeks were flushed, her eyes sparkled, she joked with her friends in her usual pert bright way. The farewell scene at the door amid the usual hail of confetti seemed to entertain her, and as they drove off she was laughing heartily. But in the car she took off her fur cap, saying that it was rather heavy, and she then exclaimed in a rather petulant tone:

"You've never said whether you liked my hair."

Morcar, uncomprehending, gravely surveyed her head. Her hair certainly looked rather different to-day, he thought—shorter, curlier. "Oh! You've had it bobbed! Yes," said Morcar, looking at it with his head on one side and rather pleased with the rapidity of his diagnosis: "I like it, Winnie love. It suits you."

"Poor Harry. You didn't notice it before, did you? Poor Harry," said Winnie strangely. She laid her hand on his for a moment and pressed it, then sat silent, her eyes averted, until they reached the station.

They were not alone again till late that night. Then, just for a moment, for a moment only, there was beauty and rapture. She lay in his arms, this perverse and wilful Winnie, astonishingly acquiescent, and looked up at him with wide, liquid, shining eyes of love. Her hair so soft and silky, her little neck which he could

127

almost span with one hand, her breast so warm and full and rich against his own—for a moment these were rapture, these were beauty. For a moment he forgot that she was Charlie's sister.

Afterwards, there was his utmost kindness. In the recesses of his mind he was rather surprised that this was the love the poets and artists made such a fuss about, for it hardly seemed to deserve so much praise. But that surprise, of course, must never be revealed to his wife. Everything that was kind and good in him he must show to her now. Winnie seemed content, reclining her head on his shoulder, drawing deep calm breaths and smiling upon him sweetly. Nevertheless, through his sleep later, Morcar believed he dimly caught a sound of weeping.

16

Wife and Child

A battle followed between Winnie and her parents of which the echoes reached Morcar near St. Eloi.

Most war brides in Winnie's position made their home with their parents pending their husband's return, and Mrs. Shaw's recent decline from health seemed to make this even more reasonable in her case. But Winnie, it seemed, was determined to be installed in a house of her own at the earliest opportunity. Her father was angry, her mother plaintive, Mrs. Morcar dubious; but Morcar felt he understood Winnie's antipathy to living with the Shaws, because he shared it himself. He was conscious, too, that he had perhaps looked glum when, parting from Winnie to return to France after their honeymoon, she had spoken, as they stood on the King's Cross platform together, of his spending his next leave at the Sycamores. Accordingly he was not daunted or much disconcerted after the first surprise when, on coming out of the line after a tour of particularly dangerous duty, he found a short note from Winnie explaining that she had found a suitable house, together with a business communication from the solicitor he had employed to draw up his will, stating the procedure necessary to undertake the purchase of Hurstcote, which Mrs. H. Morcar had informed him was contemplated, and a long alarmed letter from his mother, describing the skirmishes between the Shaws and Winnie in a veiled manner, and hinting at her own feeling that a young wife ought to remain in the shelter of her parents' roof until her husband himself could make a home for her. *I would gladly have Winnie to stay with me here if she wished*, said Mrs. Morcar, *but she seems determined on this house—which in itself I must say is very suitable.*

After the bloody raids in which Morcar had just taken part, the thought of being alive, a peaceful citizen of Annotsfield, with a house of his own, was indescribably alluring. If he were killed in the war, he did not see that Winnie would be any the worse off for having begun the purchase of house and furniture, for these two commodities were scarce and in great demand in England and he could trust Mr. Shaw to see that she sold at a profit. He made up his mind at once therefore and wrote to Winnie, Mr. Shaw, his mother and his solicitor Nasmyth, to say that the house should be bought. He had already deposited a power of attorney in the solicitor's hands, so the negotiations need not wait for his presence.

A sheaf of letters flew across to him in reply, reaching him when he was involved in preparations for the coming battle of the Somme. He opened his wife's first, drew out several sheets of notepaper headed in writing *Hurstcote, Hurst Bank, Annotsfield*, saw that the matter of the house purchase was settled and laid aside Winnie's sheets for a more leisurely perusal when he should have coped with the rest. Mr. Shaw's small contorted characters, in very black ink, informed him that Winnie's place was with her mother and she was not fit to undertake the preparation of a house in her present condition. Mrs. Morcar with her usual dignified reticence mildly commented on the strangeness of Harry's buying a house he had never seen while expressing willingness to help Winnie in every possible way so that she should not overtire herself. The lawyer informed him that he had made the necessary advance payment to the Annotsfield Building Society from Henry Morcar's savings, and Hurstcote was now Henry Morcar's property, subject to his paying them two pounds a week for the next five years. An insurance policy had been taken out in accordance with the Building Society's requirements.

Perceiving from the turn of some sentences in the letters of Mr. Shaw and his mother that Winnie was thought to be pregnant, Morcar turned to his wife's letter again eagerly. Winnie's hand was not a pretty one, mused Morcar; it was at once vehement and formless, emphatic, black-stroked but of uncertain outline. Her spelling was erratic and her grammar uncertain. But like Charlie she had the knack of vivid description; her pen flew rapidly across the paper in lively sentences full of detail spiced with malice. She was writing in Hurstcote itself, it seemed, having gone there to put a fire in for the painters. Hurstcote was a small stone house, newish, semi-detached, just on the brow of Hurst Bank; the front windows looked over the Bank across a tiny garden; the back windows looked at the tops of the trees growing in the valley. There were two sitting-rooms, a kitchen and a scullery downstairs, with a tiny but neat square hall at one side; the notât-all steep staircase had a landing in the middle from which sprang the bathroom; three little bedrooms, and a tiny hole which Harry might like for his study, occupied the second floor. There were no attics, but good cellars on a level with the ground at the back, which dropped away abruptly. Coal delivery might be a problem. There was electric light. The bathroom was too small to swing a cat in, but Winnie had always been against giving baths to cats. The kitchen stove was poor, so an uncle's wedding cheque which had previously been earmarked for armchairs was being devoted to the purchase of a gas oven. Other wedding cheques, and other of Morcar's savings, were to go into furniture. His mother was helping to choose carpets, make curtains, embroider linen. Winnie had secured a "woman" to "come in" three days a week.

It was all so normal that Harry felt soothed and happy; the shellfire seemed to die away in the distance, the oozing trench to grow dim, while a picture of a quiet peaceful little room with a view over Hurst Bank and a blazing north-country fire rose clear before his delighted eyes. It gave him real pleasure to address his reply to Mrs. H. Morcar at Hurstcote.

He thought ruefully however, as he wrote his reply, that it was just like Winnie not to mention her pregnancy in her letter to her husband. Since she had chosen to be silent, he hardly knew himself how to broach the matter to her, and after much thought compromised on a sentence written below: *Your loving husband, Harry*, which ran: *Take care of yourself and don't work too hard.*

Apparently this was satisfactory to Winnie, for in her next letter she brought herself to remark: *The doctor says I am very well*, and thereafter in an offhand allusive way from time to time she indicated her preparations for the birth, in her letters to her husband.

The child was born in September 1916, while Harry was still in the battle of the Somme. He was three weeks old before Harry knew of his existence, and christened and thriving, big and bonny, before Captain Morcar could get leave to make the boy's acquaintance.

But when this event at last took place, in the new year of 1917, Morcar at once fell head over heels in love with Baby Harry. He was a fair, merry, healthy little boy, who looked at him, thought Morcar, from his own grey-blue eyes but smiled Charlie's lively smile, kicked his delightful toes with an energy absurdly reminiscent of Mr. Shaw and waved shapely hands which seemed to Harry a miniature edition of Mrs. Morcar's. Baby Harry surveyed the new strange member of the household with solemn but friendly awe, blew a deprecatory bubble and gurgled enquiringly at him, looked pained when Winnie who was busy with his safety pins and buttons turned him on his stomach and tried to crane his neck so as to secure another glimpse of Morcar. His tiny fingers, with their perfect joints and exquisite nails, rested peacefully on Morcar's straps when Morcar nursed him; his round rosy cheek was incredibly smooth and cool against Morcar's weather-beaten face. Sometimes he rolled with furious energy on the hearthrug; sometimes he sat erect, gazing philosophically at the world and holding his own toes. He was a general favourite. Mrs. Shaw doted on him, Mrs. Morcar truly and devotedly loved him and made for him the most delicious silk frocks with incredibly complicated smocking. Those of Winnie's brothers and sisters who were still at home admired his fresh appearance and sweet disposition Whole-heartedly, while Mr. Shaw told Morcar sen-tentiously that there was nothing so lovely as a baby, dandling his first grandson on his knee the while. (This had the same results as of old in the Sycamores with Mr. Shaw's own offspring; the over-shaken baby began to soil his bib and Mr. Shaw called wildly for his daughter. This time, however, the baby had another champion, for Morcar snatched him from his grandfather indignantly.) Winnie was at her best as a mother; as she sat feeding the child or changing him or bathing him an expression of deep content illuminated her face, her restless spirit seemed calmed, her sharp tongue was blunted to benevolence. She was thoroughly competent in all essentials of child care, and even struggled to understand the newest ideas of infant welfare just come into fashion, asking Harry to explain nutrition terms to her with a humility which he found touching.

As for Morcar, he felt a degree of emotion about Baby Harry which he had not felt about anybody or anything since Charlie was killed—perhaps indeed his feeling for the child was the strongest he had ever experienced in his life. Perhaps he was cut out to be a father rather than a lover or a husband, he thought soberly, admitting to himself that Baby Harry meant more to him than his wife. But his love for the child was so deep, so satisfying, that he felt an immense gratitude towards Winnie. She had given him this child, their son; this beautiful innocent creature who was his own, his own to love and cherish, to protect and provide for.

"You've got something to do now, Harry," said Mrs. Shaw to him, chuckling feebly—she was now bedridden—as Morcar laid the child on her bed in order to wrap him more carefully in his white woollen shawl to return to Hurstcote after a visit to his grandparents.

"I don't care *what* I do for him," said Morcar earnestly, folding the shawl over in the prescribed fashion and taking the child into his arms. "I'll do *anything* for him, Mrs. Shaw." He looked about him; he was alone in the room with the ailing woman. He added in a conspiratorial tone: "All I want, Mrs. Shaw, is to come safe back and make a good home for Winnie and Baby."

"You'll have to win the war first,", the old lady warned him.

"Oh, of course," said Morcar.

His leave was up next day and he returned to France, in ample time for the Allies' third spring offensive.

17

Homecoming

It was the spring of 1919; a tallish, broad-shouldered, solid young man, with thick fair hair, grey-blue eyes, a fresh complexion and a wide mouth, wearing officer's khaki, was travelling towards Annotsfield in a northbound train. He carried his head slightly poked forward owing to a flesh wound through his left shoulder, but had been told by the medical officer that this would remedy itself shortly. His usual expression was mild and sober, but a pleasant grin curved his full lips and a merry look enlivened his eyes when occasion justified. After being crowded for many miles, the railway carriage had emptied at a junction and Morcar, left alone, was looking at himself in the somewhat tarnished railway mirror. So this was Henry Morcar, aged twenty-eight, recently Captain H. Morcar, D.C.M., now demobilised and about to re-enter civilian life. Not too bad, thought Morcar, surveying himself thoughtfully. He had a wife and a child and a house and a job, so he was luckier than most. Then why did he feel so empty and so enervated? The landscape outside the carriage window was green and smiling; there were dandelions in the hedges and lambs in the fields. In his kit he had a length of pale-blue crêpe-de-chine for Winnie, a miniature football and a crane for the boy. He had longed for this day through four dreary months since thé Armistice last November; now it was here and he felt hollow and perplexed. He winked at himself in the glass to cheer himself up. His reflection winked back and Morcar felt rather better. But not much.

"Probably need a cup of tea," he adjured himself.

He sank back on the velvet seat and hummed *Roses are Blooming in Picardy* mournfully.

All of a sudden the sun went in; great black clouds had rolled up over the horizon and blotted it out. The colour of the grass darkened all the way down the range as though one had poured gallons of black into it, thought Morcar, and wondered how much of that old designing stuff he really remembered. "But I can soon mug it up again," he told himself staunchly. Meanwhile, it had begun to rain—no, to snow. Yes, positively to snow; white flakes were driving thick and fast before a strong cold wind, which rattled the windows, tossed the fleeces of the sheep and howled through the telegraph wires. The scene had changed in a moment from spring to winter, from relaxation to effort, from a smile to a frown.

"Ah, this is more like the West Riding!" cried Morcar aloud, laughing. He sat up, feeling stimulated, and changed his tune to a local song beginning: *I will take thee to yon green garden, Where the pretty flowers blow.*

"Where the pretty, pretty, flow-ers grow," sang Morcar, pronouncing *pretty* in the Ire Valley fashion. His thoughts turned to his wife, and he smiled with pleasure.

At Annotsfield station his cheerful mood was sustained. There were no taxis to be had, of course, but an old out-porter with a barrow bobbed up and offered to take his kit-bag as far as the Hurst tram.

"How do you know I want the Hurst tram?" queried Morcar, laughing, as they walked along side by side. He put a hand on the barrow and helped to push it, with a delicious sense that he was not in the Army now and could do as he chose.

"You're Captain Morcar, aren't you? I owned you as soon as ever I saw you," said the old man. "I used to work at your grandfather's twenty years ago. Your picture were in the paper when you won your medal, think on."

Morcar, pleased by the recognition and enjoying the Yorkshire turn of phrase, tipped him heavily and took his seat in the empty tram. Here he had to wait several minutes till the proper time of departure was reached. At first he felt a feverish impatience, but presently he could not help taking an interest in the conversation, conducted in loud tones and the Yorkshire idiom, between the driver and the conductor, who were sitting together in the body of the tram. The driver, an oldish man, was describing to the conductor, who had been demobilised from the Ripon dispersal camp a few weeks ago, the behaviour of the conductress who had replaced him during the war. His anecdotes were ribald, and usually ended in the comment: "Eh, she were a one!" The conductor, laughing heartily, opined at length that her husband would have a surprise when he got home. At this the driver looked grave.

"Nay," he said: "There were no harm in her, tha knows."

The conductor, feeling that he had gone too far, agreed. "No harm—just a bit o' fun, like."

"That's right. Well," said the driver, drawing out a large watch from the folds of coat about his waist: "Time to be off.

This gentleman's wanting to get home, I daresay."

"You're right there," said Morcar.

It seemed an age before the conductor at last jerked the bell-string, the driver applied the power and the tram began its slow grinding progress up Hurst Road. But at last the tram topped the rise, at last he was dragging his kitbag off the steps, at last he was hurrying down Hurstholt Road, the bag banging at his knees as he strode. After all this delay Hurstcote appeared with an effect of suddenness at last. From shyness, or diffidence, or excess of emotion, or a real desire to examine this house, which in his feverish wartime visits he had not really made his own familiar home, Morcar paused at the little green-painted wooden gate.

The sun had come out again and the house—though rather like a birdcage in size and shape, thought Morcar, amused—looked well; he noted with pleasure, for he did not like brick, that it was built of the greyish local millstone grit. Spotless curtains of white casement cloth hung very straight at the windows and a few neat daffodils sparsely filled a diamond-shaped garden bed. Morcar unlatched the gate and swung it open. At an upper window a small face appeared and bobbed up and down; its owner, a little boy in grey, was evidently jumping on the same spot with a child's enjoyment of rhythmical repetition. The face was fair and friendly; suddenly it beamed with recognition, and vanished.

"It's Harry," thought Morcar, and his heart turned over.

He went up the garden path and tried the neat green door. It was locked; he rang the bell. Suddenly it was thrown open and Winnie stood there, dressed to go out in her squirrel coat and cap. Clinging shyly to her hand was the child, in a grey cloth coat with a velvet collar, and leggings which to Morcar's delighted amusement seemed to reach from foot to waist.

"Oh, Harry!" cried Winnie. "What a pity you've come today! We haven't a loaf of bread in the house!"

For a moment Morcar was deeply hurt and daunted. Then he rallied staunchly. This was just Winnie's usual perversity; she was really glad to see him though her words sounded otherwise; like the West Riding she was apt to mingle snow-showers with her sun. All the same, he could not quite bring himself to offer an embrace to her till he was sure it was wanted. Instead, he picked up the child and buried his face in young Harry's soft little neck. Harry put an arm round Morcar's shoulders and gave him a kiss, moist and confused but spontaneous and real, in return. Then Morcar felt his heart melt towards his* wife, and he took her in his arms and spoke lovingly to her.

Her response was cool and he soon desisted, instead displaying the presents he had brought. The football was received with ecstasy, and did some immediate damage amongst the drawing-room furniture; the crane was pronounced by Winnie "too old" for a boy only two and a half. The lovely turquoise silk she eyed in silence.

"It's too pale for a blouse," she said.

"It's meant for underneath, love," said Morcar, laughing. Winnie coloured and tossed her head.

It seemed that Winnie had been about to pay one of her regular visits to the Sycamores and stay there for tea, and in view of the shortage of bread at Hurstcote this plan was adhered to, Morcar joining her at the Sycamores after a brief visit to his mother.

He found the house greatly changed. Mrs. Shaw had died last autumn—"I *told* you, Harry," Winnie kept repeating, while her husband mildly countered with the excuse that the letter had gone astray. One of Winnie's sisters had married and gone to live in Bradford, the younger girl had become a nurse during the war and refused to return to home life now, while her two remaining brothers had been demobilised rather earlier than Morcar, one from a regiment of Sappers and the other from the R.F.C. The three male Shaws were therefore all living at the Sycamores under the care of a working housekeeper with occasional supervision from Winnie, in what appeared to be an uncertain and uncomfortable way. It was clear to Morcar, as they sat at high tea in the dining-room, that Mr. Shaw had put pressure on Winnie to go and live, at the Sycamores, that Winnie had refused, that between Winnie and the housekeeper there was a continual and bitter feud, that judging from the appearance of the table and the quality of the cooking the feud was not altogether unjustified, and that the two younger Shaws, thus suddenly grown from negligible schoolboys into young men, did not particularly enjoy living in the unmitigated company of their father.

"I don't suppose they're any more comfortable together at the mill," thought Morcar shrewdly: "It's time I was getting back." He recalled how affectionately Charlie had cared for his young brothers, and resolved to look after them himself with just as great and brotherly an affection.

"Shall I start work on Monday, then, Mr. Shaw?" he said affably. "Or would you like me to come down tomorrow morning?"

There was a pause.

"I don't know that I've much room for you at Prospect, Harry," said Mr. Shaw.

"Oh, yes, you have, Father," said Winnie at once, feeding an egg to young Harry from a spoon.

"Nay—I don't want to go where I'm not wanted," drawled Morcar with an outward calm which covered anger. "I thought I'd helped to build Prospect up a bit, but if it's viewed differently here, I can find myself another job, I don't doubt."

"Oh, aye—two, I daresay," said Mr. Shaw ironically. "We all know you, Harry—you're the man that had two jobs in one day, at fifteen years old. But I don't see that there's much room for you at Prospect."

"If you don't take Harry back, Father," said Winnie fiercely, "I'll never speak to you again. I mean it."

"I'm not talking about not taking him back," said Mr. Shaw irritably. "I simply say there isn't much room for him. He can come, and welcome, if he likes; but it'll have to be at a less salary than he had before and there isn't much prospect of advancement. I've still two sons to provide for, bear in mind."

"There was room for him when Charlie was here," threw out Winnie sarcastically.

"Charlie isn't here now," said Mr. Shaw.

There was a pause.

"We should be glad to have Harry, Father," muttered the ex-Sapper, Hubert.

"Well, I'll expect you on Monday as usual, Harry," said Mr. Shaw in a milder tone.

"I'll come tomorrow," said Morcar shortly.

"You'll do as you want, I expect—you didn't ask me when you left, and you'll do the same about coming back, I suppose. You didn't once come down when you were on leave, I noticed. But come when you like. Only don't blame me if there isn't much to do," said Mr. Shaw disagreeably.

It was not a very cheering welcome to Annotsfield, reflected Morcar as he walked homewards later, Winnie silent by his side. But the sleeping child in his arms made up for everything. Besides, perhaps Mr. Shaw was right and there was really no place for him in the business. If so, he would leave and find some other post. Now that he was back in the West Riding his textile memories were returning in a flood, and he remembered the fate of many a fine business which had sunk under the weight of too many owners' families. Anything uneconomic of that kind he despised; he did not wish to be associated with any such silly work.

"It was grand the way you stood up for me to your father, Winnie," he observed soberly: "But it may be he's right and there's no room for me at Prospect."

"Your place is at Prospect," said Winnie hardly.

"Well, we shall see," said Morcar, as he unlatched the Hurstcote gate and stood aside to let her enter. "No business can stand too many households living out of it—it isn't sense."

"Then let Eric go out," said Winnie. "He wasn't in it before and he hates working for Father."

"He's your brother."

"You're my husband."

Morcar involuntarily let out a snort of laughter, for her remark, so loving in word, was in tone so snappish as to amount to an angry retort.

"What are you laughing at?" said Winnie, quivering with fury. She inserted her key and opened the front door. "Father has a duty to provide for me too, I suppose?"

"I'll provide for you," said Morcar, vexed. He spoke rather more irritably than he meant because he did not altogether relish being let into his own house with Winnie's latchkey.

Winnie switched on the light and they found themselves in the tiny hall.

"Besides, we have to think of the boy," said Winnie. She bent towards little Harry, removed his hat and made to take him from Morcar's arms. "I'll take him straight up to bed."

"I'll carry him for you."

"No, give him to me. You ought to think of him, Harry, before you talk of leaving Prospect," said Winnie in a virtuous reproving tone.

"I am thinking of him!" shouted Morcar, suddenly losing his temper. "Who else do you suppose I'm thinking of?"

"Not of me, certainly," said Winnie disagreeably.

"I don't want him to have to go through what I went through when I first went to business," panted Morcar, turning from her and carrying the child upstairs.

"He won't—he'll be in his grandfather's business," said Winnie angrily, following.

"If there's room for him. But suppose there isn't? Your brothers will marry and have sons too. I don't want my son to be a poor relation. I want Harry to have a business of his own to go into when he grows up, and if I've got to make one for him, I shall have to start soon and build it up. There isn't room to build much at Prospect, and your father's that obstinate—if he's made up his mind not to make me a partner, he never will. You'll have to trust me to decide, love," said Morcar, regaining his good temper as he looked down at the round flushed cheek, the long fair lashes, the peaceful forehead and fair silky hair of the sleeping child. He turned to his wife as they reached the top of the stairs. "I'll go to Prospect and stay a month or two to look round, but you must trust me to do the best for Harry."

"Why should I?" screamed Winnie suddenly. "He isn't yours."

Morcar gaped at her.

"What do you mean, Winnie?" he whispered at length.

"He's not your son!" cried Winnie madly. "He's not your child! Don't you understand? He's not your child!"

For a moment Morcar gazed at his wife in horror. Then thrusting the child into her arms, he rushed from the house.

IV
Fall

18

Metamorphosis

A Few hours later Morcar came to himself to find he was standing at the edge of a remote bluff on Marthwaite Moor. A landscape of singular beauty lay before him: a vast amphitheatre where three great slopes interlocked, sweeping majestically down to the streams far out of sight below. Tonight the turbulent masses of rock and heather lay frozen into black and silver beneath a cloudless sky lit by a clear full moon.

The calm silver light, the perfect stillness, the silence, mocked him; he could have borne the torment of his heart better, he thought, in storm and rain. Even nature was out of sympathy with him, even Marthwaite Moor thought he was a fool for his pains. A fool, a fool, a simple, soft, silly credulous fool! He remembered his engagement and marriage—how Winnie had forced it, hurried it on. He remembered also that she had said: *I always loved you, Harry*—and laughed in self-derision. He had believed that? He had been flattered by that? He remembered Winnie's eagerness to have a house of her own—an eagerness with which he had softly, sentimentally, sympathised. A home of her own— to conceal her lover, her bastard child, from the eyes of her family, of course. Morcar laughed aloud, and the echoes of this cynical and raucous mirth rolled away among the rocks. Who was her lover, he wondered? Which face at the tennis club, in the Army, was reproduced in Baby Harry? He spared a moment of unselfish grief for the child, a gentle and affectionate being, guiltless, whom he could have loved. If Winnie had only held her tongue, thought Morcar cynically, as she did on my other visits, during the war—if she had only held her tongue I should never have known and I should have loved that kid like a son. Who was his father? Which other part of Morcar's life had that treachery blasted?

In this hour of frightful disillusion it was not only his relation with Winnie which floundered in filthy and putrid mud such as he had seen in Flanders; his whole life seemed to crack across its surface, to gape, to reveal obscene and squalid truths below. That old scene with the Prospect Mills weights, for instance—he now believed Mr. Shaw had known of the unstamped light weight's presence, had been a party even to its use against unsuspecting customers. That explained, thought Morcar with a knowing smile, his sudden anger against the lad who revealed the weight to the Inspector. Again, Mr. Shaw's unexpectedly affable agreement to Morcar's departure to the Oldroyds'— Morcar thought he understood it now. Mr. Shaw had had Morcar trained at somebody else's expense, securing his services again just when, and only when, they became of value. The plan had probably been in his mind the whole time. Mr. Shaw's protest, that very night— was it only that night? It seemed a century ago—that he saw no place at Prospect Mills for Morcar, what was it but an attempt to get him at a cheaper price? Morcar had been a fool all his life, a credulous gaping fool, a fool whom others laughed at, whom cleverer men bought and sold while he received nothing. No, he was not altogether a fool, argued Morcar; he had his captaincy, won by merit, he had his medal. A medal for bringing in a dead man, retorted the new Morcar; a medal for an act unproductive of good to God or man, useless, stupid, sterile. I shan't hang such a medal on my watch-chain. And what was the whole war indeed but insensate, useless? He felt a savage scorn for his uniform, his ribbon; he wanted to throw it off, to tear it up, to burn it. He remembered that he had civilian clothes at his mother's house, and swung round at once to make for them.

He found that he stood in a waste of rock and heather from which no discernible path seemed to lead; but what of that, thought Morcar contemptuously; far to the left, across a conflu- ence of two distant valleys, a narrow thread of white hinted at the road which crossed the Pennine pass at the level of the Ire Valley; he could orientate himself by that; such a small matter as being lost in the middle of Marthwaite Moor would not now trouble him. For it seemed to him as if the shock of Winnie's betrayal had peeled a thick layer of protective fat from his brain, so that the raw nerves, apt for perception as for suffering, lay exposed to every wind that blew. In the old life Morcar had been slow, placid, mild; nobody now would be more rapid in percep- tion, more critical, more ruthless than he. He pushed swiftly through the tough black wiry stems of the heather, the rusty fronds of last year's bracken, avoided the rocks and the hollows with a light quick step, gained the upper road and hurried down towards Hurst.

The little suburb slept; the pubs, the chapels, the shops, the houses, all were quiet and dark, doors shut, blinds drawn. Morcar glanced at his luminous watch, relic of trench warfare; the hands showed between two and three. From consideration less for his mother than for the scandal it might start—"I shall need all the reputation I've got," thought Morcar, setting his teeth— he did not knock on his mother's door. He had not been a soldier four years for nothing, he reflected, drawing out his knife; he forced back the trumpery catch, lifted the window easily and climbed into the living-room almost without a sound. Flinging off his khaki tunic, he lay down on the sofa and tried to sleep.

He had been through so many emotions that day that he was exhausted and slept heavily till the sound of workers' footsteps in the street outside woke him with a start. It was not yet quite daylight. He lay still for a moment and the full realisation of what had happened swept over him.

"There are two ways of taking this sort of thing," he said to himself. "Bend or stiffen. The soft or the hard. I shall take the hard."

A new epoch of his life began from that moment.

He rose, lit the fire, washed, went upstairs and looked out some civilian clothes. Then remembering that Mrs. Morcar used to keep a set of his father's old-fashioned razors, he went into her room to find them. Not hitting upon the right drawer immediately, he raised the blind, and Mrs. Morcar awoke. She peered at him, frightened. The old Morcar would have soothed, explained, apologised, but the new Morcar coldly stated his errand, accepted his mother's direction—"How old she looks without her teeth," he thought brutally—and carried the razors downstairs without further words.

His mother soon followed, dressed with her usual neatness but looking scared and pale.

"I'll have breakfast with you, Mother," said Morcar, shaving.

"Harry," began Mrs. Morcar piteously, folding and refolding a towel she held in her hand.

"Winnie and I have finished with each other, Mother," said Morcar.

"Oh, Harry!"

"That's all there is to it; there's no more to be said. So don't try to say anything," said Morcar.

"She was never the girl for you, Harry," mourned Mrs. Morcar. "I always knew it. I didn't want you to go into business with the Shaws, on that account. You should have had someone softer. But it's too late for all that, Harry," she said in a firmer tone. She came close to him and laid her left hand on his arm. Morcar found himself peculiarly susceptible to wedding-rings on women's hands, and winced.

"Yes, it's too late," he said.

"Far too late," said his mother with dignity. "Winnie's your wife and the mother of your child, Harry, and you have a duty to her."

Morcar exclaimed, then bit off the exclamation before it was completed. The full implications of his situation rushed upon him. He saw that he had to decide at once what line he meant to take about Winnie. Was he to attempt a divorce? He could not see himself publicly accusing Charlie's sister of adultery. Besides, it was all so long ago. The child was more than two years old. He had "condoned" Winnie's betrayal technically, he supposed, for all that time. Or if that was perhaps not the legal view, and a divorce remained possible, what evidence could he procure? And how procure it? Who was the child's father? Some fellow who was in Annotsfield round about the new year in 1916, Morcar calculated bitterly. If Charlie had not been killed the year before, none of this would have happened, he reflected, cursing himself again for allowing Charlie to spring up above the lip of the crater. Who would know Winnie's lover besides Winnie? Could he endure to confront her with the demand for his name? Would she ever yield it? It seemed clear to him now that Winnie had sought his protection in marriage because her lover either could not or would not give her his own. He's probably rotting in a shell-hole by now, anyway, reflected Morcar. The shell-hole brought Charlie back again, and Morcar knew with certainty that he could not in public or in private accuse Charlie's sister. He decided at once upon silence.

"Winnie and I will never live together again, Mother," he said. "I can't go into it all, but there it is. It's settled."

"But little Harry, love?" pleaded his mother.

"It's all finished and done with, Mother," said Morcar, wiping his razor.

His mother, her pale face fallen into deep lines of perplexity and distress, slowly moved away, and with a long tremulous sigh began to fill the kettle.

As they sat at breakfast together a knock sounded on the door. Mrs. Morcar's face lighted with hope, her son's became correspondingly more sombre.

"Come in!" called Morcar.

The sneck of the latch lifted, and there entered a shabby tousled lad in his teens with a nervous look.

"Mr. Henry Morcar?" he piped. "Mr. Shaw told me to come up from Prospect to you with a message. He telephoned."

"Aye. Well?" said Morcar.

"Mr. Shaw says: You need not trouble to come to the mill any more," said the boy, repeating the words in a parrot tone to show their authenticity, very clear and conscientious.

"Thanks," said Morcar drily. On an impulse he felt in his pocket and gave the lad a sixpenny piece. The boy's eyebrows twitched in astonishment, then as he withdrew he involuntarily gave a smile of pleasure. Mrs. Morcar burst into tears.

"If you've done wrong in France, Harry, all the same Winnie should forgive you," she wailed.

"It's not a question of forgiveness."

"She's your wife," mourned Mrs. Morcar, sobbing. "But you never should have married her."

"It's no use crying over spilt milk, Mother," said Morcar at length. "We own this house, don't we?"

Mrs. Morcar, startled, raised a tear-flushed face. "Yes."

"Where are the title-deeds?"

"They're upstairs," faltered Mrs. Morcar. "Why?"

"Mother, you'll have to lend them to me," said Morcar.

"But you wouldn't sell the house, Harry?" wailed his mother.

"No—only borrow money on it," said Morcar. "I'm going to set up in manufacturing on my own. Get me the deeds."

"But——"

"Get me the deeds," repeated Morcar hardly.

By ten o'clock he was closeted with his lawyer in Annotsfield. He instructed him to dispose of the incompletely purchased Hurstcote by negotiation with the Building Society, to ensure the possession of its furnishings to Winnie, and to inform her that her husband would provide her with the necessary evidence for a divorce. Meanwhile, pending the legal provision of alimony, he would contribute to her upkeep as far as lay in his power—at present, said Morcar, he could not offer her more than two pounds ten a week. The lawyer's well-meant attempts to suggest an interview, hint at a reconciliation and in other ways interpose delay, Morcar brushed aside.

"We shall never live together again, so the affair must be wound up now," he said.

The mystified lawyer hinted that possibly a legal separation might be wise.

"What would be the use of that?" said Morcar. "A divorce is what we need."

"An interview," began the lawyer.

"Any interview between myself and any of the Shaws is out of the question," said Morcar. "Please make it quite clear to my wife that I shall not initiate a divorce—I could not do so, of course," he added hurriedly—"but I am taking steps to provide her with evidence on which she can divorce me. I shall not defend any divorce suit she brings. Good-day."

By eleven Morcar was talking to his father's banker. By twelve he had money in his pocket. By three that afternoon he had rented a room and bought two looms.

19

Interview with a Merchant

"Why should you think I like to remember an occasion when I was wrong?" asked Mr. Butterworth testily. His silver hair sparser than of old, his pink cheeks more pendulous, his body plumper, the merchant sat in his private office and scowled at Morcar, loftily disregarding the patterns on the desk before him.

"Because it's the only time in your life when you *have* been wrong, Mr. Butterworth," Morcar informed him cheerfully. "If I were making a lot of cloth for you, it would make you a splendid selling anecdote. You could sell hundreds of yards of striped suiting on that story alone."

"I'm surprised you didn't stay on at Oldroyds'," said Mr. Butterworth, flipping his thumbnails.

"A private matter," said Morcar easily. He knew that rumours about himself and Winnie had lacerated his reputation, but did not intend to show a scratch on his public surface.

"Why didn't you stay at Shaws?"

"The same private matter," said Morcar, smiling.

"What is it you want from me, young man?" enquired the merchant crossly. "Is it a job? Do you want me to recommend you to a manufacturer?"

"Nay, Mr. Butterworth," said Morcar pleasantly: "I'm a manufacturer myself, you know. What I want is a good customer."

"I know the kind of manufacturer *you* are," said Mr. Butterworth rudely. "You've taken one 'room with power' in a tumbledown old place out at Denbridge, and are weaving a few pieces a week on commission."

"You're out of date, Mr. Butterworth," said Morcar mildly.

"Eh?"

"That was two years ago. I have a couple of floors now and I'm making forty pieces a week."

Mr. Butterworth snorted. "Well—I'll look at your suitings," he said grudgingly. "Though I don't suppose for a moment you're making the class of stuff I care to buy."

Morcar displayed his patterns.

"They're not bad," said Mr. Butterworth reluctantly at length. "They're not bad at all."

When Morcar left the merchant, he had a good order from him in his pocket.

20

Buyer and Seller

Morcar walked round Daisy Mills with its owner. The building was empty and for sale. He had visited it before but this was a final inspection.

The pointing of the walls was recent, he noticed; there was a good unloading platform; the up-hill-down-dale character of the ground which is at once the curse and the blessing of the West Riding had been utilised skilfully so as to harness the force of gravity wherever possible. The windows were in good condition; on the first floor he observed one large enough for perching, situated on the right side of the mill as regards light. The stone steps between the floors were naturally somewhat worn at the edges, the whitewash rubbed and greasy; more important, the lighting system was old-fashioned—though capable, thought Morcar, of comparatively easy adjustment. Morcar occasionally praised satisfactory items in order to lend an air of truth and justice to his criticisms; the items he criticised, however, were always much weightier and more expensive than the ones he praised. Secretly he considered that Daisy (as he already affectionately called her) lived up to the good report he had received of the place as a neat, compact little property, well situated just off the main Annots-field-Hudley road where it passed through the hamlet of Den-bridge, built specifically for cloth manufacture, and in good repair.

A mill in Denbridge gave him a good excuse for living out of Annotsfield, which at present he preferred for personal reasons; he still wanted to be as far away from the Shaws as was reasonably possible. Moreover, he thought it just as well that his early steps towards fortune should take place, so to speak, off the Annotsfield stage. The years when he worked twelve or fourteen hours a day would best be spent in some quiet place; by the time he returned to Annotsfield he meant to be powerful and prosperous, with a fine house and car and plenty of money to spend. Yes, Daisy was a nice little place, just the thing he wanted. He meant to buy her if he could.

There was a difficulty, however. Of course he had not the money with which to buy the mill, but he would borrow it from the bank on the security of the deeds backed by his present turn-over—he foresaw no special difficulty about that; it was risky of course and the bank would need persuasion, but they knew him there nowadays as a reputable and promising customer. He was well aware, however, having made the necessary enquiries, that to substantiate the purchase, he would have to deposit one-tenth of the price immediately, before any negotiations could begin. Five hundred pounds was the utmost cash he could spare at the moment. He could not, therefore, bid more than five thousand pounds for the mill. Yet he had heard a rumour that six thousand was being asked for Daisy. In his opinion she was worth it. He ran over in his mind for the hundredth time his resources and his liabilities; no; it was maddening to be held up by such a paltry sum, but not a penny more than five hundred pounds could he find. Not at present. There was his weekly wages bill and his monthly spinner's account to think of; old Butterworth owed him plenty but it was not due yet. Unfortunately there was another prospective purchaser for the mill, or so he had heard: a large combine to which an extra thousand pounds was a fleabite. Hang it, he must have Daisy, thought Morcar; his praises died away and he looked round him keenly for some major defective item with which he could frighten old Kaye into dropping the price.

Old Kaye, who was not really old but had a depressed in-valid-ish air, gaunt and grey, was meandering on about his reasons for selling the mill, which were purely personal—and therefore by implication did not detract from Daisy's value and charm.

"I've not been so well, you see," he said mournfully. "So I've retired and gone south."

Morcar turned aside and fingered the cable of the hoist, to conceal his contempt. If there was a type of man he despised, it was the man in the West Riding textile trade who gave up the struggle and retired to a seaside resort on the south coast. To travel was a fine thing and he meant to do it himself as soon as he could afford, but to settle in an armchair and do nothing from morning till night amongst people who had never heard of the West Riding, seemed to him quite pitiable and disgusting.

"Eastbourne?" he said affably.

"No, Southstone. Do you know it?" asked Kaye in an eager tone.

"No. I hear tell it's very pleasant," said Morcar. "Lovely air."

"That's what my wife says," Kaye told him, pleased. "You'll find it quite sound and in good condition," he added, referring to the hoist.

159

"I was just thinking so," said Morcar in a complimentary tone.

"Of course," went on Daisy's owner as the two men crossed the yard towards the boiler-house: "I shouldn't have given up, you know, if I'd had a lad to carry on after me. You'll be luckier there than me, I daresay."

The blood rushed to Morcar's face; for the life of him he could not utter a word.

"We lost him in the war," said Kaye gruffly. "The Somme."

"I'm sorry," muttered Morcar.

"You were through the war yourself, I expect."

"Yes. I'm surprised you didn't sell your business as a going concern, Mr. Kaye," said Morcar.

"Well—I thought of it, but I couldn't just get my price. Then I put a manager in, but while I was bedridden it went the wrong way. I let part of it off—but it was always needing attention, d'you see, so I thought I'd sell the whole lot up and get out. I sold the looms and such by auction."

"Aye—I think I got some of them," said Morcar. "How much coal did you run on, Mr. Kaye?"

"Twenty-five ton a week. If you want to know about pressure and that, you'd better ask our old boiler man; he lives just down the road."

"I don't know much about steam," said Morcar disarmingly.

"I'm glad there's summat you don't know much about," said Kaye. He then seemed to feel that such a tone was a thought too sardonic to employ to a prospective customer, so he dug Morcar in the ribs, laughed artificially, and added: "Boiler will give a hundred and twenty pounds, as far as I know. As you can see, she's new—as boilers go."

"And what about your engine?"

"Runs on sixty pounds," said Daisy's owner. He led the way

to the engine room without further speech.

Morcar's heart leaped. "The engine's old," he told himself.

He knew almost nothing about engines and could discern no defect in this one, but he gazed at it seriously and remained markedly silent. Kaye at his side was silent too. After a time Morcar suddenly drew out his cigarette case and offered it to the owner, as if to soften some disagreeable thing which he was about to say.

"No—I'll fill my pipe," said Kaye. He did so, slowly; pressed down the tobacco with his thumb, struck a match, lighted the pipe and puffed once or twice. Morcar for his part drew on his cigarette and blew out thoughtfully. Kaye made to turn away. Morcar did not follow him.

"I don't want to deceive you, Mr. Morcar, or say anything that isn't true," said the older man at last. "I haven't said anything about Daisy to you that isn't true. The engine isn't new, as you can see for yourself. But it's been kept in good repair, and there's years of good work left in it yet. I haven't said anything that isn't true to you, and I'm not doing so now."

Morcar fully believed him, but did not intend to say so. The two men crossed the yard again and entered the empty and dusty office. A torn strip of paper hung down from the wall. Morcar however scorned to look at it. He wished to give the impression of a sensible decent man whose complaints and reservations would be just and reasonable. Kaye perched himself on a high stool and leaned his elbows on the dusty desk. An intense embarrassment descended on the room, for the moment had now arrived when an actual proposition had to be brought into being.

"Well, Mr. Kaye," said Morcar at last in a thin reedy voice which he could not make normal: "What price are you asking for Daisy Mills, then?"

"I'd rather you made an offer," said Kaye, smoking stolidly.

Morcar cursed himself for having spoken first and thus started the interchange on the wrong foot. He paused to give the impression of thought, then said sharply: "What do you say to five thousand?"

"Six thousand is my price," said Kaye immediately.

"I wasn't naming a bargaining price," said Morcar, affecting an offended tone. "I named a fair price and my final offer."

"So did I," said Kaye.

There was a pause. "Perhaps you'd like to think it over, Mr. Kaye?" suggested Morcar.

"I'd rather it were decided now," said the millowner.

"Well, *I* should like to think it over," said Morcar, laughing. "There's yon engine, you know, Mr. Kaye, and the lighting, and the steps, and that place at the far end where the flooring's rotten——"

"If that's all you can find to say against the place you've not much to grumble at," said Kaye.

"I'm not grumbling at all," said Morcar with an effect of frankness. "Except about that engine. Some people might want you to put in a new engine, you know."

"I shan't do that," said Kaye. He spoke promptly, but his tone, Morcar noticed with glee, was slightly uneasy.

"H'm," said Morcar. He pursed his lips and appeared to meditate.

"It's got to be decided here and now," said the millowner stubbornly. "I've other folk after it if you don't want it."

Morcar wanted to say: "And you're in a hurry to get back to Southstone-on-Sea," in a silky sarcastic tone. But he wanted Daisy Mills more, so he repressed it. Instead he remarked good-humouredly: "I'll tell you in five minutes, Mr. Kaye, if that will do. No offence meant. It's just a question of what it's worth to me, you know. With that engine. I'll take a turn in the yard and think it over, if you've no objection."

Kaye gave an assenting grunt, and Morcar ran quickly down the steps and into the yard. The situation of Daisy Mills was rural and pleasant; from the yard one looked across fields up to the hills on the slopes of which sprawled Annotsfield. Morcar went at once to the low wall which gave on this prospect and arranging himself in a comfortable attitude leaned against the stones. He knew he was in full view of the office windows and had decided not to smoke lest his movements should betray his nervous tension. He wanted Daisy Mills more and more keenly every moment that he spent there, but to offer more than five thousand was impossible. There was accordingly nothing for him to think about and he could spend his five minutes in idle blankness. The only hope of obtaining the mill was that his calculated depreciation of the engine and a pretence of indifference to the purchase might stimulate Kaye to concessions. It was this last bluff which he was now engaged upon.

"Five minutes, sixty seconds each," he thought. "I mustn't look at my watch. I won't stir till I've counted three hundred—no, three hundred and fifty."

He began mentally to count at a slow steady pace which, at first agreeably rhythmical, presently became almost intolerable in its tarrying beat. He had vowed to himself to move not at all, to keep his arms folded, to look steadily in the same direction, in order to debilitate Kaye's resistance by suspense. It became a discipline harsher than any he had suffered in the Army. By the time he had counted one hundred he was bored and irritable; at two hundred he was panting and exasperated; by three hundred, weak and limp, he felt that Daisy Mills itself was scarcely worth the continuance of the ordeal. But he had vowed to himself to count to three hundred and fifty and so he went on counting.

He had reached three hundred and twenty-five when a touch on his sleeve gave him a violent start. Kaye had crossed the yard and stood beside him. Overjoyed by this sign of weakening, Morcar contrived to turn coolly and stare at him with a calm smile.

"Made up your mind yet?" said the millowner in an embarrassed and peevish tone.

"My mind's been made up all along, Mr. Kaye," said Morcar. "Five thousand's my price, and I'm not bargaining. That's what it's worth to me."

"Well," began the millowner. He suddenly broke off and shouted: "All right—have it your own way!"

"Done!" cried the delighted Morcar. "Now, Mr. Kaye," he went on eagerly, catching him by the arm in a friendly way: "You know you've done the right thing for yourself as well as for me. The syndicate would never have put up with yon engine. They're hard bargainers, too—you'd have had no end of trouble with them."

"Happen I should," agreed Kaye.

"Yes—you'd have been up and down between here and South-stone for months," said Morcar. "Selling it to me, the whole job will be finished next week."

"Happen," agreed Kaye morosely. "Well, what do we do now, then?"

"We put our solicitors in touch with each other, I suppose," said Morcar. "Mine's Nasmyth."

"Aye, but what do we *do?*" persisted Kaye.

Seeing whither he was trending, Morcar replied disingenuously: "I suppose that'll be for our solicitors to say."

"Nay, I don't know as it will," said Kaye. "Don't you as buyer pay a deposit, like?"

"Do I?" exclaimed Morcar. "Yes, of course, I suppose I do. Whatever the lawyers think proper."

"Ten per cent is the proper amount," said Kaye at once.

"Oh, is it? I've never bought a mill before," said Morcar, laughing. "Let's see. That'll be five hundred pounds, then?"

"It will," said Kaye, eyeing him shrewdly.

"Right. I'll send you a cheque tonight," said Morcar. (Kaye's face brightened.) "And then we can get our solicitors to work. Mine's Nasmyth."

"Bottomley's mine. He has the deeds."

"I want to complete at the earliest possible moment," said Morcar earnestly, his hand on the door of his cheap but service-able coupé: "I've no time to waste, Mr. Kaye; I've a long way to go."

"You've gone pretty far already for a lad in his early thirties—which is what I take you to be—it seems to me," said Kaye, smiling for the first time during the interview. "My lad would be just about your age now, I reckon."

Morcar called: "Goodbye, goodbye!" in a tone of great affa-bility, and drove away.

When he had gone a mile or two he drew up, and taking off his hat, wiped his forehead, which dripped with sweat. "Daisy's worth every bit of six thousand pound," he thought. He laughed aloud and drove on.

21

Thistledown

"Take a look at these, Harry," said Mr. Butterworth. Morcar took the folds in his hand. They were patterns of very fine soft dress cloths in elegant light-hued designs—delicate checks and stripes in subtle colourings. Morcar studied them admiringly. Their charming clear colours, in fresh and unexpected combinations, were just what he liked—old Mr. Lucas, he thought smiling, would have dubbed them far too bright—and the fine flexible tissue, soft to the touch as thistledown, was a pleasure to handle.

"French," he said.

"French," agreed Mr. Butterworth. "Dresses for women and children."

"I've seen a good many of these just recently."

"You may well—the French are importing plenty."

"They're really very pretty," said Morcar, continuing to examine them. "There'll be quite a big vogue for them, I shouldn't wonder."

Mr. Butterworth watched him, flipping his thumbnails. "Can you make me something like that?" he said suddenly.

"Well—they're woollen and I'm a worsted manufacturer. They're twice as fine as anything I've had to do with in the woollen line before. And look at the colourings! We should need an enormous number of yarn dyes—simply enormous," said Morcar thoughtfully. "It would be a big job altogether."

"Pah!" snorted Mr. Butterworth, enraged. "That's what you all say, you manufacturers. Bradford, Annotsfield, Hudley—you're all alike. I didn't expect *you* to say that to me though, Harry Morcar."

"I'm much obliged to you for your good opinion," said Morcar, laughing. "But I should need a mill-ful of fresh machinery to make cloth like this."

"And why not? What's another mill to Harry Morcar?" said Mr. Butterworth smoothly.

"What indeed? But trade's bad, you know."

"And going to be worse. We've finished the post-war boom, my lad, you can take it from me. Overseas they're repudiating their orders as fast as they can cable."

"And yet you urge me to begin a big job like this?"

"When trade's bad it's the time to think of something fresh."

"You're right," said Morcar thoughtfully.

"Of course I'm right. I spend my life being right—except about the number of threads in a stripe," said Mr. Butterworth. "Listen, Harry: if you want to do anything or get anywhere in the textile trade, I strongly advise you to tackle cloths of this type. I'm sure there's a big market coming for them. With your feeling for colour, you're the man to go into it. The West Riding can make these cloths as well as the French, surely?"

"I shan't give you the same designs. I never copy other folks' designs—or even imitate them at a distance," said Morcar.

"Well, something similar," urged Mr. Butterworth.

"And I shan't make them as well as the French. I shall make them better, or I shan't make them at all."

"Get along with you," snorted Mr. Butterworth.

Morcar pretended to take him literally and rose. "Right," he said. "I shall have to tackle the spinning end first. I'll take these patterns with me, shall I?"

Mr. Butterworth nodded. "Let me know how you get on," he said.

For the next four years Morcar worked from seven in the morning till just on midnight, five days a week. After experiments, difficulties and disappointments which seemed endless, he succeeded in spinning a very fine woollen yarn—of pure white, soft and light—and proving to his own satisfaction and Mr. Butter-worth's that he could weave it into a soft fine fabric. It was necessary then to arrange for the dyeing of nearly fifty special shades of this new yarn and to evolve scores of different designs in which to use it. The last process was sheer pleasure to Morcar; to play with the pure clear delicate colours was his weekend treat. During this period of experiment he had to keep some of his ordinary products going in order to pay his way, but this business naturally dropped for lack of his keen attention, and there came a period of inevitable changeover when Daisy Mills seemed to produce almost no cloth at all. There was indeed one frightful moment when the real money in Morcar's possession amounted to only thirty pounds. Mercifully he was by this time doing his own spinning, having acquired the millful of machinery for this purpose which he had prophesied as necessary to Mr. Butterworth; but when he reflected on his employees going about their work, calmly certain of their wages on Friday, when he reflected on the three households he supported, and on his involvements at the bank, which held debentures on everything he apparently possessed, he felt undecided whether to throw up his hands with a shriek of despair and vanish, or laugh, steel his nerves and carry on.

As it chanced the day was Thursday, market day in Bradford; he dressed in a new suit just come from his London tailors, with harmonising shirt and tie, grey-blue to match his eyes, drove to Bradford and lunched at the Midland hotel amongst a group of textile acquaintances, with whom he was the life and soul of the party, sparkling and full of fun. Most of the party went on to the Wool Exchange, so Morcar accompanied them in order to appear normal, wondering however as he passed by the effigy of Bishop Blaize (patron of woolcombers) and between the pink marble pillars, whether he would ever see these familiar sights again. It was High 'Change and the floor was crowded, but as luck would have it he bumped at once into his main creditor, a wool merchant with the long flat roll beneath his arm which indicated a sample of wool. The wool was unrolled and displayed. Morcar considered it with his usual keen eye. It was exactly what he wanted, and if he bought none he feared it might look odd. Smiling cheerfully, and saying to himself: "You're daft, lad," Morcar made a considerable purchase. The wool merchant was pleased; the contrast between his present affability and his probable expression if he knew the real state of his customer's finances amused Morcar. His reflections on his drive to Denbridge, which he accomplished in record time, were lurid; but after all, what did he care, what had he to lose? When he reached Daisy Mills he found that a couple of overdue cheques had come in, so his weekly wages bill was safe—and a section range of the new Thistledown cloth was at last ready for his inspection. He drove to Annots-field at once to show it to Mr. Butterworth. The merchant confirmed Morcar's own judgment by approving the cloth warmly. The bright charming fabrics were on the market the following season, and enjoyed a striking and complete success.

Henceforward Morcar was regarded as an expert in this type of cloth, and orders poured in upon him from all directions. Mr. Butterworth became merely one—though the one who received first attention—of his many customers. He rushed from Daisy Mills to his other place up Booth Bank on the other side of Annotsfield, and back again to Denbridge; he rushed to Bradford, to Leeds, to London, pursued always by telegrams and telephone calls; he employed an agent in Paris, he was represented in New York; he sold cloths in South America, New Zealand, China. He made eight or nine hundred pieces a week; he paid off the bank and owed no man anything; he grew rich—a warm man, in the West Riding phrase.

There were difficulties, of course. The world seemed in a wretchedly insecure, treacherous and disappointing state—but then, that was what Morcar expected of the world which held his wife. Strikes abounded. There were miners' strikes—but Morcar had laid in a good stock of coal. There were railway strikes—but Morcar had good contracts with road transport. There was a textile strike which was maddening when one reflected how eager foreign competitors were to capture British markets—but Morcar employed the time in putting in fresh machinery and making fresh designs. There were occasional private rows at Daisy and Booth. These were not numerous; out of respect for himself Morcar was a good employer, he paid Union wages of course and work with him was plentiful, whereas in too many other textile mills it was growing scarce. There was a general strike—Morcar thought this too much of a good thing, and drove a large coal lorry back and forth between Annotsfield and Manchester with success and some enjoyment. The shadow of the post-war depression, spreading continually across the world, reached the West Riding sky and hung there, continually deepening and darkening; Morcar fought it off from Booth Bank and Daisy with cool tenacity. In fact when his colleagues at the Annotsfield Club, to which he had recently been elected, were not calling him a warm man they spoke of him as a cool hand. Why should he not be cool, thought Morcar with contempt when he heard this; he had nothing to lose, everything to gain.

Nothing to lose, indeed. Though he kept three households he had no home. His wife still remained his wife, but he had not seen her since 1919. He had supplied her lawyer with evidence on which she might bring a suit for divorce against him—a gross and disgusting task which he had carried through with savage determination—but she had laid no such suit. He had increased the income he allowed her as his own increased; she should now be reasonably comfortable, he hoped, in a small way—she and her child—on ten or eleven pounds a week. He had heard no word from her since he left her on the Hurstcote stairs; he had heard no word from her father since his message on the day following Morcar's return from the War. He had seen nothing, indeed, of any Shaw, and it was now no longer very likely that he would see much of them, for his financial stratum lay far above that of a small manufacturer in a back street. He never thought of the Shaws if he could help it, and struck savagely at anything which brought them to mind.

As for his mother, she still remained at Number 102. When Morcar, in his "room and power" days, removed to small mean lodgings near Denbridge, Mrs. Morcar refused to accompany him, though he invited her to do so and the economy would have been welcome. Speaking with her usual calm dignity, Mrs. Morcar observed that it was her son's duty to make a home for his wife and child—she would not delay this, make it less obvious and easy, by assuming Winnie's duties, Winnie's place. "Neither of us will have much to live on if we live apart," said Morcar grimly. His mother set her lips and was silent, then suddenly flashed out that she did not intend to run away from the Shaws, whatever the rights and wrongs of the case. With this simple pride Morcar sympathised; accordingly he did not press her again to come to Denbridge. When after some years of Daisy and Thistledown he returned to Annotsfield he broached again, as a matter of decency and duty, the proposal that she should come to live with him, but he did not now wish for this, his tone was perfunctory and he accepted her refusal with relief. He supplied her generously with money and gave her handsome presents. But Mrs. Morcar stubbornly saved most of the income, and made little use of the luxuries, he proffered. The truth was that she had preserved her original impression, that Harry and his wife had parted because Winnie had discovered some immorality on Harry's part, in France. (A good many people in Annotsfield thought the same, he found, and Morcar did nothing to contradict this natural—as he bitterly termed it to himself—supposition.) Accordingly Mrs. Morcar disapproved of her son's conduct, and no amount of worldly success could make her waver from this disapproval. She disapproved, too, of his present way of life; always rushing about in cars and eating in restaurants, no proper home, no quiet, no family affection. He smoked too many cigars—why could he not be content with a modest pipe, like his father? She spoke in these terms to her son whenever he came to see her. Morcar, revealed now in the mirror over his mother's sideboard as a powerfully built, sophisticated-looking man in his later thirties, well-groomed, wearing a London-tailored suit, handsome shoes, expensive cuff-links, a shirt made to measure, a Bond Street tie, maintained his easy lounging posture with difficulty as he listened, and the moment she gave him an opening looked at his admirable wrist-watch and announced that he must be off; for her words flicked him on the raw. He knew the disadvantages of his way of life quite as well as his mother.

When he had first decided to return to Annotsfield and looked about for accommodation Jessopp had turned up and suggested that Morcar should employ him and his wife to keep house for him. But Morcar had no desire to remember any of the events of the day of Charlie's death, of which Jessopp emphatically formed one; besides, the Jessopps had young children, and Morcar felt that he should find young children intolerable. He therefore rejected the timid suggestions of Jessopp—who as a partially disabled soldier was unemployed at the time—brusquely, and took the ground floor of a solid house in the Hudley Road where it debouched into Annotsfield. This portion of the road, once the abode of wealthy merchants, was now a town street, occupied chiefly by doctors and dentists. If Morcar had been living with a wife and family, such a site would not have been compatible with his present financial standing, but for a man alone the place did very well. It was handy for the Annotsfield Club, in any case, where Morcar spent a good deal of his leisure time. The house was owned by an elderly couple, reputable but somewhat declined from their original status; the man was a semi-invalid in an unobtrusive way, the woman cooked and cleaned with the aid of an elderly maid of the well-trained, old-fashioned kind. The furniture was a trifle dingy, but solid and in good repair. All this was of little importance, in any case, because Morcar hardly ever ate or sat there; he used it as a sleeping apartment only.

His life outside his mills was at that time a procession of hotel dining-rooms, waiters, large cigars, plates containing the change from massive bills, drinks on trays, tables bearing the wreckage of elaborate meals above which the smoke from many cigars thickly hung and curled, glances at his watch, hurried departures and arrivals by car, golf clubs, music-hall shows, evening dress, carnations in the buttonhole. He was able now to give himself all the swift and strident pleasures of the age, and because of their contrast with his restricted youth, his sojourn in the trenches, his postwar years of incessant work, because too of a deep relief in being like other men in these at least and because he did not want to have time to think, he drank them avidly, and soon could not do without them, though fully conscious of the bitter and unsatisfying quality of the draught. He usually stopped short, however, of pleasure with women, and in any case never allowed himself to become too deeply committed in such affairs, turning a cool and derisive eye on other men's excursions on that stormy and uncertain sea. Bought favours bored him—"I've had enough of them with my wife," thought Morcar sardonically, for he considered he had bought Winnie's embraces by the protection of his name—while he should never have either the confidence or the wish again, he thought, to try for honest love—if indeed such a thing existed. Occasional Sunday luncheons in business colleagues' houses gave him glimpses of other men's home lives; wives who seemed fond of their husbands, children with curls and smiles who leaned against their father's knees and gazed wonderingly at Morcar. But such affairs were business occasions disguised; after the silver, the polished table, the lace mats, the expensive out-of-season food, the coffee, the liqueurs had played their part, the cigars were lighted, the wives vanished and the host began to talk about textiles.

For Morcar had no friends, only business associates whose hospitality he returned, lavishly enough, in hotels and clubs. Friends implied private confidences, and these Morcar was not prepared to make. He was not a member nowadays, either, of any of the associations with which northern England abounds. He did not go in for politics, national or municipal—why should he? What good had municipal service done his father? What good had his country's service done to him? He gave to charities when he was asked, but with a cool smile which discouraged further application. He had no artistic hobby, for he had never learned one. He never entered a church or chapel or any building which his mother would have called a "house of worship"; for since that moment on the stairs at Hurstcote, all religious practice was hypocrisy to him and all religious belief antiquated nonsense, mythology falsified by the experience of life.

In a word, his attitude at this time was typically that of the 1920's.

22

Christina

"Take a look at this, Harry," said Mr. Butterworth, holding out a fold of cloth.

"What, another five-year plan?" said Morcar, laughing.

Mr. Butterworth's face remained grave, however, and Morcar's face changed too as the pattern came into his own hand. The cloth was a crude imitation of one of his own earlier designs. The yarns were coarser, the colours fewer and less delicate; nevertheless the resemblance existed and might deceive those inexperienced buyers, the general public, into the belief that they were obtaining a cloth equal to Morcar's at a much lower price.

"Well, it can't be helped," said Morcar distastefully. "Imitation is the sincerest form of flattery, they say, and there's no law against it in our trade. It's a dirty trick, but nothing can be done. If people are fools enough to think this is as good as mine, more fools they, that's all. They'll find the difference in the wear."

"Aye, but look here," said Mr. Butterworth. He turned to a corner of the pattern bearing a small adhesive label of the familiar type, oval, jimped at the edge. The label was marked in writing with various figures and letters to identify the cloth, and printed in the centre: *Soft as Thistledown*.

"What the devil!" exclaimed Morcar, colouring violently. "Thistledown! That's an infringement of my trademark, Butterworth!" That this travesty should bear the name of his own beautiful cloths enraged his every instinct, whether of art or trade.

"It doesn't actually call the cloth Thistledown," pointed out the merchant.

"No—but the intention's plain," said Morcar. "Whoever made this cloth and labelled it intended to deceive the buyer into thinking he was getting one of my Thistledowns. By God, I'll sue him!" he exclaimed, his anger mounting as the scope and probable consequences of the trick came home to him. "Who is it? I'll make him rue the day he printed those labels. Soft as Thistledown! Printed! I'll sue him, I'll show him up properly, I promise you!"

"There's a bit of a difficulty, you see, Harry," said Mr. Butterworth in a soothing tone.

"Nonsense. It's a clear case. If the law doesn't think so, the law's a fathead. I'll bring the case anyway—I'll show him up—I'll let the trade know the rights of the matter, choose how," said Morcar firmly.

"Aye—but you see it's Shaw of Prospect," said Mr. Butterworth.

"By God, I'll sue him!" cried Morcar, springing to his feet. "I'll not stand——" By a violent effort he checked himself; he had been about to say: "I'll not stand bastard cloths as well as bastard sons." He struck the merchant's desk a savage blow with his fist; the pain relieved him, and he struck the desk again. "It's just what you might expect of Shaw of Prospect," he said. Finding that his voice was thick with rage, he paused, swallowed, then remarked in a tone to which he strove to give a judicial calm: "But what are the Shaw lads about? Hubert and Eric? I shouldn't have thought they'd lend themselves to a trick of that kind?"

"They're not with him now, you know," said Mr. Butterworth. "Hubert went off to Australia—he's in textiles there—and Eric's in South Africa growing oranges. Or it may be the other way round. Which was the one that flew?"

"Eric," said Morcar mechanically, staring before him.

"Yes, Eric. It's he that's growing oranges."

"I suppose they couldn't stand the old man. And I don't blame them," said Morcar viciously.

"I've heard he's a bit difficult," said Mr. Butterworth in a soothing tone. "But it's awkward for you, Harry, having worked for Shaw. He may contend that you made the design when you were at Prospect, you know. He may well contend so."

"He can contend till he's blue in the face, but he shouldn't have used my trademark," retorted Morcar. "It's no good, Butterworth—I shall have to bring a case. If I don't, we shall never see the end of it. I know——" he was going to say: "the Shaws," but managed to turn it into—"the ways of Mr. Shaw. It isn't the first time he's done this sort of thing."

"Well," agreed Mr. Butterworth reluctantly: "You may be right. It may be a bit—painful, though. In the circumstances, I mean."

Morcar gave him an angry look and went out.

He encountered the same arguments, phrased in more legal terms, from his solicitor—and one more cogent.

"When was the trademark registered?" enquired the current Nasmyth, who was now the son of the solicitor Morcar's father had employed, a University man, rather soft and sleek by Morcar's standards. "And where? At the Patent Office in

London, or the Manchester branch for textiles?"

"Neither," said Morcar bluntly. "It's not registered at all."

"Not registered?" exclaimed Nasmyth, astonished.

"I'm afraid I didn't realise it had to be registered," admitted Morcar. He felt sick with anger at his own ingenuous and ignorant omission. Put him against the Shaws, he thought, and they win, every time; in spite of his recent successes, his expanding experience, he remained naïve against their innate sophistication. If the charming name of Thistledown had to be sacrificed it would cut him deeply, in sentiment, pocket and reputation. He felt sore all over, raw to the touch, lacerated by anger and disappointment. But this time he would fight; this time he would not give in; he did not intend to be rooked by Mr. Shaw as he had been by Winnie.

"Trademarks should be registered, you know," Nasmyth was saying, shaking his head. "If I had known … However, you can claim you have established a right by usage, I don't doubt."

"I've used it for five or six years," said Morcar.

"Pity you never thought to register it," repeated the lawyer.

"It's mine by five years' usage—it's known as mine all over the world," said Morcar fiercely.

"Useful but possibly difficult to prove," began the lawyer, hesitating.

Eventually he agreed to send Mr. Shaw a letter of an astonished and enquiring turn, requesting an elucidation about the *Soft as Thistledown* label.

To this he received, on Prospect Mills notepaper, a reply in Mr. Shaw's thick small black script, curtly denying any infringement. Nasmyth thereupon repeated emphatically to his client all the considerations tending to the doubtfulness of his case and the probability that he would lose it if he took it to the courts.

"You note that Mr. Shaw has not even thought it worth while to take the matter to his solicitor," he pointed out.

"He thinks I shan't go to extremes because of family considerations," said Morcar hardly. "But he's wrong. Don't you see, Nasmyth," he urged: "To clear my own reputation with my customers, I'm bound either to secure a withdrawal from Shaw, or make his deception public. If I can't do that, I shall have to give up the Thistledown trademark myself and adopt another. I daresay I shall have to do that in any case—Shaw's ruined it by putting out poor crude stuff under that name."

"Losing a court case doesn't tend to clear the reputation," Nasmyth advised him gloomily.

"I shall press for damages," said Morcar, stubborn.

Nasmyth sighed. "I'd better get you a Counsel's opinion," he said. "And then we'll see."

"Aye, do," said Morcar. "Get it from somebody who specialises in trademarks, if there are such people—somebody up and coming, a young man who isn't afraid of a fight."

"I'm afraid you are confusing a Counsel's opinion with a barrister's brief," said Nasmyth in a dry legal tone.

"Well, you know what I mean," said Morcar impatiently.

The lawyer bowed his head to signify assent.

A few days later he informed his client that the counsel he had consulted—Harington, Edward Mayell Wyndham Harington, a rising junior with whom he had been at college, he explained—would like a conference before giving his opinion, as one or two knotty points seemed to be involved. Morcar snorted derisively at this but agreed to attend the barrister's chambers, provided the conference could be fixed for a day when he would be in London in any case on business.

The following week he found himself ascending the worn

stone stairs of one of the inns of court behind the black-coated Nasmyth. His surroundings alarmed him; he viewed the fine old square, the paved walks, the well-rolled grass, the occasional slight tree, the ancient buildings, the solid oak doors, the small old rooms, the piles of tin boxes white-lettered with clients' names, with mingled awe and derision; they seemed to him to symbolise, to sum up very accurately, in their ancient beauty, the nonsensical out-of-date processes of the law, which were entertaining to look at but death to engage in. Seeing them, all the layman's distrust of lawyers returned to him in strength; he warned himself that this was not his proper place and he had better not venture too far into it.

"If this fellow's opinion isn't very strongly favourable," he said to himself: "I'd better drop the case and change the trademark."

But what guarantee was there that Mr. Shaw, emboldened by his son-in-law's retreat, would not repeat his trick? Morcar ground his teeth and greeted bad-temperedly a man of about his own age, rather fair, rather plump, rather bald, with large pale grey eyes, a fresh complexion, very handsome cuff links and a look of mingled arrogance and power. This was presumably Edward Mayell Wyndham Harington, thought Morcar grimly. He took a dislike to the barrister on sight, which was not modified by the sound of his voice. This was strong, resonant, even beautiful in its mellow cadences, but it contained those inflexions which the north-country Morcar despised as southern affectation, and was perhaps rather too consciously employed.

"There are two points, Mr. Morcar, which seem to need clarification," began the barrister when the party was seated. "The first concerns your employment with Mr. Shaw. Was this trademark Thistledown ever used during that employment?"

"No," said Morcar. "The cloth was not then invented." It

occurred to him that this was rather strong, considering the French manufacture which had given him the idea, and qualified it by adding: "In this country."

"And when did that employment terminate?"

"August 1914," said Morcar with some satisfaction.

"Oh? There was no post-war employment?"

"In 1919 I was employed by Mr. Shaw for one night. I received no pay and did not enter his mill."

There was a pause; the barrister looked at the lawyer, who said with a cough: "The employment was terminated by a family disagreement, as I understand."

"You assure me that any disagreement that might have occurred then did not concern this cloth or trademark, Mr. Morcar?" pursued the barrister.

"I tell you that neither the cloth nor the trademark was thought of in the West Riding before 1922 or 1923," said Morcar angrily.

"1923—that was when you first made the cloth and used the trademark? Now what was the difference between the cloth you assisted in making while with Mr. Shaw and the Thistledown made by you alone in 1923?"

"How can I possibly explain that to a man who's never handled a hank of yarn in his life?" exclaimed Morcar irritably. "Any West Riding man would know the difference right away, but you—"

"Ah! You could call expert witnesses if necessary?" said Harington swiftly.

"Of course."

"A useful point," said the barrister. "My second point, Mr. Morcar," he continued in his mellifluous drawling tones: "springs from my surprise that the Patent Office accepted such a name as Thistledown as a trademark. It is a word in general use, which

182

might legitimately be used as a noun of description, for purposes of comparison, in many trades, especially those concerned with woollen manufactures. It therefore lacks distinctiveness, and might also be judged to operate unfavourably, in unfair restriction that is to say, towards other traders. However, am I to understand that the word was so accepted and registered?"

"No," said Morcar with the calm of extreme anger. "It was neither accepted nor registered. I was not aware that such registration was necessary."

"But then, my dear Mr. Morcar," drawled Harington, throwing out his hands, palm upwards, in a gesture of amused resignation: "Your case is infinitely weakened."

The barrister's fine white hands, his drawl, the way he pronounced *Patent*, his formal phrases which he evidently enjoyed, his stress on the words *trade* and *traders*, which somehow defined such matters as beneath a gentleman's consideration, exacerbated Morcar's rage to a pitch where he could no longer restrain himself from venting it.

"The fact of non-registration could have been ascertained from Mr. Nasmyth by letter," he said coldly. "There was no need to drag me here to discuss it."

"Mr. Nasmyth had reported the fact to me," said the barrister at once.

His voice was calm but his face showed a faint flicker. "He's afraid for his conference fee," thought Morcar contemptuously, and he remarked aloud: "Then why bring me here to report it all over again?" He answered himself in secret: "To show off his learning and his voice," and added angrily aloud: "I'm a busy man, sir, if you are not."

The barrister flushed—it was possible that Morcar had hit an awkward nail on the head—and raised his fair eyebrows haughtily, but drawled without apparent concern: "It was essential that I should hear your personal testimony on your business connection with Mr. Shaw, and I should like also to go into the matter of your proofs of use of the trademark—if you have time."

"Certainly," said Morcar, trying to maintain his cool tone, though he felt his head congested with angry blood: "I have time for anything which furthers the establishment of my exclusive right to this trade name."

"It is simply a *name*, I take it, not a name printed in any special manner or associated with a picture or design?"

"That is so."

"You have used it for five years, to all your customers?"

"Yes. All over the world."

"Can you show correspondence referring to this name, ordering cloths by it, and so forth?"

"Most certainly I can. Here's a specimen," said Morcar, pulling out his pocket-book and handing over a letter from a New York merchant laying a big order for *your Thistledown cloths*.

The barrister scanned it, and was about to speak when the telephone on his desk interrupted him. He spoke down it quietly, quickly and with evident displeasure, but in the same mellifluous drawl he had employed during the interview. "The drawl must be genuine, then," thought Morcar derisively. "Poor fellow!" Nasmyth was trying to fix him with a glance, and mouthing a query as to what Morcar thought of Harington. It was clear that he expected an admiring answer; Morcar, though not without perception of the barrister's acumen, which had revealed even to him several new aspects of the case, gave himself the pleasure of replying: "Nowt!" with emphasis. Nasmyth coloured and sat back, disconcerted; Morcar, looking away, saw that the barrister's large pale eyes were on him and that Harington, though doubtless ignorant of the significance of the Yorkshire word, was perfectly aware of his client's valuation of his services. Harington now laid down the telephone and stated in his smooth unpausing drawl:

"I will send Mr. Nasmyth my formal opinion in writing of course, but there is no harm perhaps in my telling you now informally of my main conclusions. It would appear that the proper course is undoubtedly for Mr. Morcar to proceed at once to register the trademark, furnishing all possible proofs of usage with his application. The proposed registration will be as is customary advertised in the appropriate trademark journal. Mr. Shaw may then choose to oppose it, in which case the onus of proof of his own use will rest on him. The Patent Office will then make a decision, which can be contested by a case against Mr. Shaw, if necessary; it would seem that Mr. Morcar will be able to prove longer and wider usage. If Mr. Shaw does not oppose registration and the trademark is registered, his case, if he then uses the trademark, will be immensely weakened by his lack of opposition. I have put the matter simply and informally and not in legal form for you, Mr. Morcar—"

"Thank you," said Morcar sardonically.

"—but that is the gist of my conclusion."

Morcar, revolving the statement in his mind, decided that it was clear and on the whole comforting. "Damn him, he knows his job," he conceded reluctantly. Aloud he said: "I am obliged to you, Mr. Harington." He rose briskly, implying, in courteous contrast to his previous hints, that the barrister was a busy man whose time must not be wasted.

"And now that our formal conference is concluded," said the barrister cheerfully, rising also: "Perhaps you and Mr. Nasmyth will give me the pleasure of your company at lunch?"

"Either he has another textile case on hand and wants to pump me, or he wants to soothe me down for Nasmyth with a view to further business," thought Morcar cynically. He felt that he had been made to look such a fool by the two men of law that it was a point of textile pride not to reveal the extent of his humiliation. "Thanks—that would be very pleasant," he said. "I'm not sure whether I'm engaged or not—there'll be a message for me at my hotel. If I might telephone?"

"By all means," said Harington affably, offering him the instrument.

The message, as Morcar expected, liberated him for the lunch hour, and the three men were soon passing through the arched entrance to the court and climbing into a taxi which speeded swiftly to answer Harington's loud smooth call. Morcar's mind for the last few minutes had been on the business which his telephone call had settled, and on returning his attention to the present he found Harington apologising with unexpected emphasis for the Bloomsbury restaurant towards which they were driving. It seemed he was meeting his wife there—a previous arrangement—better perhaps not to attempt at this late hour an alteration which might cause delay—he and Mrs. Harington were to attend an auction together—some nice pieces were being sold from Lord So-and-So's place. He did not say where the auction was to be held, and Morcar felt sure, from the pucker on the full lips and the frown on the bald brow, that the auction-room lay far away from Bloomsbury, which had doubtless been chosen for the barrister's convenience. He felt sure also that Harington had thought the restaurant quite adequate for the entertainment of Morcar until he heard on the telephone the name of Morcar's hotel, which was highly expensive and well-known, even famous. Morcar smiled pleasantly and said he should be glad to make the acquaintance of the restaurant named, as he had not visited it before and liked to find new places. At this Harington looked even less comfortable than before, as Morcar had intended. He might, he reflected, be ignorant in law, but when it came to money he could probably buy up Harington five times over and not notice it; if Harington chose to insist on his own advantages, so would Morcar.

They entered the restaurant, which was Italian and, as Morcar had expected, of good and even stylish quality—he could not imagine the barrister contenting himself with anything less than fine wines and a good cuisine. It appeared that Harington was well known there, and the business of exchanging a small table for a larger one was carried out expeditiously, which somewhat restored the barrister's good-humour. Mrs. Harington, it seemed, had not arrived. The men settled themselves and ordered drinks; the drinks came and were disposed of; the barrister looked at his watch and frowned impatiently, fidgeted, frowned again, spoke of telephoning to Kensington, decided against it, summoned again the wine waiter, who did not immediately appear. His fine voice had an edge on it when at last he said: "Ah, Christina!" and the three men rose.

"Mr. Morcar, my dear," said Harington smoothly. "Nasmyth you know of old."

The tone of his voice shouted aloud: "I want something from this man, so soothe him and flatter him." Morcar had heard this tone in men's voices before when they were addressing their wives, and he now wondered cynically to which type of wife it was addressed on this occasion—the seductive, the condescending or the motherly. He turned, and found that Christina Harington was none of these things; she was the elegant, the gracious, the beautiful. It struck him that he had never seen an elegant woman before in his life.

As Morcar made so much material which women wore, it was a habit with him, part of his work, to observe the apparel of all women. The season was spring, the day cool and bright; Christina was wearing a dress of thin black cloth, admirably cut, with a small black hat and an abundance of silver foxes. Her figure was charming, her hands slender; she had no jewellery save one magnificent sapphire ring. So much Morcar had noticed while she drew off her soft white gloves; then he looked in her face and received a shock of surprise. She was lovely, she was unhappy, she was frightened. Her complexion was milk-white, her profile most delicately chiselled, pure, clear and flawless; her eyes were dark-blue like her sapphire, deep yet bright, like the sea; her dark hair, cut short in the style of the day, curled so thickly that one might guess she had some difficulty in confining it within the limits set by her taste. Her lips, beautifully moulded, delicate yet full, were lightly touched with carmine. This style had not then penetrated to the provinces, and Morcar felt a delight, a sense of joyous release from old shibboleths, in the company of a woman of quality who thus showed her fashion. Her voice was soft and gentle; her southern pronunciation struck Morcar as childlike, touching. Harington became infinitely more real to him through her presence. At the moment she was apologising rather breath-lessly for being late; her husband, in frowning concentration over the menu, seemed to deride her apology as unnecessary yet wait for more.

"There's no need to make a song and dance about it, my dear," he said drily at length, without looking up at her. "After all, it's not the first time."

The waiter now appeared expectantly at Harington's elbow. A handsome lad of some southern nation, he displeased

Harington by tapping his order pad with his pencil.

"Don't do that," said the barrister, with an irritable gesture which knocked the pencil from the boy's hand to the floor. This result was probably unintended, for Harington flushed, but his irritation was not calmed by shame for his bad temper, but rather heightened.

"You're not the man I usually have," he drawled. "Where is Morelli?"

"Pardon—this is my table, that is his," explained the boy, smiling and waving. He added helpfully: "The sole is off."

"I haven't ordered it yet," snapped Harington. "Well, what is there to eat to-day?"

As the menu consisted of a card about twelve inches long and eight inches wide, closely written in smudged purple ink, the question was a large one, and Morcar was not surprised that the boy seemed perplexed how to answer.

"There are oysters," he began in a conscientious effort to please: "Hors d'œuvres. Smoked salmon. Minestrone. Ravioli." His stubby forefinger indicated these items on the card. Harington shook the menu to dislodge the finger, but the well-meaning boy persisted in his indications. Suddenly Harington, colouring violently, snatched a fork and aimed a jab at the intruding hand. He missed, of course; but to stab at a young waiter with a fork! A fork! Upon my soul, a fork, thought Morcar, horrified. Nasmyth, colouring, began a rapid three-cornered conversation with Christina and his client—on the weather, plays, films, anything. They tried to keep it up, but the inquisition inexorably proceeding in the background beat down their feeble efforts into silence.

"What else is there?"

"The salmi of game is best. Or the risotto."

"Answer my question. What else is there?"

"That is the best, the salmi, that is what I recommend you to 'ave."

"I ask you a question and you don't answer it. What else is there?"

Perspiring in his anguished wrestle with an unfamiliar language, the wretched boy wailed: "The sole is off."

"He means: *Only* the sole is off, the rest are all available, Edward," murmured Christina softly.

"Kindly allow me to give the order myself, my dear," said Harington, colouring with anger, so that even his bald forehead grew pink. "I am perfectly competent, I assure you. Now, boy!"

"It is late, and the fish is off," almost wept the waiter, turning in an instant from a sophisticated servant into a crumpled school-boy just promoted.

"Oh, go away and send me someone who understands the language!" cried Harington in a false-friendly tone, with a large gesture of rejection.

"There is all, all it says there, sir, only the sole is off."

"Oh, clear out! Hop it! Go away!" shouted Harington, slamming the menu so viciously on the table that plates bounced and cutlery flew. Everyone in the room looked round; the head waiter rushed up, and with an angry glance shooed the unhappy boy in disgrace away from the table. Bowing obsequiously and drawing an order pad from his coat-tail pocket, in a trice he collected orders from all four guests. He withdrew; service of the meal began almost immediately.

"Incompetent ass! Stupid donkey! Impertinent jackanapes!" said Harington in his mellow tones. He was now pale, almost livid, with rage; his mouth was compressed to a vicious line; his pale eyes shone with hate. "This place has deteriorated, my dear

Christina; we mustn't come here any more. I know you have always liked it, and indeed it used to be quite good, quite a decent little place, but we mustn't come here again. My dear Mr. Morcar, my dear Nasmyth, I apologise. Pray accept my apologies; I'm exceedingly sorry. Remember, Christina, we mustn't bring guests here again. Of course we were rather late in ordering, as that little numskull said."

During this scene Morcar sat sideways to the table, smoking, smiling a little in a non-committal way, looking down, lounging in an easy posture which he only maintained by a strong muscular compulsion. His impulse was to drive his fist savagely into Harington's hateful face, knock him flying among the crockery, then seize Christina and Nasmyth in an iron grip and march them out of the restaurant before him. He had observed already that Christina, like himself, sat very still; her stillness, it struck him now, was almost deathly, hypnotised. Even her lovely breast seemed motionless. At the barrister's last sentence, a glancing insult towards herself, Morcar looked at her quickly. Her delicate mouth was curved in an imploring, frightened smile; her blue eyes, tear-filled, like flowers in rain, were fixed on her husband in an expression of helpless anguish. Morcar's heart turned over, and he took action.

"It must be very difficult for you to grasp the intricacies of an unknown manufacture, Mr. Harington," he said. "And yet I suppose you do it continually for professional purposes?"

"Oh yes, continually, continually," responded Harington in an offhand tone. "One can always mug it up in books, you know. These things are not—excuse my saying this, my dear fellow—these things are not such esoteric mysteries as their practitioners like to pretend. I daresay, you know"—he gave a false little laugh—"that you would find me quite capable of understanding

191

wool textiles, if you tried me."

"So that *is* what he wants," thought Morcar. "I shall take you up on that," he said aloud jovially. "Now when you were advising me just now——"

He proceeded to give a succinct account of the textile trade in the West Riding as it was then organised, with a sketch of the main types of fabric manufactured. Harington, he saw, followed him closely, putting shrewd questions from time to time. "He's clever enough, damn him," thought Morcar. He was rewarded for his effort, however, by seeing Christina's lovely face relax. She smiled sweetly, kindly, gratefully, at Morcar. By the time the party reached coffee, they were all (outwardly) excellent friends.

It now appeared that Harington had obtained as much information as he needed out of Morcar, for he dropped his questions suddenly, turned the talk to amusing legal anecdotes and glided off into a discussion of mutual legal and college acquaintances with Nasmyth. As he turned to the lawyer he gave his wife a swift compelling glance and a frown, which as clearly as words commanded her to forget her stupid shyness, entertain Morcar and charm him well. Accordingly Christina turned to Morcar and proceeded to flatter him in the usual way, by asking him questions about himself and expressing great interest in the answers. It was a charming performance if rather strained, thought Morcar, admiring in detached fashion her eager look, her expressive graceful gestures, but it was quite factitious; somehow he wanted more from her than that. So he said abruptly:

"I'm not a very interesting person, Mrs. Harington. I should prefer to talk about your own chief interests in life."

Christina's face changed. She smiled, a delicate colour rose to her cheek, her blue eyes widened. It was as though the sun came out above a classic statue. She hesitated, gave a soft laugh, then plunged the hand bearing the sapphire ring into her mono-grammed black handbag. The trifles within were expensive, silver-mounted, elegant, observed Morcar, retrieving some of these as they were falling. Christina disregarded them, drew out a soft black leather folder and opened it triumphantly.

"My children," she said.

A pang went through Morcar as he took the leather case. On one side was a studio portrait of a boy in his early teens, fair and candid, with curly hair, his father's plump face redeemed by Christina's eyes. The other photograph fitted sideways into the case. It showed a child, a little girl curled up on a settee, reading intently. Her short fair hair hung page-boy fashion in a thick smooth bell. Her face was grave, clear and handsome; her absorption in the book was real and touching. *The Talisman*, read Morcar upside down. The photograph was a triumph as regards texture; the child's hair, her bare knees, her socks and shoes, her check cotton frock, were remarkably rendered.

"Edwin and Jennifer," murmured Christina. "My husband took the snap of Jenny and enlarged it. Photography is his hobby."

"Showing your offsprings' photographs?" broke in Harington's irritable resonant tones. "My dear Christina! What will Morcar think of you? It's too too naïve, too shy-making!"

"They're very handsome children," said Morcar truthfully. He glanced up to offer this compliment to his host, and for the first time saw Harington look simple, eager, pleasant. Responding to this changed expression, Morcar asked with interest: "How old are they?"

"Twelve and eleven."

"The boy looks older. You must have been married very young!" exclaimed Morcar involuntarily to Christina.

"She was seventeen," said Harington. His voice still held the pride, the pleased surprise, which his triumph long ago had caused him. At that moment it was clear that, in spite of any appearance to the contrary, he loved his wife and rejoiced in her beauty. "A war marriage."

"They're beautiful children," repeated Morcar, gazing at the portraits.

"You have children, Mr. Morcar?" said Christina in her soft hesitant voice.

"No," said Morcar shortly. He closed and returned the folder.

"Well, I'm afraid I must be off to catch my train," intervened Nasmyth tactfully. "If that clock is correct."

"Our auction, Edward!" cried Christina. She caught up her furs and drew them carelessly about her; the result, as Morcar admiringly observed, was one of modish elegance.

"Yes, I'm afraid we've run it rather close," agreed Harington, imperiously beckoning the waiter. "If you had been a little earlier, my dear—if you could have managed to be punctual for once——"

He went on in this strain until the party separated on the kerb, when he spent several minutes taking an effusive and confidential farewell of Nasmyth. It had been discovered that Morcar's destination, his London office, which lay just off Piccadilly Circus, was close to the Haringtons' route; Morcar accordingly was seated in the taxi during this conversation, side by side with Christina. Her body was quite as beautiful as her face, thought Morcar; slender, shapely, delicately proportioned. He had already observed that she was taller than her husband. She did not speak, but fixed her wide anxious look on Harington, who still delayed. She sighed; her long dark lashes dropped over her blue eyes in helpless resignation. Morcar perceived that she was really troubled lest they should be late. "He'll make it out all her fault," he reflected angrily. He jumped out of the taxi.

"I'm sorry, but I'm afraid I must be off," he said. "I have an appointment."

"Get in, get in, my dear fellow!" cried Harington, bustling him back and following him immediately into the vehicle, which was what Morcar had intended. "Goodbye, Nasmyth!" he waved airily in farewell. "Goodbye! Rather long-winded, our friend Nasmyth, I think," he remarked as soon as the taxi drove off: "Perhaps not *quite* out of the top drawer, eh?"

"Not coming from the top drawer myself, I couldn't say," replied Morcar coolly. He smiled reassuringly at Christina, who was looking frightened, and added: "The Nasmyths have been reputable lawyers in Annotsfield for two or three generations; he has a good practice—if practice is the proper word."

"This confounded fellow is taking us down the wrong street!" exclaimed Harington angrily. He tried to pull back the communicating window, clawing at it impatiently, to gain the driver's ear, but failed. "Confounded ass!" he said, sinking back. "Wants to add to his fare, I suppose."

When Morcar dismounted at his office, Harington gave the building an appraising look. Morcar with proper expressions of gratitude took his leave, paid the taxi-driver and closed the vehicle's door. Suddenly, as the Haringtons drove away, his heart burned within him. To shut Christina in with that! To leave her helpless, defenceless, enclosed with that outrageous temper, that relentless egoism! Her blue eyes shadowed by fear, her sweet face clouded with sadness, her gentle voice, her graceful hands, haunted him. A forlorn lady in an enchanted castle, who needed rescuing.

Next morning Morcar rang up the barrister's chambers.

"Harry Morcar here," he said.

195

"Yes?" said Harington. "What can I do for you, Mr. Morcar?"

He sounded cautious and prepared to snub, and Morcar felt his dislike for the man rise hot and strong. But he commanded himself and spoke cordially. "I'm afraid I was rather abrupt in your chambers yesterday," he said. "Your questions took me by surprise, and I'm afraid my response was a trifle blunter than I intended."

"Ah well, we're used to it; we men of law have to administer these shocks from time to time, you know," said the barrister in his smooth flowing tones. "Think no more of it, my dear Morcar, I beg of you."

"I wanted to atone—I hoped perhaps that you and Mrs. Harington would dine with me here tonight—I have three stalls for the theatre," said Morcar, mentioning a play he had heard Christina observe to Nasmyth that she would like to see.

"Well, that's very kind of you, very kind indeed," said Harington. His voice had now completed the transition from suspicion, through formality, to pleased surprise and finally greedy complaisance. "Very kind indeed," he repeated warmly. "I think I can answer for my wife—I believe we are free. I'll just consult my diary. Yes. I accept with pleasure."

That evening when the Haringtons came—rather late—through the revolving doors and Morcar, correct in tails and white tie, rose to greet them, he saw with a thrill of delight that the stuff of Christina's evening gown, a strange misty blue, subtly self-twilled, soft and clinging, was of his own design, woven on his own looms. The coincidence gave him an exquisite pleasure.

"I shall tell her of it some day," he promised himself.

As he had never in his life spoken to a woman of his work, he intended by this promise more than he then knew or was prepared consciously to express.

23

Lovers

Morcar became the Haringtons' close friend. The trademark problem formed a slight thread of connection, which Morcar day by day thickened into a steel rope. Eventually, by slightly misspelling the word thistledown and adding to it a daisy agreeably intertwined with a seeding thistle, he succeeded in registering the mark. A copy of the appropriate trademark journal was sent to Mr. Shaw, who did not oppose the registration, and as far as Morcar could ascertain at the time by a fairly extensive enquiry, did not afterwards use the *soft as thistledown* labels; indeed as far as could then be discovered it seemed he ceased to make his imitations of Morcar's cloth at all.

Each stage of this course of events was made by Morcar an excuse for entertaining the Haringtons, who replied by similar entertainments. With Morcar as host the trio dined together, went together to the play—where in the late 1920's in every form night after night the destruction of the old moral code was depicted or advocated—preparatory, it was understood, to the construction of a new one. Harington disapproved altogether of all these new ideas, calling them "filthy" yet unable to stay away from the interest of the spectacle. Morcar, impatient of shibboleths, accepted these new destructions as true to the facts of experience, and sympathised with Christina, who he saw yearned idealistically for a freer, finer life which they might possibly provide. With Morcar as host they danced at night clubs. In her modish long frock—long dresses were just returning to fashion, Morcar had not seen one before Christina's—Christina was a graceful though absent-minded dancer. Morcar trembled slightly when he encircled her with his arm. He had known in his life no greater pleasure than to hold her thus—her elegance of soft sweeping folds, of moulded curves, of matching jewels, all his own; her clear ivory cheek, her sweet pure profile, the dark arch of her eyebrows, her wonderful sea-blue eyes, so near to him. She was tall, but since her height was proportionate to her sex, Morcar was taller; her dark head just topped his shoulder. The waves of dark hair sprang up so thickly from the narrow central parting as almost to conceal it; Morcar looked down on the intricate convolutions of those crisp waves with tender admiration. One hand, not small but white and slender with a curve of wrist which Morcar found exquisite, lay on his arm; the other, silk-smooth, flower-cool, rested in his. She turned her head and gave him her lovely generous smile; her rich lips parted, and in her low quick tone she made some observation on the scene—trifling enough yet somehow always agreeing in sentiment with Morcar's. A whole group of objects associated with her began to spell romance for him: dark red roses, stars in a night sky, a certain shade of blue, a fluted wine-glass, the sapphire in her ring. The Haringtons on their side introduced Morcar to ballet, to opera, to picture exhibitions, to French films. Morcar's hospitality was lavish, luxurious. It irritated him that Harington should continually throw out, when offering his invitations, such phrases as: "It can't be the Savoy, you know ... I'm not a millowner ... we men of law who depend solely on our own brains for our subsistence . . the new poor ..." But he did not hesitate to buy Christina's company by pandering to her husband's taste for luxury.

The next stage in the intimacy came when Morcar was invited to their home, a small but well-proportioned house in a quiet old Kensington square. It had a graceful iron balcony, festooned with wisteria; the house-door, the old-fashioned shutters, were painted a glossy deep bright blue. Within, all the walls were parchment-coloured; the floors of polished wood were sparsely but finely covered with Indian rugs, which it seemed had belonged to Christina's father. The furniture consisted of choice "pieces"—it was a word Morcar had never heard before but soon picked up though without venturing to speak it—bought one by one at auctions, country farmhouses, secondhand dealers'. Christina's drawing-room upstairs was a place of beauty and repose, with its light walls, its delicate Indian rugs in which blue predominated, its fine old furniture mixed with a few comfortable chintz-covered armchairs, the small cherished Sickert over the mantelpiece, the group of old family silhouettes displayed on a screen, the great jars and bowls of flowers, the low white bookcases, the solitary photograph, a fine strange seascape of Harington's production, the agreeable ornaments, some of soft blue gilt-patterned glass. There were a good many objects of Indian art of one kind or another scattered about the Haringtons' house: Kashmire shawls, small brass statuettes of fine workmanship, silk panels, lacquered boards, garlanded lamps, diagrams of Rangoli picture patterns (which fascinated Morcar particularly).

Christina's father, it seemed, had been something rather high up in the Indian administration—governor of some province, perhaps; Morcar was uncertain, and Christina did not enlighten him. This seemed in some curious way to entitle Harington (not Christina) to a knowledge of India, and he often expressed strong views which might be summed up in his frequent exclamation: "Those damned natives don't know when they're well off." Nothing made Morcar recall his Liberal ancestry so clearly as to listen to Harington's tirades about India, which Harington was apt to conclude: "I'm sure your father, Christina, would have thought the same." Morcar was convinced of few things more emphatically than that Christina's father, a noted administrator whom, as he understood, Christina much resembled and greatly loved, would have thought nothing of the kind; and he was confirmed in this by Christina's silence on these occasions. She was not prepared to sacrifice her father or her children to agreement with her husband, Morcar noticed; everything else with a too generous, too lavish, too eagerly yielding hand, she threw away for his sake. "Never mind," she said in her tone of loyal, loving consolation to all her husband's innumerable complaints: "Never mind. We'll do——" something of a remedial nature, which would sacrifice her own leisure and pleasure to his incessant requirements.

Christina's father had been widowed early, and she had spent her childhood in a country vicarage in Kent, the home of her father's oldest friend, who was Edward Harington's father. Morcar drove down with the Haringtons to Bersing one weekend, and found Canon Harington a small silver-haired widower, dignified, simple, an Oriental scholar. The vicarage was large and well tended; in the centre of its smooth green lawn, lined by rosy Canterbury bells and pink sweet williams, stood a cedar tree so old its lower branches were supported by stakes and chains. The sweet green country, so warm and mild, its fruitful fields sheltered by tall windbreaks, astonished Morcar, accustomed to the harsher West Riding mould, as much as the hat-touching politeness of the villagers. (For himself, he greatly preferred the straightforward bluntness of, say, Nathan— Nathan was his Daisy foreman—but it was interesting to see these southern manners.) An old castle stood in Bersing parish; with the people who owned the castle, descendants of those who built it in Norman times, the Haringtons had a distant but clear relationship. It was at Bersing that Morcar discovered, from a chance remark of the Canon's, that the poverty, the narrowed circumstances, which Harington continually deplored, included a united unearned income, from bequests of Christina's father and Edward's mother, which approached four figures. Doubtless such a sum did not go far when one lived in London, had a son designed for the navy—the navy was traditional in the Harington family; Edward's eldest brother had perished at sea in the War—and a daughter to follow her mother at Roedean; but looking at it from the point of a man who had to "make" every penny he had, Morcar thought Harington quite well placed and lucky. Harington on the other hand seemed to imagine that when one had a mill money rolled in upon one without further effort—"your workmen go on making cloth all the time you're away, Morcar," he said, when urging Morcar once to extend his stay in London.

Every time Morcar saw Harington and Christina he witnessed some violent outbreak of temper from the barrister, similar to that against the unlucky waiter at their first meeting, or some blighting comment which mildewed the company's enjoyment. There was the morning when the marmalade on the breakfast-table was not of the thick peel-crowded variety known as "Oxford"; there was the Saturday noon when he brought Morcar home unexpectedly and found nothing for lunch except a couple of meagre chops. There were the awful weeks after a judge at some provincial assize rebuked him for insufficient preparation of a case; there was the time when the laundry had over-stiffened his dress-shirt button-holes. There were continual clashes with theatre attendants, taxi-drivers, porters, waiters, ticket-inspectors. Morcar thought he began to see a motive, a pattern, so to say a theme-song, in Harington's rages. On the surface, they were caused by some material discomfort, but beneath that lay the deeper cause, a hurt to Harington's pride. This pride was a pride of class. The Oxford marmalade represented to him his University, his social standing, his way of life, his claim; he quarrelled with all who by a lack of service, a frustration of his desires, seemed to deny this claim. This was confirmed for Morcar on the evening when, dining in Notens Square, he first met the Harington children and saw them beneath the lash. The family had been away to the sea for their summer holiday; Morcar, who remembered every detail he heard about Christina, knew the dates of this holiday very accurately and contrived to be in town a week or so after their return. He rang up Harington to offer entertainment, but received instead a jovial invitation to come to Notens Square that night and dine off a brace of pheasants which one of the Castle relatives had sent from their September shoot.

"The children are at home," concluded the barrister. "I believe Christina would like you to see them. Don't be late."

Morcar rang the bell punctually and was rewarded by finding

Christina alone in the drawing-room with her two fair children. The boy in Etons, the girl in softly coloured printed silk, short-sleeved, very full and childish in its folds, rose on his entrance; they gave him the effect of gathering about their mother and gazing at him from large hostile eyes. Edwin's were blue, though not of Christina's rich tint; Jennifer's were grey, but warm and fine, not pale like her father's. The girl was serious and handsome; the boy, a pleasant lad enough, seemed more commonplace. Their manners were excellent, courteous but unaffected and easy, as he had expected from Christina's children. Jenny poured the sherry very seriously and carefully; Edwin seriously and carefully handed it. Harington came in, late but affable; he drew Jenny towards him, and while joking about the peer's peerless pheasants, fondled her. Morcar watched him.

"Perhaps you don't care for children, Morcar?" exclaimed Harington abruptly, evidently struck by his sombre expression.

"I don't know any," said Morcar.

Harington's perceptions were keen enough when not blinded by anger; he dropped the subject and they went down to dine.

It was his custom on informal occasions to carve at a side table. He did so tonight, or rather began to do so, for on the first impact of carving-knife and bird he exclaimed angrily:

"Christina! This bird is ruined! It's not cooked! It's red raw!"

"Try the other, dear," said Christina hastily.

"The other's just the same. Ruined! Raw! Come and look at them! Come and see for yourself. Come and look, I say!"

The unhappy Christina was obliged to rise and inspect the birds, even, at her husband's command, to prod them. Harington by now was quite out of his command; his face was crimson, words poured from his lips in a scathing torrent. Christina, still holding in one hand her table-napkin, stood before him like a scolded schoolgirl. The fact that the scene was comic as well as tragic in its implications made Morcar all the more furious; it occurred to him to look at the children who, he felt sure, must be Christina's chief concern. The boy sat with hanging head, flushed, his lower lip quivering; the girl seemed cut in stone, pale and erect, gazing ahead with a look of contempt as though chiselled on her face.

"Perhaps you omitted to inform the cook of the dinner-hour?" said Harington sarcastically.

"Perhaps Cook doesn't know how to cook pheasants, Daddy," piped up Edwin suddenly in defence of his mother, in his shrill young tones.

"Be silent, sir!" roared Harington.

The make-believe fury in his voice was now coloured by a real rage, and Morcar suddenly understood that his vexation over this mishap with the pheasants arose because it seemed to indicate that his cook was not of the kind used to dealing with game—not the kind of cook his castle cousins had. His cook was not commensurate with his class; he had lost prestige, face.

"Never mind," said Christina in her lovely soothing tone: "I'll send them out to be recooked."

"And what shall we do meanwhile? Sit and twiddle our thumbs?"

"If you could possibly develop those sea-prints you spoke of, I could have a look at them before I go north," suggested Morcar easily.

"Develop in a dinner-jacket," criticised Harington scornfully. "Suitable, very."

The matter was settled so, however. Harington took his son to the dark-room in the basement; Christina, Morcar and Jenny went up to the drawing-room. Christina paused, one foot on the lowest stair.

"Go downstairs, children dear, and ask Cook to give you both a thick slice of bread and butter, to carry you on," she said.

"I'm not hungry, Mummy," said Jenny coldly.

Edwin seemed to wish to emulate this refusal, but his flesh was too strong for his spirit and he was soon munching, to judge from his father's petulant comments on the dark-room threshold, which echoed up through the house.

"I'm so sorry for this confusion and delay," apologised Christine when they reached the drawing-room. She looked flushed and weary. "You must be very hungry, Mr. Morcar."

"Perhaps he'd like a slice of bread and butter too," suggested Jenny in a tone not unlike her father's at his most sardonic.

Morcar laughed. He was genuinely amused and laughed whole-heartedly. It saddened him, however, to see how the two faces watching him brightened at the sound.

"Put on one of the new records, Jenny," said Christina.

The three sat in happy silence for nearly an hour, listening to sweet music. Morcar heard little of it, but was content to sit and gaze at Christina's face.

When at last it was reported that the birds were done, Harington could not leave the dark-room, and they spent another hungry fifteen minutes. At last they were all reassembled round the board; the table-napkins, re-folded, had lost some of their pristine freshness and Harington scowled at them, but all else was fresh and newly-set, so he passed them by. Christina joked bravely about the unusual gap between soup and game, the children smiled dutifully and Harington, who was clearly ashamed of the delay he had caused by his photographic process though not at all of his bad temper, played up well. He stuck in the fork; it was a moment of suspense.

"Ah!" he said. "Christina, Cook may be congratulated."

Three sighs of relief came from the listening family, and in spite of himself Morcar could hardly avoid breathing a fourth. As he looked about, smiling, after doing so, he met Jenny's eye fixed on him intently. They stared at each other with great solemnity for a long moment, then Morcar, greatly daring, winked at her. Jenny's thick fair eyebrows rose in astonishment; she seemed stunned, appeared to ponder; then suddenly her face changed as Christina's sometimes did, into a sunny, joyous smile.

After this incident—as it seemed to Morcar strangely enough—the Haringtons took him more closely to their family bosom. Perhaps it was a relief, an amelioration of their private nightmare, to feel that Morcar had seen them at their worst and still liked them—he was at pains to proffer an invitation very shortly after. Perhaps Harington was grateful for someone to patronise. Morcar guessed sardonically—for he sometimes heard echoes in the children's speech—that Harington spoke of him to other friends as *my wool man, my satanic millowner, my rich Yorkshire tyke—he smells of money; not out of the top drawer, of course, but a good fellow all the same.* Morcar submitted to this; he submitted too to let Harington pick his brains and achieve a reputation for industrial knowledge on the pickings. If it came to that, Morcar admitted honestly, the picking was not all on one side. The two men had a certain common interest in their æsthetic faculties, on Morcar's part undeveloped except as regards textiles. Morcar genuinely admired the barrister's photography, and took an initiated interest in his lighting and composition effects. Morcar learned from the Haringtons' pictures, their rugs, their chintz, their prints, from Harington's still-lifes and Christina's careless elegance, even from the children's party charades. Soon the three adults were on first-name terms; Morcar gladly endured Harington's version of his name, which his suave drawl turned into something resembling *Herry*, in exchange for the privilege of uttering the magic syllables Christina.

For the children, what deep thoughts went on in their young minds he could not know, but they soon called him Uncle Harry and treated him as a very present help in trouble, a staunch friend who could be relied on to take their side.

That Christina should feel him always at her hand to help her, a comforting, sustaining presence, was Morcar's aim. "This will be better perhaps," he said mildly, adjusting the position of a lamp or the angle of a chair. "We can easily telephone," said Morcar when some difficulty arose and Harington's anger threatened: "We can run over and fetch it—we can have it sent by rail—I can drop round and change the tickets in the morning." Harington's surface manners to his wife were of course those of a gentleman; he never omitted to rise when she rose, to open doors, to carry coats, to give her precedence; he taught his son to do the same under threat of fearful penalties and reviled (at considerable length) the low-bred behaviour of all who did otherwise. But he was apt to emerge from the small room downstairs used as his study and shout: "Christina!" and when she hurried to him to discover that he wanted a sheet of notepaper from the bureau or an invitation which was staring him in the face over his mantelpiece. Morcar intervened whenever he could to spare Christina the tasks which her husband's egoism thus dumped on her, against which her nature was too generous to rebel. She grew, he hoped and believed, to rely on him when he was present, turning quickly towards him in any difficulty, without ever asking for his help or admitting that she needed it. This situation, where Morcar was half in her confidence, half out, was unlikely to last, and Morcar did not intend that it should; it would come to all or nothing in the way of confidence between them, and he meant it should be all.

One of the familiar scenes of Harington's exacting temper gave him the chance he wished. It was winter and during the children's term-time; the Haringtons were entertaining guests for cocktails; Morcar, arriving early for the party by request, found the maid wearing an embarrassed air. He stood waiting while she hung his coat in the closet, taking as it seemed an unconscionable time about this simple act; then the sound of voices from upstairs told him what was wrong. He went up swiftly, and found that some error over the drinks had excited Harington's rage. He was scolding furiously; Christina, trying to soothe, succeeded only in adding fuel to the flames. Even as Morcar entered, the doorbell rang below. A look of deepened misery flashed across Christina's lovely face. Morcar had a moment's view of what it must mean to a woman to have guests arriving in her home while her husband raged. The social exposure imminent in such a situation must be hell to her.

"Hullo, Edward, good-evening, Christina," said Morcar briskly, affecting to notice nothing strained in their manner. "I'm first, but only just, I gather; two legal luminaries are on my heels."

Harington's face changed at once; an ambitious man, he was exceedingly susceptible to the good opinion of his professional colleagues. He put on a host's countenance and greeted his guests with suave affability, and the party, a large one flowing into every room, passed off well. Towards its close, Morcar found an opportunity to ask whether he and Christina would come out and dine, in view of the disruption which parties inevitably caused in domestic arrangements. Harington accepted, provided Morcar could wait awhile; he thought of taking a cottage in Cornwall for the coming summer from one of his colleagues then present, with whom he wished to begin preliminary negotiations. When all the guests save this one had gone, Harington withdrew with him into the study, and Morcar went upstairs to Christina.

She was alone in the room, standing by the fire, her arms outstretched to the mantelpiece, her dark head bowed. In that pose, her long filmy black draperies flowing about her, she looked weighted down with griefs too heavy for her strength, and Morcar's heart swelled with pity.

"Christina."

"Oh—Harry. You startled me," said Christina, at once changing her pose. She turned to him, spoke in a cheerful tone and smiled, but Morcar saw that tears stood in her blue eyes. "Have another drink? A cigarette?"

"You needn't put on your party face for me," said Morcar.

Christina raised her eyebrows. "I wasn't aware of doing so," she said haughtily. Her lips quivered, however.

"Don't try to hide from me, Christina," said Morcar. "I understand—I understand everything. You're very unhappy. If only I could do something to help you, my dear. But at least you needn't trouble to hide from me. You can trust me."

Christina stood silent, her eyes averted. She stooped and snatched a cigarette, tapping it nervously against her hand. Morcar held a match for her.

"Is it so obvious to you?" said Christina suddenly. "My unhappiness, I mean? It's a nightmare to me to feel that people in the street look at me and say: 'That woman's unhappy in her marriage.' I feel ashamed. You won't understand that. It's a woman's feeling."

"On the contrary I understand it perfectly," said Morcar

grimly. "For years I've felt that way myself."

"You?" said Christina, astonished. Her beautiful face changed on an instant, softening from lines of wretchedness to her customary lovely look of sympathy, compassion. "Are you unhappily married, Harry?" she said softly. "I'm so sorry. I didn't know." She looked round, sank to a chintz-covered settee, threw away her cigarette. "Tell me," she said.

Then Morcar, seating himself beside her, looking away, leaning forward, clasping his hands between his knees, told her about his wife. His words poured out, incoherent, jerky, commonplace, but revealing. As he spoke, it struck him that he had never told anyone, anyone at all, anyone in the world, of the true reason for his separation from Winnie. After a silence of almost ten years, it was an infinite release to speak of it, and yet an agony; he suffered in the telling, his muscles twitched, his body was drenched with sweat. "I've never seen her from that day to this. 'He's not your son,' she said, 'he's not your child. Don't you understand, he's not your child.' I've never known whose child he was," said Morcar, turning to Christina. "I couldn't bring a divorce suit—or, at least, I felt I couldn't," he amended: "Because of her brother, Charlie. My friend. My lifelong friend. I've never known whose child he was. At first I used to look in every man's face to see if there was a likeness. I still do sometimes. I've never known. Not even guessed. Charlie was killed in the war. We were on patrol together. I've never seen her from that day to this."

The sorry story was ended, and he fell silent. Christina did not speak.

"So you see," said Morcar after a while, making an effort to sound normal, looking down casually at his hands: "About feeling ashamed of being unhappy—wanting to conceal it—I understand."

210

"Poor children!" exclaimed Christina.

Morcar was astonished. At first he could not fathom her meaning, turned to her questioningly. Her blue eyes, veiled in tears, the whole curve of her body, her woman's nature, seemed to offer him such a soft and loving sympathy that he could hardly restrain himself from kneeling before her and burying his face in her hands.

"Poor children," repeated Christina softly.

This time Morcar understood. "Yes, I expect that's just what we were," he said, soberly considering. "Children. We knew nothing of life. Winnie had lived in such a narrow restricted kind of way, you know. I see that now. Uneducated. Ignorant. She left school at fourteen. I was ignorant too, in spite of my war service. Just a raw lad."

"You didn't think of forgiving her, Harry?"

"Somehow it never entered my head. Besides," continued Morcar—with difficulty, for this was the last, the deepest, the unforgivable wound: "She didn't want me to forgive her, you know."

"I'm so sorry," said Christina. She dropped the words out slowly and softly.

"You at least have your children," said Morcar, not without bitterness. "They should console you."

"Yes, oh yes!" cried Christina with her lovely smile. "Yes, indeed!" She added in a whisper, turning away her head as though it was not for him to hear: "But it's their happiness I'm afraid for."

"Count on me for help—for friendship," said Morcar earnestly. He dared not say: "For love," but added: "For anything you like and need."

"I will," said Christina. She smiled, rose, and as he stood up,

211

offered him her hand. "It's a promise," she said. "If you will promise me to believe that you have a home with us."

"I promise," said Morcar.

After that day confidence was complete between them; they felt themselves in a sense companions in misfortune. Gradually they told each other all their histories. Morcar spoke of his parents, his cloths, Mr. Shaw, Daisy Mills, Winnie, Charlie; Christina spoke of her able and brilliant father, very dearly loved, of her happy childhood in Bersing, her schooldays happy in learning, of her father's death in India, and Edward's elder brother. It was clear to Morcar that Christina had loved this brother (drowned at Jutland) though perhaps she was too young then to know it. Edward arriving back on leave from France with all the prestige of heroism and danger just after her father's death, urging her to abandon her scholarship to Somerville and marry him, marry him, had called out all her generous respon-siveness, and given direction, as she had thought then with schoolgirl earnestness, to a life lost in a maze of grief. On her side, Christina indicated to Morcar her conviction that he had never loved Winnie as a lover should, but only as a brother. Morcar smiled a trifle grimly when she laid this idea before him; he knew its truth so well, so very well, now, for his love for Christina had taught it to him.

During the following summer the Haringtons rented for some months the Cornish cottage of which mention had first been made at their cocktail party. Morcar shared this expense with them, and came to the remote little village by the sea for a couple of weeks in August and as many weekends as he could conve-niently spare. The result of this life in common was to rouse in him a mingled pity and desire for Christina which he found intolerable. On the one hand the holiday offered, as holidays are apt to do, innumerable opportunities for irritation to Harington. The Harington car broke down—in Morcar's opinion Harington was a wretched driver; he expected miracles from his machine and wrenched angrily at the wheel when they were not accomplished. The express bringing Edwin part-way on his cross-country journey was late, and minor inconveniences resulted. The cottage—really a house—which Morcar thought charming, stood on the flank of a steep hill, so that to return to it was always tiring. The domestic labour was variable in quantity and quality, and Christina's housekeeping, always a little sketchy (at least by the solid north-country standards to which Morcar was accustomed), suffered in consequence. The bathing pool, a natural hollow in the rocks, was too small for Harington to display his diving talents. The weather was too calm for the sailing in which he and his son delighted, and the sky too vacantly blue to make good background for his photographs. Jennifer did not win the children's tennis tournament in the seaside resort along the coast, as her father had expected, observing calmly, when reproached, that her victorious opponent had won because she played better. The weather was a blaze of sunshine, the high cliffs sheltered the village from any land breeze; Harington's fair skin suffered from acute sunburn and his temper was equally irritated. As usual when Christina was bowed beneath her tyrant's verbal lash, Morcar's pity, his wish to rescue, to defend, burned within him.

On the other hand, the romantic little harbour, haunt of artists, was of a singular and most bewitching beauty, a beauty which strangely matched Christina's own. The towering hills sweeping down in grace and strength to the white-sanded coves, the black rocks, the blue sea, the misty aureole which encircled the pier lantern, rosy in the twilight—all these seemed designed to stress by repetition Christina's dark curls, her blue eyes, her milk-white skin and rich carmine mouth. Morcar and Christina were together all day, sometimes in company, sometimes alone; he helped her over rocks, down fern-grown paths, into rocking boats, through the white surf of breaking blue waves; they leaned over the bridge together, walked through gorse among the blue butterflies. The sun blazed down; Christina went hatless in thin light frocks. They talked continually; he touched her hand a hundred times a day. Cornwall seemed a very long way from Annotsfield; the Cornish fisher-folk with their lilting speech seemed to make this an earlier, more primitive, remote and romantic world. Jumping Jennifer down from a high jagged boulder as they clambered down towards a cave, she fell into his arms and Morcar kissed her, the child hugging him in return warmly. When it came to Christina's turn down the boulder he kissed her lightly too.

"Harry!" laughed Christina rebukingly, in the tone she used to the children when they made a forgiveable *gaffe* which however must not occur again. "Dear me!" She ran away across the beach and kneeling, became very busy about their picnic tea.

Morcar with the touch of her lips on his knew that he could not leave Cornwall without making her his own.

For the next few days she seemed to avoid him, which maddened him yet gave him a subtle pleasure; she knew of his love, he argued, her avoidance was a recognition of its power. If her eyes met his, his burning heavy glance left her surely in no doubt of his feeling. Embarrassment, consciousness, grew between them, as Morcar meant it should; Christina looked down at his approach, she spoke to him unevenly; for his part he haunted her path so that she found him at every turning, silent and sombre.

On the last night before Morcar's departure an entertainment was given in the village by visitors. The two children were eager to go to this, for entertainments were rare in the quiet little place; they had been promised the treat and tickets had been bought. Christina however at the last moment excused herself. It had been a trying day; Edwin, entrusted with the printing of some recent negatives, had allowed them to become too dark; Jenny, commanded by her father to eschew the society of some children whom he thought not quite the thing, had been seen playing with them in a nearby cove, and when scolded had replied calmly that they were nice children and she liked them. A highly uncomfortable scene had followed this, for Jenny, usually calm and happy in disposition, was when roused as fierce and stubborn as her father. Harington, as always when you stood up to him, reflected Morcar, was defeated and retired abashed; later he became positively genial and actually helped to set the table for the evening meal, the day being one when no domestic help was available. But Christina did not recover so easily; she looked white and tired and said with more determination than usual that she meant to stay at home. Morcar suspected that she was at the end of her endurance and meant to give herself the relief of tears.

Accordingly he accompanied the party to the entertainment, meaning to excuse himself presently on the ground of his long journey on the morrow. Such being his plan, he did not attend much to what was happening on the platform, but schooled himself to sit through a few items. Almost at once, however, he found himself listening to a song:

Through the long days and years,
What will my loved one be,

Parted from me?
Through the long days and years.

Always as then she was,
Loveliest, brightest, best,
Blessing and blest.
Always as then she was.

Never on earth again
Shall I before her stand,
Touch lip or hand.
Never on earth again.

But while my darling lives,
Peaceful I journey on,
Not quite alone.
Not while my darling lives,
While my darling lives.

The words kindled his passion; he could no longer endure inaction. He rose and made his excuses. As the concert promised to be long and probably mediocre, Harington thought his departure natural enough, and Morcar returned alone to the house.

He entered very quietly, and treading lightly in his crêpe-soled seaside shoes, found Christina in the kitchen and stood in the doorway watching her without her knowledge. She was arranging great sprays of blue anchusa in a honey-coloured vase. She hummed a little to herself; Morcar found it touching to see her thus calmly happy, ministering to the joy of others, alone. A movement betrayed him. Christina turned. A warm colour flooded her lovely face. She turned quickly to the flowers again.

"What are you doing here, Harry?" she said in her courteous social tone. "Where are the rest?"

"They're at the hall—I came to see you," said Morcar. He added: "My darling," and drew her strongly into his arms.

For a moment she lay there passive, her head on his shoulder, her hand on his breast. It seemed as if she rested against his strength, at peace and happy, and Morcar rejoiced, for he knew himself loved. He kissed her tenderly, caressing with his hand her slender white throat.

"No, no!" murmured Christina. She raised her head and strove to draw away. "Harry, we can't do this."

"Yes, we can."

"But the children!"

"They won't know."

"Have you no scruples?" murmured Christina. "No feeling that it is wrong?"

"None!" said Morcar strongly.

"We shouldn't," murmured Christina, weeping. "Harry, we shouldn't."

Morcar kissed her with passion. "My darling, I love you," he said.

"And I love you, Harry," whispered Christina.

Morcar put back her rich curls and murmured his plea into her ear.

"No, no!" said Christina, starting. "No, Harry!"

"Yes, Chrissie, yes," said Morcar.

Later, when she lay in his arms, he told her about the blue frock.

"I knew you were mine when you wore it; I loved you then,

my lovely girl," he said.

Christina traced the line of his thick fair eyebrows with one finger. "Then I loved you first, Harry," she said. "I loved you before I wore your blue frock."

"When?"

"When I first saw you."

"Thank you, my darling," said Morcar. "Thank you."

He spoke with ardour; for Christina had thus healed him of the wounds dealt him by Winnie, who had never, it seemed, given him love. He did not then perceive that he was revenging himself on Winnie by compelling Christina to the course for which he had repudiated his wife.

24

Nadir

Morcar felt lonely now when he was away from Christina. He loved her, and she was the only person in the world with whom he could be completely himself. Besides this true and loving pleasure in their love, which was real and lasting, he rejoiced also that he was now as other men, with a woman of his own; nor did it displease him, since it was in the fashion of the times, that she was a mistress and not a wife. Christina wrote to him sometimes in her graceful and individual but careless hand, but he could not safely reply to her on Harington's account— nor would he in any case have known how to express himself in writing. He needed to see her, to hear her voice, to touch, to hold. Accordingly he looked forward to his visits to London as a boy looks forward to play after school, and became daring and skilful in arranging secret meetings. But he had no intention or inclination to allow his work to suffer from his play, and never went to town unless his work took him there. He would have regarded any such indulgence as silly, unmanly, excessive.

His work at present needed the greatest possible skill and attention, for the economic situation was going from bad to worse. The British manufacturers, condemned by England's return to the gold standard in 1925 to lose overseas either their profit or their market, after trying for some years to walk the razor-edge between the two fell on to one side or the other and began to draw on their capital to prevent them from falling to the bottom of the abyss. One by one they found their assets dwindling, incurred overdrafts and saw all they owned wrenched piece by piece from their hands into the banks' safes to provide "security." They cut down expenses and discharged workpeople; the purchasing power of the community diminished, the home market shrank; they incurred further overdrafts and discharged more workpeople and the market shrank still more. In 1929 a Labour government came into power, which Morcar, who had languidly voted Liberal out of habit, saw as an embodiment of high taxes, high wages, lower profits and a general disregard of the manufacturers' overseas problems. A great many other manufacturers felt the same; enterprise or initiative was at a discount, they decided, caution and economy were required. They cut down expenses and discharged workpeople; the purchasing power of the community diminished and the market shrank as before. Looms fell silent, queues at Labour Exchanges lengthened; bankers who had seemed good fellows all their lives now suddenly appeared harsh tyrants; a look of worry began to line every West Riding face.

Morcar, however, continued to prosper. He had no large hereditary mills, no long-standing commitments, no incompetent but deserving old retainers impossible to dislodge, to drag him down. No too-numerous shareholders' dividends, no bunch of expensive family households, no Excess Profits Tax still unpaid from the War, drained his profits; no huge inherited mansion built in the days before McKinley, no costly hobby of horse or plane or yacht, ate their way like moths into his substance. He was spending more in one way than ever before in his life, for in everything to do with the Haringtons he wished to be generous, lavish; but his personal expenditure in Annotsfield was particularly small, for now that he had Christina he felt satisfied and did not need to seek the drug of incessant pleasures. On the positive side, his machinery was up-to-date, his premises were small though neat—indeed they were rather too small, and certainly too widely scattered, Morcar told himself restively at times. His product was a speciality, new, adapted to the needs of the age, commanding a wide popularity in home and overseas markets. It was not now entirely his own, of course, for several other merchants and manufacturers in several countries, including England, had had the same idea as Mr. Butterworth and Morcar. But in his case it was continually refreshed by his own original talent which, Morcar felt with a modest confidence (never mentioned to anyone save Christina but the core of his life) very few designers anywhere could really excel. Accordingly, he prospered—not without anxious moments but steadily—while frowns of worry deepened on other manufacturers' brows.

Then in the autumn the American stock market fell, with a crash that shook the world. American banks closed, American merchants failed. Morcar suffered a loss which made him wince, but others suffered losses which made them stagger. Merchants who exported largely suffered heavily; for the first time Morcar saw a look of care on Mr. Butterworth's plump pink face. A fresh wave of economic depression spread all over the world in widening circles, like ripples when a stone has been thrown into a pond. Next year Morcar added the name of Hawley-Smoot to his detested Dingley and McKinley, for in an attempt to retrieve the economic débâcle, the United States imposed a heavy tariff on imported manufactured goods. European states retaliated, and tariffs spread across the world like weeds—weeds which, in the rippling economic pond, prevented free motion, entangled the limbs of trade. A kind of hush spread over the West Riding; there was much feverish activity, but little open talk; men watched each other in silence to detect the first sign of faltering. It began to be rumoured that even the great firm of Armitage, even Oldroyds', were rocking. Morcar, by the keenest, most unflagging, most expert attention to every detail of manufacture and finance, by continual thought and intensive labour over his designs, by unremitting pursuit of trade, by ruthless cutting of costs, continued to prosper. His textile acquaintances began to ask him with a peevish air how it was done, and to murmur that he was a hard man to come up against, a hard man to bargain with.

One afternoon in the spring of 1931 Morcar, in high spirits, was on his way to Annotsfield station to catch a London train when it occurred to him that his supply of ready money, though most would have judged it sufficiently ample, was perhaps not enough to have about him when he was near the Haringtons, to whom he was giving dinner late that night. "The bank—I've time," he told his chauffeur, who wrenched the wheel round and made the car leap across the square. Morcar sprang out and ran up the bank's marble steps. On the top step he encountered Mr. Butterworth.

"Hullo, Butterworth—sorry I haven't a minute—just off to town!" cried Morcar breezily, laying his hand on the merchant's arm as he passed by. "I've some Thistledowns coming along to you this afternoon," he added over his shoulder.

"Hullo, Harry," said the merchant gruffly, without pausing.

"Fifty, please," said Morcar to the cashier, rapidly filling up a cheque. While he wrote he made a lightning calculation. "Butterworth looks glum—his hair's grown very white—ill perhaps. *Or perhaps something is wrong with his business,*" thought Morcar, signing his name. "Yes, that's it; he's just come from a gruelling interview with the bank manager. He's probably just going down—the bank has a first debenture already, I shouldn't wonder." If anything went wrong with Butterworth, Morcar would not get paid—or at any rate not fully paid: "Sixpence in the pound perhaps, damn it!" thought Morcar—for the cloths he had sold the merchant recently and already delivered. "No use throwing good money after bad," thought Morcar swiftly. He made up his mind, snatched up the notes from the counter, ran out of the building and without pausing hurried across the road to Annotsfield Post Office. He telephoned Daisy Mills, glancing impatiently at his watch, and asked for his foreman.

"Nathan," he said: "That last lot of Thistledowns for Mr. Butterworth—have they gone yet?"

"They're just being loaded on t'lorries now," said Nathan in a tone of mingled grievance and virtue—virtue that the pieces were on their way, grievance that Morcar had thought it necessary to doubt his efficiency by enquiring about them.

"Take 'em off, will you?" said Morcar.

"Eh?"

"Take 'em off—there's a hitch about the finish—I'll explain when I get back."

"The finish?" began Nathan, vexed and expostulatory. "There's nowt wrong wi't'finish, Mr. Morcar."

"That's what you think," snapped Morcar. In imagination he could see Nathan as he was looking now, his serious fresh-coloured

Yorkshire face agape, his quiff of ginger hair positively bristling, with indignant non-comprehension; the picture irritated him.

"Well, you passed 'em yourself," Nathan snapped back.

"Don't let them go," said Morcar in a tone of command. "I want to find them at Daisy when I get back from London, do you hear?"

"I hear," said Nathan angrily. "But I make no sense of it. You've been fussing about getting those pieces off all t'week."

"Don't let them go to Butterworth's," commanded Morcar.

He rang off; his chauffeur was almost dancing on the kerb outside with anxiety lest he should miss his train. But Morcar was not afraid, for he felt it was one of his lucky days; by his chance encounter with the merchant and his swift telephone call he had saved himself, he felt pretty sure, the loss of a quite considerable sum of money. That he had also helped Butterworth on his road to failure, by depriving him of some stock which, easily and rapidly disposable, would have brought him some ready money at a comparatively early date, Morcar knew at the bottom of his mind but did not stop to consider.

It was the most completely selfish act, the lowest point, the nadir, of his career.

V

Rise

25

Boy off Train

"Butterworth's down," heard Morcar at the Club. "It'll push plenty of others over as well, I shouldn't wonder. How about you, Harry?"

"Not too bad," said Morcar.

"It'll about finish Oldroyds', I reckon. He owed them a packet."

"Armitages won't like it either."

"Oldroyds' are rocky already."

"They've been going the wrong way a long time."

"That doesn't surprise me," said Morcar. "What Francis Oldroyd knows about textiles wouldn't cover a sixpenny piece."

He had occasion to repeat this at intervals during the next couple of months, for the rumours about Oldroyds' difficulties grew stronger every day.

"It'll be a pity if they have to go down, though, after all these years," said opinion at the Club.

"How long have they been going, then?" asked Morcar.

"You should know; you worked there."

"I didn't take much notice; I was only a lad."

"Well, it must be at least a hundred and twenty years. Nay, it must be longer. They were in at the beginning of the Industrial Revolution, if you know when that was. I don't myself. One of them was the first to run machines in the Ire Valley, and got himself murdered as a result. Luddites and all that, you know."

"Ah," said Morcar noncommittally, and turned the conversation. He had never heard of Luddites, and saw no reason why he should interest himself in the Oldroyds' past. What interested him at the moment was the news in the papers about the flight of gold. There was a woolcombers' strike on, too, but that was normal; this gold business was out of the ordinary and it troubled him. *Bank Rate up to 3½ to check Heavy Efflux of Gold*, the newspapers said, and *Last Week the Bank of England lost £15,000,000* and *Stopping Gold Drain*—but it did not seem to stop. Morcar did not understand what the flight of gold implied—sterling and exchanges and bank rates and all that sort of thing anyway were some of these stock exchange, London, distributors' tricks, all my eye and Betty Martin, that financiers practised to do down the manufacturers, the men who actually made the stuff, thought Morcar—but that gold should leave England was all wrong. Not respectable, somehow. Gold leaving *England*. What had the Government been about? England! When Morcar thought of England nowadays he thought of Christina as well. Imagine England borrowing gold from Paris and New York! England having to ask favours! Morcar felt about that as he did when he heard Harington raging at his wife; a burning anger that he could not rescue her. The Haringtons were holidaying in Sark this summer, and Morcar was to join them presently. But he felt he could not leave Annotsfield while things were so upset.

228

In August it became known that Oldroyds' were in liquidation.

"I suppose Francis will reorganise and start again," they said uneasily at the Club. The continual disappearance nowadays of traditional textile landmarks like Oldroyds' gave a very uncomfortable, end-of-the-world appearance to the West Riding landscape.

"Like the rest of us," added someone bitterly.

"Not he! He'll get out of textiles and go south," said Morcar contemptuously. "I know him."

"The less fool he, then, that's what I say. I wish I could do the same."

"I don't like to leave a game when I'm losing," said Morcar curtly.

"And when you're winning you don't want to."

"Exactly."

"Wait till you've lost a quarter of a million, Harry; then you'll change your tune."

"I don't intend to lose a quarter of a million——"

"None of us *intend* it."

"—but if I did, I shouldn't crawl out and go south."

"He'd start again with two looms in a room-with-power, wouldn't you, Harry?"

"Summat o' that sort," said Morcar in the vernacular, joking to conceal his real feeling.

At another level of his mind he was wondering about Syke Mills. If Francis Oldroyd sold up and cleared out—"and he will," thought Morcar again contemptuously: "I know him"—the Syke Mills premises would be vacant. "Don't think of them," scoffed Morcar to himself: "They're too large for you. You'd rattle about in them like a pea in a bottle." They're well situated, in fine condition, they'd do you credit, the other side of him argued; you'd save eventually by putting all your processes under one roof—you wouldn't have this continual running back and forth between Booth Bank and Daisy. "Aye! But look what it'd cost—look at the responsibility—look how it would tie you up for years," he contended. Booth Bank and Daisy are rather hole-and corner, rather mean for what you make; if you had Syke Mills, you needn't be ashamed to show it to Christina, argued Morcar. "This is not the time for sentiment," decided his other self hardly. "It's a time to cut your overhead, not increase it. The Government are going to save ninety-six million on the budget; don't you expand yours."

Francis Oldroyd, as Morcar predicted, decided to sell up and go south; the bank took over; nobody would buy Syke Mills as a going concern; in a three-day sale the looms and other equipment were auctioned off, falling in small lots at low prices to cautious buyers. Morcar had a copy of the sale catalogue and looked it through, but found nothing he wanted; where his own type of machinery coincided with that used at Syke Mills, his own was greatly newer and superior. He dropped into the sale on the first day, not to buy anything but to look at the premises; they were quite as desirable as he had believed. It gave him a strange feeling to see again after all these years the archway where Brigg Oldroyd gave him his start in life, the private office where he corrected Mr. Butterworth, the designers' room on the upper floor where he had learned his job from Mr. Lucas. He looked back at the ingenuous Harry Morcar of those days wistfully; a nice honest lad, he judged, with all his life before him; he wished he was like that nowadays—though not if it meant giving up Christina. The huge premises, unwanted in this time of bad trade, would go for a song as compared with their real value—or perhaps a couple of songs, thought Morcar. But if he bought, it meant years of intense work to pay off the price; why saddle himself with the additional responsibility? Besides, this financial muddle is going from bad to worse, thought Morcar angrily. Cotton prices were slumping now to the tune of thirty million depreciation; Lancashire staggered under the blow. That was uncomfortably near home, a sister textile just across the Pen-nines; Annotsfield men looked very gravely at each other when they heard of this. *The Budget must balance*, read Morcar; well, I should hope so! There seemed to be some disagreement in Parliament about what economy measures should be taken; the Labour party objected to cuts in the dole. The unemployment figures were mounting; Ramsay MacDonald begged the country not to listen to panic-stricken talk. At last, in late August, the crisis came to a head; the Labour Government fell and a National one was formed to effect economies and save the pound. With a sigh of relief Morcar went off to the Channel Islands to join the Haringtons.

He had a glorious holiday with Christina. The dark rocks, the blue sea, the gorse, the butterflies, were much as they had been in Cornwall; the joys of love were greater, for he found he loved Christina more dearly than before. In the perfect intimacy of love she was at ease with him, threw off her cool reticence, her social manner, and talked to him quickly and openly, like a child, of all the happenings, large or small, of her daily life. It was inexpressibly sweet to the lonely Morcar to be consulted about the length of Edwin's shorts and the sleeves of Jenny's frock, the colour of Christina's lipstick, whether to have tea at a farm or take it in a basket, how to make a trunk close or mend a sandal—especially as Christina did not, as far as he could see, chatter with the same happy freedom to her husband. (Indeed she lacked the opportunity, for Harington's egoistic tones were always booming about himself when he was present.) This childlike dependence on him in practical matters endeared Christina to Morcar the more because on the large political questions of the day she was better informed than himself, and had an æsthetic taste which Morcar rated very highly. To be able to speak freely on every subject in life, and to know that one would be met with understanding sympathy and love, was a heavenly luxury and relaxation.

If to be with Christina was heaven, to part from her was naturally hell. Parting from her on a London station platform in the early hours of a chilly September day, with the children cold and miserable—Jenny was not a good sailor, had suffered from the night's crossing and still looked rather green—and Harington fuming in the background over some lost luggage, was certainly wretched. To part itself was bad enough, but to part thus, to part without a kiss, without a loving embrace, to part with a cool word and a casual touch of the hand, to leave her on a chilly rainy morning with all her troubles thick about her lovely head, to know that their holiday together, to which he had looked forward so much so long, was over and for months they would see each other only in rare snatched hours—yes, it was hell. He felt as if someone were digging out his heart with a spoon—a sharp-pointed grapefruit spoon, thought Morcar angrily. He breakfasted alone, called at his office, acquainted himself with the usual collection of thorny problems which accumulate during holidays, and took a northbound train, in a deep depression only slightly mitigated by the rush of the morning.

In the train, for the first time that day he opened a newspaper. The headline leaped out at him: *Gold Standard Suspended.* Morcar's heart fell with a sickening thud. So the pound was not saved after all! *We regret to have to announce today that the Government have found themselves compelled to ask Parliament temporarily to suspend ... Grave as is the financial crisis ...*

"I suppose it will be better for trade," thought Morcar wretch-edly after a moment. "But it seems a shame." He was deeply wounded in his pride, his love. England off gold! The English pound no longer changeable for gold! "Good God! What are we coming to?" thought Morcar.

He reached Annotsfield towards the end of a dull grey after-noon. It was the flat time just before the mills turn out; the place had never looked so grimy, so dead-alive, so sordid. His sunburned face and hands, his light summer suit, felt hideously out of place in this industrial landscape. He drove to Booth Bank, where the mill found him exacting and bad-tempered; he rang up Daisy, and was irritable on the telephone to Nathan. He decided to change his clothes and have a meal before going out to Denbridge to examine in the quiet of the evening the mass of correspondence which Nathan said awaited him.

In the Club he found a good deal of company, less gloom and more liveliness than he had expected. Some event seemed to have occurred locally which was attracting talk away from the gold trouble. A group of textile-trade men of Morcar's acquain-tance, sitting with glasses in their hands, were discussing it with animation.

"Young fathead!"

"Silly lad!"

"What good did he think it would do?"

"Might have broken every bone in his body."

It struck Morcar that though their comments were disapprov-ing, their tones held a wistful, almost an admiring, affection.

"What's up? Who are you talking about?" he asked, joining them.

"Francis Oldroyd's son."

"He hasn't a son," objected Morcar. "Don't you remember,

he got a Booth girl into trouble, and the child was stillborn."

"Aye—but there was another. David."

"I don't remember any son," said Morcar stubbornly.

"Well, he has one, you can take it from me."

"He married again after the war—an Armitage."

"Nay—that child was a daughter. This David belongs to his first wife. He's a schoolboy, sixteen or so."

"Well, what's he been up to?" said Morcar disagreeably—he was not pleased that Francis Oldroyd had a son while he had none.

"The Oldroyds left Annotsfield today."

"I know," said Morcar. "They've gone to the south. Good riddance."

"Aye—but this boy, you see, he jumped out of the London train when it was moving."

"What?" exclaimed Morcar.

"In the Marthwaite tunnel."

"No, it was just before the tunnel. At the top of the Ire Valley, above Marthwaite—just beyond the bridge, you know."

"Young fathead!"

"Might have broken every bone in his body."

"What good did he think it would do?"

"What did he do it *for?*" enquired Morcar.

"He didn't like the idea of the Oldroyds' leaving the West Riding, after all these years, you know."

"He has a sort of fancy for staying in the textile trade."

"More fool he!"

"Young fathead."

"How do you know he did it for that reason?" asked Morcar.

"I was in the next compartment. I saw him jump out—he threw out his suitcase first, and that attracted my attention, you see, and I put my head out of the window and heard the whole thing. His father got a shock, I can tell you."

"He might well," said Morcar. His tone was constrained. He was seeing what he had not seen for years: two boys driving iron hoops down a steep moorland path to the narrow old stone bridge at Marthwaite over the waters of the Ire. He saw the white sand of the path, the outcropping black rock, the heather purple in the summer, the bracken just beginning to be fringed with russet. The boys were Charlie and himself, a quarter of a century ago. This boy now, Brigg Oldroyd's grandson, jumping out of a train at Marthwaite——

"Young fathead!"

"Still, you can't help liking his spirit, you know."

"What good did he think it would do, poor kid?"

"Don't drink that," said Morcar suddenly, handing his glass to his neighbour. "I've a call to make."

He left the room; when he returned a few minutes later after telephoning his bank manager at his private address, he was so clearly in the best of spirits that the group perceived it instantly.

"What have you been up to, Harry?"

"Never you mind," said Morcar.

"He's been buying a mill," suggested someone sardonically.

"You've hit it, lad!" said Morcar, slapping him on the shoulder. "Come on—drinks all round on me, to celebrate."

"You don't really mean it?" said his neighbour, awestruck.

"I do. I've bought Syke Mills," said Morcar.

"Harry! Nay! You must be daft! Buy a mill *now?* We're all trying to sell ours. I need a double whisky after that. Really you're absolutely daft, Harry—I mean it."

"Nay—I can see a way to make it pay," said Morcar. He turned aside to speak to the waiter, mumbling: "Somebody has to keep things going."

26

Old Man in Handcart

It was on April 4th, 1933—Morcar always remembered the date—when he shook out the pages of the *Manchester Guardian* at his breakfast-table with a pleasant sense that at last he had leisure enough to read it through and not merely glance at the headlines after digesting the textile and cricket news.

He had just concluded a really quite terrific bout of work. Moving from Booth Bank and Daisy into Syke Mills was a sufficiently arduous and complex task, but keeping his manufacture going meanwhile and finding the finance for both operations at once was a protracted juggling operation demanding incessant attention, skill and nerve—one second's lapse and the whole lot would fall to the ground, as Morcar often told himself. He had laughed and continued to juggle successfully, but the process—which involved very long hours of brain work, very many interviews, innumerable vital decisions, endless rushing hither and thither—had aged him. He was no longer a promising young fellow with a future, but a man in the prime of life with great responsibilities, to whom many people looked for their daily bread. He had ceased to be surprised by his own wealth and took as a commonplace the luxuries and the service which it bought. His powerful body had slightly thickened, his fair hair had darkened; his tone had become commanding, and young Edwin Harington's naval cadet friends from Dartmouth called him "sir." He laughed as he thought of this now, shaking out the pages of the newspaper; it was all worth while, he thought, for he was now safely, firmly and prosperously established at Syke Mills.

One of the minor pages was headed by a photograph. Morcar glanced at it, felt incredulous, looked at it more attentively, exclaimed. The picture showed a mild respectable old man, thin, bald, bearded, with a long narrow face, a Jew possibly by his appearance, seated in a handcart, which two young men in some sort of uniform were pushing along a broad and busy street. They had evidently halted to allow the photographer to take the picture, and turned laughing, triumphant faces to the camera. Other young men, passers-by, stood around, also laughing. The appearance of the old man, however, belied any suggestion of practical joking; in an uncomfortable posture, his legs stretched out straight and stiff before him, he clutched the sides of the cart in a frenzied grip, the extreme of fear distorting his poor old face. A violent and painful pang of pity stabbed through Morcar's heart. He coloured with anger, and at the same moment on another level of his mind it occurred to him that it was a long time since he had seen his mother.

"But what are they about?" he muttered, dashing down the paper. "What on earth are the police doing not to stop it?" He picked up the paper again and found that the young men were Berlin Nazis and their victim a German Jew. "Upon my soul!" said Morcar.

He became guiltily conscious that he was not well informed as to what was going on in Germany; he knew vaguely that Adolf Hitler had become Chancellor a month or two ago, and that his opponents were supposed to have burned down the Reichstag, though the evidence was so flimsy that for his part Morcar did not believe it for a moment. But he was not fully aware, he now realised, of the implications of Hitler's rule; he had not seen the Haringtons, on whom he relied for his interpretation of world events, since Christmas.

The picture of the old man in the handcart weighed on him all day. He spoke of it at lunch to other men. Many had seen it; some shook their heads over it angrily, some asked him impatiently what he expected from a maniac like Hitler, some opined that it was time somebody tidied up Germany anyway and if Hitler could do it, good luck to him. Most concluded by observing:

"There's nothing you can do about it anyway, Harry, so come and have a drink."

Morcar agreed, but all the same that evening he drove up to Hurst Road to see his mother.

When she opened the door of Number 102 to him she started back and gazed at him incredulously, her eyes bright and her cheek pale. The word "Harry" formed itself on her lips but she did not utter it. Then suddenly drawing him in she embraced him in a fierce and prolonged grip, pressing her lips deeply into his cheek. Morcar perceived with shame that it was a very long time indeed since he had been to see his mother—when indeed had he visited her? Not last Christmas; perhaps not even the Christmas before. She had grown much older, smaller and frailer; there was grey in her light brown hair, which was now thin and very severely arranged, and her once bright complexion had faded. She still sat erect, however, as he saw when he led her to a chair; her dress, a black knitted suit with a touch of white at the neck, was fresh and tasteful, with even a touch of coquetry in a black velvet ribbon tied round her throat. Her shoes were well polished, the house was spotless, the kitchen range gleaming; a meal set out on the table had all the proper accompaniments of napery and silver. Morcar, observing his mother's workworn hands as they lay folded in her lap, admired her spirit. "There's no need for her hands to be workworn," he thought irritably: "I send her plenty of money——" but aloud, driven by an irresistible impulse which the unprotected persecuted old man in the picture that morning had put in motion, he said:

"I'm thinking of buying a house, Mother, and I want you to come and live with me."

Mrs. Morcar clasped her hands more tightly together, and said:

"I don't see why I should."

Her tone represented so exactly his own obstinate feeling that he would never go where he was not wanted that Morcar laughed.

"We're an independent family, Mother, the Morcars," he said. "But I want you to come, all the same."

"And how long have you been planning this, Harry?" said Mrs. Morcar sternly.

"Since nine o'clock this morning," said Morcar with truth.

There was a pause. His mother's lips moved as if registering an inward debate. It struck Morcar that she was much alone.

"I couldn't keep house for you, Harry, in the way you're used to now," she said presently.

This confession from one who had so greatly prided herself on her housewifery in days of old struck Morcar as infinitely pathetic.

"No, no—you wouldn't need to—a housekeeper would do all the work," he said hastily, deciding at once that he would employ the Jessopps.

There was another pause.

"I daresay I should enjoy it," said Mrs. Morcar at last in a voice which shook.

"I'm sure you would, Mother," agreed Morcar cordially, planning at once all kinds of treats and comforts for her.

"I should be glad to have no housework to do. I should have more time for my needlework, you know," said Mrs. Morcar, visibly declining to allege any other reason for wishing to live with her son.

Her glance travelled to a heap of material on the table which she had evidently thrown down on hearing Morcar's knock. His glance followed hers, and Morcar saw a cushion cover, agreeably embroidered in rose and blue. He made a long arm and picked it up, remembering with a rush that the talent on which his fortune was founded was derived from his mother. He examined the embroidery; the stitches, he thought, were not quite as perfect as of old, but the design and colouring were charming. He said so, and added:

"Perhaps you could do some of these for my new house."

"I couldn't undertake to provide them all, Harry," said Mrs. Morcar with dignity. "That would be beyond my present strength."

"You shan't do anything you don't want to do, Mother," said Morcar cheerfully. "I can't promise you'll see much of me," he added, thinking it kindest to make this clear from the outset: "But you'll see a good deal more of me than you do now."

Mrs. Morcar bowed her head in acknowledgment; Morcar knew that she was too proud, her nature too rooted in reserve, to

240

make an open reply.

The house he eventually bought was Stanney Royd, an attractive seventeenth-century residence of a kind frequent on the hills round Annotsfield; strongly built in good local stone now blackened by the centuries, with a couple of gables, many mullioned windows, a fine porch with a rose window, outbuildings which previous owners had converted into garages, a stone terrace, stone balls over the gateposts, a pretty garden with a small stream and an old sundial. Neither too large nor too small as Morcar thought, Stanney Royd stood beneath the brow of a hill overlooking one of the many valleys whose streams joined the Ire just west of Annotsfield; it was not far over the brow to Syke Mills, or along the valley to the town—not far, that is, as Morcar's cars rated distance. He liked his house immensely and had many photographs taken of it to show the Haringtons, whose help he wished to enlist in its furnishing. Edward and Christina found the pictures charming and highly approved his choice, and they both found it natural that Christina, who had such discriminating taste and knowledge in these matters, should help him to find period furniture.

Accordingly Morcar and Christina attended many sales together and corresponded considerably on the business; the Haringtons rejoiced with Morcar when a suitable piece was found, and gave shelter in their house to all kinds of small articles which Christina bought as Morcar's agent, or which were bought from small obscure shops which did not want the trouble of despatching parcels of awkward shape to the north. To Morcar this was a time of much happiness; he loved to feel that the furniture of his home was being chosen by Christina, and he rejoiced in the greatly increased opportunities the business gave him of enjoying her society alone without any query from her husband.

He assumed that it was a time of happiness for Christina too. But one day, on returning from a sale, having paid the taxi while Christina entered the house and followed her into the drawing-room with their purchase beneath his arm, he found Christina standing by the hearth with her arms stretched on the mantelshelf and her head bowed, a pose he knew betokened grief with her. The cheerful words of pleasure in their day's success died on his lips; he put down the oak cupboard and went to her quickly, saying:

"What's wrong, love?"

"Nothing!" said Christina, turning to him at once with a smile. Her blue eyes, however, were full of tears, her rich lips quivered.

"Don't lie to me, Chrissie," said Morcar in a loving tone. He put his arm round her waist, drew aside her curly dark hair and kissed her ear. "What's wrong?" She was silent. "Tell me, love," he said, coaxing her with caresses.

"Your house," began Christina suddenly in a breathless tone, fixing her eyes on his in anxious question: "Why are you buying it now? Who will live there? Is it for Winnie?"

"Winnie!"

"Edward thinks it is—he thinks you intend a reconciliation with your wife."

"Nonsense!" cried Morcar furiously. "I never heard such nonsense in my life! Don't call Winnie my wife—why on earth should you think I intend to make it up with Winnie?" Christina's body trembled within his arm, and he was ashamed of his vehemence. "I'm getting as bad as Edward, shouting at you like this," he said apologetically, dropping his voice to a more reasonable level: "But you grieved me so. How could you think I meant to be reconciled with Winnie? How could *you* think so, Christina?"

Christina hesitated and looked away. "We haven't seen very much of you these last two years, Harry," she said.

"But, love, I've been so busy—I told you; I've been moving into Syke Mills."

"I know. But——"

"Why, surely, Chrissie," cried Morcar, suddenly struck by an astounding thought: "Surely you haven't thought I was growing less fond of you?"

Christina turned to him and buried her face in his shoulder.

"You *have* thought so! Good God!" exclaimed Morcar. "How could you, Christina?" He pulled off her hat, took her face between his hands and kissed her passionately, murmuring all the endearments of vehement love. "I shall never love anyone but you, I shall never love anyone as I love you," he said. "Christina! Don't you believe me?"

"Yes—yes," murmured Christina. "Yes, Harry, I do, of course I do. It's just that sometimes there is such a long time when I don't see you, and I never know when you will come again—if ever, as the children say. Sometimes I get bouts of not liking to leave the telephone in case you call. I don't go out all day—I sit and wait and listen." She broke into tears, and sobbed: "It's terrible to wait like that, Harry, it's terrible!"

Morcar, kissing her tear-stained cheek, was horrified, appalled, by this glimpse of the abyss of torment into which he had plunged her. "I've made you wretched, Christina," he said soberly. "It would have been better for you if you'd never met me."

"No, no!" cried Christina. She clenched her hand and beat against his shoulder frantically. "Don't say that, Harry! Don't say that!"

"Perhaps we ought to part," said Morcar, more and more disturbed by these evidences of her distress. "But we shan't," he added strongly. "I shall never give you up, Chrissie, never. I couldn't bear it."

"No—neither could I," breathed Christina. "I should die if you left me, Harry. Oh dear," she added, giving a strange smile and pressing her hair from her forehead in a habitual gesture of trouble: "That's not the right thing to say to you at all. I made up my mind never to say that kind of thing to you, Harry."

"And what other silly things have you made up in your silly little mind?" said Morcar in his fondest tone.

"To ask for nothing—then perhaps it won't all seem so wrong," murmured Christina.

Morcar exclaimed. To ask for nothing, to give everything—she was too generous to add the latter phrase, but it was implicit in the former. He felt a deep shame. Just then, however, Harington came up the stairs. The lovers drew apart; Christina sank to the settee and took a cigarette; Morcar examined their purchase—an oaken corner cupboard, black with age—attentively. The necessity for this furtive behaviour, this lying concealment, had never seemed so hateful and so degrading to him as it was in that instant.

Harington came in, peevish about some adventure on the Underground. He had recently taken silk and became more and more pompous and snobbish with each successful stage of his advancing career. He bent down and kissed his wife's cheek. Anyone with a single thought to spare from himself would have observed Christina's distress, thought Morcar angrily, but the barrister had no such thought, which was after all a mercy in the circumstances. Christina resuming her usual social grace mentioned that she was tired, that they had had no tea and needed drinks, that a friend had rung up on some photographic matter and asked Harington to ring him up before dinner.

Harington showed a disinclination to leave the hearth, where-upon to draw his attention from his wife Morcar asked him in a doubtful tone whether he considered the cupboard genuine seventeenth-century. Harington, on whose recommendation they had attended the sale, defended the purchase strongly, remembered an illustration in a book in his study of a similar cupboard and went downstairs to seek it. The moment he was out of earshot Morcar began:

"Christina, this can't go on. We must arrange an address where you can receive private letters from me. You must agree."

"No. I should have to destroy each one before I brought it home, and I might forget. I'm so careless nowadays."

It was true; her carelessness, her preoccupation grew on her; Morcar thought with horror that he now saw the reason, in the emotional disturbance and distress she had revealed. He paced up and down the room, bitterly angry with himself, his thoughts turbulent, confused. But there was no time to arrange them, to think of soothing phrases—there was never any time for anything but physical love, thought Morcar with a flash of insight, in illicit relationships. He halted in front of her.

"Christina, will you leave Harington and come to me?"

"You've been a long time saying that, Harry," said Christina softly, looking away from him into the fire.

"The more fool I. Will you come?"

"How can I? The children—you wouldn't want to hurt them."

"No, of course not. They're your children. Besides," added Morcar with truth: "I'm too fond of them for their own sake, especially Jenny. But it might not hurt them—I sometimes think they'd be happier with me. It isn't as though I couldn't provide for them," he concluded, not without some pride.

"But we shouldn't have them with us, Harry," said Christina

earnestly, her beautiful face turned up to his. "The law would see to that. Edward would see to that. He'd keep them away from me."

"Well—children grow up, they leave home, they marry. Harington couldn't keep them from you when they are over twenty-one. Will you come to me then?"

"What's the use, Harry my darling? You know you yourself are not free."

"I'll get free."

"I don't see how you can," murmured Christina softly. She turned to the fire again, and her body fell so naturally, so inevitably, with such an effect of custom, into the pose of grief-stricken resignation that the phrase *acquainted with grief* came into Morcar's mind and his heart swelled with sorrow for her.

"I reckon I'd better get a Counsel's opinion," he said in a savage tone.

Christina exclaimed. "Don't be angry with me, Harry," she pleaded, looking up at him, her blue eyes wide. "I can't bear it if you are angry with me, really I can't."

"My darling, I am never angry with you," began Morcar, but before he could repeat the assurance in more convincing terms, Harington entered the room.

Immediately Morcar reached Annotsfield next day he went to Nasmyth and consulted him on the prospects of obtaining a divorce from Winnie. The lawyer, who was obviously astonished by Morcar's revelations about his wife, shook his head unhappily and thought the prospects poor. On the one side, it was fifteen years or more since Winnie's alleged adultery, for which Morcar had no evidence save her admission to him—and this, made without witnesses, she could simply deny. On the other side, looked at from Winnie's point of view: her husband had given her evidence of adultery—but it was some twelve years ago and she had taken no action, thus condoning the offence; he had deserted her, true, but then he had supplied her with a steady income. If steps had been taken sooner …

"But at this stage it would all have to be done over again, I fear," said Nasmyth. "You would need to come together and live under the same roof, and then fresh evidence would have to be offered. Of course if your wife were willing to—er—assist, by bringing a suit, Mr. Morcar—indeed she will have to be willing, or I fear nothing can be done."

"We might buy her assistance with money," said Morcar grimly. Nasmyth gave an exclamation of professional horror. "Or on the other hand, we might not. It rather depends on the state of Prospect Mills, I'm afraid."

"As far as I know," said Nasmyth, looking down his nose: "Mr. Shaw is doing rather well just now. But I can in no case lend myself——"

"If Mr. Shaw is prosperous I shan't ask you to," said Morcar.

"If you came together and then parted," proffered Nasmyth.

"I couldn't risk that—she's too clever," said Morcar, thinking of the day when Winnie and he became engaged. "Even if I could stand it personally—which I couldn't for a moment."

"If you were to see your wife—in a solicitor's presence, of course," began Nasmyth.

Morcar shook his head.

"Then a letter should be written," said the lawyer.

Morcar hesitated, then agreed.

"You'd better let me compose it," said Nasmyth. "If you write it yourself, you know, you are sure to say something inadvisable."

Morcar again agreed.

The letter was duly composed, copied, signed and despatched.

While he waited for the reply Morcar lived in a strange dream-like world. The thought of undergoing a divorce suit was exceedingly unpleasant to him, the more so as he was sure that Winnie would contrive to make him look a fool. But when he considered that by these means he might eventually secure Christina for his wife, bring her and the two children to Stanney Royd to live, the foundations of his world seemed to disintegrate and form themselves afresh into something resembling an earthly paradise. He spent some of the nights when he could not sleep in planning a delicious little sitting-room for Christina on the second floor in one of the rooms with a row of mullioned windows. The view, an endless recession of folding hills, was very fine, if one waived a mill chimney or two towards Annotsfield. It should be a delicate feminine room, an adaptation of the old to the modern, in white and that strange twilight blue which he associated with Christina—fringed white taffeta silk hovered agreeably at the back of his mind. The children could be accommodated in this room and in that; Edwin should have a car in a year or two—there was ample space in the garage. Morcar began to imagine himself strolling round the Stanney Royd garden with his wife on his arm, discussing domestic detail, flower-beds, chintz, the need for extra hot-water-rails in the bathrooms. He would show Syke Mills to Christina, he would show her Annotsfield. Happy laughter in the background would indicate the presence of Edwin and Jenny, still calling him Uncle Harry but with the shadow of sullen fear lifted from their faces. It was possible—very possible, thought Morcar cheerfully—that he and Christina would have children of their own. That these happy dreams would be obliged to wait until Jenny reached the age of twenty-one, Morcar did not for a moment believe. Let him once be free to marry, and he would make Christina leave

248

her husband, come away with him; he could trust his strength of will to overpower her own, thought Morcar, smiling. Once she left her husband, Harington's pride would ensure the necessary divorce. Morcar paced his room, sleepless, through the night, revolving all these delightful plans, and rang up Nasmyth almost before his office opened next morning.

It was not Nasmyth, however, who eventually received Winnie's reply. One morning about a week after the despatch of the letter Morcar, entering Syke Mills, thought that his clerks eyed him queerly, and on going into his private office found the reason. On his blotter, open, lay a sheet of cheap notepaper headed *Hurstcote, Hurst Bank, Annotsfield*. The blood rushed to Morcar's face as he picked it up—how like Winnie to embarrass him by sending the letter to his business address, where all his letters were opened by his secretary; she had probably not even troubled to mark the envelope personal. He read in Winnie's vehement chaotic black-stroked hand: *I shall never divorce you, Harry. W. M.*

A black rage blotted Morcar's vision. His dreams of a happy life with a wife of his own choosing crashed to earth. A boy's ingenuous loyalty had impelled him to a decision which the cynicism of his middle years had confirmed, and this decision was not revocable except by a protracted struggle through acres of mud and scandal, with no certainty of reaching freedom at the end. That Winnie should bear his name, sign herself with his initial, seemed the last intolerable insult. As he tore the letter savagely into shreds Morcar experienced, beside his bitter disappointment at the blow to his personal happiness, a sense of humiliation, of shame. It seemed to him that he stood convicted lately of sins of omission for which all the prosperous order of Syke Mills could not atone.

27

Dictators and Diplomats

The Sunday air was full of martial music, and on their way to the Palatine the party continually encountered processions of small boys marching along with a ferocious air which sat oddly on their childish faces. Christina shuddered when she saw them.

"Italian boys now belong to the State from the age of six," she said. "Imagine taking little boys of six away from their mothers and teaching them to be soldiers!"

"Your little boy has been taken from his mother and taught to be a sailor," said Harington.

"But Edwin went because he wanted to go and he's seventeen, Daddy," objected Jennifer.

"I was joking, my dear Jenny," said her father coldly. "Seriously, Christina, these Wolf Cubs are similar in organisation to our own Boy Scouts."

"I don't think they are like Boy Scouts at all, Daddy," said Jenny clearly. "They don't have to do a good deed a day or anything like that. Do they?" she asked, appealing to the guide, who spread out his hands and said: "I do not know," in a reserved manner.

"It seems strange he doesn't know a detail like that," said Christina—though she admitted the guide's real erudition she disliked him because he fixed his glowing brown eyes on her too admiringly and held Jennifer's elbow too long when helping her over Roman ruins.

"Of course he knows, my dear," said Harington irritably: "But he doesn't wish to answer. How often have I to tell you that he is anti-James and therefore has to be particularly careful?"

"James" was the name some of the English people in Rome gave to Mussolini, so as to be able to express their views of him with safety and freedom.

"I shall be glad to be back in England again," said Morcar suddenly.

"I'm sorry you're not enjoying the trip. It's your own fault you came—art and antiquities don't agree with Annotsfield, I suppose," said Harington.

"I don't enjoy the antiquities much because I don't know the history they represent, but I enjoy the art better than you do, Edward," retorted Morcar. He had long since made up his mind that he would always call Harington's bluff and never accept an insult even in joke from him—he would not buy Christina's company by complaisance of that kind. Since he knew he would never break this rule he was always able to keep his temper and speak pleasantly, and Harington did not resent his sparring. "It's just that I don't care for dictators. I don't like being in a country where people daren't speak their minds."

"You'll probably find it necessary to overlook a few little details of that kind in post-war Europe," suggested Harington in his smoothest and most sophisticated tone.

"Why? I shan't if I don't want to. We don't believe in that sort of thing in England."

"Who told you that?" enquired the barrister.

"English history," interpolated Jennifer neatly.

At this moment the guide luckily began to elucidate the *Domus Liviae* in one of his admirable historic sketches—he was not the ordinary kind of guide one hired for a few lire a day through a travel agency, but an especially knowledgeable man of high attainments and high fees, whom Harington had secured for the benefit of his daughter.

Jennifer, now sixteen, was revealing herself as a quite exceptional daughter, in whom her father took great pride. In appearance she was beginning to be very handsome, even in her schoolgirl navy blue; her thick golden hair, brushed till it shone and arranged very simply, her aquiline features, not small but admirably shaped and proportioned, her pure clear fine skin, her large grey eyes, dark-lashed, spaced well apart, her generous mouth with its candid friendly smile, the lift of her head on her strong white neck, gave her a really noble, really classic beauty. She moved with a natural grace in a rather slow and quiet way except on the tennis-court and hockey-field, when she was swift and devastating. In addition to these advantages she seemed to possess a first-class brain; her career at school was exceeding even her father's expectations, and it was already settled that she should go up to Oxford. Harington's ambitions for his daughter varied, but were always high; at one time he thought she should marry an ambassador, at another that she should become a barrister. (He disapproved strongly of women in any profession, and especially in law, except when the woman concerned was his own daughter.) Hints on the subject of marriage were received by Jennifer with anger, on the subject of the law with grave consideration; she was in love with history at the moment, and had not decided yet, she remarked calmly, whether she would go in for law or no. It was Christina's present care to defer her husband's ambitions reaching crystallization before her daughter's; if this could not be achieved she feared a terrible contest of wills. She gave Morcar an imploring glance now; he interpreted it as he had interpreted many similar glances lately, as an appeal to him to keep Jennifer away from her father if he could manage it without appearing to do so. For unluckily Jennifer and her father seemed already to disagree on almost every subject. Jennifer had her mother's integrity and sympathy, her father's obstinacy; head-on collisions between them occurred every day. Morcar could not but admire the young girl's spirited resistance to Harington, for he often longed that Christina should show the same; at the same time he often felt vexed with Jenny because her independent manner troubled her mother so greatly. This morning things went fairly well except for a protracted argument on the character of Augustus Cæsar, whom Harington admired and Jenny denounced as mean and cold-hearted—a worse danger to liberty than bloodier tyrants, she observed shrewdly, because he made dictatorship seem respectable. Harington's pride in the capacity of his young daughter to make such an observation rather dimmed his irritation at being contradicted; he muttered a little but squeezed her arm in a friendly way—it was one of the moments when Morcar liked him.

As they were returning, talking in cheerful open voices, along the Via dei Cerchi, Morcar glancing around saw that the wide road had suddenly become very empty. Supposing that the lunch hour had arrived he glanced at his watch.

"Yes, you will be late, you will be late if you do not hurry," urged the guide.

In fact they had ample time to reach their hotel and Morcar turned to the man to make a mild remonstrance, when he saw that the guide had real fear in his eyes.

"It will be better to go this way," he said, suddenly plunging off the road into some excavated ruins which lay below road level on their left. "Circo Massimo. I pray you to hasten."

Morcar glanced around again; the road now held not a single passer-by with the exception of a series of men in great-coats with soft hats pulled over their eyes, who walked slowly along the edge of the pavement towards them, at about fifty yards distance each from the other. Similar men similarly patrolled the opposite side of the road. These men, who all carried their right hands in a most sinister fashion in their pockets, resembled so exactly the Chicago gangsters whom he saw when he took Edwin to the films that Morcar felt really alarmed for the safety of Christina and Jennifer, and hurried Jenny down the white wooden steps energetically. Christina meekly followed; Harington however hung back and began expostulations.

"I can't see another forum before lunch," he said.

"It is not that—I fear that Signor Mussolini is coming," whispered the guide, his olive face mottled. "He often drives this way, very quickly, towards the drained marshes, the Pontine."

"Oh, good! We can see him," cried Jenny, skipping up the steps again.

"No, no—it is not only difficult to see, but dangerous," urged the guide. "Last month an American lady stayed to see, and took out a camera. While she—she—" he sketched in gesture the act of getting a range—"she moved backward and tripped over a stone, and all these men"—he waved towards the plain-clothes bodyguard—"thought she made a diversion while others threw a bomb. She was arrested. They were not gentle with her. After a while she left Rome."

Harington's face changed, he took his daughter's arm and turned her down the steps again. The guide hurried them rapidly across the uneven ground between mounds of ruined masonry and broken pillars; they made a detour and reached their hotel without mishap.

The incident was only one of a number which spoiled Morcar's enjoyment of this Italian holiday and made him glad to return home. Otherwise his enjoyment would have been very great, for beside the pleasure of Christina's company and of sightseeing he found that he could learn much for his work, not only from some textile displays and trade journals which he discovered, but also simply from the forms and colours of the landscape, whether of country or city, in this joyous, vivid, southern land.

"Joyous! It's not joyous now," objected Christina when he mentioned something of this. It was the day before their departure; the party were sitting in Faragli's drinking tea; the music covered their conversation. "I have heard only one man singing in the streets since I came. In the pre-James era everyone sang."

"Don't make Harry more anti-James than he is already," Harington warned her.

"I'm already completely anti-James, anti-Hitler, anti-dictators of all kinds—nothing could make me more so," said Morcar, his feeling crystallizing as he spoke.

"Well—you're entitled to your opinion, of course," said Harington.

"I certainly am," said Morcar hotly. He was puzzled by the barrister's attitude of apparent tolerance for the James régime, which seemed to him incomprehensible; he could not believe it genuine, yet could perceive no motive which might dictate the pretence of it.

"If you're going to quarrel with all the dictators in Europe, you'll have a full plate," said Harington. "Germany's rearming, has already introduced conscription. If we want to support France against Germany—I say 'if,' mind—we shall need James at our side to help us."

"England won't ally herself with a dictator," said Morcar. Jennifer looked at him gratefully.

"She won't have anybody else but dictators to ally herself with, my lad."

"Let us hope this Stresa conference will tidy it all up," said Christina soothingly.

"If the conference finishes this weekend, as they say it will, we shall have an uncomfortable journey home, let me tell you," said Harington.

His forebodings were justified. The conference terminated officially that night, and as they journeyed north on Sunday evening, they saw that all the bridges and level crossings were guarded by soldiers—it was evident that high personages, possibly James himself, were expected. When the train drew in to Stresa, they found the station crowded with soldiers, flags of many nations waving, a military band playing; the scene was lively and colourful, and though their compartment was far in advance of the centre of activity, Morcar and Jennifer leant out and watched it eagerly. Presently to their amused delight the band broke into a florid version of *God Save the King;* it was clear, though invisible to their physical eye, that the train had taken aboard some British great ones from the conference—members of the Baldwin National Government then in power, with their attendant diplomatic staffs.

This became clearer still when the party attempted to procure some dinner. When they had managed to push along the now

256

crowded train to the dining-car, they found every place taken, though they had purchased tickets for the first service long before. Some ten or a dozen other travellers, mostly Italian, were in the same predicament. Harington expostulated angrily, Morcar mildly, with various waiters, and tipped them; they shrugged and bade the party return later, perhaps about nine. Hungry, tired and a trifle cross, they returned at the hour named, to find the car crammed as before, and the same ten or dozen other travellers still sharing their plight. They leaned against the side of the corridor, gazing wistfully into the car of which they caught glimpses from time to time as the door opened. After a long wait the head waiter suddenly beckoned; all surged forward, to find that only two seats were vacant. Edward and Christina were already seated in these when the shortage was discovered, so Morcar and Jenny returned to their previous waiting-places in hopeful mood.

The April evening outside was cool, for they were now in Switzerland, but the crowded dining-car had become very warm and the door was wedged open, so the waiting file had the doubtful pleasure of a continual view of the diners within. The prospect of watching others eat disheartened Jenny, and she turned with a sigh to gaze out of the window, but the night was falling and she turned back to the car. Immediately she became very still. Morcar himself was standing in a stiff and tense position.

A party of minor diplomats, unmistakably British by dress, manner and speech, filled all the seats within their view. The dishevelled napkins, the dirty glasses and plates on the tables before them, showed that they had long since dined; they sat comfortably smoking, drinking, ordering more drinks, with the hungry, queue outside well within their sight. At first Morcar simply could not believe his eyes—or his ears; either eyes or ears must be faulty, he thought, for English people, especially people in responsible positions, did not behave like that.

"They're a trifle lit up, Uncle Harry, if you ask me," murmured Jenny in his ear.

Morcar felt relieved; yes, they were drunk perhaps and did not see, or did not perceive the significance of, the hungry waiting line. It was bad enough certainly for English Foreign Office staff to be "lit up" in a public dining-car in a strange country, but not as bad as for them to be in their senses and deliberately keep hungry people waiting while they enjoyed an extra drink. If they realised the queue's plight, doubtless they would move at once. With this in mind Morcar fixed his eyes persistently on a man who faced him, in order to gain his attention. He achieved it, and was rewarded by a lift of the eyebrows and a conscious, exceedingly arrogant and perfectly sober stare.

Morcar coloured deeply. The incident was trifling, of course, but all the same he felt profoundly ashamed. The two ladies behind him, mother and daughter, the mother aged and resigned, the daughter explosively muttering; the young advocate with the sensitive dreamy face who was next in the line; the fat jolly old man, the thin young man who made tiresome jokes; the young girl with the aunt and the merry little boy with a red white and blue scarf, named Umberto; all these people, and more behind, wanted food and were being kept from it by a handful of selfish arrogant officials who, as all those waiting knew, for the word *Inglese* was often on their tongues, represented England.

"They don't represent me," thought Morcar angrily. "I'm damned if they represent me."

"Uncle Harry," Jenny was whispering earnestly in his ear: "Don't let us go in first. Let us go away and come back later, so that we shall be at the end of the line? I should like it better."

Morcar, bending to listen to her with his hands in his pockets, nodded gravely and the two moved away down the train. A gleam of hope lighted all the faces they passed, and the queue pushed up very promptly into their vacant places.

About half-past ten all the waiting passengers at last found seats in the dining-car. Unfortunately some of them, Jenny and Morcar amongst these, were due to descend in Lausanne in ten minutes' time, so in spite of the tired waiters' good-natured efforts, their meal proved scanty.

Morcar was very silent as the party stood on the dark platform while a porter passed their hand-luggage through the window. Jenny shivered a little in the night air; Christina proffered a scarf and urged her to draw her coat-collar closer; Harington asked whether she had made a reasonably good meal, why they had been so belated, and so on. Jenny's answers were monosyllabic, and Morcar did not come to her aid as usual. He was preoccupied, troubled, deeply uneasy. If those damned officials could behave like that over the small matter of keeping twelve people waiting unnecessarily to suit their own selfish pleasure, could they be trusted to behave properly over the great matters of European politics? A faint whiff of Biblical phraseology floated to him across the years; if they are not faithful in little things, he demanded, ought they to have charge of great things? They don't represent England, he said to himself angrily. They don't represent me. They don't see things as I see them. They don't intend what I intend. We need to keep an eye on them, and I haven't troubled to do so.

It was a small matter; but as Morcar said to himself, a small sound can wake a sleeper, and when he is once wakened, he is awake. Morcar never again felt the carefree irresponsibility, the happy certainty, about British foreign policy which he had hitherto taken for granted as his birthright.

28

David

"Mr. David Oldroyd to see you, sir."

"The boy who jumped off the train," thought Morcar, startled. He felt a repulsion to Francis Oldroyd's son, a reaction against the injustice of that feeling to a lad not responsible for his father's sins, a liking for the boy's spirit and a sympathy for him because he had to see a stranger sitting in his father's place, all at once. Morcar's private office was very different from what it had been in Francis Oldroyd's time; he had banished the mahogany and installed very large plate-glass windows, blue and white paint, and furniture of unvarnished oak, chromium and blue leather, in a fine modern design. "It will be painful for him," thought Morcar, saying aloud: "Show him in." He bent to finish the signing of some letters which the typist had brought in, and when he looked up David Oldroyd was already in the room.

It was not a schoolboy, however, who stood before him, but a young man fully grown, tallish, broad at the shoulders, slender at the hips, who carried himself without self-consciousness and smiled at him pleasantly. Dark crisp hair with chestnut glints, blue eyes, strong dark eyebrows and eyelashes, olive complexion, a head broad at the temples narrowing to a determined chin. His suit of dark grey check was quite as handsome as Morcar's, and he wore (of course, thought Morcar) an old school tie. In spite of this Morcar liked him at once, whoever he was, for he had a look of such lively intelligence, such merry friendliness, such vigorous gusto, that it was really very taking. But who was he? Morcar wondered.

"I hope this is not an inconvenient time for me to call, Mr. Morcar," said young Oldroyd, colouring under the older man's stare: "Perhaps I should have asked for an appointment? I chose Saturday morning because I thought you might be less engaged. But if it's inconvenient I'll take myself off immediately. Perhaps you'd let me come another time?"

He said *orf* where Yorkshiremen said *off* and used the broad *a* and other southern modes of pronunciation, like Christina, and altogether showed he had received what was known, thought Morcar with his customary scepticism on this subject, as a gentleman's education.

"Oh, it's quite convenient this morning," said Morcar. "I apologise for my surprise, but I was expecting the boy who jumped off the train."

"Ah! My romantic past," said David lightly. "But that's nearly six years ago now, you know, Mr. Morcar."

"I suppose it is," said Morcar. "You're ashamed of it now, eh?"

"No!" exclaimed David, colouring fiercely. "Why should I be ashamed? I'm not in the least."

Morcar indicated a chair and pushed forward the box of cigarettes.

"And what can I do for you?" he said.

"You'll think I'm a sentimental ass, no doubt," said David pleasantly. "But I'm collecting and editing family papers in my spare time—that is, when I have any. And I find we have no photographs of Syke Mills. I came to ask your permission to have some taken. I thought I should come at once, before major alterations are made in the premises. I'm too late in some respects already, I see," he added with an engaging grin, looking at the chromium.

"Would you like to come round now and pick your sites?" suggested Morcar.

"That's very kind of you," said David.

Although it was Saturday morning, the mill was, in the Yorkshire parlance, "throng"; each department showed a busy preoccupation which naturally did not diminish as Morcar approached. Every loom was clacking, the spindles hummed; the warehouse was full of bales, which a warehouseman was stencilling in black with the names of far-off cities. It was such second nature to Morcar to look at what was going on, finger the cloths stacked about, step up to the perching window and so on that he found himself doing it now as usual, though he tried to refrain. He spared young Oldroyd as much embarrassment as he could by introducing him immediately they entered a room, so that chance remarks of an awkward kind should not be made, but the Yorkshire nature is downright and several workmen asked him blunt questions as to the difference between the mill now and in his father's time. Even without these, Morcar could guess that the experience was a trying one for the young man, and that he could hardly command a cheerful smile and tone as they selected sites for his photographs.

"You're very busy," remarked David in a constrained tone as

262

they turned towards the office. "How many looms do you run altogether, Mr. Morcar?"

"Nigh on two thousand. You're collecting the family history in your spare time, you said. What do you do with the rest of your time?" asked Morcar kindly, to turn his thoughts.

"I'm a cloth manufacturer, Mr. Morcar. I've rented Old Syke Mill, you know, Old Mill it's called now—my family had it in the early days. It's small, of course."

"I began with a couple of looms in one room, myself."

"My cousins are helping me—the Mellors."

"Which Mellors are those?" said Morcar, running various West Riding genealogies over in his mind. He could not track down any manufacturers named Mellor who were related to the Old-royds, and made up his mind to ask his mother—she would know.

"They're great Trades Union men," said David.

"Oh!" said Morcar, astonished.

"I've been living with them up Booth Bank, you know, for the last six years," said David easily. "I run Old Mill on a profit-sharing basis."

"And what do your Trades Union cousins say to that?" said Morcar sardonically.

"They say I'm trying to vitiate the principle of collective bargaining and make my workers betray their class," replied David promptly.

Morcar looked at him, startled. He met young Oldroyd's lively eye, and suddenly both men laughed.

"I have an Old Mill social club—welfare, you know—but I'm told that's smearing the workmen's souls with capitalist jam," went on David with his merry look.

Morcar again gave a bark of laughter. "Aye, that sounds

familiar. I seem to have heard all that before," he said comfortably. "Why do you go on, then?"

"I'm entitled to my own views. It's my idea of a transition stage," said David. "However, I don't expect you want to hear all about that."

"But do you know anything about *cloth?*" demanded Morcar, frowning.

"I took a four year course in textiles at Leeds University, if you think that counts."

"Oh, you did."

They had by now returned to Morcar's private office, and on an impulse he picked up a pattern which lay on his desk and tossed it over to David. It was one of his latest Thistledowns, supple in tissue, delicate in its hues; brilliantly successful in the market.

"That's the sort of stuff I'm making here," he said.

"Yes—I know your Thistledowns, Mr. Morcar," said David, examining it. "Charming colours—charming. Delightful design. But I think we could beat you on texture."

"Eh?" barked Morcar. "What?" He coloured violently; he was astonished and also furiously angry. "I think you'd better make that good, young man—substantiate it," he said, in a loud angry tone, using one of Harington's words to lend dignity to his sentence. "Just show me the fabric that can beat my Thistledowns."

Young Oldroyd dived into a waistcoat pocket and produced a tiny scrap of material, which Morcar seized on avidly. It was a one-colour fabric suitable for women's coats; in colour an extraordinarily deep rich blue. Morcar at first thought it a trifle too bright to be tasteful—Christina would never wear it, he felt sure—but then it struck him that the colour would suit young Jenny to perfection. He felt the cloth between his fingers; it was extremely thick and rich, almost velvety, in the handle, yet feathery, supple, light. His expert eye perceived at once all the subtle techniques which had been employed to give the cloth its special merits: the combination of woollen and worsted yarn which kept the weight down; the rich shade to match the rich character of the cloth; the repeated cropping and raising necessary for the velvet pile; the vertical wave design which gave it bloom.

"Texture is what I'm especially interested in," said David in an apologetic tone. "You can hardly judge from such a scrap really, Mr. Morcar. Now if you saw the piece—there's no reason why you should be interested, of course."

"None whatever," said Morcar brutally. There was a pause. The two men eyed each other fiercely, neither allowing their glance to give way. "Damned young whelp," thought Morcar. "Throwing himself out of a train, running a profit-sharing business—and turning up with the best bit of overcoating for women I've seen outside my own mill for years," he added, his lifelong expertise in textiles compelling him to this honest estimate. He gave a sudden snort of laughter. "I'll come along with you and look at it now, if you like," he said. "Though you're a fool, bear in mind, to show your patterns to a competitor."

"I'll risk it," cried young Oldroyd, laughing.

A few minutes later Morcar was driving himself up the Ire Valley in the wake of David's old and rather rickety but well-engined sports car, which in a young man's style, thought Morcar forgivingly, was painted white, with scarlet wings. They turned off the main road and bumped down an uneven lane which still had something of the country about it, for there were fields on either side divided from the road by low stone walls. Halfway down David slowed to have a word with a young workman who was walking up. He was bareheaded, and his reddish hair bristled in the March sunshine; short, solidly built, fair-skinned, he listened to David with a reluctant air, resting large hands on the car door, glanced at Morcar rather sourly, but eventually nodded his head. "One of the Mellors, I expect," thought Morcar. The two cars drove on and stopped in the yard of a small mill standing on the bank of the river. "Good water," thought Morcar appreciatively, descending. The outside of the mill was in excellent condition; the walls well-pointed, the wood-work freshly white-painted, the windows clean, the door a handsome (and probably political, thought Morcar grimly) scarlet. They were met in the doorway by a young man of a different type; thin, dark-haired, wearing a brown cardigan and brown tie to a brown corduroy suit. He had a well-shaped head like David's and a lively ardent air; on a closer look he was seen to have features which were a thin edition of those of the young man in the lane, his hair too though dark had reddish gleams, so probably he was another Mellor.

"This is my cousin, George Bottomley Mellor," said David. "Mr. Morcar of Thistledown fame."

"Corduroy, my God," thought Morcar, shaking hands.

"I've been boasting to Mr. Morcar about our cloth, GB, and he doesn't believe me," explained young Oldroyd.

"I think you'll find you're wrong, Mr. Morcar," said Mellor, his brown eyes sparkling. "Yes, I think you'll find you're wrong there."

He spoke in a reasonable persuasive tone, as to a child, and Morcar felt obscurely irritated. "How does he know whether I shall be wrong or not," he thought, "when he doesn't know what Oldroyd has been boasting *about?*" Aloud he grunted non-committally, and said he should be glad to see the piece in question.

266

"I was just leaving, David," went on Mellor. "The buzzer sounded some time ago. Will you lock up? I thought of catching the next bus. Matthew's gone."

He spoke fluently, correctly, in a friendly open tone and with a better accent than Morcar's. "He's a nice chap," thought Morcar: "But young, opinionated and swollen-headed. Dogmatic . Theoretical. A hothead. Not a patch on young Oldroyd. Nice chap, though. But what a pair of children to run a mill!"

As he thought thus it struck him suddenly that of late all young men had begun to seem very young to him. Last time he had been alone with Christina, he remembered too, she had laid a caressing finger on his temples and told him the touch of grey there suited him. "Good heavens," thought Morcar: "I'm forty-five. Forty-six next October. I suppose I'm middle-aged." He shook off the strange and painful thought impatiently.

"Yes—we met him in the lane. Don't bother to stay unless you want to help me to show Mr. Morcar round," David was saying.

"I won't deprive you of that pleasure," said Mellor, smiling.

Accordingly Morcar was shown the blue piece, and taken round the mill, by Oldroyd alone. As Mellor had said, the buzzer had sounded, and as he had implied, the workpeople had left; the engine was not running, the premises were silent, and no mill ever looked at its best when its machinery was still. In spite of this disadvantage Morcar was constrained to admit that he could not have arranged Old Syke Mill better himself. The machines were new and good, their location with relation to each other sensible; useful gadgets—wooden slopes, handy shelves, wheeled tables, good lighting—ameliorated the working conditions and expedited the work; the cloths on the looms were good sound stuff and suited to modern requirements; altogether there was an air of cheerful and intelligent enterprise about the place which

Morcar liked. Long before they had finished their inspection, Morcar was asking questions and giving advice as if the owner of Old Syke Mill were a favourite nephew, while young Oldroyd displayed his arrangements and his problems quite as if asking for approval and guidance.

"It's no affair of mine, of course," said Morcar presently: "But where did you find the money to pay for all this?"

"It isn't all paid for," said David, colouring. "I only wish it were. I had a small legacy from my grandmother when I was a boy—luckily when we came to go into it we found I couldn't touch the cash until I was of age, so it escaped the crash period. I used it to get more from the bank, you know, in the good old way—or the bad old way, whichever you prefer."

"Ah, the banks! That's a big subject," said Morcar feelingly.

"When I was a student at Leeds I used to think I would never allow myself to owe a bank anything," said David ruefully. "But I couldn't have started this place without them—and I believe I can make it pay, so I had to take the chance."

"Didn't your cousins invest anything, then?"

"No; heavens, no. Matthew works here, that's all. GB is at Oxford at present. Ruskin, you know."

"Ah," said Morcar. He did not know, but could pick up information without betraying ignorance, rather faster than the next man.

"GB comes here a good deal during his vacations," continued David.

"Well, what about that piece?" said Morcar, who was tired of GB—he would tire of that young man very easily always.

The blue piece was altogether admirable.

"You've had some trouble with your dyer, to get a really blue blue like that," said Morcar, admiring it.

268

"You're right—I argued with him for weeks," said David, laughing.

"What do you call the blue?"

"I haven't given it a name."

"A name's a great help in selling," advised Morcar seriously.

He went on to recommend methods of making the quality of the Oldroyd product known. In doing this he gave David advice about merchants and markets which some of Morcar's competitors would have paid large sums to hear, and set him right on one or two over-naïve suppositions carefully.

"Well—I reckon you did right to leave that train, lad," said Morcar as they sat down at last in the neat little office. "Now what about a bite of lunch with me at the Club?" He looked at his watch and whistled ruefully. "Half-past two—won't be much left," he said.

"Come out with me—that is if you can put up with a cold meal for once," said David eagerly. "I have a cottage on the hillside here, up at Scape Scar."

Finding that the young man lived alone, so that there would be no household to upset by his intrusion, Morcar agreed. They left his car in the yard and set out in David's, drove up to Mar-thwaite, crossed the river by the new bridge and dashed up a narrow moorland lane, full of stones large and small and of so uncompromising a gradient that Morcar was quite glad not to be driving his own handsome car over it. They drew up in front of two cottages just under the brow of the hill. An Annotsfield Corporation sign, white on blue, labelled the cottages *Scape Scar*; they had long rows of windows in their upper storey, such as Morcar had often seen in cottages on the West Riding hills. David inserted a large cottage key and raised the sneck on the door; they came at once into a low room with a beamed ceiling, where a substantial cold luncheon was already set. David took additional china and silver from a corner cupboard for Morcar, and they began the meal.

"I haven't had this place long, so you must forgive me if I'm still houseproud. It's an ancestral abode, as they say—forbears of mine lived here in 1812. I lived in Booth Bank with my cousins before I came here, so this seems particularly pleasant."

"How did you like Booth Bank?"

"How does anyone like a small house in a row in a West Riding street with no indoor sanitation? It was hell," said David cheerfully. (Morcar remembered his first Saturday morning at Number 102 Hurst Road, and winced.) "I had to live with some relative till I was old enough to start at Old Mill—my father insisted on that—so I thought it might as well be the Mellors. A useful experience. My father was vexed but I couldn't help it."

"Do you live here alone, then?"

"Mr. and Mrs. Ackroyd next door 'do' for me," said David. "Ackroyd was my father's chauffeur, his batman in the last war. You may remember him."

"I do vaguely," said Morcar, who at once saw the trench on the day of Charlie's death—and the shell-hole and Charlie's dead face, and Jessopp's face with the jawbone sticking out. "But why the 'last' war?"

"Don't you think we're heading for another? Or don't you?"

Morcar moved uneasily. "I don't know," he said. "I don't like the way we back away every time our toes are threatened."

"And you think it invites further toe-treading? Just my view," said David. "I hate war, but we can't just let freedom and justice slip down the drain without lifting a finger to stop them."

"It's a great pleasure to me to hear you say so!" exclaimed

Morcar warmly. "I don't know much about these things, but that's just how I feel myself."

David rose and opened the cottage door, where a whining and scratching had become audible. A rough-haired, low-hung, black and brown dog with upright ears bounced in, wagging a rapturous tail; after greeting David ecstatically, it turned mild brown eyes on Morcar and advanced to sniff at him, eventually raising itself and laying a pleading paw on Morcar's arm.

"Down, Heather, down, old boy," said David. "Please don't give him anything to eat. He's a mixture of Lakeland terrier and Scotty," he replied to Morcar's question.

"Mongrels always have the nicest dispositions, I'm told," said Morcar, stroking Heather's head and enjoying the pleasure in the dog's beautiful loving eyes.

"Yes—look at the English," agreed David. "Shall we have coffee upstairs? I live mostly in the loom-chamber because of the view."

Somewhat mystified, Morcar followed him up the narrow stairway into the room with the long row of mullioned windows. The view was certainly fine; one could see down the winding length of the industrial Ire Valley almost to Syke Mills, or up the valley to the rocky moorland. The furniture of this room was old, he noted, and in cottage style: an oak chest, an oak settle, a large round table, a couple of spindle-back chairs, a wooden clock on the wall. The table was covered with papers, some old, with seals attached as if they were property deeds, some new, typed in the modern fashion.

"I was just making out the family pedigree," said David. "But I think this would probably interest you most." He turned over the papers and handed Morcar a long narrow book backed in crumbling whitey-brown paper. "It's an account book for 1728—the

271

oldest Oldroyd document in my possession. The Old-royds were cloth-manufacturers then, as you see."

Morcar turned the leaves slowly, in astonishment. *Two packs of wooll*, he read; *woad—madder—teazles*. They were items which figured often in his own accounts.

"And is this quite genuine?" he asked. "Was cloth really made in the West Riding in those days?"

"My dear Mr. Morcar!" exclaimed David quickly, colouring. "Cloth has been woven in the West Riding certainly for seven hundred years and possibly for twelve hundred. Excuse me," he said in a tone of apology, breaking off: "The honourable antiquity of the cloth-trade is rather a hobby-horse of mine, and I'm apt to gallop away when people question it. But you've read all the books on the subject, of course."

"No, I can't say I have," said Morcar slowly. "In fact, I can't say I've read any of them." He turned the pages of the account-book, fascinated. *Note that a pack of wooll as many pounds as it cometh to so many pence it is a lb*, he read. "That's still true of course," he thought, "for wool-packs still hold two hundred and forty pounds—as many pounds in weight as there are pennies in a pound sterling. I suppose the old chap found it useful when he was costing his cloth."

"I've masses more of a similar kind," said David. He threw back the lid of the oak chest, and revealed a tumbled mass of books and papers. "I'm going to sort them all out," he said, speaking eagerly. "When we left Syke Mills a lot of these were turned out and put to be burned in the boiler fire, but luckily I rescued them. And then I got some from a great-uncle who took an interest in these things—he left me his papers when he died. They're really interesting. Here for instance is a copy of a letter from an ancestor to Richard Oastler. Here's an Order Book for

1835. See the tiny patterns stuck at the side? *Wanted by waggon immediately*— that has a modern ring. Here's the poster of a meeting about settling spinners' accounts. This is the correspondence about the first steam engine in Old Mill, with Boulton and Watt, you know."

"Oastler!" thought Morcar. "Boulton and Watt! Loom-chamber! Hell!"

"I have the modern accounts too," went on David, nodding towards a row of tall ledgers in the low bookcase: "A sorry tale they tell! But I'm boring you, Mr. Morcar—I'm apt to forget that everybody doesn't share my zeal for the antiquities of the textile trade." He made to close the lid of the chest.

"Nay," said Morcar slowly, stretching out a hand to prevent him: "It's very interesting."

As soon as he had spoken he realised that he had accented the last word on the *est* syllable, a Yorkshirism of which he knew he was sometimes guilty, for Christina teased him about it. He looked quickly at David to see if the young whippersnapper were laughing at him. David was indeed smiling, but with a look of such friendly candour, such gentle affection in his agreeable young eyes that Morcar was not offended but encouraged.

"I'm a West Riding manufacturer, you see," explained Morcar. He sounded hesitant, laborious, because he was speaking with a sincerity he had hitherto used only to Charlie and to Christina, in the whole course of his life. He intended to express that he had no pretensions to be a gentleman or a scholar, but only to make good cloth, and he saw by David's nod that he was understood.

"Everything about the West Riding textile trade is dear to me," said David. "Its past, its present and its future."

"I've been too much concerned with its present only, perhaps," said Morcar slowly, fondling Heather's ears. "With my own small part in the present, perhaps I should say." He hesitated, and added: "I should like to learn about its past, though. But I must be off!" he exclaimed, as the clock struck an hour and he was visited by a mental picture of his laden desk.

"I'll turn the car before you get in—it's rather awkward," said David, hurrying downstairs. "No, Heather, you can't come."

As they drove through Marthwaite village David suddenly checked the car.

"Look at that," he said.

A poster outside the village newsagent's read: *Germany's sensational Rhineland move.*

Morcar exclaimed.

"I'll hop out and get a newspaper," said David.

They bent over the Annotsfield evening paper together. *German Troops Re-Enter Rhineland: Sensational Move by Hitler This Morning: Germany Sheds Last Shackles of Versailles.*

"That next war we were discussing is beginning now," said David grimly.

"Aye! They're at it again. I reckon I shall soon have to get down my old tin hat," said Morcar.

They looked at each other and knew that they were friends.

29

West Riding

It seemed to Morcar that he spent the next twelvemonth walking the West Riding and listening to David Oldroyd's talk about its long and fascinating story.

David knew every mile of the West Riding countryside— every fold of the sweeping hills, every high and lonely purple moor, every outcrop of sombre rock, every bracken-covered hillside. He knew every wood whether of oak or pine, every stretch of sweet short springing turf, every clear brown foaming stream, every waterfall, every mossy stepping-stone. It sometimes seemed to Morcar that David knew also all the dancing delicate mauveblue harebells, the buttercups and daisies, the pink and white clover, the tall spiky purple thistles, the nettles of acrid scent, the red sorrel, the blatant dandelions, the crimson foxgloves, the white hemlock, which edged the sloping fields; the long bulrushes with thick black heads which lined the becks, the tiny green fronds of the ferns which clung to the niches of the rough stone walls. David knew all the lean tough grasses which battled

275

undaunted with the wild bleak winds. David knew every lane and every path, whether by moor or fell, by wood or stream— nay, thought Morcar with affectionate amusement, even the dog Heather knew them, and would pause expectantly at some almost invisible moorland track or gap in the wall. David knew the soaring larks singing in the blue, the black and white lapwings which somersaulted through the spring twilight squeaking their harsh leathern cry, the grouse which cried *go-back go-back* amongst the heather; he knew the black-faced moorland sheep with their defiant hazel eyes, their fleeces shaggy and ragged in spring, close-fitting jackets of fawn velvet after shearing-time.

Morcar had seen these things, more or less, all his life but had not paid them much attention; now David made them into a design, a pattern.

The pattern was this. The hills of the Pennines rolled down the centre of England in interlocking spurs, which formed a chain. The West Riding links of this chain were part white lime-stone, part hard dark millstone grit, coated with peat, fringed with coal, pocketed to the south with iron ore. Millstone grit, said David, cannot grow rich grass or deep abundant grain. It cannot pasture many cattle, it cannot grow fields of waving corn; oats, and the sparse rough grass short-haired sheep can feed on are, with heather, its only produce. But coal and grit country are rich in springs and streams. So it is that our hillsides are seamed by innumerable hillside cloughs, countless narrow winding valleys, each with its tumbling thread of water. In the West Riding, said David, you are hardly ever out of the sound of tumbling water. And so these rough, sweeping interlocking hills of millstone grit, crowned with dark rocks and purple heather, with their cold turbulent becks rushing swiftly down from the moorland through the fields to the little river in the steep wooded valleys below—these, said David, are the cause of the textile trade. Wool and soft water; coal and iron when you find you want them; no good living to be had by farming alone; these, coupled with human invention and human need, add up to weaving cloth.

The story is indelibly stamped, said David, on the West Riding land and the West Riding life.

Look at these grey stone homesteads scattered about the folds of the hills, with the long row of windows in their upper storey. Those are the homes of the hand-loom weavers of old; their looms stood in those rooms with many windows, built thus to give ample light to the loom-chamber. Scape Scar is such a weaver's cottage; my Bamforth ancestors wove cloth there two hundred, three hundred years ago, said David; here are the house-deeds, here is a will bequeathing the loom and the spin-ning-wheel, to prove it. They wove a piece or two a month and grew oats on their scrap of land, from which they made oatmeal porridge and oatcake; this fine old chest is a meal-ark, said David; you find meal-arks mentioned often in the old diaries. As for oatcake—well, in this water-colour sketch on my wall, dated 1816, a cottage woman is baking the spongy brown ovals; we still eat and enjoy it to-day—here on our supper-table to-night you see it, crisp and brown.

The weaver carried his piece on his shoulder, left arm akimbo, down the many moorland miles along tracks like these, said David, to market; when he grew richer, perhaps he had a horse or a donkey. My ancestors carried their pieces thus ten miles down the Ire Valley to Annotsfield; they bought a stone or two of wool there and carried it back to Scape Scar and sat down to spin and weave again. The wife spun for her husband.

Look at these beautiful old single-span bridges across the

valley streams, said David; those are packhorse bridges; their parapets are built thus low so that the cloth across the back of the horse should swing clear of them.

In the old days, said David, the cloth was displayed on a church wall or a bridge in the towns; on the bridge in Leeds; on the church wall in Bradford and Annotsfield.

Oh, the cloth trade is much older than *that*, said David; there's a letter in the British Museum from Charlemagne in 796 to the king of the northern midlands in England, asking that woollen cloaks sent to him might be made of the same pattern as used to come to him in the olden time—it's a pity the first record of West Riding textiles is about woollen goods not up to sample!

Well, yes, perhaps that is a bit far-fetched as to date, said David; but old Yorkshire law cases, way back in the thirteenth century, speak of men named Webster and Walker and Lister, which as you know mean weavers and scourers and dyers of cloth. Webster isn't a common name in the West Riding now? No—there were too many weavers after a while to use it as a distinguishing appellation. Tax records in 1396 show that there were then three hundred and fifty-seven cloth-makers in Yorkshire, not counting those in York.

Yes, there are records. You see there was a fourpenny tax on each piece of cloth offered for sale, said David; it started in 1353 and went on for about four hundred years, I seem to remember. A lead seal had to be affixed to the cloth to show the tax had been paid. In 1468 nearly five thousand cloths were sealed thus in Yorkshire. The clothiers were always having rows with the king's tax-gatherers about this tax; they petitioned the king about it continually. In 1611 there was a terrific bust-up about it; suspecting that some manufacturers were evading the tax, a tax-collector broke into some bales of cloth travelling by pack-horse to London, while the drivers were sleeping the night at an inn on the Great North Road. The drivers woke up sooner than was expected, and there were heads broken.

Of course by that time some of the weavers had grown rich by weaving and become yeomen clothiers; they farmed several acres of land, ran three or four looms, dressed their own cloth, employed weavers and croppers and apprentices and paid them wages. Your own house, said David, Stanney Royd you know, is the home of a yeoman clothier. I should think your study and Mrs. Morcar's bedroom were the loom-chamber.

As a matter of fact, said David, the owner of Stanney Royd in the seventeenth century was quite a notable figure during the Civil War; he was a great Parliament man, you know—sent lots of money to support the Parliament's army against King Charles, which was fighting then in Yorkshire. Some people say he was present at the siege of Bradford.

Oh, that was in 1643, said David; the Royalists besieged Bradford, fired down the streets with cannon; the Puritans, clothiers and weavers chiefly, hung woolsacks on the church tower to protect the men defending it. I've seen an old print of the incident.

Yes, it's still the same church tower; you ought to look at it next time you go to Bradford.

Yes, we've played our part in English history. Usually a stubborn, independent, freedom-loving part. We rebelled against William the Conqueror, under an earl of your name; we fought the tyranny of King Charles; we're nonconformists, argumentative, hard-headed, practical, stiff-necked. As Charlotte Brontë said, we're difficult to lead and impossible to drive. We're stubborn folk, we West Riding clothiers.

As you say, the Civil War upset the textile trade a bit, agreed

David; they suffered strong blasts of adversity, as they put it in those days.

You're right; we've met with a good many blasts of adversity, one way or another, through the centuries; but we've survived, you see. We've adapted ourselves, given a new turn to our product, recovered our markets and prospered.

Look at this Piece Hall; it's one of the earliest. Our own Cloth Hall in Annotsfield came thirty years later. It was taken down in the 1890's, you know; the Annotsfield Free Library is built on its site. All the Piece Halls and Cloth Halls in the West Riding were built in the eighteenth century. By that time the cloth trade was far too great for church walls and bridges to serve as markets.

The Halls usually had a large central room for the market, with many small rooms where the manufacturers kept their cloths. The bargaining was conducted in whispers.

Yes, the Yorkshire clothiers still sent cloth to London by pack-horse train to be sold there; they sent it overseas too—there are grumbles about missing the convoy, which go on for a couple of centuries.

Old Sam Hill, who lived in this ruined house in this hilltop village where we are now standing, sold cloth all over Europe. Holland and Belgium and France of course, but even as far as Russia. Yes; uniforms for Russian soldiers. Have you never seen his letter-book? His pattern book? Oh, you should; let's drive down to the museum and look at them. Sam was a tough *hombre*, said David, smiling, a real West Riding individualist; you should read his letters when the quality of wool and soap he bought didn't quite please him. Vitriolic. He had a thirty-thousand pound annual turnover. Not bad for 1737. I should think he employed half a hundred weavers, who wove the yarn he provided on their own looms in their own homes, for wages. The Domestic

System, you know; Defoe gives a marvellous description of it in his *Tour through England*. It was about that time the Scape Scar weavers, Bamforths, began to weave for my other ancestors for wages. This paper-backed folio gives a list of William Oldroyd's "out-weavers" for 1759; there's a Jonathan Bamforth and a Matthew Mellor amongst them.

Heather! Come here, Heather! Come here, sir! Oh, well, we may as well go down the lane, since he's so determined. Heather's quite an historian; he knows all the sites of historical interest, he's visited them with me so often. This one is really rather interesting. See the water-wheel? This is one of the first mills in the West Riding to run textile machinery by water-power. The use of water as power drew the textile industry from the hillsides to the valleys, where the streams were broader and stronger. It was the beginning of the Factory System.

Oh, from 1790, 1800 or so onwards.

Of course, my own mill, Old Syke Mill, was the first in the Ire Valley to run frames by power, said David.

Didn't you know that? Oh, yes; an ancestor of mine was murdered by his workpeople for introducing cropping-frames run by water-power. Shot. Just at the top of the lane. They took an oath and called themselves Luddites. They attacked other mills, too—quite a large-scale unrest. 1812. A horrible lot of hanging to finish with.

The Industrial Revolution? Well, it depends whether you date it from water-power or from steam. First they invented textile machines to run by water-power, then they discovered the power of steam, then they harnessed the steam to the machines. My ancestors put a steam engine into Old Mill about 1817. Steam made the West Riding the seething smoke-blackened forest of mill chimneys it is to-day. Let's hope electricity

281

will take the smoke away again.

This is John Wood's house—you know, the manufacturer who supported Richard Oastler in his fight to free children from working long hours in the mills. In fact, said David, it was Wood who persuaded Oastler to take up the cause. They dined together one night when Oastler had been making an anti-slavery speech about the West Indies, and Wood told him there was slavery nearer home which needed attention. Yes, I'm sorry to say, children were working fourteen or fifteen hours a day, from seven or eight years old. They passed a Ten-Hour Bill eventually and put a stop to it. One of the earliest examples of industrial welfare legislation.

This is the inn where the first weavers' union was formed. My cousins' grandfather was one of the founders, explained David. They called the first textile strike in 1883, you know. He's my grandfather as well, you see. Yes, I'm pretty well mixed up with the West Riding textile industry—but then, we all are; I daresay if you investigated your own ancestry you'd find you were pretty much in the thick of it.

"It often seems to me," remarked David diffidently one day a few months later: "That we're beginning another industrial revolution now. If so, I should like to take part in it."

"You mean we're beginning to use another form of power-electricity?"

"No. I mean the way the industry is run," said David. "You'd probably think my ideas on the subject quite fantastic, but I should like to talk to you about them some time."

"I shall be glad to listen," said Morcar truthfully.

"Could you bear my cousins to be present at the discussion?"

"Why not?" said Morcar staunchly, though with much less pleasure.

30

Argument of the Century

"Well, here we all are. I told my father you smoked cigars, Mr. Morcar, and he's sent this box. I hope they're all right."

"It's very kind of Colonel Oldroyd," said Morcar stiffly.

"Cigarettes behind you, Matthew. Pipes for you and me, GB."

The four men were sitting in the Scape Scar loom-chamber; Morcar in a spindle-back chair by the hearth, the two Mellors on the settle, David sprawling on the oak chest by the windows. The hour was dusk, the time was the spring of 1937; the lights down the Ire Valley sparkled agreeably.

"I shall now set the ball rolling and horrify all present," continued David, "by stating my belief that Trades Unions and Employers' Federations are a pair of horrible legacies from the nineteenth century. I say horrible advisedly. Bodies which exist to secure material advantages for themselves by imposing regulations on somebody else are in my opinion horrible. Trades Unions and Employers' Federations both do that. I think an industry should be organised *as a whole*, with two objects. One: honourable service of the community by its products. Two: honourable living for all who produce the product."

"Well, my dear David," said GB in his pleasant reasonable tone: "You can have your organisation any time you want, if only enough of you vote for the Labour Party. Nationalisation is the answer to your problem."

"You and my father, GB, on opposite sides, can always be relied on to toe the party line."

"Russia," began Matthew Mellor ardently.

"Aye," cried Morcar, interrupting him: "And without seeing what they're toeing. Sorry," he added hastily, with a glance at the Mellors: "But I understand we are to handle this problem with the gloves off."

"By all means," agreed GB pleasantly. "Far better. The only way to any real progress. But come now, David, you know that Trades Unions were and are absolutely necessary to combat bad working conditions and secure proper rates of pay."

"Oh, I daresay," agreed David. "In past and present times I agree they may have been necessary. But I'm talking about the future. Wars have been necessary sometimes in the past, but I don't like them, I want to get rid of them. In the same way, I hate this tearing of the textile trade into halves."

"Well, you can blame capitalism for that," said GB with a trace of acerbity.

"Yes, that's true. As soon as a man has to weave on another man's loom the interests of the two are different. How are we going to get those two interests together again?"

"He's told you," said Matthew in a loud peevish tone: "By nationalisation."

"It's the only thing, David," said GB. "You may as well admit it. I suppose your idea is some kind of Guild Socialism?" he added politely.

"Guild Socialism has been tried once already in the textile trade," said David.

"When? Of course you're much better informed about textile history than any of the rest of us," said his cousin.

"Oh, in York, in the middle ages," said David. His tone was rueful as he went on: "Unfortunately it didn't work—or rather, it worked too well. The innumerable regulations about payments, apprentices, numbers of looms, weights and dimensions of cloth and so on, kept the York clothiers too busy keeping them to make any cloth. The York trade just decayed and vanished, and the industry journeyed west, to the tough, hard-headed individualists of the West Riding."

"There you are, you see," said Morcar, delighted. "That's just what I've always said. Individual talent and enterprise are what make progress. Over-organisation kills. Your whole argument is vitiated by your own showing. And so is yours," he added, turning to the Mellors.

"If you look at Russia," began Matthew, bristling angrily, while GB replied in his reasoning tone:

"No The York failure is only one of the facts which have to be remembered. There are others, you know, Mr. Morcar, such as low wages and bad conditions. Surely everybody nowadays would rather never wear cloth again, for instance, if it involved the awful child labour of the early nineteenth century. If we can't have a certain product without exploiting the worker, then we must give up the product."

"That's understood," said David.

"Of course it's understood," said Morcar angrily. "I don't want to exploit the workers, good heavens. I want to pay them a good wage for reasonable hours. But there comes a point when wages are so high and output so low that the price of my product is too high for the overseas market to pay. Then what happens?"

"The industry as a whole should decide how to tackle that problem," said David.

"The State should decide it," said Matthew.

"Life or death, comfort or starvation, for the workers shouldn't depend on a private person," amplified his brother.

"My own comfort has always depended on me," threw in Morcar. "But the point is—"

"Your life is fascinating, Mr. Morcar, but thoroughly antisocial," GB told him with a smile.

"I don't see that," said Morcar, colouring. "I've made these charming cloths which weren't made in bulk before. Millions of people—not by any means necessarily rich people—wear them with pleasure. The price is lower because I've popularised them and given them a bigger sale. I pay proper wages and give employment to hundreds of workers."

"But it's all done from the wrong motive," smiled GB.

"You must excuse me for thinking that a cloth trade is a trade to make cloth," said Morcar, getting hot, partly with anger, partly with the unaccustomed effort to express himself on abstract subjects. "Now look," he went on: "There's just two things I want to make quite clear. The first one is this: About the profit motive. I don't give a damn for the profit motive really."

"*You* don't, Mr. Morcar!" exclaimed the younger Mellor, his brown eyes sparkling with polite and amused incredulity.

"Tell me another!" invited Matthew with derision.

"Of course I want to earn a decent living wage, the same as everybody else," said Morcar. "I want to support my family, I want to be able to travel and do as I like. But I don't really care about heaping up an immense fortune. If I had children of course, perhaps it might be different; I should want to give them the best that could be had—same as everybody else. But profit isn't what I really work for—I do it for the fun of the thing."

"He means he'd be perfectly willing to run his business not for private profit," explained David, "provided that——"

"Provided I were free to run it as I liked," said Morcar.

"If public money and public interest are concerned, no one person can be free to run anything as he likes," said GB, frowning disapprovingly.

"That's just what I'm saying," argued Morcar. "All the fun goes in a controlled industry. I like there to be lots of separate units, doing as they like."

"I expect the Saxon thanes in the Heptarchy said that when Alfred the Great wanted to unite and organise England," remarked GB.

"I don't know history as you do," said Morcar impatiently. "I'm not a scholar, I haven't had your advantages. But I do know the textile trade. I've worked in it since I was sixteen. I love wool, I love colours," said Morcar, getting excited: "Designs are a real pleasure to me. And I love managing the finance and taking a bit of a risk, I love pulling off a good order. There'll be no fun in industry if it's all to be nationalised, regulated, if we can't move a step without filling up five forms, if we can't use our own originality and judgment. You can take the profit and I shan't call out, but take the freedom and the fun's all gone. Nay, if industry's to be like that I shan't be in it. I'd rather go to sea. And if you think you won't miss me and my like, if we leave textiles, you're wrong, for you will. Originality, individuality, that's the mainspring of a trade like ours. I've got it. Will your nationalised manufacturers have it? I say they won't, they can't."

"There's a good deal in what you say, Mr. Morcar," said GB judicially: "But you have to remember that industry is what you describe with such horror, already, for your workmen. It's regimented as far as they are concerned. They have no scope for originality, individuality, enterprise, in minding a machine."

"There's not much fun in it for us!" supplemented Matthew emphatically.

"Then there ought to be; they ought to enjoy output as much as I do."

"No, they can't," objected David.

"Nathan does."

"It's no use pretending that dull jobs aren't dull," said David.

"Nationalising won't make 'em any brighter."

"Yes, it will, because the motive for them will be different," said GB.

"Serving the State," said Matthew, turning his round blue eyes resentfully on Morcar, "instead of a private employer."

"Besides, there'll be a chance for the workers to rise to administrative positions. There isn't now."

"I rose all the way by my own efforts."

"Not quite all the way," said GB judicially. "You had a grammar school education and some small capital—or access to it."

"There are never many jobs at the top, think on. I'm not saying the universe is arranged perfectly," said Morcar with a good deal of heat. "I'm just saying what I feel. Lively intelligent chaps used to like to go into industry but now they don't, they go into the professions if they can, because they're so hampered in industry with these everlasting regulations." It occurred to him that even the Mellors were an example of this; the lad with brains, GB, took scholarships and went to Oxford and would go off to teach or be a Trades Union official or something; Matthew was left to go into textiles because he wasn't clever enough for anything else. "It's a bit hard on the textile industry," said Morcar with feeling, considering the pair on the settle. Fearing he had made his thoughts about them too clear, he went on rapidly: "And now for my second point. I'm sick and tired, and all employers are sick and tired, of always being the villain in the piece. Whatever the employer does nowadays is wrong. If he's a bad employer, well naturally he's blamed, but if he's a good employer, he doesn't get any credit. He's accused of interfering with the workers' private lives, trying to vitiate the principle of collective bargaining, make the workers betray their class, and all that sort of claptrap. The fact is, you Labour chaps don't *want* good employers—you'd rather have bad ones that you can make a song and dance about. Tell us what you want employers to do. Go on, now. Tell me."

"We don't want any private employers at all. We want industry to belong to the State. We want a classless society," said Matthew tensely.

"And where do I come in, eh? Men of my kind, I mean? The chaps with the ability and the enterprise?"

"Nowhere!" cried Matthew in a high fierce tone, his upper lip quivering. "Such as you ought to be liquidated."

"Well, that's candid, anyway," said Morcar grimly. "Now we know where we are."

"Come, come!" said GB soothingly. "You will manage a mill, of course, in the newly nationalised industry."

"Thank you for nothing," said Morcar angrily. "We're going round in circles in this argument."

"Yes—because that's the crux of the problem, don't you see," urged David. "It's the problem of the century. The relation of the individual to the community. How to keep freedom for the individual without hurting the community, and how to serve the community without hurting the individual. In totalitarian states the community exploits the individual. In capitalist states individuals are free to exploit each other. How are we to combine the two objects of industry? How are we to combine freedom and security? These are the real problems of the twentieth century."

"I wish you joy of solving them," said Morcar.

"Well, I mean to have a damn good try," said David. "The textile trades in northern England were the first to be mechanised, the first to start the Industrial Revolution. I should like the wool textile trade to be the first to solve the problem in the new social industrial revolution."

"You're daft, lad," said Morcar cheerfully.

"We agree on that, anyway," said Matthew sourly.

"But it's a nice kind of daftness," said GB in his pleasant reasonable tone. "He means well."

"We all mean well," said Morcar.

"I'm not so sure of that," growled Matthew.

"It depends whom we mean well *to*" said GB. He avoided looking at Morcar, while Matthew glared at him.

"Oh, to hell with them," thought Morcar. But he felt uneasy when he saw that David too was avoiding his eyes, gazing down the Ire Valley with a grieved and thoughtful air.

31

Meeting

"It's very good of you to help my boy, Morcar."

"Not at all," said Morcar stiffly.

He was bored and uncomfortable. He did not like being Colonel Oldroyd's guest for the weekend at the Southstone-on-Sea hotel where he and his wife and daughter now resided. (Nor did Morcar like the hotel much; it was not as luxurious as those to which he was now accustomed.) He had only accepted the invitation with the greatest reluctance, because he felt it was his duty to come. It was true that he had tried to help David—recommending him to merchants, speaking well of his prospects at the bank, commending his products when any chance presented itself, and so on. It was therefore natural and proper, it was only right, admitted Morcar, that the boy's father should want to know what kind of man it was into whose hands, so to speak, his son had fallen. A visit to Francis Oldroyd was proper and must be paid.

But it was a nuisance. Sitting in a deck-chair on the Promenade near a bandstand, listening to light music played by chaps in frogged coats, with Francis Oldroyd at his side, was not Morcar's idea of a pleasant Sunday morning. The scene was pleasant enough, of course; the cliff gardens were thronged with an upper-class holiday crowd in light suits and bright dresses; the sun shone; the grass was exceedingly neat and green, the flowerbeds were colourful; far below, the blue-grey waters of the English Channel were crinkled by a slight breeze; shipping in great variety passed along the horizon and afforded topics for conversation. Still, Morcar was bored. It was a nuisance having to sit here, to walk slowly beside Colonel Oldroyd, whom rheumatism contracted in the trenches in the last war or an old wound or both condemned to a limp and a stick, to behave genteelly, to listen politely to talk in which he was not at all interested, to be urbane with a man he despised and disliked. Above all it was annoying to waste here a day which he might have spent with the Haringtons. He had succeeded in minimizing the visit by not coming down till tea-time on Saturday, and by explaining that it was absolutely essential for him to leave soon after lunch to-day, in order to catch the evening express to Yorkshire and be at Syke Mills first thing on Monday morning. The thought of the evening express comforted him now; only a few more hours, he thought, and steeled himself to these hours as a test of endurance.

The band now played the National Anthem, and all the deck-chair occupants of course rose to their feet. Francis Oldroyd sprang up and stood rigidly to attention with that over-emphasis which former officers of the aristocratic, conservative, gentry type always gave to this action, thought Morcar irritably. The Colonel's quick movement dislodged his stick, which fell to the ground. Morcar found himself obliged, from the merest human decency, to pick it up. It was a handsome dark cane bearing a silver band engraved with its owner's name and address.

"Thanks. David gave me this," said Francis Oldroyd, smiling.

"There is that in his favour," admitted Morcar to himself. "He's fond of the boy."

The two men walked slowly away in the direction of the hotel. Oldroyd was a fine handsome fellow still, admitted Morcar grudgingly. In spite of his limp he carried himself well; his red-fair hair had thinned but he was fresh-complexioned still and had not lost his good slender figure—indeed he appeared to weigh rather less than of old—nor his attraction for women. His clothes were a trifle worn, but of excellent cloth and cut; he wore his hat at a debonair angle. His manners and speech were those of a gentleman, while Morcar to his fury found his own accent growing more and more north-country with his growing boredom. "Still, he's fond of the boy," Morcar reminded himself. "Treasures his presents."

Oldroyd's thoughts had meanwhile taken a different turn, along the lines of a different association, to the cause of his lameness.

"You and I were in the front line together, were we not?" he said. "Just for a short period. I remember when your friend was killed—Corporal Shaw, wasn't he? A very bright keen lad. At Ypres in 1915, wasn't it?"

"Aye. Boesinghe," replied Morcar shortly.

"He was dead when you brought him in, I remember."

"I remember you thought so."

"Why, didn't you think so?" enquired Colonel Oldroyd in astonishment.

Morcar struggled with himself.

"Yes and no," he brought out at last.

His host looked at him and seemed to consider. "He was certainly dead," he said at last. His tone was firm but had an undercurrent of understanding and sympathy. "He had gone before he reached the trench. We tried his pulse and all the tests, you know, while you were out rescuing the other fellow."

"Jessopp."

"Yes. You had a well-deserved decoration for the double rescue, hadn't you?"

"I can't talk about it," said Morcar hoarsely.

"Ah, there are my wife and David," said his host, immediately changing the subject.

"I don't want his damned sympathy and his damned tact," raged Morcar perversely.

David's stepmother came up talking rapidly in a light smooth voice, as usual. She was a faded but still pretty blonde; a nitwit but probably satisfying, thought Morcar crudely; she thought everything her husband did quite perfect, which was probably soothing to a tired man. Her clothes, very light and summery, were expensive and well-chosen by Annotsfield standards, but lacked the metropolitan elegance of Christina's.

"Are you tired, Francis? Are you tired, Mr. Morcar? We shall be late for lunch if we don't make haste. Fan will be late for lunch if she doesn't make haste. We couldn't get seats—we had to stand all the time. Fan was sure she could get seats round the other side. David thought she couldn't but she was sure she could. She went off by herself. Daughters nowadays are not what they used to be, Mr. Morcar. Of course Fan's a sweet girl, and *so* devoted to her father. She'll be late for lunch if she doesn't make haste. There's Fan!"

"No, I don't think it is, Ella," said David soothingly. "I don't think that's her dress. She has a pale green silky dress to-day."

"No, she hasn't, dear. What are you thinking about, David? She had her primrose chintz frock at breakfast."

David smiled but made no reply; Mrs. Oldroyd however continued the argument all the way back to the hotel, and during the moments while they had drinks and waited for the arrival of her daughter. These were protracted.

"Have you been in Southstone long, Mrs. Oldroyd?" enquired Morcar, trying to stem the tide of chatter.

"Just two years. Fan found the country so dull, you know. Of course for a pretty girl like Fan, a little country village is rather dull. Her name is Frances really, of course, after her father. Fan is just her short name. But we think it suits her. Oh, here's Fan! Why, David, you were right, dear, she had her green dress! I *am* surprised. I'm sure she had her yellow chintz at breakfast. Didn't you think she had her yellow chintz at breakfast, Francis? Fan, dear, you're very late. Shall we go in now, Francis? I'll lead the way with Mr. Morcar. David would like Fan to live with him, you know, Mr. Morcar, but Fan is so devoted to her father."

In Morcar's opinion—for he was hungry, and the child, who couldn't be more than seventeen, had made no apology for keeping the party waiting—David's stepsister was a selfish little minx who wanted smacking. But he realised that if he had been a younger man he might have taken a different view, for she was certainly very pretty. Small and extremely fair, with a heart-shaped face, long silky lashes, a brilliant complexion, eyes of turquoise blue and a rosebud mouth which usually wore a mutinous pout, she struck him as spoiled and wilful. She's like a blonde kitten, he thought now, as she took up the luncheon menu and criticised it savagely in a small light voice; the kitten's coat was of a velvet, an altogether delicious, softness, but her claws were sharp and naughty.

"I'm afraid there's nothing suitable for you, Francis," said Mrs. Oldroyd, scanning the courses. "He's on a diet for his rheumatism, you know, Mr. Morcar."

"Never mind—I'll just have vegetables," said her husband.

"Daddy, why don't you *talk* to the management? Why don't you *insist* on having something to eat?" said Fan. "It's absurd, really."

"Never mind, my dear."

"Is there any fish for Colonel Oldroyd?"

"I'm sorry, madam; there is none left."

"Never mind."

"It's absurd, Daddy, for you to have no lunch," said Fan, tossing her silken curls.

"It's of no consequence, my dear," said her father mildly. "Probably better for me. I'll have vegetables."

"What shall we do this afternoon, Daddy?" enquired Fan.

"Perhaps Mr. Morcar would like to see something of the surrounding country," suggested her mother.

"I have to catch the three-fifteen to town, unfortunately, Mrs. Oldroyd," Morcar reminded her.

"Me too," said David.

"Oh, David!" chorussed all three Oldroyds. They all fell silent at the same moment and regarded him reproachfully.

"Your father will be very disappointed, dear," said Mrs. Oldroyd at length timidly.

"You might stay a bit longer, David; you really are a washout as a brother," said Fan fretfully.

"Of course if you must get back for business reasons," began Colonel Oldroyd in a wistful tone.

"I'm afraid it can't be helped," said David.

Morcar felt vexed by the young man's persistence, which made his own departure less easy.

"When will you come again, David?" asked Fan sharply.

David hesitated. "In a couple of months, perhaps. Fan, why don't you come and stay with me now you've left school? I should like so much to have you with me."

"At Scape Scar? No, I thank you," said Fan emphatically. "All moors and stone walls and mill chimneys and people saying: 'Nay, love.'" She sparkled round the table for appreciation of her imitation Yorkshire accent, which was certainly accurate and revealed, if she only knew it, thought Morcar sardonically, her own Yorkshire origin. When she reached Morcar in her tour of eyes, she blushed suddenly and her silken eyelashes fell. She's remembered that I speak like that, thought Morcar, and he kept his eyes in her direction so that she should meet them again when she looked up. She blushed again, more deeply—a pretty pastel shade certainly, thought Morcar. "If I leave Daddy and Mummy at all," said Fan in a tone of virtue: "It will be to go to London."

"Fan wants to go to London and work," explained her mother.

"What at?" demanded Morcar brutally. It was clear to him that Miss Fan Oldroyd wanted not work, but escape from family control. "As a mannequin, perhaps?"

"No!" thundered Francis Oldroyd.

"Oh, Daddy, you're so silly about these things, darling," said Fan with a pout, laying her hand all the same affectionately on her father's. "You have such old-fashioned prejudices. Pre-Noah, actually."

"Your father likes to have you beside him, Miss Fan," said Morcar.

Fan pouted. "I think I ought to be doing some *work*" she objected with her little air of virtue. "David thinks so too. Don't you, David?"

"Yes. But you must train first, Fan; untrained labour is a waste and a nuisance."

"I would rather you stayed with us, Fan dear, until you get married," said her mother fondly.

Fan's mutinous little face flamed. "Mother, don't be so *vulgar!*" she exclaimed angrily.

"Fan!" said her father.

"Sorry, Daddy, but really!"

"Shall we have coffee in the lounge?" suggested Colonel Oldroyd. "There isn't much time if you must really go so soon."

His tone held such a depth of disappointment and mild resignation that in spite of himself Morcar felt sorry for him. "What a life!" he thought. "Fancy living in a small hotel, surrounded by women, with nothing to do all day." "You know David has really made a very good beginning at Old Mill," he said in an earnest confidential tone into Colonel Oldroyd's ear as they moved together into the lounge. "I think you're going to be proud of him." The beam of pleasure in Francis's anxious eyes quite touched Morcar. Yes, he's fond of the boy; David's the main part of his life now. "You can rely on me to look after him," said Morcar. "I'll just give him an eye—without appearing to do so, you know."

He nodded conspiratorially, and Francis nodded back. "I shall be most grateful," he said, lowering his voice as they approached the rest of the party. "I can't tell you how glad I am that you came down this weekend—I'm most relieved and grateful."

"Not at all," said Morcar.

"I'll just see the porter about a taxi, Father," said David.

"Fan will drive you," said his father.

Morcar looked towards Fan, expecting the customary pout and contradiction, but to his surprise Fan seemed pleased and acquiescent.

"The Sunday three-fifteen is a boat train from Dover. Let's drive over and catch it there. You come too, Daddy," urged his daughter.

"Yes, go, Francis," urged his wife.

The plan was agreed. To give father and son a chance of private talk together, Morcar sat in front beside Fan; she drove with verve and skill and landed them at the station with just the right number of minutes to spare. Her fair hair, uncovered, blew back from her pretty little face, which was now smiling and happy; it was clear that she loved speed. She gave David a warm sisterly hug in farewell, then left him with his father, and climbing on the step of the railway carriage which Morcar had just entered, put her head in through the open window and gave Morcar precise instructions how to arrange his coat and case. With her hands over the door and her face framed in the window opening she looked more like a kitten than ever, and Morcar could not help but smile.

"David is very fond of you," said Fan abruptly. Her tone indicated that the admission was virtuous on her part since she saw little reason for David's preference, and Morcar's smile soured a little.

"I'm very fond of him," he said staunchly, however.

"I'm glad he's got you to look after him," said Fan. "Because, you know, he's full of these dreadful Socialist ideas. Like the Mellors. Have you met the Mellors?" Morcar nodded; he had never felt so sympathetic towards the Mellors as at that moment. Fan looked over her shoulder at her father; finding him deep in talk with David, she turned back and whispered: "David's mother was a Mellor, you know. I always think she gave poor Daddy a hell of a time. Of course he doesn't say so to us—"

"I should think not, indeed," said Morcar repressively.

"—and she was very beautiful and all that, but she left Daddy once because of her Socialist Mellor ideas, and David seems to have inherited them, or something. Daddy's often worried about him."

"I don't think he need be," said Morcar, exasperated by these unsuitable confidences. "Get off that step now and let your brother in."

"Half-brother," said Fan.

"It's the same thing. Get off the step—I want to say goodbye to your father."

"How domineering you are!" pouted Fan.

"David!" cried Morcar as the train began to move.

David leaped in and Morcar extended his hand through the window to his host, who hobbling rapidly alongside managed to grasp it. To Morcar's vexation the clasp seemed to throw Colonel Oldroyd slightly off balance, for he staggered a little and a flicker of pain passed over his face.

Morcar vented his annoyance at being the cause of this, together with all his other annoyances of the weekend, by saying abruptly as soon as the train was out of the station:

"I don't know why you didn't stay the night as they wanted you to do, David. It's a long journey for such a short stay. Surely Old Mill can run one day without you."

"I wanted to stay," said David soberly. "But my aunt and uncle are in a good deal of trouble just now, and I feel I ought to be with them."

"The Mellors?"

"Yes. I didn't mention it to my father, because he dislikes the Mellors and I didn't want to upset him. It's Matthew, you know."

"What has Matthew been doing?" growled Morcar.

"They heard on Friday that he's been killed."

"Killed?"

"Yes. In Spain. Didn't you know he went out there to fight against Franco?"

"No, I didn't. I knew I hadn't seen him about lately," said

Morcar uneasily. "But I didn't realise he'd gone to Spain. Young fathead! What good did he think it would do?"

"It was a matter of conscience. I know he wasn't a favourite of yours," said David.

"Nay! I'd nowt against him. He stood for his side same as I stand for mine," said Morcar. "And as to Franco, I agree with Matthew entirely. I can't abide dictators."

"It's especially hard for my uncle," said David in a warmer tone: "Because you see he's always been a pacifist. He was terribly upset when Matthew went."

"You've got some odd relations, David. No offence meant."

"Which do you think are the odder," said David smiling: "The Oldroyds or the Mellors? Which are the most useful?"

"Your grandfather was a fine chap and gave me my first job," evaded Morcar hastily. "You're rather like him."

David laughed, and Morcar shook out his Sunday newspaper in self-protection.

As they had not a great deal of time to spare to catch their northern express they hurried down the platform as soon as the train reached Charing Cross. Sunday travel was disagreeable to Morcar, his feelings had been both ruffled and moved by his weekend with the Oldroyds, David's disclosure about Matthew Mellor had depressed him and the uncertainty about the northern train was vexing, so he was in a gloomy mood. Suddenly he heard his name called in its variations:

"Uncle Harry! Morcar! Harry!"

He looked round and saw Harington, Christina and Jennifer bearing rapidly down upon them.

Immediately the world took on an entirely different aspect. He looked at Christina fondly. She had lately been "growing her hair", as the phrase went; the experiment was now complete and the result was charming; Morcar longed to run his fingers through those dark rich curls. On the coast the season had been summer, here in London it seemed early autumn; Christina was dressed in delicate black and wore her fox furs, with no ornament save her sapphire ring; as always she had the air of elegance, of sophistication, of tragic loveliness, which to Morcar was the essence of high romance. *Loveliest, brightest, best,* he thought. In her presence he forgot entirely about David for some moments, and then his introductions were perfunctory. Harington explained rapidly that a detail had come up in a brief on which he was working which concerned industrial practice. He wanted an elucidation of the meaning of an industrial phrase, and remembering that Morcar had gone to Southstone for the weekend had enquired about evening trains to the north and deduced that he would travel to London by the one which now stood at the platform. He knew there was very little time, had brought the car and would drive Morcar to King's Cross and tap his brains *en route.* David made an unexpected factor in the situation, but Harington was so pleased with himself over the success of his deductions that he took this factor in his stride and packed David in with his wife and daughter; the party were on their way in a few moments.

This good temper did not last. Harington always drove badly and became annoyed by any vehicle or pedestrian impeding his progress; to-day he drove execrably and became correspondingly bad-tempered, because Morcar could not give the information he wanted. Since the detail concerned cotton manufacture, Morcar considered Harington's expectation unjustifiable, but the barrister saw the matter differently.

"I can give you the name of a man who can tell you what you want," offered Morcar.

"My dear Harry, how many times have I to repeat that I need

the information today—or at latest first thing tomorrow?"

"Would the name of a book containing the information be of any use?" put in David suddenly.

"Yes—if it were the kind of book I could get from the London Library," conceded Harington.

David promptly named a book. Harington looked over his shoulder at the young man rather peevishly. Knowing the barrister's thought processes so well through his sensitiveness for Christina, Morcar could read Harington's mind now; he was thinking that it was all very well to have one vulgar rich north-country manufacturer in tow—one, would pass as an amusing eccentricity. But two! Impossible! Morcar grinned to himself, but took no steps to smooth David's path—he did not wish anyone from Annotsfield to become friendly with the Haringtons. Accordingly the remainder of the transit between the stations was occupied with efforts on David's part to be agreeable which were received with snubs from Harington. They reached King's Cross and began to descend from the car. David said suddenly:

"I wonder if you know a sort of cousin of mine, sir, who lives down your way? Sir Richard Bamforth? He's something in the Treasury."

Harington's face changed so abruptly that Morcar perceived Sir Richard to be something very considerable in the Treasury.

"I know of him," said Harington.

"Come along, David, or we shall miss this train," urged Morcar irritably.

They all hurled themselves from the car and ran on to the platform.

"Well, come and dine with us next time you're in town," cried Harington as the two travellers sprang into the train.

Astonished by the tone of this invitation, which would have

been suitable if addressed to him seven or eight years ago, Morcar looked round, and perceived it was intended for David, who was saying "Thank you, sir," gratefully.

The train left at once. Morcar had no chance to look into Christina's eyes, to exchange a private word, to touch her hand. His disappointment was savage. Moreover, he was not pleased by the barrister's invitation to David. He was not pleased that David had met the Haringtons at all, and wished again that the boy had stayed in Southstone, as his father had obviously desired. Morcar did not want Annotsfield to know of his friendship with the Haringtons, because it seemed to him that any such knowledge was the first step towards the discovery of his relations with Christina. (He regretted even that Nasmyth knew it, but Nasmyth was a lawyer and presumably knew how to hold his tongue.) Any West Riding manufacturer who saw Morcar with Harington and Christina would know at once, Morcar felt sure, that Morcar was with the Haringtons either for the sake of business or for the sake of Christina. To them Harington would be an insufferable bore, and they would dismiss with derision any suggestion that Morcar took pleasure in his company; when they found that business was not in question they would draw the inevitable conclusion. Now one West Riding manufacturer—not a typical one, perhaps—had seen Morcar with the Haringtons and knew of the friendship. Possibly a meeting was inevitable some time, reflected Morcar, between two groups of people of both of whom he saw so much. But the invitation to dine, to further intimacy, was not inevitable; it would not have been given if David had not, so to speak, forced it.

"Well—you played your ace," said Morcar to David sourly, sinking back in his corner seat.

"Yes," said David. He coloured. He was still standing; he

looked at Morcar defensively. "It was too soon in the game, you think?"

"What game?" said Morcar in a rough tone.

David did not enlighten him. Instead, he said politely: "Will you excuse me now, Mr. Morcar? I'm afraid I haven't a first-class ticket on this part of the journey."

"Quite right," approved Morcar, mollified in spite of himself by this example of sound economy. "Always keep down your overheads. Be off with you to the thirds. I'll see you perhaps at Annotsfield."

When David had gone Morcar took up his newspaper again. But he found it difficult to concentrate on what he was reading. The figures of the four Oldroyds—the lame colonel defeated by the slump, the silly adoring wife, the naughty kitten Fan, David so exceptionally able and noble—mingled with those of the Haringtons—the snobbish hateful Edward, the ingenuous young Edwin away at sea, the noble handsome Jenny and his own darling, his beautiful beloved Christina. The two Mellors wove in and out of the mazy dance while his mother—for whom he had bought a special kind of deck chair in Southstone on Saturday on Mrs. Oldroyd's recommendation—sat in the background sewing and watching. He felt sorry about that violent but sincere young fool Matthew, vexed that Fan should vex her father, pleased in a sad way that David should travel first where his father could see him and third elsewhere.

"I'm getting cluttered up with people," thought Morcar savagely, turning his paper with a jerk that tore the sheet. "I must cut them all out except Christina."

But he knew he could not cut them out; he cared too much for them.

32

Presages

The curtain rose to reveal an extraordinary backcloth, of a kind which Morcar privately designated surrealist, though probably inaccurately. Strange whorls and lobes in clashing crimsons, bold powerful planes in black, a couple of uneven yellow ovals which might or might not be eyes, a hint of a starfish and something resembling a huge scroll of ribbon, brought to mind uncomfortable words like cosmos and cataclysm, and suggested an action to come which without doubt, reflected Morcar, recalling the Victorian anecdote with amusement, would be quite unlike the home life of the great Queen. He seemed to remember now a remark from David that the décor was meant to suggest a human heart.

"Fan won't like it," thought Morcar with a grin, as Verchinina entered and with her head held down as if in deep thought whizzed her arms in violent arcs which Fan's expensive boarding-school would certainly regard as unladylike.

The ballet was *Les Présages*; the party—a dinner, Covent

Garden, supper and dancing—was an offering to the children by Morcar on the occasion of Fan Oldroyd's birthday. Morcar sat at the end of the row with Christina between himself and her son, who was at home on a brief leave; then came Fan, very silky in close-fitting fashionable white which revealed every curve of her charming little body; Harington was enjoying himself between Fan and his daughter, each so striking of her kind; Jenny also in white looked classically handsome where Fan looked sexually attractive; David at Jenny's left completed the party. Fan, now engaged (more or less) in a secretarial course and installed in a Kensington hostel of Christina's choosing, was sampling the delights of London with avidity as far as (perhaps indeed a little further than) her limited means allowed. She had expressed a desire to see a ballet, but Morcar felt certain she had expected the sort of chorus *ensemble* found in musical comedy, something cheerful, pretty and in the vulgar sense stylish. The dissection of the heart's problems offered her by Massine would probably both puzzle her and excite her derision.

What was it all about anyway, wondered Morcar, as male figures leaped wildly across the back of the stage. He flicked on his lighter and examined the programme. *The subject of the ballet,* he read, *is man's struggle with his destiny.* Quite a big subject, thought Morcar sardonically. *The first scene represents life, with its diversions, desires and temptations.* Ah, thought Morcar—watching the dancers with a keener interest and reading his own interpretation, the meanings of his own life, into the work of art before him—that is very true, that is just like life; one has aims, one has ambitions, one lowers one's head in preoccupation, gazes within, dreams, swings one's arms in a violent effort of thought to reduce the world to understandable patterns; then bevies of sensual images come swirling lightly in, events rush upon one distractingly, the ordered movement breaks and disintegrates. One tries continually to return to one's original aim, the thought, the clear forward movement, but the other figures continually break in upon it.... What a mess my life is, thought Morcar; nothing is as it should be except Syke Mills and possibly David. I hope to God these four young things here will make a better job of it than I have. He felt moved and troubled, and if he had had the right to do so he would have taken Christina's hand to seek reassurance.

But now the stage was empty for a moment, the music changed to a beautiful slow melody which Morcar found thrilling, passionate and tender. He glanced at the programme again: *In the second scene is revealed love in conflict with the baser passion which shatters the human soul. The beauty of love is imperilled, but prevails.* Morcar looked up quickly at the stage; from the right two dancers entered. Lichine in strange bright green, his arm about the waist of his lover, supporting her: Baronova in strange bright red, on her points, her lovely arms extended upward in hope and aspiration: advancing slowly, with rhythmic pauses, to Tchaikovsky's poignant and romantic music. Their progress was solemn, noble, beautiful; an ardent devotion, a tender respect, seemed to sustain them. Morcar was profoundly moved. Yes, he thought; that is love; that is how I feel towards Christina. The lovers danced together; ah if we only had time, thought Morcar, those noble evolutions would represent the movements of our souls towards each other, not merely of our bodies. But now the *corps de ballet* rush in—they are lovers too, no doubt, thought Morcar irritably, but I wish they would keep away and not confuse the issue. But what is this? Morcar sat up abruptly. A hateful batlike figure in dusty black rushes upon the scene; sinister, agile, hideous, with an effect of malignant glee, he threatens the dancers in powerful ugly gestures. Oh no, this is intolerable, thought Morcar, his heart contracting; the woman is thrown from her lovely poise, her beautiful serenity, by this hateful sordid black-winged destiny; her movements become anguished, exaggerated, contorted; she droops and wavers, her body tosses in anguish like a flower in a storm; destiny seizes her, drags her across the stage, she struggles to escape; the other women suffer the same torturing anguish. The man springs forward to try to rescue his love; he seems to attack the hateful black figure, to batter against it—in vain; he sinks back, defeated, exhausted. The woman—will she be carried quite away, hopelessly imprisoned? No; with a supreme effort which Morcar watched in terror lest her fragile form should be torn apart by the strain, she wrenches herself free, and dancing always, with poignant effort gradually regains her flowerlike grace and balance. The others take courage; the black destiny with a last malignant sneer, a threat to return, leaves them.

And now the lovers are alone. After these terrible ordeals, these devastating changes and chances, at last through the power of their love they struggle upright. They resume their first noble pose; the woman raises her arms once again in steadfast aspiration, the man's arm holds firm about her waist; they support each other. Moving once more in their old stately rhythm, they leave the scene with a tragic dignity, ennobled by the ordeals which have tried them. Their love, for the moment at least, has proved stronger than human destiny.

Morcar's feelings were so intense during this presentation of his own anguish of love that he feared he must have betrayed himself. He glanced along the row of his guests in apprehension. Tears trembled in Christina's blue eyes and she gazed at the dancers with a tragic intensity which matched her lover's.

309

Edwin's fresh young face gaped, soberly intent; Fan looked very young and frightened; Harington's suave mask was wrinkled into keen æsthetic appreciation. What of the two good young souls beyond, wondered Morcar; what of Jenny and David? Their heads bowed slightly towards each other, their candid eyes wide, they gazed entranced at the moving and beautiful parable.

With a shock of surprise and alarm, followed by a strange joy, Morcar saw that Jenny's hand was clasped in David's.

33

Peace with Dishonour

Then it was 1938. In Morcar's life two parallel actions progressed throughout the year. There was a public action: England's descent into the abyss of appeasement and humiliation. There was a private action: the division of all Morcar's acquaintance into parties on opposite sides of this abyss. These actions presented themselves to his memory as a series of three-cornered conversations between himself, Harington and David Oldroyd, with Christina and Jenny as auditors and judges. The conversations were not always conducted in the presence of all five people concerned; Jenny was now up at Oxford, achieving her usual brilliant success in work and games, and David could not often be away from Annotsfield. But across the country by letter and report and talk, from David through Morcar to Harington, from Jenny through David and Christina to Morcar and Harington and back to David and Jenny, the argument raged.

"You talk the most amazingly sentimental claptrap sometimes, Harry," drawled Harington at dinner on New Year's Day. "I've examined all that modern Jewish-German art pretty carefully, and I can assure you it was thoroughly decadent. Needed cleaning up. Besides, don't you think Hitler's treatment of the Jews is really rather natural? They'd grabbed all the best jobs in the land."

"Those who can hold the best jobs are entitled to them," said Morcar.

"If we acted on Hitler's principle in this country," said David, grinning: "We should be building concentration camps for Scotsmen."

Harington, who prided himself on a remote Highland strain in his blood, coloured and told him not to be absurd.

February came; Anthony Eden resigned from the post of Foreign Secretary. It was a little difficult to know what went on behind the scenes, but it seemed clear enough to Morcar that Eden thought Germany and Italy should show some signs of repentance of their ways and give some guarantees of mending them before Great Britain could consent to meet them in friendly fashion at the conference table, while the Prime Minister Chamberlain was ready to take them by the hand without these preliminaries.

"Why should we trust countries which have broken every promise made so far?" said David. "Let them show they mean good faith by keeping, even though belatedly, their promise to get out of Spain."

"David is prejudiced about Spain," said Harington when he heard this from Morcar, "because of that preposterous cousin of his who got killed there."

Jenny attended a protest meeting about the resignation, in Oxford, David a similar meeting in Annotsfield.

"Though why they should protest about an act of purely personal pique I own I cannot understand," said Harington.

"I don't know the ins and outs of the thing, but I don't think

England ought to change her Foreign Secretary to please Germany and Italy," said Morcar.

"The negotiation is a business matter which must be put through in a business style," said Harington. "If Eden is an obstacle to the bargain, he must be dropped."

"I wouldn't do business with firms which never kept their promises to pay," said Morcar. "Besides, look what a strong bargaining point their presence in Spain gives to the totalitarian powers."

In March, Germany seized Austria. Liberals and Jews committed suicide; beatings, tortures, concentration camps began.

"And we stand by and do nothing!" raged David.

"What does the young firebrand want us to do?" demanded Harington, when this was reported to him by Jenny.

"He wants us to tell Hitler to stop, in accordance with our previous guarantee to Austria," wrote Jenny.

"What good would that do? Simply involve us in a war not our own," contended her father.

"David says it *is* our war," reported Jenny. "Our respect for international obligations is involved."

"Besides, from the practical point of view I think he's right," urged Morcar. "We let the Japs get away with snatching Manchuria, and these totalitarian states have been snatching ever since. If Hitler gets away with the seizure of Austria, he'll just go on to seize something else. Next it will be Czechoslovakia, then Poland, then the small Balkan nations, then when he's got them all under his thumb, it will be the turn of France and England."

"You're very well informed nowadays, Harry," sneered Harington.

"Aye—I've taken to reading a book or two."

"Under David's guidance, I suppose?"

"Something of that sort," returned Morcar equably.

"You're entitled to your own opinion, Harry, of course," said the barrister, smiling and looking contemptuously down his nose.

"Yes, I am," said Morcar.

"He wouldn't be entitled to it in Hitler's Reich. Uncle Harry would be in a concentration camp in Germany," commented Jenny in her next week's letter.

In April the Anglo-Italian agreement was signed, recognising the Italian conquest of Abyssinia. It was Easter, and the party were together, in a houseboat which Morcar had rented on the Thames. David wore a face of gloom as they listened to Morcar's portable radio on the upper deck. Everything around them was very English and pleasant; the grass was green, the water silver, the willows' graceful branches swayed in the gentle breeze, the swans arched their long white necks proudly. But David's thoughts darkened the landscape.

"Other nations can now expect nothing but expediency from England," he said.

"Don't be so exaggerated, David," said Harington.

"I was only quoting the *Manchester Guardian*."

"Oh, the *Guardian!* Cut your losses—it's the only sensible thing to do," pronounced Harington. "Surely you as a business man appreciate that principle, Harry."

"Aye—but these are somebody else's losses," objected Morcar.

"If the recognition of the conquest of Abyssinia saves the peace of Europe, the sacrifice is well worth making."

"It is expedient that one man die for the multitude," said Jenny suddenly.

"Jenny!" exploded Harington.

"Why don't you take out the punt, dear?" said Christina hastily.

When the two young people had gone upstream Harington turned to Morcar and said:

"Of course I have no right to object to your other guests, Harry, but I wish very much you would avoid inviting us with that young man again."

His tone was smooth but his face a mask of fury. Morcar enquired mildly: "What has the boy done wrong?"

"I can't endure these long-haired young Bolsheviks who want to plunge Europe into war for their own silly ideas!" raged Harington. "What does he think will happen to London if England gets into a continental scrap? Damned young fool! I should be greatly obliged, Harry, if you would refrain from introducing young men of that sort into my house in future."

"You invited David Oldroyd to your house yourself, I had nothing to do with it," said Morcar, angry in his turn. "If you don't wish him to visit you again, tell him so."

"What's the good of that when the harm's already done?"

"Harm?"

"Don't pretend you haven't noticed it—don't pretend you haven't eyes in your head!" raged Harington. His bald head was flushed, his pale eyes bloodshot. "He wants to marry Jenny, as you very well know. He told Christina so at Christmas."

"Well, why shouldn't he?" said Morcar, to whom Christina had confided David's intentions.

"Because he hasn't a penny and because he's an uncouth West Riding manufacturer—he's not a suitable match for my daughter," barked Harington. "On top of that he has these outrageous views, which he's imparting to Jenny."

"Edward dear, you know that's not true," said Christina soothingly. "David was educated at Winchester, he isn't uncouth, his hair is short, he's very personable. He has pleasant

315

relatives—there's Sir Richard Bamforth after all. From what Harry says, his father's people have been figures in West Riding history for two hundred years."

"I don't want Jenny to go and live in a barbaric hole in the West Riding!" raged Harington.

"I resent your attitude to Yorkshire," said Morcar hotly. "But if what you say is true and we need civilising, then that gives all the more scope to Jenny."

"And what would the happy pair use for money, as Edwin would say? That boy hasn't a penny except what he earns—"

"Neither have I, if it comes to that."

"—and his premises are mortgaged to some bank or other. He told me so himself."

"The bank are financing him," explained Morcar.

"How can he possibly provide for Jenny properly?"

"Well—he'll be my partner one of these days," said Morcar.

Christina exclaimed; Harington, halted in mid-diatribe, quite gaped at his host; Morcar himself tried to conceal his surprise at his own decision. It had sprung from his lips before he was altogether aware of it, but once uttered he knew he had made it long ago.

"Of course if you say that," grumbled Harington unwillingly: "The matter wears a rather different aspect. But there are dozens of young men I would sooner Jenny married than young Oldroyd."

"But if they are in love, Edward?" said Christina.

From his wife this was an argument which Harington could not easily counter, since it was part of his pride to regard his marriage with Christina as an ideally happy love-match. "It's his confounded politics, my dear," he grumbled. "These wild ideas—there's no future in them."

"Don't forbid him the house. Please don't, Edward," begged

Christina. "It would make Jenny very unhappy. Give her time to decide for herself."

Harington snorted angrily but allowed himself to be guided by his wife.

Morcar thought it well, next time they were alone together in Yorkshire, to give David a mild warning of the opposition he was likely to encounter from Jenny's father.

"Oh, that's just the usual Œdipus-complex stuff," said David calmly. "He wouldn't approve of anyone who wanted to marry Jenny, even if he'd chosen the lad himself."

"That may be," said Morcar, wondering who (or what) Œdipus was. "But it's your political ideas he can't get over."

"I can't help that," said David. He paused and added: "I think myself it's my lack of cash he objects to."

"That will remedy itself, I don't doubt," said Morcar.

"To some extent," agreed David. "But not very far, I fear."

"I thought I might remedy it by giving you a small partnership in Syke Mills," said Morcar, taking the plunge.

The blood rushed to the young man's face. "That's awfully good of you," he said. *"Awfully* good!" he repeated on a note of astonishment. "And very tempting. Especially as it would bring me back to Syke Mills. But I'm afraid I mustn't accept."

"Why not?" barked Morcar.

"I have these peculiar economic ideas, you see," said David. "You don't care for them and they're all I care for."

"I thought Jenny was what you cared for?"

"Jenny and I care for the ideas," explained David. "We share them. At least," he added in a murmur, colouring: "It's no good our marrying, if we don't."

"Well—the offer stands open. I shan't take an answer now so you needn't go on talking," said Morcar, drowning David's expostulations. "It isn't all for your sake, so don't think so. I'm fond of Jenny and want to see her happy. And whatever Œdipus may be, take my advice and let sleeping Œdipuses lie."

David laughed. "I'll try," he promised dutifully.

In September, the Sudeten Germans within Czechoslovakia demanded incorporation in Germany.

"It seems a natural and reasonable demand," said Harington. "They are German nationals, not Czechoslovakian."

"Let the problem be settled in a reasonable way, then," said Morcar, "by negotiation."

"Nonsense!" said David. "Hitler deliberately stirred them up so as to have an excuse to attack Czechoslovakia."

Hitler made a speech at Nuremberg. The ranting, raving voice shouted over the radio to the world.

"Naturally he feels the matter deeply and has to play it up a little for his own people," said Harington.

"Damned rude. Asking for trouble," said Morcar.

"Deliberately inflammatory and provocative," said David. "Part of the plan."

An ultimatum was presented to Czechoslovakia, to expire at midnight. Chamberlain flew to Godesberg.

"I must say I don't like an English Prime Minister going to Hitler," said Morcar. "Hitler should come here."

"He won't."

"Well, if he won't, that shows how low we've fallen."

"I'm glad to see you still have some patriotic feeling," sneered Harington.

"It's not a question of patriotism, it's a question of law and outlaw, of judge and criminal," said David.

"I don't trust Chamberlain with England's reputation," said Christina uneasily.

"I'm afraid he will sell Czechoslovakia," said Jenny.

"My dear, if appeasement is to be achieved, sacrifices will have to be made."

"Whose sacrifices?"

"No matter whose."

"It is expedient that one man die for the multitude," commented Jenny as before.

"Appeasement means you'll do anything for peace which doesn't inconvenience yourself," defined David.

The conversations between Chamberlain and Hitler were suspended, for Hitler raised his demands and at the same time continued to entrain troops towards the Czechoslovakian frontier.

"Too much even for Chamberlain," said David.

"It seems to me that David was right, and this Sudeten business was simply an excuse to attack Czechoslovakia," said Morcar.

Hitler declared his intention of mobilising on the morrow unless the Czechs accepted the Godesberg ultimatum. Chamberlain spoke over the wireless to the British nation. He observed that however much one might sympathise with a small nation confronted by a big powerful neighbour, he could not undertake to involve the whole British Empire in a war simply on that account. *If we have to fight, it must be on larger issues than that. ...*

"Good God!" exclaimed Morcar, incredulous. "Hasn't the man ever heard of justice?"

"Chamberlain argues like the maidservant who excused her illegitimate child on the ground that it was a small one," said David.

"I see no analogy," contended Harington. "We must take a realistic view."

"But justice doesn't depend on the size of what is involved, surely, Edward?" said Christina in a puzzled tone.

"Allow me to know a little more about law than you do. A thief who steals much receives a longer sentence than one who steals less."

"But both are judged guilty against the law, and branded as thieves."

"Justice," said David, "is a principle, not a unit of measurement."

"Mr. Chamberlain," said Jenny, "has no principle, only a policy."

"You'd have to look far to find a better Prime Minister for England to-day."

"No, I wouldn't," said Morcar. "There's Churchill. He supported Eden in the House."

"Churchill as Prime Minister? Never!" exclaimed Harington.

Two days later the Union Jack, according to the newspapers, hung beside the Swastika.

"Ugh!" said David.

"How Chamberlain can stand those brutes slobbering over him I can't imagine," said Morcar.

"I feel profoundly humiliated, profoundly ashamed," said Jenny.

"We must face the facts and take a realistic view," said her father. "Do you want war? Do you want London to experience air-raids?"

"What's the use of life if you're disgraced, enslaved?" said Jenny.

Hitler invited England, France and Italy to meet him at Munich. Two Czech representatives were also there, but not present at the meeting, remaining merely "at the disposal" of their allies. On the last day of the month Chamberlain surrendered completely to the threat of force, giving Hitler everything he asked for, including partial occupation of Czechoslovakia on the morrow. The day was Friday; as it chanced Morcar and David dined at the Haringtons' that night.

"Peace with Dishonour!" exclaimed Jenny as they sat at coffee.

"We've saved our skins by throwing Czechoslovakia to the wolves," said David bitterly.

"Aye—I keep thinking of decent little Czech manufacturers having to turn out and leave their mills and everything at a day's notice or stay under Germany's rule," said Morcar.

"You'll find they won't leave," sneered Harington.

"By God! If it was me I'd leave," exclaimed Morcar feelingly.

"What, leave Syke Mills?" jeered Harington. "Thistledowns and all?"

"Yes!" said Morcar.

"I feel so disgraced, so ashamed," said Jenny. Her lower lip quivered; her whole face was distorted by the effort to control her tears.

"My dear child, you're making yourself ridiculous."

"You're making yourself ill, Jenny darling. Do try not to mind so much," urged Christina.

"You really must control yourself," said Harington sternly.

"Daddy, I can't. This is the blackest page of English history. Our name will be execrated by every right-thinking nation. We've betrayed justice and righteousness and democracy and everything I hold dear."

"Really, Jenny! You're becoming hysterical."

"She's quite right, sir, all the same."

"Kindly allow me to know what is best for my own daughter,

Oldroyd," said Harington, handing Christina his cup.

"I met murder in the rain, It carried an umbrella like Chamberlain," murmured David.

"It's all very well holding these jejeune ideas when you haven't to put them into operation and watch the results," said Harington. "Statesmen have to consider consequences; the responsibility for consequences rests on them. The point is simply this: Are we to make these small sacrifices—"

"But it's not we who make them. Haven't you heard the story of Chamberlain and the souvenir, Mr. Harington?" said David. "Chamberlain when asked for his umbrella as a souvenir of Munich, replied: 'Oh, I can't give you that; it's mine.'"

Morcar laughed, Christina and Jenny exclaimed bitterly, at this. The goaded Harington flushed.

"If I could be allowed to finish a sentence in my own house," he said savagely, "I should be extremely grateful. The point is simply this: Are these sacrifices to be made, or are we to subject Europe to air bombardment?"

"Well," said David: "If we've given in to Hitler out of fear, let's at least be honest and admit it, and not talk guff about Peace in Our Time. I don't enjoy belonging to a nation of funks, myself."

"Leave the house, sir!" shouted Harington.

David put down his coffee cup with meticulous care and flung out of the room.

Jenny slowly rose. No longer a girl but a tall young woman with a handsome head, she made a singularly striking figure in her white evening frock, which flowed about her in lines of such classic simplicity that she had quite the air of a statue from a master hand. At the moment her face was almost as white as her frock, and her great grey eyes blazed.

322

"Father," she said—it was the first time Morcar had ever heard her use this appellation—"if David goes, I go too."

"Don't be so ridiculous, Jenny," said Harington petulantly. "I thought you had more sense than to indulge in these histrionics."

"Jenny, dear," pleaded Christina.

"I can't help it, Mother," said Jenny, her lip quivering, tears springing to her eyes. "I can't stay here where everything I love is hated and everything I hate loved."

"But darling, what do all these political things matter? You love your father. These questions of principle are above your head."

"You talk like Chamberlain, Mother," exclaimed Jenny.

"Let me remind you that I am your legal guardian until you are of age," said Harington, white with fury and jealous love.

Jenny seemed to consider. "Very well," she said at length. "But as soon as I am twenty-one, I shall marry David."

She began to move slowly towards the door, but her youthful dignity broke before she reached it and she ran from the room.

"Jenny!" called her father fondly. "Jenny, my dear!" After a moment's hesitation he went out after her, and could be heard pleading: "Now let us be sensible, Jennifer," as he followed her upstairs.

Morcar turned to Christina. She sat with head bowed, her face in her hands. Her attitude showed the delicate white neck beneath her dark curls, which it was one of Morcar's pleasures to caress, but at this moment he dared not touch her. He paced about the room once or twice, but finding her pose of tense grief did not change, said pleadingly:

"Don't worry so, my darling. It's nothing. ... It will pass."

"No, it won't. It's my fault."

323

"How do you make that out?" said Morcar in a tone of fond derision.

"It's—what we've done. We've sinned, we've indulged in unlawful pleasure, we've followed the devices and desires of our own hearts," murmured Christina. "This is the payment."

"Nonsense! That's old-fashioned superstitious rubbish," said Morcar uneasily. "I believe in cause and effect, not in providential interference."

"So do I. If I'm estranged from my husband, how can I expect Jenny to love her father, or Edward to understand his daughter?"

"I haven't noticed much estrangement," said Morcar, with a bitterness he knew to be unjust but could not control.

"Oh, Harry! I love you and I don't love Edward. That is enough," said Christina.

"Listen, Chrissie. Jenny and her father disagree in their principles, not in their affection. Jenny's principles are right and Harington's are wrong."

"Yes, I agree there," said Christina with a sigh.

"And principles come before affection."

"That's what I said," murmured Christina, giving him a strange anguished look.

Harington came into the room. "She seems calmer now," he said in a self-satisfied tone. "What are you two looking so serious about?"

"We're discussing the relative importance of principles and affections," said Morcar drily.

"What a couple of bromide merchants you are!" was Harington's cheerful comment.

324

34

Mustard Gas

As Morcar put his car in the Stanney Royd garage he saw that there were lights in the downstairs windows; presumably his mother was waiting up for him. He sighed, for he was feeling depressed by the incidents of the evening, and considered whether to put his head into the room just to greet her and then withdraw at once on the plea of work to be done. But he was hungry and remembered pleasurably the decanter, the syphon, the sandwiches which awaited him; besides, he had hardly seen his mother this week and he supposed it was dull for the old girl. He sniffed, hung up his coat in the downstairs cloakroom and went into the lounge. Mrs. Morcar, neat and fresh in a grey silk dress with a lace front, wearing her black velvet neck-ribbon tied in a coquettish bow at one side, sat erect in a high-backed armchair beside a bright fire. As usual, she had a piece of embroidery in her hand.

"Well, Mother," said Morcar, kissing her.

"You've brought a gust of cold air in with you, Harry," Mrs. Morcar reproved him.

"Well, it's a cold night; it's November," Morcar excused himself in a mild filial tone. "Any messages for me?"

"David Oldroyd rang up to say he can't dine tomorrow; it's one of his training nights."

"Ah," said Morcar thoughtfully. He poured himself some whisky, noting with amusement that his mother gave the depth of the golden liquid in the glass a stern appraising glance.

"What is *he* training for?" asked Mrs. Morcar.

"He's joined the Territorials," replied her son.

He was well aware of the significance of his mother's emphasis on the pronoun, but did not wish to respond to it; he munched sandwiches in silence and looked at the fire.

"Well, Harry!" exclaimed Mrs. Morcar at length in an impatient tone. "Is that all you're going to say? Aren't you going to tell me anything about the class?"

Morcar sighed. He described how he had parked his car beside Annotsfield Town Hall, had found the appropriate side entrance, had read the notice *To A.R.P. Class, Room* 27 and had found Room 27 after some wandering along echoing stone corridors. He described the instructor, a St. John's Ambulance man, very neat and dapper, with a genteel accent and a toothbrush moustache, who proved to be Annotsfield's best hairdresser; he described the twenty-five pupils in the class—a mixed bunch of men drawn from various income levels. One or two of them he knew socially; one turned out to be the Syke Mills foreman, Nathan; one was a chapel-keeper's son whom Mrs. Morcar knew, the lame son. After the first shock of seeing each other there, Morcar and Nathan grinned at each other, and found themselves sitting together in a double desk. They were all provided with notebooks and pencils; the hairdresser dictated notes to them hard for a couple of hours. He had a blackboard and wrote on it very rapidly and legibly, with various coloured chalks. It seemed that he had been a member of the voluntary St. John's Ambulance' Association for years—it was his hobby—and had recently taken a special gas instruction course. He rapped out chemical terms very briskly; Morcar and Nathan found them difficult to spell, but helped each other out when possible. The instructor had on the desk in front of him a small wooden box fitted with pigeonholes, in each of which stood a tiny gas tube containing liquid gas. Towards the end of the class the tubes had been handed round and each pupil had been invited to take a very brief sniff, so that they might learn to recognise the various gases by their smell. Nathan's ginger quiff almost stood on end at this suggestion and Morcar himself had gaped a little, but they both sniffed manfully. Phosgene smelled like musty hay, lewisite like geranium, mustard gas like garlic. At this point Morcar stopped abruptly.

"And is that all you learned?" demanded Mrs. Morcar, disappointed.

"More or less," said Morcar.

"But what did you take notes about?" demanded Mrs. Morcar.

Morcar was silent. He turned over in his mind the information he had imbibed that evening and tried to find some which. could safely be imparted to the dignified, bright-eyed, innocent old lady before him. But he could find none. He simply could not bring himself to tell her that every single droplet of gas spray would cause a burn the size of a shilling, and that these gases could be sprayed from an aeroplane flying so high as to be barely visible, carrying a couple of tanks holding twelve gallons apiece. Lung irritant was deadly—lethal, said the instructor with unction; it made you cough and choke, you felt nausea, vomiting, pain in the chest. After a short time these symptoms wore off and you felt well—but this period was particularly dangerous. Lung irritant patients were stretcher cases from the start. Mustard gas of course was very much worse; Morcar had written down in neat tabular form ten reasons for the pre-eminence of mustard. Mustard was a blister gas. The instructor had passed round a few photographs showing the kind of blisters induced by mustard. They were horrifying, nauseating. His mother would not sleep a wink if he described them. She would have nightmares if he so much as hinted at these achievements of twentieth-century civilisation. He was not sure that he could sleep many winks himself.

"It's too bad!" exclaimed Mrs. Morcar, suddenly bursting into angry tears. "You never tell me anything, Harry. I might as well not live with you, for all the notice you take of me. Here I am stuck out here in Stanney Royd away from all my friends and you never tell me anything."

"I'm sorry, Mother," said Morcar soothingly. "But it was all so horrible, you know."

"You're so reserved, Harry," scolded his mother. "You've always been so reserved, so stolid. I can't think why you don't confide in me more fully."

Unfortunately this called before Morcar's mind a vision of his mother's face if he told her all the things about his life which she did not know, and he smiled ruefully. It was a tactical error. Mrs. Morcar interpreted the smile as one of insult and derision; she gave an angry sob, bundled up her embroidery and swept out of the room.

Morcar sat on for a while, his feet stretched to the blaze, thinking. It was impossible that he should ever reveal the horrors of gas warfare to his mother; it was his duty to protect her from the knowledge even if his uncommunicativeness caused her another kind of pain. Next week the A.R.P. class was to deal with types of gas masks, he understood; they would be less horrible and he must remember to describe them all to Mrs. Morcar. Tomorrow at four o'clock he was to take his driving test; he had volunteered as an ambulance driver and must show his abilities on a large lorry; that too could safely be described to his mother. If war came—and he was pretty sure it would; when Hitler had digested Czechoslovakia he would be ready for his next meal—if war came he meant to be out in the streets, right in the thick of it, doing a useful job as he had done last time. It seemed strange that he should be too old to fight—he, Harry Morcar, whose body was still so completely strong, tough and virile. But an ambulance driver would be useful. Or perhaps he would become an Air Raid Warden. Whichever was the more useful, the more dangerous. Somebody cool and tough would be needed if there were mustard gas about; that was certain. Mustard. Ten reasons for the pre-eminence of mustard. Mustard was very persistent, mustard was soluble in fats and soaked into human tissue, mustard was very stable, very penetrative, not easily detected, had a cumulative action, had a delayed action. Respirators protected eyes and lungs but left other parts of the body vulnerable, to mustard.

"That's only eight," thought Morcar uneasily, ransacking his memory. "It's not so easy to learn at forty-nine as it is at nineteen. This A.R.P. business is going to be a damned nuisance," he thought, as he went out to the cloakroom to extract his notebook from the pocket of his coat. "A night every week for the class, and mugging the stuff up in between."

An hour later when he went up to bed he was sorry to see light still streaming from beneath his mother's door. He sighed, knocked and went in.

Mrs. Morcar's room was in his opinion hideous, for she had

brought all her old solid Victorian furniture with her from Hurst Road and it clashed horribly with the Jacobean style of the house, but if she was comfortable he was satisfied. He noted with pleasure that the inset radiator was glowing and the light above the bed well-placed. Mrs. Morcar in a blue woollen bed-jacket of her own design was sitting up in bed, busy with some fine white embroidery in a small frame. Her quick uneven strokes as she plucked the needle from the taut linen revealed her agitation. She looked so small and spirited, and so defenceless against phenomena of the mustard gas kind, that Morcar was touched; he pushed back the blue eiderdown—it shocked Mrs. Morcar's frugal eye to see anyone plump themselves down on a satin eiderdown—and sat down at her side on the bed.

"Now, Mother," he said in his kindest tone: "Calm down and go to sleep."

Mrs. Morcar gave a slight toss of her head, which was enclosed in a neat grey net to match her hair, and said nothing. Morcar, eyeing the frame, saw that she was embroidering his initials on a cambric handkerchief. The monogram, one of her own design, was shapely and pleasing.

"I'm sorry if I grieved you," said Morcar.

Mrs. Morcar, turning tear-filled eyes on his, suddenly dropped her needlework, took up his hand and pressed it against her withered but still soft cheek, then turning it over softly kissed the palm. Morcar was deeply moved, yet at the bottom of his heart deeply angered too. It was the first time in his life—at any rate since he outgrew infancy and could remember—that his mother had so openly shown him her affection. If she had done that once, just once, in his childhood, he thought there would have been confidence between them. If she had done that just once, he thought he might have told her the truth about Winnie on that morning after they had parted for ever; the young man would have received his mother's counsel, he would have acted differently, his life would not now have been the inextricable tangle it had become. The exclamation: "You're twenty years too late!" rose to his lips, but he repressed it. He sighed, forced a smile and said nothing.

"You've been a good son to me, Harry," wailed Mrs. Morcar tearfully.

"Now, Mother!" urged her son, embarrassed.

"But Harry dear," faltered Mrs. Morcar: "You've not been a good husband and father."

Morcar sprang to his feet. "Mother, don't speak to me of that!"

"I must, Harry."

"Mother, leave it alone."

"I can't, Harry. Look. Look at this. I've been wanting to show it to you a long time, but you're so reserved." She took a folded newspaper from the table at her bedside.

Morcar took it from her hand. For a wild fleeting moment the hope crossed his mind that Winnie had died. But he saw nothing of the kind in the square of newsprint his mothered offered him. He unfolded the paper and glanced at the top; it was a copy of the *Annotsfield Record* bearing a July date of 1938, the current year.

"What do you want me to look at?" he said roughly.

Mrs. Morcar refolded the paper to show a paragraph headed *Technical College Successes*. Her trembling wrinkled finger moved down the lines. *Textiles: Fourth year Course*, he read: *C. H. Morcar*. A violent anguish stabbed his heart; his whole body seemed to wince, to shudder, to be ready to dissolve.

"Your son. My grandson, Harry," quavered Mrs. Morcar.

"You see, he goes to the Technical just as you did."

"I see he's only passed third-class," said Morcar hoarsely.

"He's at Prospect Mills," quavered Mrs. Morcar. "He oughtn't to be in that horrid dark place with Mr. Shaw, Harry, he ought to be at Syke Mills."

"Never!" exclaimed Morcar with passion.

"Harry, I want to see him."

"You can't see him here."

"When I lived in Hurst Road I used to see him about, quite often. He always spoke to me. But here I never see him."

The maddening thought of Winnie's derision of his mother's interest in a grandson not her own stung Morcar.

"In another minute I shall tell her the truth," he thought savagely. "And why not? Why take the blame? Why spare her? Why spare Winnie?" He took a breath and began: "Mother." But then the thought flashed across his mind: "The truth would blister worse than mustard." He bit his lip and turned away.

"You must do as you like, Mother," he said. "But for my sake, don't approach Winnie, and don't have the lad here."

35

Marching as to War

The next pictures in Morcar's mind were those of defensive preparations for war. He remembered the events of 1939 by his own preparations, for they marched with those of England—or possibly, thought Morcar, sometimes a trifle in advance.

In March Hitler annexed Czechoslovakia and Morcar passed his anti-gas examination. He felt a fool writing answers on lined foolscap sheets for a couple of hours, and still more of a fool sitting like a schoolboy in front of a uniformed police inspector meekly naming the defects in an imperfect gas respirator and stating the necessary strength of cleansing formalin solutions. Still, he passed; Nathan also passed.

Two days later Mr. Chamberlain observed at Birmingham that there was one thing he would not sacrifice for peace, and that was liberty.

"He's coming round to my way of thinking," said Morcar.

"Aye—getting quite bold," replied Nathan.

The two were standing outside the improvised gas chamber, waiting for their test. They put on their Civilian Duty Respirators, tested them with care, entered the hut. Nothing whatever happened and Morcar felt jolly. Then the instructor gave the signal to remove the masks. The pastille burning in the corner gave off only a mild tear gas, but Morcar suddenly foresaw damage to his eyes, his nose, his lungs—it took all his courage to await the signal for departure; he longed to dash immediately from the room.

"I don't know as I want to do that again in a hurry," remarked Nathan soberly as he removed his mask and smoothed up his front curl.

"Same here," said Morcar.

Hitter annexed a chunk of Lithuania—a country which Morcar had to look up on the map—and sent forces to East Prussia which presently began to seep over into Danzig. Morcar drove a lorry in his gas mask, drove a lorry up and down the steep twisted streets of the West Riding in a practice blackout, lifted patients on to stretchers in a practice raid.

The following week Mr. Chamberlain announced that Britain would go to the support of Poland if her independence were threatened, and Morcar began a special "rush" course, three nights a week, in First Aid. He wrestled with anatomy; Mrs. Morcar was required to hear him recite the names of bones and the position of major pressure-points; he bandaged everyone in range, not unskilfully, and argued the respective merits of large and St. Johns arm-slings with Nathan.

In April Mussolini annexed Albania and President Roosevelt sent a message to the totalitarian powers urging them to declare that they would not make armed attack upon any of a long list of countries which he named.

"Seems to be a good sort of chap, this Roosevelt," said Nathan.

"Aye—for an American," said Morcar.

"Perhaps we shan't need all this after all," went on Nathan, as they sat waiting their turn to have their rendering of a bandaged femur judged at the practical examination.

"I shouldn't like to bet on it," said Morcar.

Britain established a Ministry of Supply and introduced a Conscription Act; Morcar was asked to become Chief Air Raid Warden for Stanney village and district. He accepted, and with a good deal of hard work established the necessary posts and personnel.

Hitler laughed at Roosevelt's speech and said that Danzig must be reunited with Germany. Morcar and Nathan inspected the Syke Mills basements and decided which to strengthen for an air-raid shelter. Morcar employed an architect to draw up the plans.

In May, Germany and Italy signed a political and military alliance. Britain guaranteed the independence of various small nations and signed a treaty with Turkey. Morcar bought up several thousand yards of lining material and had it dyed black.

In June and July, Great Britain tried to sign a pact with Soviet Russia, while German "volunteers" oozed thickly into Danzig. Morcar built his air-raid shelters, and strengthened a cellar at Stanney Royd.

During the last few months Morcar had seen very little of David Oldroyd, for though they were both busy on defence work, their tasks were different owing to the difference in their age. When Morcar caught an occasional glimpse of him he noticed that the boy looked wretched. He was not altogether surprised at this, for he knew that Harington was doing his best to keep Jenny and David apart. The barrister did not indulge in an open break but strove to undermine the friendship insidiously; he did not forbid David his home, but forebore to invite him to it, which in view of the distance between Yorkshire and London, Yorkshire and Oxford, had much the same effect. But Morcar could not feel very troubled about the young lovers. With Christina and himself on their side, they had powerful allies; they were very young; after all Harington could not prevent Jenny's marriage when she came of age if she were really determined about it; Old Mill was (he understood from many indirect indications) doing very nicely; and Harington was essentially a coward as well as a bully in personal relations. Still obstinately persisting in his view that Hitler's appetite could be appeased by the chunks of Europe he successively swallowed, Harington intended to go abroad for his summer vacation, but Morcar opposed this so emphatically, refused so entirely to set foot across the Channel, to approach the lair and place his head in the mouth of the wolf, that Harington was shaken and reluctantly consented to remain in England. To please Jenny it had been arranged that the family should spend a week at the Malvern Festival after their time at the sea. Morcar was so busy rushing off all possible exports with one hand so that they might escape the hazards of war, and turning over to the manufacture of khaki with the other, that he could not be absent from Annotsfield for long, but he joined them for a few days at Malvern.

It was a pleasant experience, a delightful interlude. The sun shone, the little town was crowded with enthusiastic young people in light flannels and bright frocks; one took coffee on the lawns in the morning and waited for Jenny to emerge from the lectures; in the afternoon one watched Jenny playing tennis, or drove through the hilly green countryside; in the evening after an admirable dinner—the hotel was good—one walked along to the theatre and saw a play. Jenny commented shrewdly on these plays, and it was interesting to observe how often her remarks coincided with those of the critics in the better newspapers. Harington's delighted pride in Jenny made him less disagreeable than usual; Morcar shared his pride and Christina's fond affection for their daughter. It struck him, however, that Jenny was not quite her usual self. Never a bouncing or kittenish type, Jenny had usually a good deal of ardour, a joyous smile and a nice wit at her disposal; this week she seemed quiet, listless, preoccupied. Considering that she played tennis for her college, her game seemed dull; her grey eyes lacked sparkle and she argued with her father rarely. On his side Harington seemed to take an almost apologetic tone with her, as if trying to please. "To appease, is the word," thought Morcar. One day the barrister offered to drive his daughter a considerable distance to see some battle site of the seventeenth century—the seventeenth century, it seemed, was Jenny's special period. Morcar and Christina were left together; they drove off towards the Wye and spent a gloriously happy day in each other's company. As they walked back along a woodland path to the lane where they had left Morcar's car, their fingers interlaced, Christina's lovely face suddenly clouded and she exclaimed:

"Poor Jenny!"

"What's the matter with her? I've noticed something wrong."

"It's David, you know. He was to have come to the Festival—not as our guest, just on his own at another hotel. A much cheaper hotel of course, poor pet."

"But why hasn't he come?" said Morcar, astonished. "He loves her nearly as much as I love you."

"Nearly?" said Christina, smiling and swinging her lover's hand.

"Nearly," replied Morcar firmly.

She glanced up at him from her deep blue eyes; Morcar drew her towards him and they kissed.

"It's David's week in camp with his Territorials, you know," explained Christina presently. "Jenny wanted to change our dates, but Edward wouldn't."

"And David couldn't get out of it—camp, I mean?" said Morcar reflectively.

"No. If there's a war, those two poor children will take it very hard. And Edwin at sea. Perhaps there won't be a war, Harry?"

Morcar shook his head. "I'm afraid there will," he said.

After this Malvern was less bright to him. He seemed to see a shadow slowly creeping up from the horizon, menacing the throng of lads and girls, so earnest and full of high intent at the theatre, so lively and chattering on the lawns. Morcar had seen such a shadow creep up on another generation of harmless well-meaning lads and girls. This shadow now would soon blot out the sun for all these happy children; fingers of the shadow were already laid across the hearts of some, as for instance Jenny.

The shadow grew and deepened; suddenly, on the morning of his departure, it leaped halfway across the sky. Morcar had to keep a business engagement in Bradford that noon, and made an early start for home. As he stood on the sunny steps of the hotel in the early morning, waiting for the garage supervisor to bring round his car, a man came up bearing a stack of newspapers. He bought one, opened it wide and read that Russia had concluded a pact, not with Great Britain but with Germany.

"It won't be long now," exclaimed Morcar.

"Your car, sir?" said the hotel porter, who was standing by to receive his tip.

"No—the war," said Morcar grimly.

He drove home swiftly. "You may as well get the fixings up for those blackout curtains," he said to the Syke Mills carpenter.

Next day Mr. Chamberlain announced in the House of Commons that he stood by the guarantee to Poland even without Soviet Russia. Morcar rang up a building contractor and ordered a load of sand, in bags, to be sent to Stanney Royd.

Hitler demanded that a Pole should be sent to Berlin to sign terms of agreement; Mr. Chamberlain announced that we were ready for peace and ready for war; Morcar ordered the Syke Mills skylights to be fitted with sliding shutters.

On Friday September 1st Morcar took a small portable radio to the mill with him, as an announcement was expected at half-past ten. In his private office, very clean and fresh because it had received its annual repainting during Morcar's holiday, he set the radio on his desk, switched it on and sent for Nathan. They listened together, and heard that Germany had invaded Poland at five-thirty that morning. Nathan's face was so disgusted as to be comic.

"Whew!" said Morcar.

He reached for the telephone and bullied the building contractor about the sand for Stanney Royd.

The sand was delivered on Saturday, but not in bags; the bags came separately, empty—there were so many orders for the government and local government, explained the contractor apologetically, that really he had not had time to fill them.

Morcar spent Saturday afternoon and evening buying a few necessary items of equipment for his Stanney Royd cellar shelter, and fixing them.

On Sunday, sitting at breakfast, with the sun pouring into the side windows, he heard the announcement that if Germany was not out of Poland by eleven that morning, Germany and Britain would be at war.

He went at once to the telephone and rang up the Haringtons. By a lucky chance he managed to make the connection, though with considerable delay owing to the emergency, as the operator phrased it. Christina answered. Morcar's heart always leaped with pleasure when he heard her voice, but what he had to. say today must be said to her husband. He asked urgently for Harington and soon heard the barrister's drawling arrogant tones. He wondered a little how Harington would feel now on the verge of war, with all his optimistic prophecies falsified; but there was no time for tactful sparing of his feelings.

"Edward—send your family up here to be out of the way of air raids," urged Morcar. "My mother will take care of them. I've plenty of room at Stanney Royd."

"Thanks. Many thanks. I haven't considered what we ought to do yet," drawled Harington. "I may send Christina away to her father."

"I shan't leave London unless you do, Edward," said Christina's voice in the distance.

"You'll do what you're told, my dear," snapped Harington. Then making his voice mellifluous again, he said to Morcar: "I can't yet believe it will really come to anything."

"I'm afraid it's too late to hope any more," barked Morcar: "We shall be at war in a couple of hours."

"I daresay you're right. I still feel it was all quite unnecessary," drawled Harington in a peevish resentful tone. "But now that we are in it I suppose we must do our best."

"Yes. Well. You can all come here, think on," cried Morcar as the connection began to fade.

He smoked a cigar sitting beside the wireless, and endured a church service and some musical inanities until a quarter past eleven. Then the Prime Minister's voice—the voice of a business man defeated in a bargain, thought Morcar, though the words had. dignity—announced that England was at war.

Morcar went out into the garden, took off his coat, rolled up his sleeves and began to shovel the sand into the bags. Jessopp came out to help; he held the bags while Morcar filled them. Mrs. Morcar, erect, undaunted, watched him from the kitchen windows. It was a glorious sunny September day. Red Admiral butterflies zigzagged about the garden; the trees were scarcely tipped at all with gold. Something cold touched Morcar's hand.

"Why, Heather!" exclaimed Morcar, stooping to pat the dog. "Come to help me, eh?"

Steps rounded the corner of the house, and David Oldroyd appeared.

"Sandbags?" he said, sketching a salute to Mrs. Morcar.

"I'm going to put these in a parapet round yon cellar window— I've got it nicely fixed up inside," said Morcar. "Give me a hand."

David took off his coat and began to tie the ears of the bags. Morcar thought he seemed quiet and unlike himself.

When the sand was all bagged and the bags stacked in a neat redoubt around the window of the strengthened cellar, Morcar invited David down to inspect the new air-raid shelter. He was justly proud of its neat lay-out. Steel props supported the strong old roof, which consisted of two huge slabs of stone. There were four comfortable chairs, for Mrs. Morcar, her son— "though I shall be out on the warden's job usually, I expect," said Morcar—and the two Jessopps. There was a table, two pitchers of water, some mineral syphons, china, first aid appliances, cards, books. A hammer, a hatchet—"to cut our way out if the house comes down on top of us," said Morcar—a couple of flashlights, a kettle with special fuel and a new oil stove completed the amenities.

"Very neat and nice," said David.

His tone was flat and perfunctory, and Morcar felt a boyish disappointment, for he had expected his arrangements to be admired and praised.

"You've done something similar at Scape Scar, I reckon?" he said as they wriggled through the cellar window (to test the escape route) into the sunshine. "And what about Old Mill?"

David hesitated.

"I suppose I shall have to give up Old Mill," he said slowly.

"Give it up?" exclaimed Morcar, horrified. "Why?"

"I'm of military age, you know," said David. "I shall be a soldier, not a manufacturer, for the next few years."

"Ah," said Morcar. His tone was preoccupied, for he was seeing in swift startling flashes many pictures of his own early life: Charlie and himself enlisting, Charlie winding a puttee for the first time, Charlie in the shell-hole. Charlie's face, dead, and his own 1919 face in the mirror in the train to Annotsfield.

"In fact, I'm a soldier already," David was saying soberly. "I've got my papers—I leave tonight."

"That doesn't mean you need give up Old Mill. Why should you?"

"I've nobody to leave in charge. I shall have to give it up."

"Nay—I'll run it for you!" said Morcar strongly.

David exclaimed, flushed, and began to stammer incoherently in a voice which shook.

"I shall ask nothing a year as a wage, and then you can double it from time to time to show your appreciation," joked Morcar.

"But, Mr. Morcar," stammered David. "I can't accept—it's too good—of course I should be profoundly grateful—but—"

Intensely embarrassed, Morcar put a deterring hand on his

arm. "Say nowt, lad," he begged. Looking away, for he was moved, he saw the dog Heather sitting on his haunches, surveying the sandbags from his brown eyes with a judicial considering air. "Tell you what—I'll keep Heather for you too," said Morcar, pointing to the dog. "Unless you'd prefer him to go to your father."

"I think Heather would prefer to stay in Yorkshire," said David.

36

Export Group

It was March 1940. Morcar was out for a walk with David, who had a few days' leave. The two men came out of the gate of the park to high fields, and struck up a stony lane towards the moor. David stooped and released Heather from his lead, and the dog bounced rapturously ahead.

"It's grand to be out here again," said Morcar, sniffing the keen air appreciatively. "I never seem to do any walking now you're away, David. I wish you were back home, lad."

"I might as well be back home for all the good I'm doing in the Army, at present," said David bitterly. "The Army! My God!" But he had vented his vexation on this point already and was never one to press his own affairs at the expense of his listener's; he turned instead courteously to Morcar's grievance. "You know, the idea of this new Export Council seems thoroughly sound to me—I can't understand why you don't like it. According to the *Cash and Carry* Act in the United States, we can only get munitions from there by paying dollars and bringing the stuff across the

Atlantic ourselves. Our dollar reserve is getting very low, so we must earn more dollars. The only way to earn dollars is by selling our products in the States. We make the cloth, we sell it in U.S.A., we use the purchase price to pay their munition manufacturers for aircraft and tanks and guns. They get the cloth, we get the munitions. God knows we need munitions," concluded David.

"I know all that," said Morcar testily, though conscious that he understood the matter better when thus simply stated.

"So we must have more exports—we must have an export drive."

"We must have more exports, but I don't see any need for a Drive, or a Council, or a Group, or any of these things with high-falutin' names," growled Morcar. "I've exported scores of thousands of yards of wool tissues, as the Board of Trade calls 'em, in the last twenty years, and I don't need any Government official to teach me how to do it. Especially when they've never been in a mill in their life, and most of them haven't. Look at Edward Harington!" he went on, for this was a sore point with him: "Here he is with a high-up job in one of these Ministries or Departments or what not, pretending to be an expert on industrial relations. He doesn't know a single thing about industry except what he's picked up from me."

"That might be not inconsiderable, however," said David, smiling.

Morcar snorted.

"Everyone in wool textiles doesn't know his job as well as you do," urged David. "This Export Group will co-ordinate the export effort of the whole industry."

Morcar snorted again.

"You don't mean you intend not to co-operate?" said David in alarm.

"I shan't have much choice, seemingly," said Morcar in a disgruntled tone. "If the Government sets up an Export Group for the Wool Textile Industry or whatever the name of the thing is, we shall have to do what it says, choose how."

"You form one of a Sub-Group, and the Sub-Group elects its own representative to the Export Group, as I understand it."

Morcar groaned. "All this *jargon,*" he muttered crossly.

The two men reached the open moor, and paused to admire the turbulent hills which, in *mat* shades of green and sepia, rolled tumultuously away in every direction. The wild March wind roared round their ears and stung their faces; dark grey clouds chased each other swiftly across the sky, occasionally throwing to earth heavy spears of steel-coloured rain. In the distance Annotsfield, its mill-chimneys agreeably miniature, clung precariously to several hillsides. Heather galloped away, his black pointed ears emerging occasionally above the sombre stems of the plant which gave him his name.

"By the way, where's your cousin GB nowadays?" asked Morcar, as his eye identified the distant slope of Booth Bank.

"R.A.F."

"Of course I shall co-operate with anything that's intended to help win the war," said Morcar in a milder tone, reverting to the Export Group. "But you can't expect me to like it—any more than a dog likes being put on a lead."

37

Disasters

It was April 1940. Mrs. Morcar and her son sat at luncheon in Stanney Royd. Morcar had switched on the wireless so that they might hear the one o'clock news.

They listened. An involuntary gasp of horror came from both. The dog Heather, asleep by the hearth, awoke abruptly at the sound and pricked his rough black ears. They all remained silent and motionless for a long moment while the BBC droned out details.

"Ring the bell, Harry," said Mrs. Morcar at length in a stifled tone. "I can't eat anything after such disasters."

Morcar glanced with distaste at his own full plate and vigorously pressed the bell.

38

Call to Sacrifice

It was May 1940.

Morcar entered the lounge of the Annotsfield Club.

"… and so Churchill is Prime Minister at last."

"Thank God!" said Morcar.

"You needn't be so chirpy about it—he only promises us blood, toil, tears and sweat."

"Who cares?" said Morcar.

39

Volunteer

"… men of reasonable physical fitness and a knowledge of fire-arms should give in their names at their local police station."

Without waiting to switch off the wireless Morcar snatched his hat, sprinted to his garage and drove as fast as he could through the blackout down to Stanney. But of course by the time he reached the Police Station there was a long queue of middle-aged men like himself, waiting to join the Local Defence Volunteers to guard England against invasion.

40

From Dunkirk

It was a glorious June morning; the sun poured down strongly, a steady golden blaze. Morcar felt tired. He had been up all night consulting with the military authorities about the organisation of the Annotsfield and District L.D.V., of which it seemed he was to be partly in charge, and now he had to walk over the brow from Stanney Royd to Syke Mills. He had sent his car and chauffeur to the station overnight to help with the men from Dunkirk, and it had not yet returned.

The Germans had swept through Holland and Belgium, rushed into France, cut the French and British armies in two, driven the northern armies back on the Channel ports. With a thousand little boats—"If only *I* had a boat!" wished Morcar—the British people were getting out their men. The boys were pouring back from France, pouring north into safe centres to be assembled and sorted into units. The West Riding, a little-bombed area hitherto, was crammed with these returning soldiers; it was said that there were already twelve thousand in

Annotsfield alone. They were met at the station by all kinds of cars; lorries fitted with benches, ambulances, buses, private vehicles, tradesmen's vans. They were taken first to a de-lousing station, poor lads; then they were sent off, the less tired by foot, the exhausted by car, to depots, hospitals, billets. There were some of these walking along the Ire Valley Road towards Morcar now; a group on this side, a solitary lad on the opposite pavement. Their khaki was stained and filthy; they carried unco-ordinated scraps of equipment; one was in his shirt, none had caps, only one carried a gun. They looked worn, dirty, tired, unshaven, but they did not—thank God, thought Morcar—look defeated. Suddenly a shout rose behind him; he turned; one of the group had recognised the weary lad across the road and with a shout and an outstretched hand ran to him. The boy stood still and looked stupid; he swayed with fatigue, he was too tired to hold up his head. Then the hand of the other fell on his arm, he looked up, gave a hoarse cry, and suddenly they were in each other's arms, they kissed each other.

"Brothers. Parted on the Dunkirk beaches, I expect," thought Morcar. He blinked his eyes and walked on rather faster. "I mustn't be late at the mill or they'll get worried," he thought, instinctively preserving the social fabric of habit. The sun blazed, the sky was brilliant azure, the trees, bright fresh green, stood as still as though cut out of cardboard. "Thank God there's no wind," thought Morcar, seeing a picture of Channel waves. He met another group of rather older men, with filthy sweating faces.

"Got a fag, mate?" asked one hoarsely.

He gave them all the cigarettes he had about him, and could not forbear asking: "How are things going over there?" though he knew it was a silly question.

The man addressed, a corporal, grimaced and remarked in a low tone, turning aside from the others:

"I give France a fortnight."

And then it will be our turn, thought Morcar, reading this in the corporal's eyes.

"Jerry'll soon knock all these down," said another man, looking around him at the undamaged buildings.

The thought of Christina in London during an invasion with only Harington to protect her stabbed Morcar again, as it did so often nowadays; he turned into a small post-office and sent the Haringtons a wire, saying: *Expecting you today please come at once dont delay any longer.* But he had no hope that Christina would come, nor could he even wish that she would. Harington's government job obliged him to remain in London and Christina had refused to leave him. Morcar admired her courage and loved her the more for it; he wanted her beside him, out of danger, but could not really wish her in this hour to do less than her duty to England.

"I can't guarantee when this will arrive, sir," the elderly news-agent-postmaster was saying. "In the circumstances …"

"I know. Well, do your best," said Morcar hastily. He was glad that they had avoided mentioning the war, but as he went out of the little shop could not help saying over his shoulder: "No wind today."

"No wind," agreed the postmaster with deep feeling, nodding.

Morcar was hot and tired by the time he turned in under the Syke Mills archway, but he set his hat at a jaunty angle, put on a calm and benign expression and greeted his office staff cheerfully.

"There's a gentleman to see you, sir," said his secretary. "He wouldn't give his name."

Morcar frowned slightly out of habit, at this announcement, then reflected that the caller was probably an L.D.V. man and took off the frown again. He gave the girl a few rapid instructions about papers and appointments, then passed into his private office.

A small old man, grey-haired, weazened, shabby, smoking a pipe, stood waiting, looking out of the window. At the sound of Morcar's entrance he turned. It was Mr. Shaw.

Morcar felt such a violent nausea at the sight of Winnie's father standing on Syke Mills premises that for a moment he could hardly prevent himself from retching.

"What do you want?" he demanded hoarsely.

Mr. Shaw took his pipe out of his mouth.

"Your lad's in France," he said.

Morcar was silent, stupefied by the many violent and contra-dictory emotions which seized him.

"Winnie wanted me to come and tell you."

"Aye. Thank you," said Morcar.

The moment was broken by his chauffeur, who came in hurriedly, apologising. A trainful of Dunkirk soldiers had arrived just as he was leaving to come to Stanney Royd that morning, and he had thought Mr. Morcar would wish him to stay and help till the convoy was dealt with.

"Quite right," said Morcar. With an effort he detached his eyes from his father-in-law's, and addressed the chauffeur. "Drive Mr. Shaw down to Prospect Mills," he ordered.

"Yes, sir."

"Thank you—I'll be grateful," mumbled Mr. Shaw.

"And come back here quickly for further orders," concluded Morcar.

"Good-day to you, Harry," said Mr. Shaw, going out.

Morcar forced a mechanical smile and a mumble.

When he was alone he stood for a long time without changing his position. *My* lad, he thought. So Winnie has never told her father. The boy is Mr. Shaw's grandson, choose how—it looked as though the old chap were fond of him. C. H. Morcar. He's Charlie's nephew. He's just an English soldier, like those I met in the street just now. Morcar tried to imagine the scene on the Dunkirk beaches—sand, waves, groups of men, ships off the shore, aircraft continually swooping, the noise of bombing and guns. There were no pictures of it yet in the newspapers. Too terrible, he supposed. In the hour of England's trial, all personal grievances should be laid aside. Laying aside his personal grievance, here was Winnie, Charlie's sister, his wife after all, in the deepest trouble. She was the boy's mother, and the boy was in France. Take what he, Morcar, would feel if David were in France—but thank God he wasn't as far as Morcar knew, he was engaged in a training course preparatory to a commission—take what he would feel if David were in France and multiply it by ten or so, nay perhaps by a hundred for a mother and son, and you would have what Winnie was feeling. If Christina were in France now. … A pang stabbed Morcar's heart. Poor Winnie! She had asked her father to tell him. "Aye," thought Morcar grimly: "She turns to me when she's in trouble." In the hour of England's trial it was proper that all English people should behave in a way worthy of their country. All personal grievances should be laid aside.

Morcar came to himself to find his chauffeur staring at him.

"They've rung up from the station—they want me again to help with the billeting, sir," he said with an effect of repeating an unheard statement.

"All right—drive me up to Hurstholt Road first and then be

off with you," said Morcar, taking his decision.

A few minutes later he pushed back the wooden gate of Hurstcote, walked up the asphalt path and rang the bell. He was not at all sure, after all, that he had done right to come; at sight of the name on the gate, the diamond-shaped bed full of scarlet geraniums, the white casement curtains hanging in strictly vertical folds, his feelings were so terrible that he doubted his capacity to carry through an interview with Winnie with any decency. The door opened: a small middle-aged woman, sallow, thin about throat and arms, with crimped light-brown hair, wearing an ugly bright green frock and a cretonne apron, stood before him. For a moment he did not recognise her; then he saw her reddened eyelids, her cheek mottled by weeping.

"Well, Winnie," he said.

"Harry!" exclaimed his wife. "You've come, then." There was a pause; they gazed at each other. "Well, come in," said Winnie at last, stepping back to allow him to pass into the house.

Morcar smiled mournfully as he went in; her tone was characteristically acid, and in spite of his considerable fortune, Syke Mills, Stanney Royd, his fine car and all the appurtenances of his wealth, he felt for a moment humbled and schoolboyish before her superior sophistication, as in days of old. He struggled to assert himself, at first unsuccessfully; then he thought of Christina and at once Winnie and her surroundings fell into proper perspective. The furniture in the little front room was crowded and tasteless, the air was stuffy, Winnie herself, poor girl, was far from sophisticated in her appearance—she was not dowdy, but worse: smart in a naïve provincial manner. Her attempts at fashion, far from being intimidating, were pathetic.

They faced each other across a cheap light oak table with an imitation tapestry strip on which stood a bowl scantily filled with

355

one bunch of bought pink sweet peas.

"Well, Winnie," began Morcar gravely: "Your father told me—your boy's in France."

Winnie nodded. Her chin quivered, and Morcar saw that she could not manage to speak.

"I'm sorry, love," said Morcar kindly.

Winnie said nothing; her fingers played a slow idle tattoo on the table; with head bent she watched them intently.

"If there's anything I can do," hesitated Morcar. "But I'm afraid there isn't much, and that's the truth."

Suddenly a strange sound, between cry and groan, broke from Winnie's lips; her shoulders heaved convulsively, she buried her face in her hands and burst into wild screaming sobs.

"Nay—nay!" urged Morcar, alarmed. He moved round the table towards her, patted her shoulder, put his arm about her waist. The hard unyielding corset, the knot of tie-laces, he felt beneath his hand made her seem all the more pathetically naïve. "I do feel for you about your boy, Winnie love," he said. "I do indeed."

"My boy?" screamed Winnie. She turned to him, clutched his arm, beat her clenched fist against his shoulder. Her hazel eyes blazed, her sallow cheek flushed; she looked like the Winnie he had married twenty-four years ago. "My boy!" she repeated scornfully. "He was your boy too, Harry! Yours!"

"You told me he wasn't, you know," Morcar reminded her.

"You fool! Of course he was yours. How could you ever think he was not yours? He's the living image of you—always has been."

"Now come, Winnie," said Morcar in a calm equable tone: "Don't let us have a scene. You told me the boy was not mine and you've never said anything else all these years."

356

"You never gave me a chance. I kept hoping you'd come back and I could explain. When you had that row with Father over your Thistledowns I made sure you'd come and see him," said Winnie with a laugh full of malice. "I urged him on about those pieces—I made sure that would stir you up. And then when you asked me to divorce you—I refused because I made sure you'd come and see me and I could explain."

"Now look, Winnie," said Morcar, beginning to be disturbed—Winnie's mode of making the announcement of her son's parentage was so totally unlike the conventional style, so characteristic of her perverse and wilful spirit, that it alarmed him. It was so like Winnie to scold where another woman would have shed imploring repentant tears, that for the first time the possibility that she might be telling the truth shot through his mind. "Now look, Winnie. Since we are here together, with England in such trouble and the boy in France, let's have the truth out, once and for all. I won't hold it against you. Who is the boy's father? Who was your lover, eh?"

"You were his father, you fool! I never had a lover," raged Winnie, striking at him with her fist.

"Tell me the truth."

"I *am* telling the truth. As I hope for his safety," screamed Winnie, "I swear it."

"Good God!"

"He was yours, Harry."

"But why on earth did you say he wasn't?"

"I hated you for coming back alive, an officer with a medal," shouted Winnie, her eyes gleaming viciously, "while Charlie was dead and cold. You left him to die!"

"I did not!" shouted Morcar.

"Yes, you did. You went off rescuing Jessopp and winning a

medal, instead of looking after Charlie."

"Charlie was dead when I got him back to the trench."

"Who says so?" cried Winnie with derision.

"Colonel Francis Oldroyd, D.S.O.," replied Morcar with profound satisfaction. "We had it all out together a few years ago."

Winnie slowly dissolved before his eyes from a half-mad virago to a shaking weeping woman. "Oh," she wailed. "Oh, Harry! Oh!" She staggered against the table and her head sank on her breast.

"You'd better sit down," said Morcar, who felt hardly able to stand himself. He guided Winnie to a chair. She slipped from his arm and sank down awkwardly; her head lay sideways, her face went white, her eyes closed. Morcar drew out his travelling flask, unscrewed the top, poured out a strong dose and held it to her lips. "You'd better drink this brandy," he said.

Winnie sipped the brandy, sighed, lay still. Morcar stood gazing down at her. He could not yet sort out his emotions, but at the moment he was most conscious of an understanding for Winnie's hatred of himself. It was exactly the same kind of illogical, unreasoning resentment about Charlie's death which he had felt for years against Francis Oldroyd. After a moment Winnie seemed to revive; she sat up and put one hand to her head. Morcar sat down on a chair nearby and bent towards her.

"But listen, Winnie," he urged. "If you hated me for Charlie's death—I understand that, yes, I understand it. But if you hated me, why did you marry me?"

"I always loved you, Harry," said Winnie mournfully, looking at him from liquid eyes. "You won't believe it, I expect, but it's true. That's partly why I hated you, you know—it was so maddening; I went on loving you for years, ever since I was a

358

schoolgirl, and you never looked at me as a woman at all. You never loved me, Harry."

Morcar tried to utter a lie, but it stuck in his throat.

"I was very very fond of you, Winnie," he said at last gravely.

"Yes, I know," said Winnie. "That's what I mean. Poor Harry! You never loved me. Poor Harry! I don't regret it though—I have Cecil."

"Cecil?"

"Your son, Harry. Don't you even remember his name? You were in France when he was christened, of course. Cecil Henry Morcar, I called him. I wanted him to have your name, of course, and the initials—C. H.—they're the beginning of Charlie, you see. I called him Cecil after we parted—you see it annoyed Father if I called him Harry. Father was very angry with you at the time. Of course he thought we'd quarrelled and you'd deserted me. But I didn't care. I had Cecil, all to myself. That's Cecil, there."

She pointed. Morcar looked across at a window table, and saw the photograph of a fair, ingenuous, weak-looking youth with a dreamy face. Morcar could not yet look on the boy without repulsion. Cecil! What a name!

"Yes, I have Cecil," repeated Winnie fondly. Then her face changed terribly and she cried: "No, no! I haven't got Cecil! He's in France!"

Morcar exclaimed and sat back in his chair. Her flippant disregard of his own feelings, although her quick intelligence made her perfectly aware of them, angered him. She had laid his life in ruins by a perverse, frivolous and monstrous lie, and now when he had built it up, laid it in ruins again without appearing to notice that she did so.

"You've done me a very great wrong, Winnie," he said sternly.

359

"I did you a wrong when I married you, Harry, but not when I made you leave me. You do better without us Shaws—we're not your sort."

There was too much truth in this for Morcar easily to contest it. But the boy! Morcar felt a deep repulsion from the notion of any son of his who had Winnie for a mother; he did not want to see him or know anything of him. But the thought of his son being brought up by the Shaws was none the less unbearable.

"I can't understand you, Winnie," he said. "I really can't. Here you've brought the boy up in a mean poor way, when he might have had every advantage that money can buy."

"You wouldn't have made all that money if you'd stayed with us. Besides, we haven't been poor. You've been generous, Harry—you were always generous," said Winnie, lightly jeering as of old.

"But didn't you ever feel you wanted him to have more? To go to a University, to travel, to see a bit of life?"

"I kept thinking you and I would come together again and I could explain everything. And you see we have," said Winnie brightly.

Morcar exclaimed with anger and pain.

"It's too late for us to come together now, Winnie," he said harshly. "You should have come and told me this years ago."

"Would you have believed if I had?" asked Winnie pertly.

"I don't know. I don't know why I should believe you now," said Morcar.

"But you do," said Winnie. Her tone made this a statement and not a question, and Morcar resented the way she carried off her outrageous story.

"I don't see why you should take it so calmly for granted," he began. "You told me a lie once—"

"Oh!" screamed Winnie violently, pointing.

Morcar turned to the window; a soldier in khaki, dirty, dishevelled, without cap or rifle, was fumbling at the gate. A torn service respirator hanging limply from his shoulder impeded his efforts. As Morcar looked, the little wooden gate swung abruptly open, destroying the leaning soldier's balance; he staggered and fell on the asphalt path.

Morcar hurried from the house, but Winnie, her arms outstretched, ran ahead of him with all the speed of anguished love. She dropped on her knees beside the young man in the path.

"Cecil!" she cried. "Oh, Cecil!" She put her arms about his body, tried ineffectually to turn him to a more comfortable position, supported his head against her knee. "Cecil!" she cried again, rocking him in her arms.

"I'm all right, Mother," whispered the soldier.

Morcar had now reached the pair. He put his hands beneath the soldier's armpits and raised him to his feet; drawing one of the young man's arms over his own shoulder and gripping him round the waist, he supported him into the house. Once within the door, he felt the weight on his muscles double; Cecil's feet dragged; he had fainted. Morcar lowered his son carefully to the settee. He thought of him now without reservation as his son, for in spite of the grime, the tousled hair, the unshaven chin, the slack mouth, the expression of fear stamped on the unconscious features, it was almost exactly his own face Morcar looked into— not his face as it was now, but as it had been, say when Charlie died. Cecil's eyelids fluttered for a moment, revealing mild brown eyes.

"I thought his eyes were the same colour as mine," said Morcar in a whisper.

"Babies' eyes change colour," replied Winnie in the same tone.

Morcar laid his hand on the young man's forehead; it was dry and burning.

"He's ill," he said. "We'd best get him up to bed."

He grasped Cecil beneath the arms again, and instructing Winnie to support his feet, used his strength to carry the boy upstairs. Winnie, her face contorted into a mask of anxious grief, uttered small fluttering sounds of concern as they went—"Cecil! Oh! He's ill! Cecil!"—and hung over her son as he lay on the bed. Morcar sent her for hot-water-bottles, while he undressed the boy. Cecil had a fine strong body, he discovered; he was taller than his father, more like Charlie than Morcar in figure, but had Morcar's solid shoulders. As Morcar began to draw his stained shirt over his head Cecil feebly put out a hand to stop him and gazed up anxiously into his father's eyes.

"I can't stay here," he muttered hoarsely. "I'm just on my way to report. It's as quick by Hurst Bank as up the valley road, you know."

Morcar promised soothingly to notify his whereabouts to the report centre at once and drive him there as soon as he was fit to be moved, and Cecil sank back, relieved. Morcar continued his self-imposed task, his heart torn by anger and grief. Cecil's speech had struck him painfully. The young man's accent was rough, his tones slow and grating. The expression on his face was ingenuous and perplexed. He did not look or sound in the least like Edwin Harington or David Oldroyd. "If only he's honest I don't mind," Morcar told himself, minding bitterly the while: "But the Shaws have had him all these years."

Winnie came into the room at a quick stumbling run, carrying hot-water-bottles wrapped in towels. She bent over Cecil murmuring soothing words, put the bottles to his feet, adjusted his pillows, smoothed back his tumbled fair hair and gently kissed his forehead. Cecil's eyes did not open, but his face relaxed into an expression of content and ease. In spite of the hideous green dress which hurt the eyes in this brilliant sunshine, in spite of the too-bright apron, the frizzed hair, the lined face damp now with sweat as a result of shock and hurry, as she stooped over her son Winnie seemed to Morcar to symbolise a noble motherhood. He left mother and son together and went to the telephone. He summoned his own doctor urgently, ascertained the proper military authorities and notified them of Cecil's whereabouts, giving Mr. Shaw's name as the owner of Hurstcote and omitting his relationship to Cecil, so that the story sounded simply as if Cecil had fainted on a stranger's threshold and been taken into the house from mere humanity. He also tracked down his chauffeur and sent him to Prospect Mills to fetch Mr. Shaw.

By this time the doctor had arrived; he pronounced that Cecil had a touch of pneumonia—"soaked to the skin boarding a boat off Dunkirk, I expect," said the doctor—and must not be moved. Morcar suggested a night nurse; the doctor said it was almost impossible to find a free nurse at this moment and he could not undertake to attempt it, but he gave Morcar the addresses of several private nurses and nursing homes. Meanwhile Mrs. Morcar could probably manage.

"Yes, I can manage," said Winnie eagerly.

The doctor gave instructions for treatment and hurried away. "He'll pull through—he's young and strong—just needs careful nursing—keep him quiet and warm," he said on the doorstep. Morcar telephoned five addresses, learned two or three more, put in a trunk call, secured an elderly private nurse and promised to fetch her from a country home that afternoon, then returned to his son's bedside.

He glanced round Cecil's room as he entered. It had little character or taste. Cheap light-coloured furniture, perfectly clean but a good deal battered; a highly floral eiderdown in cheap sateen; a small hanging bookcase partly filled by a few battered school-stories and a couple of paper-backed thrillers; on the mantelpiece a studio photograph of Winnie, coloured, in a brown satin dress and two rows of very artificial pearls, and a snapshot of a pale landscape with a white house in the distance, which Morcar guessed to be the home of whichever it was of the Shaw boys who had gone to South Africa. Between these, in the place of honour, a used cricket-ball rested on a small black stand bearing a silver label. Morcar bent to read the inscription; it recorded that C. H. Morcar had taken ten wickets for a total of ten, in a match between Annotsfield College and a certain north-country public school, in June 1931. Morcar smiled, and turned towards his son with a slightly less painful feeling round his heart.

Winnie was seated beside the bed, her hands tightly clasped, directing on Cecil a fixed gaze of anxious loving care. As Morcar approached she turned and looked up at him.

"Harry, I'll divorce you if you want," she said, her words tumbling over each other in her haste to utter them: "There are new laws now, I daresay it won't be so difficult—I'll divorce you, I'll do anything you want, Harry, if you'll only look after him, look after Cecil."

Morcar exclaimed.

"Listen, Winnie," he said. He stooped down, took hold of her shoulders, turned her to face him. "Tell me the truth, now. Why did you keep the boy away from me all these years?"

"I wanted him for myself. I never had anybody for myself

364

after Charlie died. Cecil loves me. You didn't, Harry," panted Winnie, looking away from him. "I was lonely. You never loved me. You never loved me, did you, Harry?"

Morcar sighed. "No," he said gravely at length, releasing her arms. "No. I'm afraid I didn't, love. I'm sorry, Winnie."

"Never mind," said Winnie brightly, though tears sprang in her red-rimmed eyes. "That's all over now. I'll divorce you, Harry, I'll do anything you want—if you'll promise me to look after Cecil."

"I promise," said Morcar.

41

Alone

Nathan coughed and looked at his watch. "Shall we turn on t'wireless?" he suggested.

England lay under the threat of invasion. Warned by the dreadful fate of Holland and Belgium, the British Government were taking precautions against parachutists. Every road, every village, must be guarded; all open spaces must be watched by patrols. Concrete road blocks were to be made, barbed wire to twine round them provided; road signs were to be obliterated, maps withdrawn from circulation. Leaflets were being printed instructing householders what to do in case invasion came. The hills and dales of the West Riding were too steep and confused to be suitable for hostile aircraft landings, but their stretches of wild moorland, remote from the eyes but near the sites of towns, were ideal for paratroops and must be watched. Morcar was so busy with details of L.D.V. organisation, with indenting for weapons, with arranging training, with discussing sites and enrolling new members, that there were days when he had barely time to eat

366

or sleep, and entered Syke Mills only at odd moments for hurried conferences with Nathan. This was such a day; he had driven himself away from Stanney Royd on L.D.V. business before seven that morning without even seeing a newspaper, and had been on the rush ever since. Accordingly he welcomed Nathan's reminder cordially.

"Aye, do," he cried. "Perhaps we shall hear by now what France has decided."

"Nay—we heard that on t'last bulletin, Mr. Morcar," said Nathan stolidly. "France has asked for an Armistice."

"Oh," said Morcar flatly. He felt a tide of blood rushing to the surface of his body. France! Gone! France! We shall be invaded in a week, thought Morcar. Well! Let 'em come, damn them! Aloud he said in a mild tone: "So we're alone in the fight now, seemingly."

"Aye—the others have all gone down," said Nathan.

There was a pause.

"Well—we know where we are now, anyway," said Morcar.

"That's right," agreed Nathan, nodding. He stretched out his hand and turned the knob of the neat wall radio which Morcar had installed in the Syke Mills office, without further comment.

"Nathan takes it very well, I must say," thought Morcar admiringly.

42

Patrol at Dawn

"It's going to be cold up here in the winter, if it's like this now," thought Morcar, stamping his feet.

It was just before dawn on a day of September 1940, and Morcar was doing duty at one of the posts manned by the Ire Valley battalion of the Home Guard, as the L.D.V. was now called. The blackness of the night was slowly lifting into a sombre indigo blue, and Morcar began to be able to discern the features of the wide and massive landscape about him. The post, a small stone building with a loopholed protective wall across the entrance, stood high in the Pennines, just below the brow of a long rocky ridge, from which immense sweeps of tough grass and black stones rolled down to a main road far below. On either side at a distance of a hundred yards or so stood a circular erection of blackened brick, from each of which waved continually a short white plume of bitter smoke—a cold breeze brought the smoke to Morcar's nostrils. now and made him cough. Across a broad valley another such white plume oozed into the dark.

These marked smoke-vents, airholes to the long railway tunnel crawling deep through the Pennines beneath Morcar's feet.

By one of those ironies to which those are subject who live their lives in one circumscribed region, this Home Guard post faced, across many miles of rolling moorland, the rocky bluff on which Morcar had stood on the night he parted from Winnie in his youth, so that a visit to the post recalled that night to him always. He thought of that night now as the outline of the distant ledge came slowly into view against the northern sky. But that old anguish had gone from his mind like a drawn tooth, leaving perhaps a dull ache, a void, behind. For did he really wish that the incidents of that night had never happened? Did he wish his separation from Winnie had never taken place? Did he wish he had lived a narrow quiet life with Winnie and Cecil? Did he wish he had never met Christina? No; bad as some of it was, wasted as some of his capacities, many of his years, had been, he preferred his life as he had lived it to what it would have been if he lived with Winnie. Did he wish he had never married Winnie? Ah, that was a different matter; he wished that hard enough. But he no longer resented upon Winnie the actions which sprang from her contorted, convoluted love. The tragedy of their lives was not altogether her fault, as it was not his; the social pressures of the age had been too strong for them. "Poor children!" Christina had said when she heard the story; this was what Morcar thought whenever he stood in this Home Guard post now.

The sun rose; the sky brightened from indigo to royal, then suddenly turned pale and clear; light poured over the vast land-scape, revealing the high massive ridges, the long slopes, the gulley of the infant Ire, the black rocks, the dark heather seamed by velvety peat, the tough dun-coloured grass tossing restlessly in the wind, the stretches of russet bracken, the dark grey road. There was not a parachute in sight.

"Well, they haven't come to-night," thought Morcar cheerfully.

He hummed happily to himself, and leaving the post, climbed a few yards up the hill to a point where he could see down the Ire Valley towards Annotsfield. A dirty sheep or two flounced out of his way as his heavy boots struck the rock; down in the road the first lorry of the day crawled up the hills between Lancashire and Yorkshire. From this height Morcar could see, deep down in a snug green hollow, the village of Marthwaite. Its canal was tiny but smooth and clear, the Ire running unevenly, ruffled, beside; there was the old church where David's ancestors were buried, the new bridge and the old packhorse bridge, the row of solid little stone houses, a scattered handful of mill chimneys. The bluff of Scape Scar cut off Marthwaite from the rest of the valley, but from this great height Morcar could see over the bluff to the next village—not as far down as the canal, the river, but to the chapel gable and the mill chimneys. And so it would go on down the Ire, thought Morcar: little houses where people were quietly asleep or just waking to the toil, the fearful anxieties, of the day; little houses, large houses, mill chimneys. A deep love suddenly rushed into his heart for the West Riding, which he watched here to guard; these are my people, he thought, I must protect them, no enemy shall harm them if I can help it. His mother, Winnie, Nathan, the Jessopps, the workpeople at Syke Mills and Old Mill and all the other mills whose chimneys were now just beginning to exhale smoke; even the dog Heather; for that night they had all been in his care.

And even as he looked, his love seemed to stretch out all over England. To the camps where David and Cecil were training.

To London, where Christina and Harington, and Jenny and Fan Oldroyd, were being subjected, said the newspapers, to violent day and night raids from enemy planes. To Kent, where Canon Harington and his vicarage had perished from enemy action; a German plane, swerving away from the London defences, had crashed and the old house, the yew, the Canterbury bells, the sweet Williams, the Canon's books, were all burned, while the old man lay buried beneath fallen masonry. To the coast, where Francis Oldroyd was engaged full time in Civil Defence—David had begged his stepmother to come north to safety, but she would not leave her husband. To the air, where as he understood G. B. Mellor was a Pilot Officer in a Spitfire, fighting for the mastery of the air in the battle of Britain. To the sea, where young Edwin Harington, out of sight, almost out of hearing, helped to bring in convoys. For that night, yes, for that night while he was on guard, the safety of all these had in some measure been in Morcar's care. He felt that he could never again lay down that charge, that burden.

"They're my people and I must take care of them," thought Morcar.

43

Nocturne in London

The siren sounded just as the taxi drew up at the door of the Department which enjoyed Harington's services. Morcar felt nervous—not of possible enemy planes overhead, but lest in his lack of experience of London air-raids he should commit some naive action below the general level of London behaviour. The taxi-driver and the Ministry reception clerk, however, seemed to take no notice of the warning, and this reassured Morcar; he could play indifference as well as the next man.

He filled up a form; the clerk telephoned; an elderly uniformed messenger led him along corridors and up steps into a small room with some of its windows boarded up, where two girls, one dark, one blonde, typed and answered the continual summons of a knot of telephones. The girls were good-looking and well dressed, with south-country accents and friendly manners; they put Morcar into a large leather chair and handed him a newspaper and informed him that Mr. Harington was in conference but would see him presently. A buzzer sounded above an inner door;

the elder of the two girls, the dark one, rushed into Harington's sanctum with a notebook, rushed out again and began to telephone the Minister's private office. The other girl typed incessantly, except when a messenger came in with an armful of large envelopes and a locked despatch box, from which she immediately drew masses of files. Red and green labels protruded from these marked URGENT; VERY URGENT; PRIORITY; and so on; Morcar read them upside down. As far as one could judge from the blonde's conversation, high personages, people whose names one saw in the newspapers, telephoned continually demanding Mr. Harington, and were continually sidetracked to someone else of less importance. It was a new scene to Morcar and he watched it with a smiling interest; he felt like a schoolboy waiting to see a headmaster, but did not mind.

At last he was ushered into Harington's presence. The room was large and agreeably furnished in a spare modern style; a plain cord carpet, a large empty desk, a couple of comfortable armchairs. Some admirable modern posters of an advisory nature, issued by Harington's Department, hung on the walls.

"Well, my dear Harry, what can I do for you?" enquired Harington, shaking his hand. His tone was suave but his expression was fretful; it was clear he regarded Morcar's visit as the crowning exasperation of a harassed morning. "I'm sorry I had to keep you waiting but you had no appointment."

Morcar began to remind Harington that, as his Department well knew, he was to visit the United States in the course of the next few weeks to assist in the export drive. At this point a concealed apparatus above the lintel hooted violently in three short blasts.

"Is that a new type of all-clear signal?" enquired Morcar with interest.

"No—that means imminent danger," drawled Harington.

"Oh. I suppose people go into the basement and that sort of thing."

"I really don't know," said Harington with cold impatience.

Gunfire and heavy thuds sounded in the distance and came nearer, and Morcar had to shout the remainder of his explanation. His visit to the U.S.A. was decided after consultation with other textile interests whom he was to represent, and the Export Group had supported his application for an exit permit and travelling facilities. He had come to town to-day to pick up his permit and passport and submit his papers to the censorship bureau. But now there seemed to be some hitch about his permit, while as for travelling facilities, they were apparently nonexistent—the steamship lines had told him they had no ship whatever sailing to the United States in December.

"All that has nothing to do with this Department, my dear Morcar," said Harington impatiently.

"Really?" said Morcar, astonished. "I understood—"

"You should go to another Ministry," said Harington, giving its name.

"Oh. In that case I'm sorry I troubled you," said Morcar, rising.

"Not that I suppose for a moment that they'll be able to help you," drawled Harington. "But they're the proper channel, you know." He pressed the buzzer, and instructed the dark girl to make an appointment with the appropriate official for Mr. Morcar.

"I shall see you tonight, perhaps?" said Morcar, taking his leave.

"At home? It's very doubtful, I'm afraid," returned Harington shortly. "I'm sleeping here at present. I can't leave."

The all-clear sounded as Morcar left the building, but an alert came as he sat giving luncheon to Fan Oldroyd (who was now like everybody else working in a Ministry) and again two or three times during the afternoon. Hurrying from one government office to another with eventually satisfactory results, Morcar observed that nobody appeared to take any notice of these short raids at all, except to raise their voices occasionally when the gunfire drew near.

"They're a remarkable people, these Londoners," he said to himself. "Even Harington."

He made this observation as he was walking down Shaftesbury Avenue, which had suffered very recently from bombs. Some buildings had vanished altogether, some had become mounds of pinkish rubble; window-frames gaped blackly, fringed some-times by sharp spikes of glass; the iron porches of theatres were twisted and blackened. Hose-pipes lay in massive curves across the road and A.R.P. personnel were busy about them. The surface of the road was charred and muddy. The day was dreary, and the whole scene struck Morcar as indescribably cheerless. In Charing Cross Road a huge hole gaped, round which buses carefully steered their way—the hole was large enough to accom-modate a couple. Some premises, façades merely through which one saw sordid ruin within, bore a notice stating they were unsafe for entry or human occupation; several bookshops thus lacked interiors, and the assistants, pale and red-nosed from the November cold, sold only from the outside stalls, wrapped up in mufflers and thick coats. Here and there a little shop, its windows boarded, its doors hingeless, propped against the wall, or vanished altogether, bore a scrawled notice announcing: *Bombed out but not sold out; business as usual.* Blasted houses, divided in two as if by a giant knife, exposed the intimacies of private life to the

375

public view: a dressing-table, a washstand, a bed with a striped mattress, perched aloft in the third storey, inaccessible now to any but a climber's foot, beaten upon by wind and rain. These soiled relics of what were once warm human habitations depressed Morcar particularly. There's nothing romantic about being bombed, he thought; it's just a miserable, uncomfortable mess. And therefore it takes all the more courage to stand up to, he concluded.

The winter afternoon drew towards its close, and Morcar began to experience a strangely poignant feeling of brooding anticipation. The dusk gathered, but no lights appeared save the dim pinpoints of hand torches and tiny circles on the buses; half-seen figures stumbled along as though through greyish mist, and entered screened doorways with an effect of relief. Everything seemed waiting, waiting. Morcar found the phrase "the doomed city" reverberating in his mind; it was perfectly possible, he reflected, and indeed not unlikely, that when if ever the war was over, London would look like the ruins he had seen in Rome, on the Palatine. A pang of angry grief went through his heart at the thought. Dark closed in, the muffling choking dark of the London blackout. The blackness seemed to press down on Morcar's head, so that it was with difficulty that he straightened his neck and walked upright. The edges of pavements became pitfalls to be negotiated with attention; each passer-by offered a possible collision. The streets became unfamiliar, so that one continually felt lost, as in a nightmare. Morcar had promised to meet Jenny at the bar of a hotel not far from the Admiralty where she was now working. He negotiated the screens and the black curtains with careful patience, and entered a foyer which seemed of dazzling brilliance by contrast with the murk outside. At once his spirits rose; here at last was a familiar scene. Not quite familiar,

376

he discovered presently, for there were very few people having drinks; the waiter with whom he entered into talk explained to him that nowadays people liked to get home before the night raids started.

Jenny was late; he had ceased to watch the door for her when suddenly she came towards him, radiant in a hooded coat of bright warm blue. Morcar had time to recognise the stuff as of David's manufacture before he saw, following Jenny as she threaded her way through the empty tables, David himself. David—in battle-dress, which Morcar had not seen before— looked well and lively, much happier than when Morcar had seen him in the spring. After greeting the young people cordially, Morcar commented on their cheerful looks.

"David's happy because he's training for something danger- ous," said Jenny, glancing at her love with mock reproach and real admiration.

This was a sentiment Morcar understood. "What are you up to, then, David?" he eagerly enquired.

"I'm afraid I mustn't tell you—it's all very hush-hush," replied David with a smile. "It's not at all dangerous yet, just bookwork, mugging up the necessary knowledge. I've just been to the War House—I have to get back to camp tonight."

The drinks Morcar had ordered came; he paid for them, sat back, and raised his glass to the young pair. It gave him pleasure to see them together, for they were most admirably matched in body, mind and spirit. They replied suitably to his toast but then fell silent, and as Morcar contemplated them it struck him that of course they wished to be alone. Hastily he rose and explained that he must go; they smiled at him kindly but with obvious relief and sent messages by him to Christina.

"Mother doesn't know David's here—it was an unexpected

visit. Tell her I may be a little late. I know it's her night at the post and she can't wait dinner for me. I'll scrounge something for myself when I get in," said Jenny.

The Underground was bright and cheerful, the Kensington streets correspondingly black to Morcar's eyes; although he knew them so well he lost his way twice and was profoundly thankful when at last he found himself on the Haringtons' door-step. He fumbled for the bell and rang; the door was opened almost immediately by Christina.

"Oh, Harry, I'm so glad you've come," she said in a tone of relief. "You're rather late—I was afraid I should have to go out and leave you." She drew him in and closed the door. In the bluish light of the wartime hall lamp Morcar saw that she was dressed in dark blue jersey and slacks. "It's my night on duty," she explained.

Morcar was so familiar with every cadence of her voice that he knew at once Harington was not in the house. He picked her up in his arms and kissed her vigorously.

"No, no, Harry," said Christina.

"Why not? Winnie served divorce papers on me yesterday," said Morcar cheerfully, taking off his coat, "I shall be free next year."

Christina made no reply, but drew him into the dining-room. The windows were boarded; the dining-table had been pushed to one end of the room; the other end was arranged as a sitting-room, with a small table, a radio, and armchairs.

"We're living in this room at present," explained Christina. "Safer downstairs, you know. Besides, there's a good deal of glass all over the drawing-room and we haven't managed to get the windows boarded yet."

She rang a handbell—blast had put the other out of order, she

378

explained—and told the elderly maid to put a portion to keep hot for Miss Jennifer and then serve dinner.

"I must go to the post. Will you walk there with me, Harry?" she said when the meal was over.

"Of course. I should like to see as much of everything here as I can," said Morcar gravely. "So that I can tell them all at home what it's like."

Christina put on a dark coat on which was stitched a blue armlet with the letters C.D. in yellow, slung her respirator over her shoulder, and balanced a steel helmet marked with a white W on her head. The tin hat slipped sideways on her dark curly hair; in this position it framed her lovely face enchantingly, but was not much use as a protection against falling shrapnel.

"Your strap's too loose," said Morcar in an experienced tone. He took off the helmet and adjusted the buckle. "That's better?"

"Yes, thank you," said Christina, smiling up at him.

Morcar took her face between his hands beneath the helmet, and kissed her—her sea-blue eyes, her rich mouth, the tip of her nose for a joke, her mouth again. Then the pair set out for the post.

"You're a warden, then?" said Morcar, drawing her arm through his and interlacing their fingers.

"Yes. Jerry's late tonight," said Christina, looking up at the sky. It was now crossed by white shafts which swayed and stabbed: the searchlights. "Haven't you had any raids in the West Riding, Harry?"

"Yes. But in Annotsfield we've only had an accidental stick or two. We hear the enemy go over night after night, of course. We get plenty of yellow and purple warnings. But they're always on their way to somewhere else."

Christina guided him down a flight of steps into the basement of a house which was fitted up as a Wardens' Post. It had the same characteristics as posts in Stanney and Annotsfield, reflected Morcar; the same items of essential report equipment, the same kind of neat supplementary improvisations—only, here they had all been used. The wardens, here as at home, were both men and women, mostly middle-aged, drawn from every income level. There was the banker, the tradesman, the housewife, the plumber, the shop assistant, the Civil Servant. They all greeted Morcar with great heartiness, especially when they learned he had been a warden himself. They hinted, tentatively, a polite curiosity as to why he had given it up.

"There isn't much air activity round our way," explained Morcar. "And all those hills of ours take a lot of watching."

Perceiving his interest to be genuine, the warden in charge of the post suggested that he might like to see the people sheltering in the Underground station. Morcar eagerly agreed, and as no alert had yet sounded, the warden offered to take Morcar and Christina there. He guided them down the spiral staircase which led to the Underground platform. It was a bright hell, thought Morcar; beneath the glare of the electric light, against whitewashed walls, lay the uneasy bodies of men, women and children, wedged against the stone stairs on either side by mattresses and rolled-up clothing. Late-comers with heavy bundles under their arms sought anxiously for a vacant stair. The platform below was crowded along the walls to the white chalk marks which defined the limits of the sleeping accommodation. Flushed children wandered excitedly from group to group, or tossed restlessly on improvised beds, unable to sleep; some of the shelterers read, some knitted, some simply lay and stared, bright-eyed, at the light; some sang mournful songs which seemed to cause them a cheerful hilarity. At one end of the platform members of the Women's Voluntary Services, in their neat green suits, with a nurse in a white coat, dispensed cups of tea, advice and sympathy. Behind them, signs indicated emergency lavatory accommodation. Electric trains arrived and departed at regular intervals with an effect of callous disregard, a couple of yards away from the feet of the sleepers. The heat and the hubbub seemed to Morcar quite appalling, but nobody looked downcast or anxious.

"What a people!" thought Morcar.

The warden led Morcar aside into an unused whitewashed tunnel, and proudly showed him tiers of iron bunks.

"These will be ready for use soon, and then they'll be able to get a real night's rest."

As they emerged thankfully into the cool air, the siren sounded. Its long wailing rise and fall depressed Morcar; at that moment he echoed Mr. Churchill's wish that the sirens could be taught to bark defiance at the enemy, for the final sinking cadence seemed to retreat from hope and prophesy destruction.

"I must be off!" shouted the warden, running.

Christina seized Morcar's arm and dragged him along briskly, but paused when they reached the top of the post's basement steps. "The gunfire's distant yet," she said. "I needn't go down for a moment or two. You must go and shelter in our house, Harry."

"Christina—I may not see you again before I go off to the States," began Morcar hurriedly.

"Oh, Harry! Are you going so soon?"

"In a week or two."

"By air?"

"No. Sea."

"But won't it be very dangerous? The submarines seem very active just now."

"Dangerous! That comes well from you, in London!" exclaimed Morcar. "I'm glad it's dangerous, he went on quickly: "I'm tired of being safe. If you think we enjoy it up in Yorkshire, being safe while you down here have air-raids every night, you're wrong. To hear about the blitz on the wireless and be able to do nothing to help—it's hell. Truly it is, Christina. Besides, we need the dollars," he went on, swerving away from a feeling which embarrassed him. "We must push up our exports so that we can buy more tanks and planes. When I get back, my divorce will come on. I shall be free with any luck by next autumn. I'm putting all this badly because of the alert," he said hurriedly, as the gunfire increased ominously and pink flashes lit up the sky. "Before the divorce is made absolute we must be careful of course, but afterwards you'll come to me, won't you?" Christina was silent, and Morcar put his arm about her and urged her: "You'll fix it up with Harington about a divorce, or come to me and let Harington divorce you, won't you?"

"Yes, Harry, I will," said Christina deliberately: "As soon as the war is over."

"No, no! Don't wait for the war—we may have to wait for years," said Morcar urgently. "We've wasted far too many years already."

"I can't do it now, Harry. I can't leave Edward and Jenny in London during the blitz. I can't break up Edwin's home when he's on the high seas."

"Yes, you can."

"I can but I won't," said Christina. "You would despise me if I did, Harry."

A prolonged whine in the air increased to a shrill but heavy roar and ended in a violent concussion. The blast seemed to rock the houses; some windows fell out along the street, Morcar's coat was dragged from his shoulders and Christina swayed in his arms. Before they had quite recovered their balance they were pushed aside by the warden in charge, who rushed up the steps crying vehemently: "Incident by the Underground!"

"I must go—goodbye, Harry!" cried Christina, running after the warden. "Stay the night at our house—don't try to reach your hotel."

Morcar groped about for his hat, which had fallen off, and, sheltering in doorways or surface shelters during the worst moments, made his way back to the Underground station. The sky was full of the reeling shafts of searchlights and the sudden flashes of gunfire; planes grated continually overhead, as it seemed to Morcar, very low; bombs whined and thudded; broken buildings rumbled heavily to earth; shrapnel spattered the roadway like rain; glass tinkled in sudden cascades from the window-frames. Morcar's predominant sensation was one of anger; to think of Christina enduring this hell of danger every night made him almost mad with rage. It came to him as he crouched angrily behind a glassless shop front that, once he was divorced, he could force Christina's hand by telling Harington himself of their liaison. This idea made him chuckle grimly.

The raid had not finished when his train reached the Strand, but it had become a point of honour with him not to stay in a shelter while Christina was outside one. His walk through the streets was dangerous and highly uncomfortable, and several wardens and policemen shouted at him impatiently to get inside, but he persevered, and reached his hotel in safety.

44

Lease and Lend

The winter of 1940–1941 was an awkward though interest-ing time for an Englishman to visit the U.S.A., for a vast argument which vitally concerned England was in the throes of nationwide discussion. The proposed "Lease and Lend" Act, to enable the President *to procure any defence article for the government of any country whose defence the President deems vital to the defence of the United States*, had just been laid before Congress; if passed, England would be able to secure munitions even when her dollar reserve became exhausted; if not passed, England would soon have to conduct and furnish the war against Hitler without any American armaments.

As Morcar made acquaintance with the teeming life, the myriad aspects, of the great continent, the argument for and against this Act raged round his head. He gazed with admiration at the soaring beautifully proportioned New York skyscrapers (the view of which from the Bay he thought fully equal to Venice) and was amused by the effect their express elevators had upon his entrails; he felt the sub-zero bite of the winter wind, heard the grinding of the ice across the frozen lakes and rivers, flew over the jagged peaks of the Rockies and the vast rolling prairie plains, and respected the courage of the pioneers who crossed and tamed them. He travelled in the handsome olive-green steel trains with their poignant clanging bells, their powerful head-lights, and chuckled at American ingenuity as he buttoned himself into the seclusion of his berth behind neat green curtains. He blinked doubtfully at the brilliant but uncoordinated whirling traceries of Broadway; he appreciated the æsthetic grace of the long unswerving slope of Fifth Avenue; he opened wide eyes at the complex subtlety of the garb of its crowds of well-dressed women. (Christina, he felt, would think the New York fashions excessive and Jenny didn't count because she cared little for fashions, but little Fan Oldroyd would dote on them.) And wherever he went he heard about him the echoes of the national argument. *This is not our war.... This is our war.... Our national security is not involved in a British defeat.... Here are free men like ourselves struggling to preserve themselves and their freedom.... England is of course fighting for her existence, but it is not our battle.... Britain is standing alone in defence of liberty.... Britain is despotic, arbitrary and tyrannical.... No, democracy is not dying.... America first....* With his mind full of pictures of bombed London, bombed Hull, bombed Sheffield, bombed Liverpool, Morcar found that the phrases he overheard sometimes assuaged but more often inflamed the prejudices he had taken with him across the Atlantic.

Of course, thought Morcar, half crossly, half amused: the Americans have quite the wrong idea about modern English life. They think in terms of dukes and coronets, footmen and lodge-keepers, curtseys and caste. When Morcar told them he had never seen a duke in his life and didn't intend to if he could help it, they gazed at him in astonishment; when he explained that in the West Riding dukes and such-like were not much thought of, they gave him a glance of incredulous suspicion and turned away. They thought England was still 'way back in the 1850's or whenever it was that those feudal times flourished, thought Morcar vaguely, uncertain himself. They expressed surprise at the short a's and general intelligibility of his accent, and when Morcar, blushing a little, informed them that several millions of north-country British spoke as he did, they said politely: "Is that so?" with complete disbelief. Nay, they even put every Englishman down as a dyed-in-the-wool Tory, reflected Morcar indignantly, a real George III. Morcar could well understand how they felt about George III, for he felt like that himself about the Spanish Armada when he chanced to remember it. But what exasperated him so was that Americans seemed never to have heard that the English disliked George III quite as much as they did, both at the time and later; that the majority of English people—certainly all the business men in the West Riding—couldn't agree with them more, as David would say, in the poor view they took of that stupid and tyrannical king and his actions. Americans had never heard of how the West Riding fought Charles I, the siege of Bradford and all that kind of thing. Of course he himself didn't know much American history, admitted Morcar honestly.

If the Americans knew little of ordinary peacetime life in England, naturally they had even less idea of English life during the war. How could they have any idea of that strange existence, in Mr. Churchill's words so grim yet gay? But at least many of them seemed eager to hear of it, and listened with sympathy to what he could tell. Stumbling and stammering, Morcar found himself answering volleys of questions after dinner-parties, in club cars and train washrooms, at the drugstore counter; talking to "small groups" at luncheons, at last positively standing up and addressing Rotarians in quite a formal way, describing the blitz and the blackout and the sound of the siren, and what it felt like to spend sixteen days crossing the Atlantic in a small ship whose captain had been torpedoed twice before. After Morcar had finished his business engagements, he was stuck in New York for several weeks, trying to find a passenger ship home when no such ship existed; with time on his hands, nothing to do but haunt the British consul's office daily, he talked gladly to everyone who wanted to hear. "You're English, aren't you?" said the taxi-driver. "Yeah, I knew you were English soon as I heard your voice. I was over there in 1918. Things seem kind of bad over there today, don't they?" Morcar explained just how bad they were. "Kind of sad," commented the taxi-driver. The negro redcap, pointing to the label on Morcar's case, asked if he had recently crossed the ocean. Morcar explained that he had just come over from England. "How is it with you in England?" asked the man earnestly. As they stood outside the platform gate in the palatial station, Morcar described the air raids. "You are doing a pretty fine job out there, yes *sir,*" concluded the porter, solemnly shaking his fine dark head.

On the other hand there were incidents not so pleasant. There was a young reporter who came up after a Rotarian lunch which Morcar had attended, and in a brisk unfeeling manner asked Morcar all sorts of questions offering to show that the British barrage balloons were useless, the anti-aircraft guns antiquated, the Army defeated, the Navy all washed up. Morcar kept his temper and answered as politely as he could, till the lad said in his cool efficient tone: "Now just one final question: Do you think England has any chance of winning the war?" "Yes!" shouted Morcar, crimsoning. The reporter looked astonished by

387

so much vehemence. "Sorry to sound violent," apologised Morcar affably: "But it's a kind of personal matter with me, you know." There was a lady in Detroit, too, who remarked in a doubtful condescending tone: "Well, it does *look* as if England were doing all she could before asking for help."

But on the other hand, again, every hotel had a collecting tin on its reception desk for British War Relief. Morcar earned many a sour look from reception clerks by shaking these tins to see if they contained any contribution; they were always most generously heavy with coin. His hosts' wives seized eagerly upon him and enquired what would be the most useful articles to include in their Bundles for Britain. Clergymen called upon him by appointment and asked what would be the most efficacious method of assisting British youth. One day, every shop window in Fifth Avenue showed some labelled British goods: whisky and cloth and gloves and books. Many had beside them the packing-case in which they had travelled, to prove that they had genuinely crossed those dangerous submarine-haunted three thousand miles of sea. *Britain delivers the goods*, read Morcar, gazing into a window decked in red white and blue; his heart was touched and he felt kindly towards every retailer on the Avenue. On the night after one of the big fire raids on London Morcar chanced to be dining with a party of business acquaintances in a famous New York restaurant. The headlines that morning had been terrible; Morcar had cabled to enquire about the Haringtons' safety but had as yet received no reply. At the dinner he exerted himself to be lively and cheerful, but found difficulty in sustaining the part. One of the guests turned to him and observed in a friendly candid tone: "I'm afraid your country took an awful bad beating last night." In spite of himself Morcar winced and coloured. The man's eyes rounded with concern, he called up a waiter and whispered instructions. The waiter nodded and went to the orchestra, and the strains of *There'll always be an England* filled the room. The merchant beside him turned a beaming happy glance on Morcar. Between appreciation for the feeling which had prompted the orchestral request, embarrassment at this public exposure of his wound, and concern for his country and his love, Morcar could hardly speak or eat. It was several days before he received a cable from Harington saying laconically and not altogether reassuringly: "All unhurt." The cable was brought to him as he sat in the barber's shop in his hotel. As he looked up after a long sigh of relief and fumbled beneath the white gown to get a quarter out of his pocket, he found the eyes of bell-boy and barber fixed on him sympathetically. "Bad news from England?" asked the barber, razor poised in hand. "Not too bad," said Morcar.

Morcar did a great deal of business and met a great many business men, and it was naturally their ideas which he encountered most frequently. Business, thought Morcar with grim amusement, surveying with relish. the greatest turnover in history, was more than just business in the United States; it was something between a sport and a religion. A sport—something like scalp-hunting, thought Morcar; a Red Indian fortitude was certainly necessary to engage in it; as they said, it was a great life if you didn't weaken. A religion—the finest buildings, the magnificent sky-scraping towers, were business premises. Were these business Americans as democratic as they made out? Well, yes and no, thought Morcar. The power of wealth was such that Morcar gasped at it; if you had dollars enough, you could get away with things for which in England you'd find yourself in gaol. The things Capital and Labour said to each other and did to each other, too, would have made the hair of Fred, the shop-steward at Syke Mills, stand on end. On the other hand, Morcar could but remember the incident of the janitor at the New England factory of a cloth manufacturer he had met as a merchant's guest. The manufacturer's natural suspicion of a foreign rival had yielded to his pride in his own product, and he took Morcar out to his plant to show him round. The janitor, a stout elderly man in spectacles, after admitting them suddenly threw his arms round Morcar's neck. "Eh, lad!" he exclaimed: "You're a Yorkshireman! I owned you as soon as ever you spoke." Mildly disentangling himself from the embrace, Morcar admitted this, and suggested that the janitor likewise hailed from the county of the white rose. "Yes. Bradford," agreed the janitor. Now Morcar was not a man who put on dignity or gave himself airs, but all the same he could not imagine the Syke Mills door-keeper behaving with quite such carefree sociability to one of Morcar's guests. He had to admit that there was a feeling of equality in the janitor's behaviour greater than you could find in England.

On the other hand, Morcar sometimes slyly told himself that he now understood how he himself appeared to David Oldroyd, for that was just how the American business man appeared to him. Fresh from the united effort, the sinking of all differences in a common purpose, of wartime England, the rugged individualism of American business practice in January 1941 struck him (to his own surprise) as somehow Victorian, old-fashioned, out of date.

Thus his reactions swayed back and forth between vexation and liking, until one day the decisive event took place. He was in a train northbound towards Canada when he heard of it. A spring blizzard veiled the landscape; it was indeed "snowing to beat hell", as a tall, large, loose-jointed man in a rather high white collar, a salesman travelling in dry goods, who sat across the aisle from Morcar, remarked with feeling. The train stopped—very late because of the snow—at a wayside station, and a lad ran in with newspapers in the usual way. Morcar glanced at the headlines. Such a gush of relief and happiness filled his heart that he could not keep silence. He leaned across the aisle.

"Well, sir," he said eagerly: "I see the Lease and Lend Act is passed."

"Yeah," agreed the drygoods salesman without expression, nodding. Then he seemed to recollect something about Morcar—his accent perhaps—and looking towards him again, added kindly: "Make a difference to your country, I daresay?"

"It certainly will," said Morcar with fervour. "Make a difference to Hitler, too." He paused, then suddenly cried out joyously: "I forgive you the McKinley tariff!"

"Pardon?" murmured the salesman politely, perplexed.

"And I'll throw in Dingley as well," said Morcar.

"Uh-huh?" rejoined the salesman, still more perplexed.

"And America's not joining the League of Nations after the last war, and wrecking the Economic Conference in 1933, and every darned thing," said Morcar with joyous emphasis: "I forgive you them all!"

"Well now, that's a new viewpoint to me. In my country," said the salesman with mild courtesy: "We usually reckon we have to forgive yours."

"Well, let's call it quits," offered Morcar, laughing: "Then we can start afresh."

The drygoods salesman gave a non-committal murmur but a friendly smile, and asked Morcar what it was like to be in an air-raid. His eyes bulged with sympathy and alarm as Morcar gave him a blow-by-blow description.

45

Convoy

"That can't be the ship!" exclaimed Morcar, looking down from the high 14th Street pier at a small deck, red with rust, which seemed chiefly occupied at the moment by heaps of scrap iron and lengths of chain.

He knew at once, from a slight movement on the part of his companion the shipping clerk, that he had said the wrong thing; this certainly was the freighter in which he was to cross the Atlantic homeward. For a moment he felt quite daunted at the thought of spending weeks in that tiny space amid Atlantic waves; then he rallied, for after all there was nothing in the world he desired more at the moment than to get back to England. "Ah—I see it is," he said blandly, reading out the freighter's name, which was painted on the bows. "Quite a neat little craft." Little was the word, he thought; there was scarcely room to walk. He saw himself pacing up and down a few yards each way, like a caged lion.

"Better not to mention her name, either here or at home.

She's about seven thousand tons," murmured the clerk. "With eleven thousand tons cargo."

"Ah," said Morcar non-committally. He had no idea whether this tonnage was large or small, so (in the language he had recently learned) he played his cards close to his chest and offered no comment. The clerk strolled on and Morcar strolled with him; behind them trailed the six other passengers, silent and doubtless rather daunted, like Morcar, but like him resolute to get home. "Ah!" he exclaimed in a different tone. The after-deck offered an animated scene. A group of men were busily engaged, under the supervision of a ship's officer, in securing a couple of aircraft to the deck by means of strong wires and bolts. The aircraft, which travelled minus their wings, were painted brown and green in dingy camouflage. It was clear to Morcar from the excited bearing of the men and the many shouted orders of the mate that aircraft formed an unaccustomed cargo for the little freighter, and he felt proud to be sailing in a craft which was taking planes to beleaguered England. The whole party seemed to experience a similar rise of spirits; they hung over the pier railing and watched intently.

"I hope we get them home to England safely," remarked one of the passengers, a New Zealander.

"God knows they're wanted!" exclaimed Morcar with ardour.

A third aircraft was rapidly attached to the fore deck. The heaps of scrap resolved themselves into rivets and wedges, the chains into neat coils; the loose rust was swept overboard, the iron decks took on the appearance of an old-fashioned firegrate after the application of blacklead. When all was clean and neat—shipshape, I suppose, thought Morcar—the passengers were allowed to board the *Floating Castle*, as Morcar decided to call the ship. (It was not her name but somewhat resembled it, and he was sure no ship called *Floating Castle* had ever been entered at Lloyds, so to name her thus was not careless talk, gave no secrets away to the enemy.) Presently the immemorial signal blasts of a ship about to sail blared out bravely, the little ship backed out from the pier, turned and headed for the ocean. The voyage had begun.

Now they were passing the Statue of Liberty, now she was only a distant silhouette with a pointed halo, now the waves began to be larger and to slap sharply against the side of the *Castle*, ruffled by the afternoon breeze. Morcar stood watching the lofty pinnacles of New York recede as the ship went down the bay. A phrase came into his mind, a tag from some forgotten lesson of his schooldays, Shakespeare he supposed: *cloud-capp'd towers and gorgeous palaces*. They were all of that, he thought admiringly, and he felt a real sadness of farewell as the island of Manhattan swam away till the skyscrapers looked like a cluster of tall pink and white flowers rising from a blue-grey sea of foliage. He should like to come and see them again after the war if he had any money left after the war to do so, which at the moment seemed highly improbable for any Englishman. Yes, he felt quite sad. He was saying goodbye to a people he had grown to like, goodbye to ease, goodbye to luxury, goodbye perhaps to life itself—but all the same he would give an arm, thought Morcar strongly, to be back in England at that moment. England was beleaguered and beset; Christina—well best not think of that, thought Morcar, turning from the bulwarks to pace restlessly up and down. The passenger deck, a tiny square which he could cover in a few strides, was far too small to relieve his sense of impatient longing; he descended to the iron deck below, walked the ship from end to end, entered into conversation with any officer, apprentice or seaman who would talk with him.

He should never forget that voyage, thought Morcar, a series of pictures of its progress were stamped indelibly on his brain. The *Floating Castle*, a freighter of the British merchant marine, usually plied between New York and the Far East, but had come as a reinforcement to the Atlantic battle. All aboard were of British nationality; the captain, English, had been a Royal Navy man, axed in the days when naval disarmament was made a reality by Britain if by few other countries; the crew were Malays, the stewards Singapore Chinese, the officers English, Welsh, Scots and Belfast Irish. Morcar at first had a tiny but cosy cabin to himself; the bedlinen could not be described as spotless, for it was stained with great daubs of rust, but it was brilliantly clean; the sunlight on the waves outside reflected quivering flashes on the ceiling through the open porthole; the white paint shone, the neatly dovetailed equipment tickled Morcar's sense of humour.

The *Floating Castle* went peacefully up the coast and after some delay by fog turned into Halifax harbour. No doubt Halifax was to its inhabitants a pleasant place, homely and kind and not without beauty, but to Morcar it represented a hell of frustration and suspense. The huge harbour was already crowded with craft when the *Castle* arrived, so that it was clear a convoy was in process of preparation, and Morcar hoped to be off homewards at break of day. But after hours of eager expectation this hope was disappointed, and a couple of days later the hope of joining the next convoy was disappointed again. The weather was hot; the passengers, who had already read all the worthwhile books in the little ship's library and were falling back on sermons and manuals, grew languid, the officers a trifle snappy; the Captain and first mate often went ashore carrying brief cases and returned hours later looking portentous with knowledge which they did not reveal.

Morcar occupied himself by assisting the carpenter to paint the name *Floating Castle* in large white letters on an enormous loose plank. This was to be displayed horizontally on the deck, explained the third mate, for the purpose of recognition by friendly aircraft. It was as he was painting a nicely curled S, on the hot June Sunday morning, that the third mate rushed up to him with round eyes and a gaping mouth, and told him that Germany had invaded Russia. Morcar was so dumbfounded that he stood at gaze until an angry shout from the bridge recalled him to himself, and he saw that he had dropped a large white splash of paint on the ship's woodwork. In the afternoon he heard over the captain's radio a relay of Mr. Churchill's speech swinging Britain unreservedly to Russia's side. The captain asked him what he thought of these developments.

"Well—we aren't alone any more," said Morcar thoughtfully.

Next day when the Captain returned from shore he summoned his passengers to the upper cabin which they used as a lounge, and told them that the Admiral of the next convoy was to make the *Floating Castle* his flagship. There would be gunners aboard, there would be signalmen—and there would probably be little room for passengers. Some of the passengers might be transferred to other ships, and some just left behind in Canada. An awful silence descended on the cabin as he said this. Left behind! After the Captain had gone each passenger seized upon the first mate in turn and explained to him why it was imperative that he, if no other, should travel on the *Floating Castle*.

"We could double up, three or four in a cabin," suggested a quiet little man who had left an American wife and child to rejoin his former British regiment.

"We could all accommodate ourselves in this cabin—it is sufficiently spacious," suggested a Frenchman who was proceeding to

396

England because, as he explained to Morcar, he was French.

"The lounge will be occupied by gunners and signalmen," said the mate in his dourest tone.

"We could sleep on the floor in the dining-saloon," suggested Morcar.

The mate snorted.

Several days passed full of anguished suspense. Morcar paced the deck in silence and thought of England and Christina; the other passengers paced up and down likewise, with frowning brows, their minds doubtless full of troubles which however they kept to themselves. Then suddenly two passengers were taken off to another ship—an oil-tanker; three were squashed into one tiny cabin, and a couple of whom Morcar was one were allowed to sleep, as he had suggested, on the floor of the saloon. All their luggage except the most absolute necessities was thrust into the hold. Four gunners and a machine-gun came aboard, half a dozen A.B.s from the Royal Navy came aboard, a yeoman of signals came aboard, lastly with all proper ceremony the Admiral himself came aboard. A small spare elderly man with seaman's eyes and a fine head, summoned from retirement to this honourable and dangerous task, dapper, courteous and a martinet, he installed his bed in the wheelhouse and remarked casually that he never drank at sea. This dictum prevented all the ship's officers from taking a drink at sea, and from sheer decency the passengers were compelled to a similar abstention.

Morcar was not much of a drinking man nowadays but he felt the deprivation more than he expected, for his nights in the saloon were singularly uncomfortable. The floor was hard, the bedding scanty, the changes of watches woke him in the small hours, the feeding of the augmented ship's company in shifts occupied the saloon at hours both late and early. ("Eat all day," as one of the Chinese stewards remarked to him mournfully.) To preserve the necessary blackout on deck, doors were closed at night, portholes were screwed up rigorously; the resulting heat and stuffiness were most unpleasant. To smoke on deck after dusk was absolutely forbidden; to smoke in the dining-saloon was frowned on. Day clothes had to be worn all the time, with the addition of life-jackets while the ship crossed the danger zone. Morcar longed for a fresh supply of shirts but could not get at his suitcase, and finally took to washing the couple he had by him and ironing them under the instruction (and with the iron) of the Chinese steward aforesaid. "I'm getting too old for this sort of work," growled Morcar to himself, as he lay in a life-jacket on the floor of the saloon in a mid-Atlantic gale, holding to a screwed-down chair to prevent himself from rolling. The Captain, however, and the Admiral, neither of whom had more than two hours' consecutive sleep throughout the voyage, he knew to be older men than himself, and Morcar did not really mean to grumble. The voyage was one of the great experiences of his life, and he would not have missed it for anything.

For at last the *Floating Castle* had left Halifax, one of a number of other such small grey ships, plodding steadily in neat parallel rows across the stormy Atlantic. There were long low tankers carrying precious oil, there were squat ships carrying precious food; there were slightly larger ships like the *Floating Castle*, laden probably with armaments and certainly with aircraft. At night the lines of these little ships on their way, silhouetted blackly against the rosy west, had a picturesque, romantic air; Morcar counted them and silently wished them well and said goodnight. When light came again in the morning they looked grey and stolid but somehow perky and undaunted, still plodding along in their neat rows. Morcar counted them again, and sometimes had a disagreeable surprise, for one or other of the little ships was missing. Consulting the mate off duty anxiously on this point, he discovered that owing to what the mate called a speeded-up turnaround, cargo ships had little rest nowadays, and their engines little time for overhaul in port; consequently there was apt to be trouble in their engine-room. Could they make repairs quickly enough to catch up the convoy and maintain the necessary speed, or must they fall behind and take another course? The Atlantic in the early summer of 1941 was uncomfortable for unescorted freighters, so the little ships made superhuman efforts to keep up with the rest; the engine-room being exhorted to these efforts by the bridge with some profanity. There was a lame duck of this kind in Morcar's convoy; several times he mourned to find it fallen behind, rejoicing later when the Captain, coming down sleepless and unshaven to snatch a hurried meal, related with several fond expletives that the determined old bitch had caught up the convoy once again. Sometimes, too, Morcar had frights of this kind which he afterwards found to be unjustified, because when he looked for them at dawn and thought them missing, the little ships were merely "out of station." They had slipped a little from their place at night, and were now straggling or bunched, their lines uneven, jagged. As soon as the light revealed this they scurried back, hoping to regain their station in the huge parallelogram before receiving a rebuking signal from the *Castle's* bridge—for the Admiral's comments on these occasions were apt to be caustic.

In spite of the discomfort which the fact caused him, Morcar rejoiced daily that the ship he travelled on was the commodore ship, the flagship, of the convoy. From the *Castle's* mast flew the instructing flags; it was the *Castle* which did the hooting and the yellow-eyed heliograph-blinking and the talking; the *Castle's* bridge gave the orders, prepared the navigation, plotted and changed the course. The passenger who shared the saloon as bedroom with Morcar had been a yachtsman in his youth and could read signal flags and Morse; he regaled the company with the convoy's messages except when they were made in code. Morcar found the process of guiding a hundred and fifty little ships in zigzags across three thousand miles of submarine-haunted ocean sufficiently enthralling, especially as it was with the *Castle* that the escorting destroyers communicated. At first the convoy was shepherded by a single sloop, which came along-side every morning to talk to the Admiral. The sloop (if that was the right name for it) had anti-aircraft guns which were always manned, and depth-charges which were always at the ready. The commander—or captain or whatever he was, thought Morcar vaguely—was a young man, with a fresh unlined face and an eager expression, quite a boy really, not much older probably than Edwin Harington. Owing to the zigzag course taken by the convoy to keep its various rendezvous, the weather was sometimes very hot and sometimes very cold. Sometimes the bearded seamen on the destroyer were clad in white shorts and little else, their brown skins glowing; sometimes they were muffled up in navy blue, seaboots and oilskins. The young commander was always spruce, however, clean and shaven and brushed, whether in white or blue or streaming oilskin, duffel hood or gold-laced cap. Sometimes this young man spoke to the Admiral through the megaphone; he had just the same kind of voice, the same expressions and intonations, as young Edwin.

One morning the sloop came near as usual but was silent, speaking only in code flags, which Morcar's bedfellow could not follow; but later in the day the passengers guessed what it was the commander had to tell, for the *Castle's* lookout sounded the bell which meant ships in sight. A mere landlubber like Morcar could not at first perceive them, but after a while two tiny grey dots were discernible far away on the horizon and presently there appeared some more—they were additional Navy escorts coming to the rendezvous. From that time onward the convoy often met additional escorts; each time they appeared Morcar knew he was one stage nearer to the special danger zone.

Part of the nightmare quality of the voyage at this stage was due to the oddness of the time-table. For convenience in making rendezvous, the convoy had adopted a time-scheme which its geographical position did not justify. Accordingly for some days it was mid-morning by the official time before the sun rose, and one could read on deck easily at ten o'clock at night. One afternoon during this distorted period the sloop came up to the *Castle* and enquired whether the Admiral would care to listen to the B.B.C. news. As all the convoy ships' radios had been sealed before leaving port, lest they should give warning to enemy submarines of their presence, the suggestion was accepted with delight. It was mid-Atlantic; the sea was dark-blue and rough, the wind strong and cold; the sun, fitful in the morning, was now withdrawing behind stormy clouds; the existence of land was almost forgotten, almost incredible. The sloop had rigged up a loud-speaker on the bridge. There were the usual atmospheric cracklings. Suddenly, clear and strong across the water, Big Ben struck nine. England! Oh, England! thought Morcar. Though he strained his ears he could make little of the news bulletin across the rising sea, but the sound of the English voice was music. It was a south-country voice of the la-di-da kind which Morcar had often derided, but when it ceased he felt lonely. The sun had vanished; the scene was emphatically the middle of a submarine-haunted and stormy ocean; England was very far away. Without speaking to any of his fellow-passengers Morcar turned and went below.

And now the danger zone was reached. The sloop had long abdicated and retired to the parallelogram's flank; grim swift destroyers now surrounded the convoy, and one led the way, zigzagging in front with an effect of dancing. But one afternoon suddenly the sloop leaped across the *Castle's* bows, and Morcar saw something dropping from her stern. "Are those depth charges?" he wondered privately. The other passengers, leaning silently against the deck railing, looked as if they were wondering the same. They soon had their reply; for Morcar felt a grinding jolt below, as if a mighty hand had shaken the *Castle's* engines from their bed. "Is it a submarine?" wondered Morcar. Now the sloop began to signal the leading destroyer with the heliograph, blinking very rapidly. The passenger who could read Morse earnestly watched the flashing light, and his fellow passengers watched him no less earnestly. Suddenly he began to laugh.

"What's up?" said Morcar. "What's the message, eh?"

"The message signalled," gurgled the passenger gleefully: "The message signalled is: 'Sorry you've been troubled. Think it was only fish.'"

Next morning Morcar was woken by the sound of loud and varied gunfire. He sprang up hastily. He was already dressed and in his life-jacket; now he slung his small bag of necessaries over his shoulder. The mate had explained firmly the rule that if the ship were sunk and one had to "go over the side", nothing must be taken which had to be carried in the hand. Any ship which paused to pick up drowning men was risking her own crew's life; she could not wait while cases or bags were passed from hand to hand, or while people with impeded grasp slowly climbed the swaying rope ladder. Morcar hurried out of the saloon towards the companion-way, but was turned back by the mate, who ran down to present the Captain's compliments to the passengers, and inform them that an air raid was probably imminent. The convoy had just driven off a hostile scouting plane which would probably summon others; the passengers would please stay below, wearing life-jackets and ready to take lifeboat stations instantly. The passengers smiled and nodded obedience, buttoned their coats, fingered their scarves, hitched up their money-belts. Morcar's heart was beating fast, but not with fear, with anger. From where he stood he could see the wired planes in their camouflaged wrappings. Are we to lose them, he thought; are they going to the bottom of the Atlantic? We need them so much at home. He looked at them with a grim wrath, and wondered.

Planes sounded in the distance and the sound grew loud. Morcar's lips tightened. "Here they come," he thought.

The mate ran half down the companion-way and leaned over towards the passengers. He was grinning. He jerked his head back towards the sound of aircraft. "Ours," he said.

The passengers, talking and laughing at the top of their voices, streamed up on deck, and looked gratefully at the planes which circled round the convoy, swift black pencils in the sunshine.

That night a gale blew up. Huge waves, dark green, pointed, white-capped, raging, threw the little ships about; the convoy's speed was slowed, the low-decked tankers shipped seas so continually that foaming water poured from them like a long white satin ribbon. Morcar eyed the respective size of waves and *Castle* lifeboats speculatively. The third mate, who had been torpedoed before, remarked as he went towards the bridge that if he had to "go over the side" that night he should make for one of the rafts which were suspended forward.

403

"Rafts'd be safer than boats tonight, I reckon?" suggested Morcar.

The mate made an expressive grimace. "Boats wouldn't live long in this," he remarked cheerfully.

Next day Morcar would have been glad of the big green waves and the driving wind, for fog fell, and the little ships all vanished from sight behind a chill grey curtain. It felt lonely.

"I shouldn't like to be torpedoed in a fog," thought Morcar.

But now at last the convoy was nearing home. Some of the escorting destroyers, having shot off a black drifting mine or two by way of farewell, bade the Admiral respectful goodbyes and leaped away towards the land, blue and hilly, which had risen on the *Castle's* starboard. The convoy presently divided, right and left; some of the little ships glided away, became mere masts and funnels, disappeared. The lame duck whose fate had caused Morcar so much anxiety limped successfully into an Irish port. Now the remaining ships stretched out into a long single line, the *Floating Castle*, flying a fine new red ensign, proudly leading. Presently the *Castle* passed lightships and buoys and reached the harbour bar. Silvery barrage balloons dotted the skyscape; a bell-buoy gave out its continual clanking warning. Morcar perceived that this was the entrance to the Mersey estuary.

A pilot came aboard. The mate went below to his cabin and emerged in his best uniform and muffler, wearing a pair of clean white gloves. The convoy passed slowly down the narrow mine-free channel. Other ships were anchored close beside; their men came up on deck to see the convoy from America reach England. England, thought Morcar, smiling all over his face, which was a good deal sunburned and weather-beaten by this time: England.

And now they were quite close to the Liverpool docks; Morcar could clearly see the Liver building, with the great golden Liver bird still perched on top. All round were battered buildings and charred docks, and the Liver building itself had a chip out of it, but as long as the bird poised there with outspread wings, Morcar felt that Liverpool was in existence. The mate in his white gloves was now standing right up in the bows of the *Castle;* he looked round towards the Captain on the bridge who, addressing him formally by his name with the prefix "Mr," adjured him to let go. The anchor chains rattled, the ship's motion ceased. The convoy had crossed the Atlantic safely. The Captain, his eyes red-rimmed from fatigue and lack of sleep, ran down the bridge to greet his owner's clerks who now boarded the vessel; he poured a heavy glass of whisky and drank it neat, while the Admiral stood by, mildly beaming. The precious oil, the precious food, the precious planes—they were all safe home. It was twenty-seven days since Morcar had left New York.

The Liverpool station was not in full working order owing to bombings, but a little train took Morcar to a junction where he caught an express. It was Saturday night. The train held many simple English families returning from a country jaunt, the children clutching drooping flowers. They all looked hot and tired and definitely shabby; but they were patient, quietly cheerful and kind, as always. Morcar thought of their scanty food rations, their scanty clothes rations, their almost nightly aerial visitations, and gazed at them with loving admiration; he felt there was nothing too good for these people, nothing.

He went up the steps of Stanney Royd about eleven o'clock. He had contrived to telephone from Manchester, and the door stood wide to welcome him. As his footsteps sounded on the threshold Heather, barking furiously, scurried out from the drawing-room. Mrs. Morcar followed. She fell on her son's neck, weeping, while Heather, almost hysterical with joy, whined feverishly and clasped his paws round Morcar's ankles.

Morcar looked through his correspondence and found that in his absence his undefended divorce suit had gone through; Winnie had obtained a *decree nisi,* in a few months he would be altogether free. A recent note from David reassured him about the Haringtons' safety. Morcar spent the weekend in a dream of happiness, strolling about the green Stanney Royd garden, looking at the loved West Riding hills. He was at home, in England; he could claim Christina for his own. He planned to go to London next weekend, to be married to Christina by next year's summer.

On Monday morning, before he even visited Syke Mills, Morcar went into the best Annotsfield bookshop and gave a large order for books to be despatched at once to the *Floating Castle.*

On Wednesday he received a very courteous and pleasant note from the shipping company to which the *Castle* belonged, thanking him for the fine parcel of books, which they were sure would be greatly appreciated by the merchant seamen in their employ. Unfortunately the *Floating Castle* had already left Liverpool on an outward voyage. Should they reserve the books for her, or give them to the crew of some other of their vessels?

Morcar's face lengthened as he read. So the captain and crew of the *Floating Castle* were already back on the Atlantic! So the voyage which to him had been such an extraordinary event, such a dangerous ordeal, they were already repeating! This was the "speeded-up turnaround" of which the mate had spoken. Evidently at this stage of the submarine campaign no ships could be spared, no men had time to rest on leave. The lifeline between Britain and America was strung out very thin; stretch it even a little further and it might break.

"And if it's like that for the Merchant Navy," reflected Morcar: "I expect it will be just as bad for those destroyer men."

He thought of the commander of the sloop: that lad so fresh and fair and young, so like Edwin Harington. He sighed, and put down the shipping company's letter very soberly, with a look of disappointment on his face. Christina's right, thought Morcar sadly; you can't break up the home of a lad who's fighting the battle of the Atlantic. We must wait.

46

Son

Morcar's recent travels had made him tired of hotels, and for his London visits he installed himself in a service flat overlooking Hyde Park. He was asleep there one wintry morning in the December following his return from the U.S.A. when the telephone rang at his bedside. The call was so early that he snatched up the instrument in some alarm, and cried: "Harry Morcar here," very urgently.

The caller evidently successfully pressed button A in a call-box, for pennies could be heard falling; but he or she remained silent.

"Who's this?" said Morcar. It was a locution borrowed from American acquaintances which Morcar enjoyed using, but it seemed to upset his caller, for there was no reply. "Who's that?" said Morcar, reverting to normal.

A Yorkshire voice said hesitantly: "This is Cecil."

"Oh!" said Morcar. As always when his former wife or his son entered his life, he felt a painful constriction. As the young man said no more, he forced himself to utter the enquiry: "Is there anything wrong with your mother?"

"No. No, Mother's all right," said Cecil. "At least, she was last night when I left her."

"Did you bring me a special message from her, perhaps?"

"Not specially," said Cecil.

At the end of his ideas, Morcar waited for some other explanation of the call, but none came. He said at last: "Where are you?"

"I'm in London on my way back from leave. Mother told me your address. She got it from Granny. She said I was to ring you up," said Cecil.

His mild grating voice sounded wistful, and Morcar, remembering his promise to Winnie, which he had hitherto implemented only by a generous provision of money through alimony and codicils and settlements, suggested hurriedly: "Come and have lunch with me."

"Shall I?" said Cecil. His voice was now relieved and shy, yearning and happy all in a breath; it was clear that his father's invitation had struck the note expected.

"Yes, of course. Don't be later than one. Well—better say quarter to, then we can have a drink together."

"Thank you," said Cecil. As far as one could judge from his tone, he seemed to be expressing astonished delight, but with the young people of today one could never tell, reflected Morcar shrewdly.

"Do you know how to get here?"

"I'll find out," said Cecil cheerfully, hanging up the receiver.

Morcar had to attend a committee meeting at the Board of Trade that morning, and was delayed longer than he expected. On his return the porter, to whom he had given instructions to admit Cecil, told him that Private Morcar was in the flat waiting for him. Cecil's name always stung Morcar, and he had to pause as he unlocked his door to compose his features into a suitably welcoming smile.

His son was sitting in an awkward position on the window seat, gazing out through the fine large windows at the Park Lane scene, busy even in wartime, and the frozen grass and bare branches of the Park beyond. He was also humming a song beneath his breath. He stood up to greet his father, his fair ingenuous face beaming. It was odd, thought Morcar, shaking hands though his flesh crawled at the touch of his child by Winnie, how some lads—David for instance—looked handsome in battle-dress and others emphatically looked otherwise. The neat workmanlike suit gave David a fine figure, broad shoulders, narrow hips, long legs, flat belly, but Cecil's tunic was at once too large and too small—"it fits where it touches," thought Morcar, using a West Riding phrase angrily. It certainly did not touch the back of his neck, but clasped his waist too closely; the general effect was to make the lad look over-solid, ungainly, bulging, countrified. "Of course he's a private and David's an officer—the cut will be poorer perhaps," thought Morcar, trying to be fair and make excuses. He enquired Cecil's taste in drinks, but finding that the boy usually drank only beer, did not know the names of other drinks and had probably never had any kind of cocktail in his life, he set about mixing him a mild gin and lime. Cecil remained standing, gazing at him.

"Sit down—sit down and make yourself at home," said Morcar. In spite of himself his voice was irritable, and Cecil's mild brown eyes clouded like a scolded dog's as he obeyed. "The cigarettes are on the table beside you. Help yourself," said Morcar more kindly.

Cecil brightened and took a cigarette. As he briskly snapped his lighter, his head on one side, his eyelids lowered, he looked more manly, and the voice in which he began again to croon his previous ditty was a deep and quite pleasing baritone.

> *"Has anyone seen the Colonel?*
> *I know where he is.*
> *I know where he is.*
> *I know where he is.*
> *Has anyone seen the Colonel?*
> *I know where he is—*
> *He's dining with the Brigadier.*
> *I saw him, I saw him,*
> *Dining with the Brigadier I saw him,*
> *Dining with the Brigadier."*

"What's that you're singing?" said Morcar, amused.

Cecil coloured. "It's just a song we sing. It goes through all the officers, and non-coms. too. And the private. They're all doing something off the line of duty, more or less, except the private."

"And what's the private do, eh?"

> *"Holding up the whole damn line, I saw him,*
> *Holding up the whole damn line."*

"Perhaps that shocks you?" said Cecil suddenly, colouring again.

"Shocks me?" exclaimed Morcar, aghast.

"Disrespectful to the officers?"

"Don't be a fool, my boy; I'm an old soldier myself." It suddenly struck Morcar as intolerable that this boy, his son and

411

Charlie's nephew, should seem ignorant of this cardinal fact. "Your uncle and I joined the B.E.F. together in August 1914," he said stiffly. The scene of Charlie's death rose once more, for the thousandth time, vividly before his eyes. "I was with your uncle when he was killed," said Morcar gruffly.

"Yes, I know," said Cecil. His tone was respectful, and Morcar hazarded the guess that whatever Winnie might have thought about that incident herself she had at least not poisoned her son's mind against him. He found himself actually feeling grateful to her. It was very uncomfortable.

"Well, let's go down to the restaurant and have some lunch, shall we?" he said.

"Shall I take my coat?" asked Cecil in his simple Yorkshire tones.

"No—we'll come up here again afterwards," said Morcar. It's like taking a child about, he thought furiously; he hasn't the least idea how to conduct himself.

This impression was deepened in the restaurant, where Cecil was quite astray with the menu and not very certain in his selection of forks. It was so long since Morcar himself had felt uncertain about forks that when he saw Cecil waiting for his father to begin a course, his eyes fixed in anxious inquiry on Morcar's right hand, Morcar did not at first understand what he was about and even looked down at his hand himself to see if there were anything odd about it. There was nothing odd; he picked up a fork and attacked his hors d'œuvres; Cecil with a look of relief did the same. Then Morcar understood the situation. "He's nervous," he thought. "Ill at ease. Afraid of doing the wrong thing. Afraid of me." A rush of pity came into Morcar's heart, and for the first time that day he connected the big clumsy young man before him whose ill-cut fair hair stood up in a tuft on the crown of his head, with the sleeping child in neat grey coat and gaiters whom he had carried in his arms from The Sycamores to Hurstholt on a night twenty-two years ago, and fondly loved. He exerted himself to talk, to set Cecil at his ease. But he found this impossible to achieve. He tried all kinds of topics, all methods of approach—the jocular, the man-to-man, the cynical, the hearty. To each Cecil said: "Yes," in his slow grating Yorkshire tones. "Yes," he said, and "No," and "I don't know really," interspersing these conversational gems with a nervous little neigh of a laugh. "My God," thought Morcar: "The boy is a noodle of the highest order."

In despair he fell back upon textiles.

"I noticed you took your textile course at Annotsfield Technical," he said. (He remembered that Cecil had passed only third class, but did not mention this.)

"Yes," agreed Cecil.

"We've had some ups and downs in the wool textile trade during the war, I can tell you," continued Morcar.

He thought he discerned a faint gleam of interest in Cecil's placid brown eyes, and decided to continue. "In any case it's the only thing I really know how to talk about," he thought.

"Well—of course you know we've had Wool Control since 1939," he said. "Wool's been rationed since two months after the war began. We've had three war jobs to do for the country in the textile trade. First of all we had to clothe the Services. We began doing that about July 1939, and got pretty well ahead. But of course a lot of stuff was lost at Dunkirk, as I don't need to remind you, Cecil. Besides, there were. all these Free French and Free Poles and Free Dutch and so on to provide for. The Dutch are very particular about the stuff for their naval men, which is what you might expect. And now this women's conscription act has passed and we shall provide uniforms for the girls as well. That was the first job, though, clothing the Services. And the easiest. Then there was the Export Drive."

Morcar sighed, and Cecil looked mildly interrogative.

"You see we wanted munitions and food and such from the U.S.A. and other countries, and the only way we could pay for it was by selling them our products, because our dollar reserve was exhausted and we'd already sold all our foreign investments," explained Morcar—rather wearily, for he had explained it so often before, to Americans. "So the Government did everything it could to encourage us to export. We formed an Export Group to stimulate export, and some of the leading West Riding men visited North and South America to stimulate export, and some of us visited the U.S.A. privately to stimulate export—we thought of nothing else for months but stimulating export. I came back with plenty of orders. Then the Lease-Lend Act passed and export to the States wasn't so vital. But still it was useful, I should have thought—it gave the Americans something in return for their goods, choose how."

His voice was thick with resentment and Cecil ventured to enquire: "But didn't they want it?"

"No! The Americans complained that materials secured by England under Lease-Lend were being made into non-war products and exported into their markets. Of course," said Morcar thoughtfully: "If it were so, you can see how it would annoy them."

"But we don't get wool from America, do we?" objected Cecil.

"No, of course not. But the Government have gone and promised not only that Lease-Lend material won't be used in that way, but also that all our export trade shall be reduced to the absolute minimum necessary to buy us food and munitions. So our export drive has gone into reverse. We're just throwing away our export

414

trade in order to win this war. Chucking it into the gutter. Of course," said Morcar hastily: "If it has to be done to win the war, well it has to be done, that's all. But what a mess we're going to be in after the war! Whew! I don't like to think of it." He fell silent and stared ahead, envisaging the mess. "However," he resumed in a determined tone: "We're making all sorts of plans already to cope with it. It's export or expire with this little island, you know."

"What do you think about Pearl Harbour?" enquired Cecil after a pause.

Morcar shook his head in grave concern. The truth was that in spite of his irritation about his sacrificed exports, he felt almost as sensitive about Pearl Harbour as an American. "It's a bad do," he pronounced briefly. "Now the third task of the textile trade in wartime," he went on, veering away from the uncomfortable subject: "Is of course to provide cloth to clothe the civilian population, at reasonable prices."

"Utility cloth," said Cecil brightly. "What is it exactly? Grandfather talks about it but I don't just understand it."

"It isn't any one special cloth," said Morcar crossly, wincing at the introduction of Mr. Shaw into his favourite topic. "Utility cloths can have any kind of colour and decoration. The only thing standardised about utilities is their price. The scheme is just a means of compelling the manufacturer to make a considerable amount of cheaper cloths, that's all. Otherwise, you see, he'd tend to make mostly expensive cloths, which give him most profit. Utility cloths must have their selvedges marked with a sign like this." He drew it with a spoon edge on the table-cloth. Cecil craned forward and examined it with interest, the waiter with a stately disapproval, tempered by his memory of Morcar's excellent tips.

"When will they be on the market?" enquired Cecil mildly.

"They're pretty well ready now. Coffee, waiter," said Morcar, lighting a cigar. "Well, that's what the textile industry has to do, and the problem is how to do it with less than a third of our normal labour. The Government told us last spring we've got to concentrate—close some of our mills and let the work be concentrated into those that are left, so that they can run full all the time. Nucleus firms, they call them. Syke Mills, of course," said Morcar, "is a nucleus firm."

A look of fear sprang into Cecil's eyes. "Do you think Prospect Mills will be a nucleus firm?" he asked. "Or will it be concentrated?"

"I should think it will be concentrated," replied Morcar. "But it won't matter," he added impatiently. "Your grandfather will go on trading in his own name, only he won't be making the cloths he trades in. Some other firm will be making them for him."

"He won't like that, Grandfather won't," said Cecil.

"I don't think he'll mind so long as he gets the money," said Morcar brutally.

"I shall mind," murmured Cecil.

"You were working at Prospect before the war, were you?" "Yes," nodded Cecil.

"Well—I expect you're bored with all this textile talk."

"Oh, no; it's very inter*est*ing," said Cecil, accenting the word on the wrong syllable in the Yorkshire fashion.

Morcar was well aware that he spoke it thus himself sometimes, but this did not lessen his irritation at hearing it on the lips of Cecil. "Nay—you'll think yourself back in Annotsfield Technical," he said, rising. He felt vexed with himself for having exposed his beloved textiles in talk to Mr. Shaw's grandson.

Cecil rose to follow him, upsetting his coffee cup as he did so, and they returned to Morcar's flat.

416

"This is a posh kind of place, isn't it?" said Cecil, looking round him with a smile of childlike pleasure.

"Yes, I suppose it is," agreed Morcar drily. It struck him, however, that this spontaneous expression of opinion, the first Cecil had emitted, was in a way a kind of confidence on the young man's part, a kind of indication that he was enjoying himself. Morcar for some reason felt soothed, and his voice was kinder as he asked the time of the train Cecil had to catch to rejoin his unit.

"My pass doesn't expire till eight tomorrow morning," said Cecil slowly, beginning to put on his khaki greatcoat.

"What time do you leave town, then?" said Morcar, helping him.

"There's a train just after midnight," began Cecil diffidently. "I thought of going to a theatre," he explained in a sudden burst of confidence: "Only I don't know which one to choose or how to get in."

Morcar, repressing a sigh, took up the telephone and arranged the evening with his customary efficiency. He decided offhand that Cecil would probably enjoy best a simple type of leg-show, booked a box—the only four seats available—at a suitable revue, rang up Jenny and Fan at their respective government departments and secured their company for the theatre and supper afterwards. When he finally put down the telephone he found his son regarding him with shining eyes, smiling eagerly.

"It'll be a wonderful evening, won't it?" said Cecil.

"I hope so," replied Morcar drily.

When towards the close of the wonderful evening the party were seated at a table eating expensive though scanty viands and listening to such dance music as wartime could afford, it struck Morcar that while Cecil was certainly simple and naïve, he was not perhaps such a noodle as his father had at first thought him. Though he had met the two girls for the first time that evening and the theatre had afforded few opportunities for talk, the young man's behaviour to Jenny and Fan respectively showed a sound common sense, an instinctive appreciation of character, for he treated Jenny with serious respect, Fan with affectionate amusement. In accordance with wartime custom the four were not in evening dress. Jenny and Fan wore the dark business clothes in which they had coped with the secrets of the national war effort all day, Morcar had a dark lounge suit and Cecil was of course in battledress. While Jenny's plainly cut frock and simply dressed hair became her fine serious face admirably, Fan's very fair smooth curls, black suit and fluffy white blouse gave her the appearance of a black kitten with a white forehead and waistcoat. Morcar told her so in a tone of compliment.

"How do *you* manage to look so spruce, Uncle Harry?" Fan teased him in return. "Every time I see you, you wear a different suit and tie. Have you used all your coupons? Do you buy your suits in the black market?"

"Good heavens, no!" exclaimed Morcar, horrified.

"Then how do you manage always to be so smart?"

"Well, to tell you the truth, young lady, I had fifteen suits in my wardrobe when the war started."

The two girls laughed; Jenny's laugh was soft and low, Fan's high and silvery.

"My, my! Fifteen! What ostentation!" cried Fan severely.

"Nay—just advertisement. If you make cloth you've got to show it off."

"Good wine needs no bush," said Jenny with mock solemnity.

"It needs the landlord should seem to drink it with enjoyment, though," ground out Cecil slowly.

"That's very true," approved Jenny.

"And witty!" cried Fan on a sarcastic note. "Oh, how witty! Really I don't know how you think of all these witticisms, Cecil."

Morcar glanced at his son with some fear that he would be hurt by Fan's sharp tongue, but Cecil's wide smile persisted, and he continued to gaze at Fan as if he enjoyed her. She was certainly a pretty if naughty little thing, thought Morcar appreciatively; full of sex and very silky.

Cecil's thought processes had now ground to a conclusion, and he remarked to Fan:

"You're so sharp you'll cut yourself one day. That's a Yorkshire saying, you know," he added hastily.

"You needn't tell me that. I'm as Yorkshire as you are," returned Fan in her sharp little tone.

"You've been away a long time though," said Cecil.

This simple answer somewhat disconcerted Fan, and the distant music reaching their ears rather more loudly at that moment, she glanced over her shoulder and exclaimed pettishly:

"Can't we dance, Uncle Harry?"

"Why not? What about you, Cecil?"

"I've got very big boots on," hesitated Cecil.

"Three-quarters of the population of Great Britain are wearing Army boots tonight," pouted Fan.

"Have those statistics been checked by your Reference Division, Fan?" queried Jenny, smiling.

"I hadn't thought of that, Miss Oldroyd," said Cecil.

Though mild, his tone undoubtedly held a note of sarcasm; Fan looked a trifle taken aback and Morcar, amused, felt that perhaps Cecil was better able to hold his own with his own generation than his father had imagined. (After all, he reflected, Cecil was Winnie's son.)

"If you'll risk the boots I'll risk annoying you by treading on your toes," continued Cecil.

Fan pouted again and tossed her head, but without further speech rose and led the way to the dance floor.

"Do you want to dance, Jenny?"

Jenny shook her head. "I'd rather talk about David."

"What exactly is he doing now?" said Morcar, drawing his chair a little closer to hers.

"Learning to jump. By parachute, you know." "Is your father still adamant?"

"No, I think he's weakening. He says now that all he asks is that we should wait for a few years. David's father says the same. Colonel Oldroyd says he hasn't any money to help us with, and David has no right to marry till he's paid for Old Mill. He thinks it would be wrong, dishonourable even, for David to marry while he's still in debt to the bank."

"If we all went by that principle," said Morcar with derision: "Very few West Riding manufacturers would be married." Morcar at present kept Old Mill going; the business paid its way and was gradually clearing off the bank's mortgage. But he could not divert any of his own orders to Old Mill, as he would gladly have done to give David a helping hand, because of the stringent wartime Wool Control regulations.

"I think Colonel Oldroyd feels it particularly because since poor grandfather's death Daddy seems to be rather affluent," explained Jenny.

"Aye. And I daresay also he has a horror of debts to the bank," said Mbrcar feelingly.

"But what does all that *matter*, Uncle Harry?" said Jenny earnestly. "It's all out of date. I'm working myself—I'm earn- ing—I always intend to work. I shouldn't like it if David were rich. We don't *want* to wait. After all, there's a war on. Suppose David.... Parachuting isn't a particularly safe operation."

"Well," began Morcar.

They put their elbows on the table and went into the whole situation thoroughly. Jenny was prepared to marry David against her father's wishes, and David was prepared to marry Jenny whenever and on whatever terms Jenny thought desirable, but they both naturally preferred the happier solution of parental consent, David on his father's account and Jenny on her mother's, whose life would certainly be made a misery if her daughter made a runaway match with a man whom she liked and her husband disapproved—a protégé, moreover, as Morcar reflected uncomfortably, of her lover's. Whether it would be wise to bring Colonel Oldroyd and Mr. Harington together or not was a subject of endless discussion between the young people, Morcar and Christina. Jenny, who had met David's father and liked him, desired a meeting between the two; Morcar felt that it would at least convince each father of the other's gentility but that they might easily quarrel—both were proud and wilful men, devoted to their children. Christina strongly opposed a meeting at present. She seemed to fear Harington's temper now even more than of old, and this fear told Morcar a sorry tale of what she had to endure from her husband in private. David thought a meeting proper and therefore desirable, and made many efforts to arrange one; but the onerous duties of Harington in the Civil Service, Colonel Oldroyd in Civil Defence and David in the Army made real difficulties which in their turn provided admirable excuses for the reluctant fathers. David and Jenny considered themselves engaged and this was tacitly conceded by both families; but Jenny now reported that when she had begun to wear a ring which David had given her, a terrible scene took place with her father. It was so terrible, reported Jenny, that her mother had wept, and therefore she herself had not worn the ring in her father's presence again.

"Have you heard from Edwin lately?" said Morcar by a natural transition, to which Jenny of course did not hold the key.

"Yes. He's still on the Atlantic, so far as we can discover."

Morcar and Jenny were so deep in the whole Harington-Oldroyd problem that they were surprised to find Cecil and Fan back at the table apologising for their long absence. Looking up, Morcar found that the room now presented a dreary appearance of diminishing activity; he paid his bill and the party left.

They went out into the deep blackout of wartime London. It was as though a black velvet curtain hung always a few inches before their eyes. Nothing tried Morcar's patience and courage more than the blackout, and accordingly he made a point of walking with a jaunty air and a firm step. This was nearly his undoing, for as the four crossed the bottom of the Haymarket on their way to an Underground station, Morcar tripped over the invisible edge of a traffic "island" and began to fall headlong. He was saved from at worst a broken kneecap and at best some very severe bruises by Cecil, who gripped his arm as with a vice, swung him in an arc and with his other hand restored him to his feet. The young soldier's muscles must have been like iron to achieve this, for Morcar was nowadays a heavily built man. Morcar felt shaken and breathless and somewhat humiliated; his arm ached from Cecil's grip and he became suddenly conscious, from their expressions of concern, that he was very much older than his companions. He made light of his discomfort and continued to escort the two girls briskly towards their station, bought their tickets and directed them paternally towards their trains. As they vanished down the escalator a vague

422

conversational cough sounded at his elbow. He turned to find Cecil, smiling diffidently and holding a ticket in his large hand.

"I see I can go from this station to Victoria," said Cecil in his slow Yorkshire voice. "So I'll say goodnight. It's been a wonderful evening."

He broke off, seemed about to speak again but hesitated, seemed about to hold out his hand but changed his mind. Morcar suddenly realised that Cecil had coughed to attract his attention because he had no other mode of engaging it, for there was no mode by which he could address his father without offering to wound. If the day had been embarrassing to Morcar, what had it been to Cecil? If life had been painful to Morcar owing to his complex family situation, what had it been to his fatherless son? Nothing of this showed in Cecil's manner; there was no resentment, no anger, neither cynicism nor self-assertion; his mild brown eyes, fixed anxiously now on Morcar, seemed simply to admit his own inadequacy and plead that his father should not be vexed. It occurred to Morcar that Cecil was a good boy, honest, affectionate, conscientious, decent, like so many thousands of his age who wore the British Army's uniform. He liked him.

"I specially enjoyed hearing all that about textiles," blurted Cecil suddenly with an embarrassed smile.

"I'll go with you to Victoria and see you on the train," said Morcar.

47

Not in Uniform

Southstone looked very different from the seaside holiday resort he had seen on his last visit, thought Morcar as he turned on to the front at Francis Oldroyd's side. Something must be allowed for the difference between summer and autumn, of course, but more was due to the difference between peace and war. The sea, grey and stormy, held no visible shipping, and Morcar guessed at the mines beneath those tossing waters. The cliffs were wreathed in barbed wire, with machine-guns snugly tucked into their hollows and mobile anti-aircraft guns mounted on their summits. Parts of the Promenade were wired off for various security reasons; the church had suffered from an incendiary, the traffic road was marred by three large bomb craters. The flowers in the beds had given place to vegetables of an edible nature, traces of which still remained in a few long tangled leaves, though most of the turnips and leeks and onions had been harvested and eaten. Of the houses, some were bombed to dust, some were hollow ruins, some had broken windows; the remainder were occupied by Army and Air Force. There were no visitors in bright-coloured frocks to be seen, no bandsmen in frogged coats; only the khaki and light blue of such of the island's defenders as chanced to be off duty.

"But don't you see there was no choice," said Morcar with some irritation in reply to his companion. "The Government instructed us to concentrate the industry in order to economise labour, and we had to do as we were told."

"Wasn't it a voluntary scheme? I understood so," said the other, frowning. His limp was much more pronounced than on Morcar's last visit, and his handsome face looked thin and care-worn. He still wore his hat at a debonair angle, however, even if the old school tie was a trifle shabby. Morcar reminded himself that the south coast of England in wartime was not a particularly comfortable place to live in—sleep, for example, was a rare luxury.

"Up to a point," began Morcar, mollified by these reflections.

"It's a little hard for me to understand, in that case, why my son should be the one to suffer."

"He won't suffer," snapped Morcar, vexed again.

"But Old Mill is empty, as I understand."

"At the moment it's crammed full of food under the Government's food-dispersal scheme, because of the bombing. They pay rent for it."

"That won't bring in quite the same return as when my son ran the building as a mill, I fancy."

"But don't you understand, David's firm is still in existence. David Oldroyd Ltd continues to trade under its own name, but Henry Morcar Ltd makes the cloth in which Oldroyds trade. After all, Colonel Oldroyd," urged Morcar slyly: "Syke Mills and Old Syke Mill will be under one management again, as I understand they were in your father's time."

"But not under the same name!" exclaimed Francis Oldroyd.

His tone was poignantly regretful. "He cares after all!" thought Morcar, astounded. The idea that Francis Oldroyd was not a willing deserter from the West Riding but a wistful exile, flashed across his mental sky with an effect of forked lightning. "He must have been wretched, all these years," thought Morcar.

"Stranger things have happened than that they should once more become so," said Morcar gravely in an entirely different tone. "Perhaps I ought to tell you—I've the greatest respect for David's abilities, and I mean to make him my partner after the war. If the young fool will accept," he added to himself silently.

"I understand you have a son of your own to provide for, Mr. Morcar," said Colonel Oldroyd stiffly.

"Aye. He's in Africa at the moment. Landed at Casablanca. But that's nothing to do with Syke Mills. He won't be working there."

"David, I believe, thought it might be otherwise," said Oldroyd as before.

"No." (I will *not* have Mr. Shaw's grandson at Syke Mills, thought Morcar.)

"They talk a good deal about the industry together, I fancy."

"David and Cecil?" said Morcar, amazed. "Why, have they met?"

Oldroyd glanced at him. "I understand that my daughter made them known to each other," he said sharply.

Morcar's exclamation was cut short by the sound of a very near siren, which wailed up and down the scale in an ear-splitting fashion. A distant drone of aeroplane engines began immediately.

"We're having a lot of these tip and run daylight raids just

426

now," said Colonel Oldroyd, hobbling rapidly towards an old suntrap shelter across the road which, glassless, the paint peeling from its gilded little dome, offered a somewhat pathetic reminder of happier days. "From converted fighters flying singly. They drop a bomb or two and run for it, and shoot us up on their way home. Down!" he cried suddenly in a loud warning shout.

He flung up one hand in an instinctive pointing gesture as he crouched and—rather slowly and clumsily because of his stiff leg—began to lower himself to the roadway. Morcar looked over his shoulder and was horrified; an enemy plane, huge, tilted, in distorted perspective, seemed already below the level of the house-tops and swooping straight towards them. The noise of its engines throbbed painfully in his ears, he could see the swastika on the upper surface of its wings quite distinctly. He threw himself on the ground and buried his face in the crook of his arms. The roar of the engines seemed to fill the whole air, leaving only just enough room for a sudden whing and spatter of bullets followed by a running tinkle of broken glass. Still the engine-roar increased; there was an awful moment when Morcar thought the German would crash directly upon their bodies; to keep his head down, refrain from looking up at the swooping peril, required a continued act of courage. Then the noise diminished as if the plane had passed the lowest point of its arc and lifted; another second and its drone was far away, out over the sea. The anti-aircraft guns had now opened up vigorously; Morcar, climbing stiffly to his knees and then his feet, saw the sky above the Channel dotted with sudden puffs of white which drew a network round the aircraft. One puff turned black and expanded explosively.

"By God, I believe we've got it!" exclaimed Morcar, dusting himself down with one hand and shading his eyes with the other as he gazed out to sea. A distant whine began to pierce his ears: "Yes, I believe we've winged it," repeated Morcar with great satisfaction, glancing towards his companion. Then he exclaimed, for Colonel Oldroyd had not risen from the ground.

Morcar hurried to his side and knelt beside him. "Are you hurt, Oldroyd?" he asked anxiously—then exclaimed again, for he saw the bullet-hole.

Oldroyd made an attempt to raise himself on his arms, but blood gushed from his mouth with the effort and he slipped to the ground again. The movement knocked his hat crooked; Morcar gently pulled it off and laid his hand on the wounded man's shoulder in a protective and consoling gesture. He looked around for help; a group of R.A.F. men over the way were clustered about a couple of their number, one of whom sat on the ground bent double, the other clutched his shoulder. Morcar shouted to them, but his voice came thinly. Suddenly a grey-painted ambulance, clanging its bell, rushed round the corner in search of casualties. Morcar raised his hand and shouted again to summon it. The driver swung it towards him; the First Aid men sprang down, pulled out a steel stretcher, laid it beside Colonel Oldroyd, gently rolled him on with the aid of his overcoat, covered him with a grey blanket. They knew him, and spoke his name regretfully. With the swift efficiency of much practice they raised the stretcher and pushed it along its grooves to its place in the ambulance. Morcar, dazed and bewildered— the whole affair had occupied only a couple of minutes—climbed in beside the stretcher, knocking his head against the lintel of the ambulance door as he did so.

"Now then, sir—you can't stay in there. Get down please. There's other stretcher cases, you know, and every minute counts," said one of the First Aid men kindly. "We're taking him to the Victoria Hospital; you can follow us there." He laid a hand on Morcar's arm and made to usher him from the vehicle.

"You'll be all right, Oldroyd," said Morcar in a strained voice which he strove to make natural, bending over the stretcher. "I'll just go along and tell your wife—I'll stay with her till you're comfortable. I'll let David and Fan know presently, when we see how you are. Don't worry about anything."

The dying man, his eyes full of the knowledge of his plight, looked up at him with a contorted smile. "Thanks. I wish I'd been in uniform," he whispered.

48

Marriage of True Minds

"*The wedding has taken place at St. Something-or-other's, Knights-bridge, London,*" thought Morcar, mentally composing the notice in the *Annotsfield Recorder* while waiting for the arrival of the bride: "*Of Major David Brigg Oldroyd, D.S.O., and Miss Jennifer Mary Harington, only daughter of Sir Edward Mayell Wyndham and Lady Harington, of 3, Notens Square, London. The bridegroom, who is the only son of the late Colonel Francis Oldroyd, D.S.O., and Mrs. Oldroyd, has had a distinguished career in the Army.* They won't be able to say what he's done in the Army," mused Morcar, "for none of us are allowed to know. He wears a maroon beret so presumably he's Airborne. It's my belief he parachutes into France, or Greece, or Jugo-slavia, or Norway or some of those places, to help the Resistance Movements, but of course he won't say a word about it. *Colonel Oldroyd was formerly a textile manufacturer in the Ire Valley, and in peacetime Major Oldroyd was connected with Old Mill in that district. The best man was Pilot Officer G. B. Mellor, the bridegroom's cousin. The service, fully choral, was conducted by*— a couple of bishops, they look

430

like to me," thought Morcar, craning his neck to see the clergy as they came out of the vestry: "But of course I'm not up in these things. However many choir boys are there? I wonder how much Harington has to pay them per head? Ah, here comes Jenny. *The bride, who was given away by her father—* Harington looks in a vile temper; he grows smaller and more vituperative every time I see him—*the bride wore a dress of ivory satin, originally worn by her great-grandmother on her bridal day.* Dearest Jenny," thought Morcar fondly: "How nobly beautiful you look! A wedding is a sacred thing to you. *Her full court train was carried by two little friends of the bride. Her veil of Brussels lace was lent by the bridegroom's stepmother. She carried a bouquet of white roses, the white rose being the emblem of Yorkshire, the bridegroom's native county. The single bridesmaid was Miss Frances Oldroyd, stepsister of the bridegroom, who wore a picture gown of dove grey, with a diamanté headdress, and carried a posy of white gardenias.*"

Morcar had heard all these details discussed very fully on the previous evening and in Christina's recent letters, so that the wedding group held no surprises for him. What he was unprepared for was the effect of the ceremony on himself. It was so long since he had seen David for more than passing glimpses that the young man had become an idea to him rather than a person. But now he found the person much finer than his imaginings. David had been a graceful, handsome, lively lad; he was still handsome, and all his movements had the ease of well-coordinated muscles, but he was now a man—a man who had had to take decisions involving life and death and accepted the responsibility without shrinking. He had broadened and toughened; his complexion had bronzed and his forehead was not now unlined; when he laughed at a joke his eyes lit up with the merry look Morcar knew of old, but in repose his face was rather stern. The first impression the onlooker received of him was that of a striking and daring personality with an iron will, pursuing without reservation and in spite of every difficulty an ideal end; it was only in intimacy that the charm of the old David—the friendly gaiety, the happy sparkle, the loving goodwill—warmed the air. Morcar viewed him now with a respectful admiration which strengthened his former affection for the boy. As David and Jenny stood at the altar together and spoke the old vows which pledged their faith through all the chances and changes of life—David in a strong ringing tone and Jenny on a note quieter but no less warm and firm—Morcar felt a deep emotion. This is what life ought to be, he thought, as David put the ring on Jenny's finger; those two are good as sunshine and true as steel; their love is enduring and noble. His own petty preoccupations seemed to fall away from him, and the true significance of human life, all its tragic grandeur, its high romance, its aspirations so eagerly pursued amid such sordid and petty conditions, its amazing endurance, its sweetness and its pathos, seemed to open out before him. The more venerable of the two clergy was now approaching the climax of the service.

"Forasmuch as David Brigg and Jennifer Mary have consented together in holy wedlock," he intoned, "and have witnessed the same before God and this company, and thereto have given and pledged their troth either to other ..."

Morcar forced himself to think of his own wedding, to think of it with forgiveness and understanding and acceptance. Yes, and with repentance too, thought Morcar suddenly; for to be stupid, to be unperceptive, to be ignorant of one's capacities and aims and nature, to take the line of least resistance—these were also crimes.

There was a moment of great pain and stillness as the realisation of his own share in his disasters pierced his heart.

Then he heard the words: "I pronounce that they be man and wife together." The organ pealed, the choir broke into a hymn about perfect love, the congregation stirred and smiled cheerfully. The ceremony was over; David with his wife on his arm followed the clergy into the vestry, and Morcar sat down and folded his arms and shrank into himself while the guests discussed Jenny's dress.

A young fellow in R.A.F. uniform hurried out of the vestry and came towards him. As he approached Morcar saw that it was G. B. Mellor, looking well and spruce in his airforce blue.

"Mr. Morcar," whispered GB, bending over the pew end with his usual air of reasonable persuasion, his brown eyes very sparkling and expressive: "They're expecting you in the vestry. David wants you to sign the register as a witness. So does Jenny. They're expecting you—they'll be disappointed if you don't come. Lady Harington sent me for you particularly. You'll come now?"

"Oh, very well," growled Morcar. He felt soothed and flattered, rose and followed P.O. Mellor with alacrity. It was pleasant to be in the vestry with all his friends; pleasant to kiss Jenny, whose beautiful face, though rather paler than usual, was radiant with joy; pleasant to shake David's strong warm hand and meet his friendly glance; pleasant to tell the pretty Fan she looked like a fashion plate and to admire Christina, who as usual to Morcar looked the loveliest, the brightest, the best of them all. The wedding march pealed out cheerfully and the procession arranged itself in couples; David and Jenny, GB and Fan, Harington looking crosser than ever with the weeping Mrs. Oldroyd hanging on him. Suddenly it struck Morcar that he, of course, was standing in the place of David's father: he offered his escort to Christina, who accepted it, laying her gloved fingers very delicately on his arm. The verger threw the vestry door wide and they marched out and down the aisle. Morcar held his head well up and smiled rather more than usual to cover his intense pain and embarrassment. To walk thus, at a wedding, with Christina still another man's wife, was almost more than he could bear. "This is the second wedding I've attended in my life," he thought. "Well, they say third time does it. The third one shall be mine and my love's."

The reception at Claridges at first went very well. Christina was always a most accomplished hostess, and today her beautiful desire to make others happy achieved full consummation. Her step was light, her smile gay, her lovely eyes sparkling, in her joy for Jenny, as she moved from guest to guest.

The young men gathered round David.

"How many times have you jumped, old man?"

"Seven."

"Where?"

"Oh, here and there, you know."

"Have you met any Norwegians?"

"I've met representatives of all our Allies at one time or another."

"Have you met any Russians?"

"One or two. They're very nice personally, but can't talk about anything but the horrors of the war."

"Natural, after all."

"Oh yes, entirely natural. They'll pour out a whole glass of vodka and drink it off in one gulp, as a toast to Stalin. Drinking's an international language," said David, laughing. "I can follow them fully, there."

"David, it's time for the wedding cake," said Christina, flying by. "Will you go up to the table, dear? Have you a sword or something to cut it with? Where is Jenny?"

"I don't know," said David, looking about. "I haven't seen her lately."

Amid jokes from his friends about letting his wife run away from him, David, laughing and retorting, moved towards the buffet table where the wedding cake stood in state. Morcar followed. He was interested in this cake, for it was a present from his mother. Mrs. Morcar was fond of David and devoted to Heather (which oddly enough had increased her fondness for the dog's owner, thought her son with a smile) and by infinite contriving of "points" and conserving of rations, especially fats and sugar, had at last amassed sufficient materials from which to make a sizeable wedding cake of good quality. The cake, in three tiers, with a thin coating of sugar, had been baked and decorated by an Annotsfield confectioner, Morcar with infinite precaution had conveyed it to London, and here it was, the cynosure of all the eyes of a very fashionable party. Their exclamations had already been such as to delight Mrs. Morcar's heart, for no minute passed without someone declaring that it could not be edible but was an excellent fake, and hearing with amused admiration the family's assurances that all three tiers were completely real, nothing *ersatz* about them. A hubbub now arose in the neighbourhood of the cake, Harington's voice could be heard in a peevish drawl, and Fan and several other young people began to move rapidly through the crowd in different directions, calling out for Jenny. Morcar who was taller than many of the guests craned his neck and stood on his toes and caught sight of her; she was standing in an alcove, her fine head bent beneath its crown of lace and flowers, listening with grave attention to GB, who was talking to her very earnestly—no doubt the young idiot was describing his ideas of the future world socialist state, thought Morcar with impatience. He pushed through the crowd in

435

Jenny's direction, and reached her at the same moment as her father.

It was not likely that Sir Edward Mayell Wyndham Harington would find Pilot Officer G. B. Mellor a very congenial guest, reflected Morcar quickly, and he saw at once that Harington was furious at finding Mellor thus in private talk with his daughter. Besides, poor fellow, thought Morcar sardonically, Harington didn't want Jenny to marry at all; he only yielded because in England in 1943 it simply wasn't possible to refuse one's daughter to an officer in an airborne division—a man with a D.S.O. too. The prevailing mental climate made such a refusal impossible. "I don't suppose he's pleased about the cake, either," thought Morcar with relish. It was clear that, whatever the cause, Harington was very angry; his pale eyes gleamed, his full mouth was pinched into a vicious line.

"What are you about, Jenny?" he cried in a loud angry drawl. "Why are you neglecting your guests? Where are your manners? Is this a sample of your behaviour as a married woman? This is hardly the mode of life in which you have been brought up!"

His tone was so loud and his voice naturally so resonant that his rebuke was audible for quite.a distance; some of the guests made discreet grimaces at each other and Christina, who came up just then, look daunted.

"Sorry, Sir Edward. My fault," said GB in his pleasant reasonable tones with a smile.

Harington disregarded him. "Come along, Jenny," he said urgently, seizing his daughter by the elbow. "Come quickly. Don't keep your guests waiting any longer."

"Yes, Father," said Jenny calmly. She gave her father a steady look and withdrew her arm from his grasp, then moved with her usual dignity towards the buffet.

A number of guests at once closed round Christina, laughing and chattering to enable her to recover from her embarrassment.

An hour or so later, when David and Jenny had left for an unannounced destination on their honeymoon and the crowd of guests were thinning out, Morcar thought he perceived on Fan Oldroyd's part a determination to leave with him. Her mother naturally wished her daughter to return with her to the hotel where she was staying, but Fan was full of excuses about the need for her to go back and finish some work at the Ministry which enjoyed her services, before joining Mrs. Oldroyd. Seeing that Fan's services were not on a very high level, Morcar doubted the necessity, but he thought she perhaps had some communication to make to him from or about David, so he aided her contrivance, and promised privately to wait for her at the hotel entrance. Fan vanished and reappeared in her ordinary clothes, and they drove off in a taxi together. Fan chattered lightly and quickly about the wedding—the beauty of Jenny's frock, the luscious taste of the cake, David's secrecy about his duties; Lady Harington always looks so lovely, Sir Edward is such a sourpuss, I think G. B. Mellor a prize bore; a pity Edwin couldn't be at the wedding—he's in the Mediterranean.

"Come now, Fan," interrupted Morcar impatiently: "If you've something to say to me, say it."

"Very well," said Fan: "Only don't be cross or I shall be nervous."

"You nervous?" queried Morcar, sceptical.

"Yes. How," said Fan, obviously about to take the plunge: "How would you like me for a daughter-in-law, Uncle Harry?"

"Not at all," said Morcar crossly, vexed by this trifling.

"You are cruel!" exclaimed Fan.

Morcar glanced at her in astonishment. A feeling he had never heard before from her shook her voice, a dark colour roughened her smooth delicate cheek.

"Nay, Fan," he said: "Surely you're not in earnest?"

Fan nodded, her rosebud mouth quivering.

"Now, Fan," said Morcar gravely: "Don't get silly ideas into your head. Cecil isn't at all suitable for you to marry." He was ashamed to say that his own son was not sufficient of a gentleman for her, and paraphrased: "He isn't the man your father would have wished you to marry."

"Poor Daddy! I'm fully aware that Cecil isn't the kind of man people expect me to marry," said Fan clearly, her head held high. "But you see, I just fell in love with him. He's so big—and so *simple*. He's perfectly maddening really," smiled Fan, wriggling her pretty shoulders impatiently.

"Then you can just fall out of love again," said Morcar in a hard tone. "I shan't encourage the match—you wouldn't make Cecil happy."

"Oh?"

"No. You're an idle naughty little parasite," Morcar told her brutally. "You must marry a man who's not merely rich but also hard and sophisticated, who'd be able to keep you in order."

"Idle! I like that! I work eight hours a day! And night duty and weekend duty and firewatching! And why should you be the judge anyway?" panted Fan. "Cecil loves me."

"Rubbish."

"Well, he writes to me."

"If you come to that, he writes to me," said Morcar, thinking of the Service cards in large schoolboyish handwriting which reached him from time to time. "I had a card last week; I reckon he's landed in Italy."

"Exactly! Of course he writes to you!" burst out Fan. "He

adores you! Didn't you know that?"

"Don't be so ridiculous!" exclaimed Morcar. He felt harrowed, sickened, disgusted as if by something obscene; sweat broke out on his forehead and he could not meet her eyes.

"But of course he does. He's made a romance out of you. He took that course at the Technical because you did, he took to bowling at cricket because you did. You didn't know that? You see, you don't understand him in the least. I tell you he loves me. He writes to me."

"Did you write to him first, Fan? Now tell the truth," said Morcar hoarsely.

"No. To be honest, I meant to, but there wasn't time. He wrote to me that very night, that very night when we first met, you know. He must have written in the train. I mean to marry Cecil, Uncle Harry, and it's no use your objecting."

"Fan," said Morcar very earnestly: "Take my advice, I beg of you. Don't hurry Cecil. Don't push him into marrying you. I'm divorced from Cecil's mother, you know, Fan; we never—I—"

"She pushed you into it?" said Fan pertly.

"Yes. And I don't want another tragedy of that kind in the family."

"You don't believe me when I say that Cecil loves me, do you?"

"No."

"Well, here's one of his letters," cried Fan, diving into her bag and fluttering rapidly through all its numerous and varied contents. She picked out a much-worn airgraph and handed it to Morcar.

Darling little Fan, he read, *I think of you day and night, with your sweet little voice and pretty ways. I wonder if you ever think of me?* Morcar snorted. He handed the letter back. "All right," he said in a tone

439

of disgust. "He loves you. Or thinks he does. I give in."

"Darling Uncle Harry!" cried Fan joyously. She threw her arms about his neck and kissed him. It occurred to Morcar as he extricated himself from her embrace that Cecil might find marriage with her decidedly agreeable.

"But what you'll make of him, I'm sure I don't know!" he exclaimed in a tone of despair that was not all humorous. "He doesn't seem to me to have an idea in his head."

"He's very reserved," Fan defended her choice. "I expect you were very reserved when you were young, Uncle Harry. Didn't anybody ever tell you that you were very reserved?"

Morcar uneasily remembered his mother's remarks on this aspect of his character. But surely he had never been anything like Cecil! His uneasiness probably showed in his face, for Fan remarked comfortably:

"Cecil is very like you *in every way*, Uncle Harry."

"I hope he'll have a happier life," said Morcar gruffly.

"I'll try to make him a good wife," said Fan, at her sweetest.

"No, you won't; his slowness will exasperate you," said Morcar out of a full heart. "And, my God! I've only just thought of it: What battles you'll have with his mother!"

Fan smiled. "I shall enjoy that," she said. "I shall never forgive his mother for keeping him away from you."

"Fan!" exclaimed Morcar. "If you take that line *I* shall never forgive *you*! Listen: If Cecil and his mother and I have had our lives messed up—"

"As you certainly have," interrupted Fan emphatically.

"—it's because his mother's feelings about Cecil and myself and her brother were too big for her, not because they were too petty. She's a tragic figure."

Fan looked at him thoughtfully. "Well, I'll try to remember

that," she said. "You must remind me if you see me getting too horrid to her, or too impatient with Cecil."

"A nice quiet life I shall have of it!" said Morcar with feeling. Fan's silvery laugh tinkled, and she patted his hand with her small rosy-tipped fingers. "I'm glad you're going to be my father-in-law," she said with affection.

"The feeling isn't mutual," growled Morcar, nevertheless squeezing her hand heartily.

Later in the evening, after dining alone, he felt so troubled by this new development, so perplexed between his undoubted duty to Cecil and the duty he felt towards Francis Oldroyd's daughter and David's sister, that he dialled the familiar number and asked for Lady Harington.

"Oh, is that you, Harry?" said Christina's voice eagerly. "I'm so glad you rang—I'm all alone and feeling dismal. Edward had to go back to the Ministry."

"Have you had any dinner, love?"

"More or less."

"I know what that means. I'll come and fetch you—we'll have some supper somewhere. Where would you like to go?"

"Let's try one of those little Chelsea restaurants."

Afterwards they walked a long way down the Embankment, pausing sometimes to look over the parapet at the dark river. Morcar drew Christina's arm through his and clasped her slender fingers. The autumn dusk had fallen, and the blackout hid them as it hid many other lovers. In the occasional dim gleam from the blue lights of a passing tram soldiers could be seen from every nation in the world—from every good and decent nation, Morcar corrected himself. British of all kinds, Americans, Dutch, French, Poles, Czechoslovakians, a Chinese Embassy official, a Russian sailor—they were all gathered here for the final assault

441

on Germany's Europe. The lovers passed a scrawl chalked on a wall: *Open the Second Front NOW.*

"Considering we're fighting on about eleven fronts already," said Morcar, vexed: "I must say that slogan irritates me."

"Yes. And yet my heart echoes it," murmured Christina. "Partly for selfish reasons."

"Are you still determined not to leave Harington till after the war?"

"Yes. Surely it won't be long now!"

"Not long, my darling," said Morcar fondly. A tram passed; in its hooded light he admired Christina's deep blue eyes and lovely profile. "You're very beautiful, Chrissie," he told her.

"It's sweet of you to say so. I begin to feel rather antique, with a daughter married."

"If you'd like a catalogue of your attractions, I have it ready."

"Probably better *not*, in this public place," said Christina, laughing. "Won't it be lovely when the war's over and the lights are up, and dear old Big B has his face illuminated," she added, as the clock struck the hour.

"When we're married we'll come and walk along here one night and remind ourselves about the war and laugh about the blackout."

"It sounds too good ever to come true."

"Nonsense!" said Morcar robustly.

"Jenny's safe at any rate."

"Yes. It's a completely good thing, her marriage. But listen, pet," continued Morcar: "I want to talk to you about Fan Oldroyd. I'm worried about her."

"You mean because she's in love with Cecil?"

"Oh, you know that?"

"I've seen them together. It's rather obvious, I think."

"I didn't know you'd met Cecil at all."

"I've seen him once or twice with the other young people."

"He'll never set the Ire on fire," sighed Morcar.

"He's a good boy, and I respect Fan more than I ever thought I could, for loving him."

"Well—if you think it's all right for Fan and him to marry, I shan't worry," said Morcar more cheerfully. "But oh, Chris! What a time I shall have between Fan and Winnie! I can't leave Cecil to fight that battle alone, I shall have to help him."

Christina laughed softly, then hesitated. "What will Winnie think about me?" she said.

"I'm afraid she'll take it hard," admitted Morcar. "But I can't help it. Our orbits don't cross much. I wonder whether it would be a good idea to take you to see her after our marriage. What do you think? It would help her, perhaps, to keep her end up with the neighbours. Or would she resent it? Could you bear to go?"

"I'll do anything you think will help her, Harry," said Christina.

"Well, don't let's think about any more awkward and difficult things tonight," said Morcar comfortably. "Let's just be happy together."

49

Honeymoon in Wartime

Under the wartime Petroleum Control Morcar received a
small allowance of petrol so that he could use his car for
business but not for any other purpose. The police handled any
infringement of the regulations strictly. If he made any non-busi-
ness excursion or even détour, nay, as he sometimes grumbled,
if he so much as ran round to the back entrance of Syke Mills
instead of the front, he was liable to prosecution. Since he had
crossed the Atlantic in the company of petrol-carrying tankers
Morcar thoroughly understood the need for the restriction and
made no attempt to evade it; accordingly he spent his free time
(if any) at the weekend in walks near home rather than in jour-
neys further afield, for which, even if they had been legal,' he
had not sufficient driving fluid. On the Saturday afternoon
following David's wedding he was walking along a path beside
the upper reaches of the river Ire.

The countryside was looking particularly beautiful at that
moment. The equinoctial gales had blown themselves out and

been succeeded by a period of calm; the sky was high, a clear pale blue, with long feathers of small scalloped white clouds lying quietly across it from horizon to zenith. Below, the West Riding landscape, often so sombre, wore today an autumn coat of infinitely delicate and subtle blending, employing the whole range of colour comprised in the idea of tawny. The green of the trees was dulled towards bronze, and tipped with many shades of yellow; bright golden leaves drifted down in gentle showers, painted the ground and swam in the pools. The upper fields had a pale russet bloom which exactly matched the fading flower of the heather on the moor above; the bracken, just turning brown along the stream, on a distant hillside where it caught the sun glowed vivid red. The rocks and the rough stone walls struck a sepia note to match a distant cluster of mill chimneys; the tumbling restless water was the colour of honey in the shallows, but beneath the packhorse bridge richly auburn. Even the occasional brown and white bullocks conformed to the colour scheme. Morcar observed all this with a designer's eye, and longed for the day when he should once more be able to blend colours without wartime limitations of costs or shortages; he observed it as a man, and longed for the day when he could display its beauty to Christina.

It had seemed to him for some moments that a scuffling noise came from the nearby bracken; now he saw that his impression was justified, for the tall fronds were violently agitated in succession as if by the passage of some animal. Suddenly he laughed, for a small thick black tail appeared above the sea of brown and green; he whistled and called, and out bounded Heather. The dog ran towards him with a friendly eye and a wagging tail, then a few yards from Morcar halted, took a few steps in the opposite direction and halted again with a look of perplexity.

"What are you doing here? Where's your master, old chap? David!" called Morcar.

Presently his call was answered, and David, with his pipe between his teeth and his wife on his arm, came round a fold of the hill. Greetings followed, while Heather leaped about them all ecstatically.

"I knew you must be somewhere in Yorkshire, when I got home the day after the wedding and found you'd called for Heather. Where are you? Don't tell me if you want to keep it a secret."

"No secret—we're at Scape Scar," said David and Jenny together.

"Really!" said Morcar. He smiled broadly; he felt delighted that Jenny should wish to come to her husband's home for her honeymoon. She's a true helpmeet, he thought. "How do you like it here, then, Jenny?" he asked.

"I love it," said Jenny simply. "Partly for itself, and partly because it seems so peaceful after London."

"Aye. We don't look to have suffered much from the war in the West Riding, and that's a fact," said Morcar, turning and walking beside them. "Of course we have rations and restrictions and blackout and Home Guard and Observer Corps and fire-watching and National Savings and Salvage and all that, the same as everybody else—and bereavement," he added, thinking of Nathan, whose quiff had faded that week—he had lost a son in the R.A.F. "But we've not been in danger all the time, like London and the south coast and Hull and so on. Our houses are still mostly whole."

"Yes. And somehow the people don't look as tired and shabby as in the south," said Jenny.

"True. And yet you know, it hasn't been easy," said Morcar.

"Up here we have all the irritations of the war and none of the excitements. And to tell you the truth, we West Riding folk don't like not being in the forefront of the battle."

"You'll be in it after the war all right," said David grimly.

"Well, that's fair enough. We shan't cry about that; we'll take our share."

"With depreciated machinery, interrupted markets and a labour shortage, you're going to have a pretty grim task pushing up your exports to earn food for England," said David.

"We've got plenty of plans to cope with it," said Morcar stubbornly. "And what's this about *you* and *your?* Why don't you say *we*, eh?"

"Why not indeed?" said David. A shadow passed over his face and left it stern. "There's nothing in the world I want more than to be back at Old Mill, with the war won and Jenny at Scape Scar," he said. "But the war isn't won yet, not by a long chalk."

"And if I can get Christina at Stanney Royd," thought Morcar: "The picture would be perfect." Aloud he said: "Have you taken your wife into the textile world at all?"

"We've inspected Old Mill, and looked at the outside of Syke Mills and Prospect Mills," said David, smiling again.

"*Lucus a non lucendo*" commented Jenny.

"Now what does that mean?"

"She means Prospect Mills is called Prospect because it has no prospect," said David, laughing.

"Neither physical nor financial," added Jenny.

Morcar snorted. "You're too clever for me," he said. (He did not want to discuss Prospect Mills in any case.) "I shall take it ill of you if you don't come inside Syke Mills before you leave, choose how."

"We'll come on Monday morning if that's convenient," said David.

"Come home to tea with us now, Uncle Harry," urged Jenny.

"Nay—not on your honeymoon. I'll see you Monday morning," said Morcar, turning. "I'll go on my way now and leave you to yourselves, bless you. Call the dog."

Heather stood with one paw uplifted and looked after him regretfully, but followed David.

Morcar saw the newly married pair before Monday, however. As he was sitting at midday dinner with his mother on Sunday he was summoned to the telephone, and when he answered it heard Jenny's voice. She sounded breathless as she told him that David had been recalled from leave.

"What, from his honeymoon?" raged Morcar. "They must be daft! I wouldn't go if I were he."

"It can't be helped. David has been—expecting it. In a way. It's something special," said Jenny. "He's catching a train from Leeds at three. I shall go back to work tomorrow."

"Isn't David going to London?"

"No."

"You'd better come here for the night, love," said Morcar. "Wait now—how are you getting to Leeds?"

"We're having a taxi from Marthwaite," said Jenny. "I'm in Marthwaite now. It's all arranged."

"Oh, no, nonsense!" said Morcar. "I'll come and fetch you from Scape Scar and take you to Leeds. And bring you back here afterwards. And if the police prosecute, they can prosecute and be damned," he added to himself, firmly sacrificing his precious petrol.

"Very well," agreed Jenny simply. "Thank you, Uncle Harry." She sounded forlorn, perhaps not far from tears, but courteous

448

and controlled, as always.

"I'll be with you in ten minutes," said Morcar.

Accordingly an hour or so later he found himself at a Leeds station. The platform was crowded and the train was crammed; soldiers, sailors and airmen, ATS, WAAFS and WRNS, with their kitbags, were deeply engaged in saying goodbye to their wives, children, husbands and parents. Wherever Morcar looked he saw an affecting scene of farewell. David and Jenny stood silently together, their hands tightly clasped, gazing into each other's eyes. Morcar withdrew and stood aloof, so that they might be alone together. He longed for the train to start. He knew that this was a selfish wish and kept himself from looking at his watch, but if the train did not leave soon he felt he should break down and cry like a child. At last porters began to be urgent that passengers should take their seats. Reluctantly the uniforms climbed into the train. The platform looked strangely neat and empty; the women left behind—they were mostly women, thought Morcar, pitying—stood very still, in their Sunday best, their heads turned up towards the carriage windows, their eyes fixed on one beloved face. Jenny stood thus, her cheek very pale, her grey eyes very wide; David, frowning, gazed down at her intently. Suddenly David stretched out his hand and Jenny laid her hand in his; they drew together and kissed, Jenny standing—an infinitely pathetic detail, Morcar thought—on tiptoe.

And now the train began to move; the lovers' embrace was over, their fingers slipped from each other's grasp. Jenny tried to keep pace with the train, but it was not easy to thread her way amongst the other women.

"Harry! Harry!" called David suddenly in an urgent poignant tone, leaning far out of the window.

Much moved by this form of address, on David's lips not usual, Morcar flung himself forward and sprang to the step of David's carriage, holding on by the handle.

"Look after everything for me, Harry," said David quickly.

"I will, lad. Goodbye and good luck," said Morcar, releasing his hold and dropping to the platform.

"Goodbye," said David.

50

Death of a Hero

Morcar kept the cutting from the London newspaper folded in his pocket-book. It grew worn and old; the paper yellowed, the print faded, the creases deepened into slits; but it remained one of his most treasured possessions. From time to time, when he felt that his ideals needed encouragement, he drew it out and read it carefully.

The Story of a Great Englishman

The story of the death of Major David Oldroyd can now be told, though the resistance movement in Europe to which he acted as liaison officer must not yet be more closely identified.

The eyewitness from whom these details were obtained later became a member of the resistance movement and is now in England. His name cannot be given, as he has relatives still living in his native country.

Major Oldroyd was executed after a mock trial, after being in close captivity for about a week.

With him perished an American officer, a Czechoslovakian officer and ten other prisoners belonging to the country's resistance movement.

It is believed that the American and the Englishman were not tortured. Some of the resistance members had been deliberately blinded, and some bore wounds and sores. Major Oldroyd appeared to have broken his arm, for he wore a sling over his left shoulder, but not otherwise to be hurt.

The story of young Oldroyd's daring leadership of the movement, his bold denunciation of Nazism at the trial, and his fearless bearing on the way to execution, excited the admiration of the whole country and particularly the young men, greatly stimulating the resistance movement and adding to the difficulties of the Nazis. It was Oldroyd's task to supervise the supply of arms by air to the resisters, and it was while engaged on this task in the mountains that the party fell into the hands of a collaborationist patrol.

In order to impress the people of the neighbouring village, a mock "trial" was staged by the Nazis in the village hall, into which they drove all the villagers as spectators. A collaborating officer of the country, whom the eyewitness called "the Captain" and stigmatised as brutal, depraved and detested, was put in charge of the trial.

The eyewitness saw David Oldroyd sitting on the floor of the hall with his back against a pillar, smoking his pipe, which one of his fellow-prisoners helped him to light. When he was called up to be questioned and jerked roughly to his feet by the guards the pipe fell from his mouth and broke on the floor, and one of the guards put his foot on the pieces and stamped them into fragments. The villagers groaned their disapproval and the Captain shouted angrily for silence.

Oldroyd waved away the interpreter and answered the questions in the language of the country. He spoke quite quickly and eloquently. He had a fine ringing voice which could be heard distinctly all over the hall; it was a pleasure to listen to him. He was a handsome man, too, with a very pleasant smile and lively blue eyes; he looked neat and correct in spite of his imprisonment. It was observed that his khaki uniform bore no insignia, and when asked for his rank and regiment he did not answer; he gave his name however as David Burg (Editor's Note: Probably a mishearing for Brigg) *Oldroyd. The Captain questioned him closely about his political opinions.*

"Why should you, an Englishman, come and interfere with the government of our country?" said the Captain. "What right have you to come here and stir up the people to wage war against us?"

Major Oldroyd answered: "I came because this war is not a struggle of nation against nation. It is a fight for justice and freedom and the brotherhood of man, against oppression and cruelty and tyranny. It is a fight for love against hate, for the good in man against the evil."

At this the people applauded, and the Captain cried out savagely: "Here we shoot men with such opinions!"

Major Oldroyd shrugged his shoulders and replied: "That will not kill the opinions."

"But it will kill you," said the Captain, laughing.

"I am ready to die for freedom," said Major Oldroyd. "And I am proud to die with these brave men, who believe in freedom, as my companions."

Here the crowd demonstrated again in Oldroyd's favour by clapping and stamping and shouting, and the guards quelled them by beating the nearest over the head with the butts of their rifles. An old woman rushed up to the platform and shook her fist at the Captain. He jumped up and struck her across the mouth so that she fell to the ground bleeding.

The Nazis must have seen now that the crowd was against them and that the trial was not serving their purpose, for a Nazi officer rose from his seat on the platform and whispered urgently in the Captain's ear, and he hurried the proceedings to a close. The trial, if you can call it a trial where there were no lawyers and no witnesses and no jury, was all over in less than half an hour, and all the prisoners were condemned to death.

Major Oldroyd then formed the condemned men into a square, and placing himself at their head, marched them off to the castle between the guards. He whistled an English tune for them to march to, and the others took it up and sang it. It was not a tune the eyewitness knew. The contrast between their brisk neat marching and the exaggerated antics of the guards excited the deri-sion of the crowd, who were country people, not accustomed to seeing the goosestep. As the prisoners marched off, Major Oldroyd raised the salute of the resistance movement: the clenched fist. The Captain struck his hand down violently. But Oldroyd called out to the people: "I give you the salute of freedom!" and raised his hand again.

Outside the castle the men were halted and made to dig a trench for their common grave, in a field. Major Oldroyd was unable to wield a spade prop-erly owing to his broken arm. A young man sprang out of the crowd and offered to dig for him, but was driven back by blows from the guards.

When the grave was finished the condemned men were lined up against the outer wall of the castle and executed by machine-gun fire. They all died raising their hands in the freedom salute.

The spectators were sobbing. Many present declared that the men's calm cheerful courage was due to the fine example of the English officer. "He was a very brave man and a very kind one," a resistance officer said later. "We loved him very much. We shall remember him all our lives. He will always inspire us. He is one of those who make friendship possible between nations."

51

Never on Earth Again

The siren warbled for the seventh time that night. Morcar, busy with the agenda of the committee on wool textile industry reconstruction which he had come to London to attend next day, called in a preoccupied tone:

"Keep away from those windows, girls!"

Receiving no reply, he pulled off his new reading glasses quickly and looked up from his desk, first at the large sheets of glass—once a pleasure, now in the summer of 1944 a menace—and then across the room. Through the windows—from habit the amount of view added to the flat's rent came into his mind, then he remembered that he was trying not to think that kind of thought nowadays—through the windows the Park over the road made a beautifully calm and sunlit picture, and the two young women by the hearth made a beautifully calm and sunlit picture too. In both cases the appearance of calm lied, thought Morcar, for the Park lay under the threat of an approaching bomb, and Jenny and Fan bore perplexities in their fair young heads and griefs within their breasts. Indeed it was not like them to be so still, he thought; in the odd, bright, careless clothes the young affected nowadays, made for movement, their immobility looked strange. But it seemed they were both deep in reverie; Jenny's handsome intelligent face, Fan's usually so shrewd and saucy, were both blank as if their owners had withdrawn from the façade. Well! They had plenty of think of, certainly, with the problems of their future all unsolved; Fan's young man, if he could be called hers, was in the Normandy battle—while as for Jenny! Now that he looked more searchingly, there was tension and not relaxation in their pose; Jenny upright on the settee, Fan folded in acute angles on a low stool, maintained their balance by a brooding concentration.

The two girls, who were friends in spite of their different natures, had dined with him, as they often did when he was in town; they found his flat easier to meet in physically than the cottage attic Fan occupied up at Hampstead, easier psychologically than the house of Jenny's parents in the select Kensington square. Morcar loved to have them with him; he had recently discovered that he was by nature a genial, lively, sociable man who liked the company of young people, lonely through no fault of his own. If he had discovered this afresh after so many arid years, it was through these young men and women who were especially dear to him; for if Cecil was his son, David Oldroyd had been better than a son to him and Fan was David's sister, while Edwin and Jenny were Christina's children; the lives of the five were closely interwoven with Christina's and his own.

Christina! His mind flew to the blue door, once so richly glossy, faded now in wartime but to him always the symbol of elegance, beauty and romance, which would swing behind Jenny when he took her home tonight. It was not in his code to approach the mother by way of the children; he kept Edwin and Jenny out of the problem, never used them as a means of meeting his love, would not accept the casual invitation to enter which Jenny was sure to offer tonight; indeed it sometimes seemed to him that half his life was spent in hiding his feeling for Christina from those whom it might hurt. But to be near Christina's daughter was to be near something of Christina, and so Morcar liked to be near Jenny. Outwardly she did not resemble her mother, for everything about Jenny was strong and fair and candid, while Christina, with her dark thick curls, her lovely tragic eyes, her sweet profile, her delicate skin and charming hands, had an air of uncertainty, of indecision; but the mother and daughter shared a loftiness of soul. Jenny was always complete and staunch and whole, whether in grief or joy; Christina ever frustrated—her very dress, though so delicious, was nowadays often marred by some slight careless omission, some unexpected roughness, which betrayed her deep inner trouble; but the generous warmth, the delicate integrity, of their spirits was the same. They loved each other, too, in spite of Harington. At the thought of Christina's husband Morcar's heart filled as always with rage and pain, for though he hated Harington he found it impossible to despise him. Sir Edward Mayell Wyndham Harington was no weakling and no fool; he knew his job, he was high in his Department, his acquaintance with powerful people and his sophistication were both immense. He was in the inner circle always, he knew how things were done. In his own way, too, he loved Christina, though it was a way which blighted, frosted. "My darling," thought Morcar with tender pity. Oh, if only the war were won! Now that we've landed in Europe, thought Morcar hopefully, surely it can't be very long. And then? Would Harington yield? Bracing himself for the struggle, Morcar wondered.

In the distance a faint throb, like a distant road-drill, began to pierce the air, and steadily though at first almost imperceptibly grew in volume. There was something unpleasant, even sinister, in the persistence of the long-drawn-out unceasing very gradual crescendo, the endless murmured repetition of the same vibrating note.

"Here she comes," said Morcar. He sighed with exasperation, shut his glasses in their case with a snap and rose.

The murmur was now much stronger and more clearly defined and not to be mistaken for anything but the sound of an approaching flying bomb.

"It's coming this way," said Morcar, putting a hand under each girl's elbow to help them up. "Best get into the hall."

"You always think they're coming this way," pouted Fan, nevertheless rising obediently, for the murmur had now become a penetrating grind.

The absence of glass in the entrance hall window, whence it had disappeared in one of the earlier blitzes, made it a useful refuge when fly-bombs were overhead. Fan lounged at the side of the boarded-up gap, Jenny sat down on a stiff hall chair. Morcar looked around and unhooked the mirror from the wall.

"What are you doing with that, Uncle Harry?" said Fan as he clasped it in his arms.

"Admiring the Morcar profile, love," said Morcar genially. "What else?"

He laid the mirror carefully face downwards on the floor.

The noise in the air grew and grew, until it seemed as if a heavy railway train rolled overhead, They all looked up, expecting a diminution as the bomb passed by, but the sound increased to a clamorous roar.

"Down! Down!" cried Morcar suddenly. "Under the table!

Quick!" The girls slipped obediently to their knees, Fan in a single graceful jerk, Jenny heavily, for she was with child and near her time. "I'll have her out of this tomorrow, Admiralty or no Admiralty," thought Morcar, helping her: "I'll get her up to Yorkshire where she'll be safe. She owes it to the child. If there is any tomorrow," he added grimly. He felt something at his knees, and found the girls trying to pull him down; but there was no room for him beneath the table, and he shook his head. The raucous thunder of the fly-bomb now crammed the air. "Nay, this is ours, this is it," he thought. "If the engine cuts out now, we're for it." The noise abruptly ceased. "Ours! Well," thought Morcar, jocularly speaking Yorkshire to himself to keep his spirits up: "If we're bahn to die, we may as well die thinking o' summat fine, choose how. England!" thought Morcar.

He wondered what went on within the two fair heads below. The girls were looking up at him; Fan wore a sardonic defiant grin, Jenny a fine quiet smile. Through his own mind now raced pictures of his life; things he had not thought of, people he had not seen, for years, came up before him fresh and vivid as when they were real, but with the added significance lent to them by later events.

"Scenes from the life of Henry Morcar," he thought sardonically. "Well! I hope this is not the last of the series."

In silence they waited for the bomb to fall.

The impact was terrific, so that Morcar shut his eyes and crouched. The floor waved sickeningly, plaster flaked thickly from the ceiling and rained down on their shoulders, glass crashed and tinkled and went on crashing and tinkling, outside there was the long rumbling groan of collapsing buildings, a stifling brown dust rose about them, something heavy flew across the room and struck the wall within an inch of Jenny's head. It was the lock of the door, Morcar discovered, cautiously opening his eyes; he had stupidly forgotten to stand the door ajar, and the blast had cut the lock as neatly out as if the heavy panelled wood were made of butter. Five long nails securing the lock had buried themselves in the wall.

Slowly the noise subsided; the floor settled into the horizontal plane; everything was suddenly very still except the glass, which went on tinkling and crashing, and the brown dust in the air, which circled upwards in slow sinister curls. The all-clear sounded. Morcar drew a long breath.

"Well!" he said.

Fan sprang up and began to shake herself and Jenny free of plaster. Morcar gave Jenny his hand and helped her to her feet.

"We're alive, it seems," he said, astonished.

"Seems so!" said Fan, perky as ever though trembling slightly.

All of a sudden they began to laugh and talk at the top of their voices. Look at the lock! Look at those nails! Look at the plaster! Look at the dust! "Oh, Uncle Harry!" cried Fan, running in and out: "Look at your bottles!" He went towards the sitting-room. For some reason he seemed to be limping uncomfortably; he glanced down and found that the blast had removed the sole from his left shoe. His decanters and bottles had leaped from the sideboard; some had accomplished the leap safely, more had perished. The windows were now open spaces surrounded by jagged spikes; the mirrors were all cracked, pictures were awry. There did not, however, appear to be any structural damage to the walls. Fan, with little fluttering exclamations, began to tidy, to repair such damage as was not beyond her skill, to restore cushions, to straighten pictures.

"If I had a broom," she said, "and a dustpan, I could do wonders with that glass."

The hall porter came in with a rather mottled countenance, to see if anyone were hurt. The bomb had struck a building at the back of Morcar's flat, about fifty yards distant, on the side away from the Park.

"Fifty yards!" marvelled Morcar. "If it's like that at fifty, what is it like at ten?"

"Don't, Uncle Harry!" Fan begged him, pretending to shudder. "Porter, could I have a broom?"

"You'd best not touch anything, miss, unless you wear thick gloves," recommended the man. "And don't sit down, sir." He indicated to Morcar a cretonne-covered armchair of which every inch was penetrated with pointed slivers of glass.

"I think I'll take these young ladies home. Perhaps you can clear up a little meanwhile?" said Morcar.

Jenny had picked her way to the glassless window and was looking out. The other two now joined her. The brown dust was settling, and the space where it had previously formed a house could be seen. "That's dust to dust indeed," thought Morcar. Rescue workers were already on the job, searching the débris for casualties. The other dwellers in the street, with that gay courage which Morcar could not sufficiently admire, were already out in the roadway shaking their carpets to remove the glass, making jokes to each other about their experiences during the falling of the bomb.

"I shan't have to do my washing-up, anyway, 'cos there ain't no china left to wash," cackled a Cockney voice.

"I thought the cat was blasted in the bath, but it was only a bottle of red nail-polish," floated up in very Oxfordian tones.

"A great people," thought Morcar, smiling, reminded somehow of his grandfather's deathbed. "Well, girls; I think we'd better go while the going's good."

He went into his bedroom to change his shoes. The telephone rang. Morcar picked it up impatiently.

"Harry Morcar."

"Oh, Harry, is it you? Oh, Harry! Are you safe? Is Jenny there? Is she safe?"

"We're all quite safe, Christina," said Morcar soothingly.

"Wasn't that one near you, then?"

"Yes, it was rather," said Morcar. "Just at the back of our street. The flat's knocked about a bit, but nothing much really." Because while they waited for the doodle-bug to fall he had been thinking of all the long course of his association with Christina, he was off his guard and his voice was particularly loving. He looked up to find Jenny standing in the doorway gazing at him. Startled, he went on hastily: "Jenny's here—would you like to speak to her? I'm bringing her home at once."

"Yes, oh yes. Be sure to come in, Harry," said Christina in her soft graceful tones. "I was so worried about you. Bring Jenny now—Edward is troubled about her being out."

"She must come up north with me tomorrow," said Morcar firmly.

"Yes, I quite agree. Edward quite agrees. Is that you, Jenny my darling?"

When Jenny had spoken a few reassuring words the three left at once, and reached the nearest Underground station without hearing another siren. On their way Fan saw a half-empty bus which she said would take her all the way home, but Morcar suggested grimly that if the bus were empty it was empty for a very good reason; Fan must travel cosily under ground or cease to consider herself his daughter-in-law elect. Fan pouted but smiled, and obediently descended into the safe earth. She went north, Morcar and Jenny west towards Notens Square.

"Oh, what a bore!" exclaimed Jenny as they emerged at the Kensington station, pointing. The *Alert* board was displayed, and indeed another flying-bomb could be heard approaching through the air. "How many is this since dinner?"

"Eight, I think."

"I counted seventeen in bed last night," said Jenny. "Seventeen loud ones, I mean; I don't count them if they're a long way off."

"Jenny, you must give up your job and come north," said Morcar firmly. "You owe it to David's child, you know."

"I begin to think perhaps I must," said Jenny thoughtfully.

They were interrupted by the noise of the bomb, which came flying directly overhead. The summer dusk was beginning to fall, and the red glare in the tail could be seen distinctly. The doodle-bug, emitting its hideous steady roar, whizzed in a business-like manner diagonally across the street just above housetop level, curved around to the left, and dived. One minute its graceful form, tilted at a steep angle, could be seen silhouetted against the greenish sky; the next there came the loud explosion, the rumbling groan of falling buildings, the crash and tinkle of falling glass, the swirling brown dust, the nauseating heave of the pavement beneath their feet.

"I should get tired of these if I lived in London," said Morcar in a peevish tone. "Come along, Jenny—we'd better hurry before the next one comes along. Yes—there goes the all-clear."

He took her arm and urged her forward, but to his surprise she hung on him heavily and did not move.

"Anything wrong?" he asked quickly.

Jenny's face was white. She looked very steadily in the direction where the bomb had fallen.

"My God!" cried Morcar. "You don't think—"

On a common impulse they started forward. "I don't think it

was anywhere near Notens Square," said Morcar.

"No, nor do I," said Jenny. "Still, one wants to know—"

"Of course," said Morcar. "Naturally. One wants to know. Just to be sure. One gets these frights and afterwards of course laughs at them. I don't think it was anywhere near."

His voice grew more and more uneasy as they drew nearer, till at last it was thick with anguish, for he saw all the familiar apparatus of rescue preceding them along the streets. They hurried, panting; their feet felt leaden, as in a nightmare, they seemed to walk for hours and find themselves still in the same dreary place.

"Some people say we get so many bombs in this district because Montgomery has his headquarters somewhere near," panted Jenny. "But I don't know if it's true."

"I don't think they can be steered much," said Morcar. "These doodle-bugs, I mean."

"No. I expect not."

"We're nearly there now, love," said Morcar soothingly. "And then we shall see."

They turned into the Square. Pushing past Civil Defence men, heavy rescue men, ambulance, police, they at last turned the corner whence they could see the Haringtons' house.

But there was no house there.

Morcar gave Jenny into the care of neighbours, and flinging off his coat, went to work with the rescue men who were lifting beams and dragging away stones. He worked with frantic haste and energy; sweat poured down his face, he tore his hands and strained his muscles; he used his strength to its full force, as he had never really used it before.

Darkness fell; powerful arc lights were fixed in the street. A crane was brought and rigged, and at last came into action. The men worked on and Morcar worked with them.

In the early hours of the morning they drew the crushed bodies of Edward and Christina Harington from the ruins.

Never on earth again
Shall I before her stand
Touch lip or hand.
Never on earth again …

Epilogue

To Work

It was touching, thought Morcar, to see how the shops in Annotsfield had all contrived with the limited means at their command to make some display of red white and blue. Those which owned flags of course hung them out proudly, but bunting and paper were in short supply in the England of 1945, and all of these commodities on view were relics of a more abundant age. But the dress shops had dresses of red white blue, hat shops had raked out the oddest looking old millinery of the right colours to show their delight in the nation's victory; shoe shops sported red bedroom slippers, old white ballroom sandals, blue wooden shoes of wartime manufacture; even fishmongers had secured flowers of the proper shades and arranged them on their marble slabs. All had left their blinds undrawn so that their rejoicing might be visible. In the streets, the girls wore red white and blue snoods round their hair, the children were dazzling in bows and coloured handkerchiefs; even the men, though rather shame-faced about it in the British fashion, sported neat rosettes in their

466

buttonholes. The radiators of cars and buses were decked with ribbons and small flags.

Morcar made his way to the Annotsfield Town Hall, for it had been stated in the *Annotsfield Recorder* that two hours after the official announcement of victory the Mayor would conduct a brief expression of the general thanksgiving there. A roaring happy crowd was waiting for the Mayor to appear on the balcony, and listening to the bells of the churches, which were ringing in changes and peals. Just as he arrived a squad of cheerful-looking soldiers, even the sergeant mildly beaming, marched up and arranged themselves in a square in front of the Town Hall, which was festooned with flags and fairy lights. The soldiers began to play military marches; the drummer in his leopard-skin banging away with great gusto. Policemen, smiling all over their faces, wrestled amicably with the crowd and answered innumerable questions. Babies crowed and wept, the shrill voices of children made an incessant treble vibration, everyone laughed and chattered at the top of their voice. "Let the little 'uns through!" cried a woman in the front row suddenly, turning. On a common impulse the crowd obeyed her; a narrow lane was made down which the children were pushed, and soon a deep fringe of small boys and girls, laughing, tossing their heads, restlessly jumping and pointing in joyous excitement, was formed in front, where the view of the proceedings would be uninterrupted. Press photographers climbed the buttresses of the Town Hall and snapped the scene from various angles.

The mace-bearer came out on the balcony; the Mayor in robes and chain, the Town Clerk in wig and gown, the Mayor's chaplain in his best black, followed him. The crowd fell silent and gazed up intently. In a Yorkshire voice uneven with emotion the Mayor read out a simple speech, to which the crowd— though many of them could not hear, for the loud-speakers crackled—listened respectfully. The Mayor called for three cheers, and a shy ragged sound began which presently became rolling and deep-throated. The chaplain now stepped forward and conducted a brief service. The people sang the doxology (which they did not know very well, observed Morcar; he himself had to fish it out of his boyhood's memories) and repeated the Lord's Prayer in a mumble. Then a couple of soldiers wearing white bandoliers raised trumpets to their lips.

The strange high notes of the *Cease Fire*, so melancholy even in triumph, rang out over the crowd, who were suddenly very silent. Their faces, very still and sober, revealed that their thoughts were with those whom they had lost during the war. Morcar thought of Christina. He missed her bitterly, painfully, continually. He was achingly lonely without her. He thought now of her beauty, her lovely compassion, her gentleness, her eager wish to make everyone happy.

> *Always as then she was,*
> *Loveliest, brightest, best,*
> *Blessing and blest.*
> *Always as then she was …*

"If I caused you suffering by my selfish passion, my darling," thought Morcar: "I beg your forgiveness. You were the true and only joy of my life."

He thought of David. *One of those men who make friendship between nations possible.* For love against hate, for the good in man against the evil.

The sound of the trumpets died on the air. The band struck up *God Save the King*, and the crowd, stirred to cheerfulness again, sang it heartily.

468

The ceremony was over; the Mayor withdrew, the soldiers marched off, the crowd began to disperse.

It had all been very simple and provincial, thought Morcar, walking towards the car park; the Mayor's speech had not been particularly eloquent, the trumpeters' tone had not been particularly silvery, the decorations were just what were left from former years—indeed it seemed to him that he had seen those fairy lights at intervals since his early childhood. But it was all *real*, thought Morcar; honest, genuine, and truly of England, that is to say sober, kindly, spontaneous, democratic; performed decently and in order.

Morcar found his car and began to drive slowly, with the deliberate patience taught by the endurances and frustrations of the war, through the crowded streets out of the town up the Ire Valley.

He foresaw that the period before him would be the busiest of his life—nay, that it would make all other busy periods of his life look like a holiday. It was Morcar's duty, as one who had survived and suffered comparatively little in the war, to do well by his county and his country. He knew it and accepted it all gladly: To see that Cecil (and those like him) who came home had a good home and a good job to come to; to ensure that the abilities of Jenny (and those like her) were not frustrated, wasted; to harness the restless energy of Fan (and those like her) so that it would be used for the common good and not tear her to pieces; to care for the future of David's child. The Haringtons' affairs lay chiefly in Morcar's hands, for Jenny had begged him to help her with them and young Edwin was still in the Far East and heaven knew when he would be back again. The Oldroyds' affairs lay chiefly in Morcar's hands, for he was David's executor and in that capacity Francis Oldroyd's widow was also apt to take her troubles to him. Baby David lay now in his pram (Mrs. Morcar's gift) on the terrace at Stanney Royd—Morcar's heart warmed now as he thought of that sunny and endearing infant, so like Jenny, so like David.

But there was something else that formed part of Morcar's duties. "Look after everything for me," David had said, and Morcar had replied: "I will, lad." I reckon he meant the wool textile trade as well as his own affairs, thought Morcar soberly. It wouldn't be like him to think only of himself. I won't think only of myself either; I've learned my lesson. For Morcar, the death of Harington symbolised the death of what was evil in the old England. Much that was lovely had perished with the old England, even as Christina perished with Harington. But the birth of the little David symbolised the survival of what was good. Morcar felt it was his part to help the growth of the good England. His grandfather and his father had served the community after their fashion, and he must do the same in his.

He remembered the day when he had argued with David and the Mellors at Scape Scar about the future of industry. Our problem is threefold, he thought. To make good and charming cloth so that people may feel happy and comfortable when they wear it. To earn food, to earn life and hope, for Britain by exporting our product. To make the industry provide a good life for those engaged in it. "Not easy to combine those three!" thought Morcar. How was it to be done? How to plan intelligently for the industry as a whole, and yet keep the sting, the fun, of individual independence and achievement? How to combine freedom with security, for all who worked in it? And make a good product spring from both? How to provide good houses, good education, good wages, good hopes of advancement, for all workers in the industry, without raising the price of the product beyond what other workers could afford to pay? How to reunite the whole industry so that it pursued a single aim, instead of consisting of opposing parties following separate purposes? He remembered how David had wanted the wool textile trade to be amongst the first to solve the problem in the new industrial revolution, the revolution which was to be social as well as industrial.

"Well," said Morcar thoughtfully: "I promise you, lad, we'll have a damn good try, choose how."

The conditions, national and international, were about as difficult for an experiment as could be imagined. The stern (though necessary and justifiable) wartime taxation had greatly depleted his own financial reserves. All personal ambition was gone from him; he had no desire to take as reward for his services more than those services were worth to the community as a whole. But he did not want private industry to die from inanition until something stronger had grown in its place; he conceived it to be his duty to keep Syke Mills running until, and indeed after, a gradual transformation had been accomplished. It would be a difficult task. The trade's machinery needed renewal, its export markets had been cut to less than half, its labour was still absent, would be absent till world peace was secured. And what of that peace? Would the nations' friendship, moulded by the pressure of war, would their idealism, still survive? Well, at any rate we can see that our own holds out, thought Morcar soberly. "If necessary, alone—that's what we said during the war. We'll keep to it in peace as well."

The day was a national holiday, and Morcar had intended to spend what was left of it quietly at Stanney Royd. But on an impulse he swung his car through the Syke Mills archway—the iron gates had long since gone for salvage—and drew up in the yard. He dismounted, unlocked the mill door with his private

471

keys and made his way into his office. To work, thought Morcar. He sat down at his desk and drew from a drawer his own especial ledger, in which he estimated the production, labour and costs figures of Syke Mills. After scanning it for a few minutes and making some mental calculations he laid it aside, and drew from another drawer a strip of blue designing-paper and a cloth-covered board on which were arranged some tiny skeins of coloured yarns. Morcar sharpened his pencil, hunched his shoulders, smiled and set to work. To work! To work! To work for the good of all..... It was an ideal to which he was proud to have risen. To work for the good of all.

472

A NOTE ON THE AUTHOR

Phyllis Bentley was born in 1894 in Halifax, West Yorkshire, where she was educated until she attended Cheltenham Ladies College, Gloucestershire.

In 1932 her best-known work, *Inheritance*, was published to widespread critical acclaim and commercial success. This was in contrast to her previous efforts, a collection of short stories entitled *The World's Bane* and several poor-selling novels. The triumph of *Inheritance* made her the most successful English regional novelist since Thomas Hardy, and she produced two more novels to create a trilogy; *The Rise of Henry Morcar* and *A Man of His Time*. This accomplishment made her a much demanded speaker and she became an expert on the Bronte family.

Over her career Bentley garnered many awards; an honorary DLitt from Leeds University (1949); a Fellow of the Royal Society of Literature (1958); awarded an OBE (1970). She died in 1977.

Lightning Source UK Ltd.
Milton Keynes UK
UKOW04f1441020913

216399UK00001B/10/P